DAKOTA

OTHER WORKS BY MARTHA GRIMES

The End of the Pier
Hotel Paradise
Biting the Moon
The Train Now Departing
Cold Flat Junction
Foul Matter
Belle Ruin

RICHARD JURY NOVELS

The Man with a Load of Mischief
The Old Fox Deceived
The Anodyne Necklace
The Dirty Duck
Jerusalem Inn
Help the Poor Struggler
The Deer Leap
I Am the Only Running Footman
The Five Bells and Bladebone
The Old Silent
The Old Contemptibles
The Horse You Came in On
Rainbow's End
The Case Has Altered
The Stargazey
The Lamorna Wink
The Blue Last
The Grave Maurice
The Winds of Change
The Old Wine Shades
Dust

POETRY

Send Bygraves

Martha Grimes

DAKOTA

A NOVEL

VIKING

VIKING
Published by the Penguin Group
Penguin Group (USA) Inc., 375 Hudson Street,
New York, New York 10014, U.S.A.
Penguin Group (Canada), 90 Eglinton Avenue East, Suite 700,
Toronto, Ontario, Canada M4P 2Y3
(a division of Pearson Penguin Canada Inc.)
Penguin Books Ltd, 80 Strand, London WC2R ORL, England
Penguin Ireland, 25 St. Stephen's Green, Dublin 2, Ireland
(a division of Penguin Books Ltd)
Penguin Books Australia Ltd, 250 Camberwell Road, Camberwell, Victoria 3124, Australia
(a division of Pearson Australia Group Pty Ltd)
Penguin Books India Pvt Ltd, 11 Community Centre,
Panchsheel Park, New Delhi—110 017, India
Penguin Group (NZ), 67 Apollo Drive, Rosedale, North Shore 0632,
New Zealand (a division of Pearson New Zealand Ltd)
Penguin Books (South Africa) (Pty) Ltd, 24 Sturdee Avenue,
Rosebank, Johannesburg 2196, South Africa

Penguin Books Ltd, Registered Offices:
80 Strand, London WC2R ORL, England

First published in 2008 by Viking Penguin, a member of Penguin Group (USA) Inc.

1   3   5   7   9   10   8   6   4   2

Library of Congress Cataloging-in-Publication Data

Grimes, Martha.
Dakota / Martha Grimes.
p.   cm.
ISBN 978–0–670–01869–7 (alk. paper)
1. Drifters—Fiction. 2. Amnesiacs—Fiction. I. Title.
PS3557. B48998D35 2008
813'. 54—dc22   2007041715

Printed in the United States of America
Set in Bembo
Designed by Daniel Lagin

To the fan at a Coral Gables book signing
who cried, "Bring back Andi Oliver!"
Thanks.
Here she is.

The thoughts of others
Were light and fleeting,
Of lovers' meeting
Or luck or fame.
Mine were of trouble,
And mine were steady,
So I was ready
When trouble came.

—A. E. Housman

DAKOTA

KINGDOM COME

I

Through the trapped heat of a late August afternoon, the girl walked along the red scoria road, occasionally stopping to shift the weighted backpack.

Behind her the Dakota badlands withdrew. She was sorry for this. She had taken comfort in a landscape that had remained unchanged for so long, for hundreds of millions of years: vast wedges of rock, some flat-topped, some spiked, and capped with the same red clinks, like sedimented brick.

She liked to think of the badlands as unchanging, but even rock changes, in the end. High wind and hard rain had eroded the strata, and the Little Missouri River had carved it like sculpture. There were scars left by the dried channels of older rivers. Not even the badlands were a match for the elements, with hard rains forming gullies down the surface of the rocks and leaving them with the look of deeply pleated skirts. Seams of bentonite turned the surface blue. And there were black coal seams that could burn underground and turn it brick red. Like her red scoria road.

And there was the silence. She had never known such encompassing silence.

Back in a café in Medora, where she'd had breakfast more than a week ago, the waitress poured coffee and said, "It's Indians gave the badlands their name; they said 'land bad,' I guess because there wasn't anything to be done with it. I mean, you couldn't farm it or hunt on it or trap."

"Or, maybe," the girl said, "the land was bad because they thought it was sinister."

"Well, does it look sinister to you? It don't to me." The waitress was holding the coffeepot by a finger as if daring the coffee to spill.

"No," the girl said, "but, then, we're not Lakota."

The endurance of land. It changed; it was always changing, but in no time she could ever measure, which lent it the illusion of permanence. How different it was for humans, who could so easily slip away, could be gone in the moment between looking away and looking back, invisible as a breath in fog.

She looked to be eighteen or twenty or even more, hard to say. She was wearing faded jeans and a faded blue shirt beneath a quilted vest and the heavy backpack she had to keep shifting between her shoulders. The khaki backpack, the bleached-out blue of the clothes, and her pale hair, lighter than corn silk, almost as pale as the moon, matched the dusty landscape she walked through, as if the land had drawn her into it.

The road was an old one and no longer traveled much, as cars and trucks took Interstate 94 or one of the state roads. This one was more a local road, and for the girl there wasn't any living thing for miles around, empty fields that might have belonged to farms, or belonged to nothing.

Until now she had seen no animals. But up ahead was a donkey standing in the corner of a fenced field, the corner where an even lesser road, perhaps one belonging to whoever owned the donkey, met up with the one she was walking on. The donkey was still harnessed to a cart full of wood and fertilizer that looked as if it were meant for something, but there was nothing.

The girl slowed down and stopped, then walked up the dirt slope and stood by the fence. Closer to it, she saw the donkey was not in good shape. She could see that the abrading of the cart and the halter had rubbed sores into its skin. Blackflies hovered, but the donkey seemed too tired to flick them away with his tail. She looked along the post and rail fence for a gate or some opening, didn't see one, and so tossed her backpack over it. Barbed wire ran along the top of the fence. She thought it was just another one of those devices meant to menace, but that served no other purpose. A horse who could jump the fence could certainly manage another couple of inches to clear the wire.

She put her foot on the second rung of rail and dropped down on the other side. From the backpack she took a small bottle and a cloth. She ran her hand down the donkey's neck, inspecting the sores. He was a pretty donkey, a lovely silver-blue color with a white blaze and deep-set eyes. But he looked wasted. Well, what was he supposed to eat in this corner of the field? There was nothing but burned grass, brown and stiff.

She always carried food in her backpack—apples, oranges, sugar, and anything that came in foil packets, such as cat food. There was also cheese, and buns. She kept a sharp knife for cutting. She brought out an apple and an orange and cut both in half. She peeled the orange, not knowing if animals liked the skin. The donkey probably would have eaten anything, but that was no reason not to take a little trouble. He finished off the apple in no time and she held out the orange, which was juicy and would serve for water, or a little of it. There was no water, none in this field. People just hadn't a clue, had they?

While the donkey ate the orange she got to work on the sore places that she could get to. The harness would come later. The liniment was one she had made herself; there was an anesthetic in it to keep the alcohol from burning too much. Then there was a salve that felt cool on her own skin, so she thought it would make the donkey's feel the same way. For serious pain, she still had a couple of vials of the painkiller that she'd stolen from the pharmacy in Santa Fe more than a year ago. A year and a half it had been since Santa Fe. She wondered how stable this drug was. Buprenex was something like morphine, and although she'd figured out how much you could safely give a coyote or a wolf, she hadn't used it on bigger animals. Maybe she should just use her homeopathic medicines, Ledum or arnica.

When she applied the salve to one of the sores, the donkey flinched, but that was all; he didn't rear back or strain against the harness, and he let her put it on other sores without resisting.

She was watching the fields as she did this, watching for someone. The farmhouse and barns and the other farm animals were out of sight, obscured by the natural rise of ground. She considered investigating, but decided not to; what, after all, would she find out? She couldn't figure out what this donkey was doing here.

She finished with the antiseptic and inspected the harness. She detached the cart. It was as if she had derailed the donkey from his old life, and she guessed it was now up to her to make a new one for it.

She walked along the fence looking for an opening and found a weak spot where a part of the wire had come loose because the rail had rotted. She had wire cutters. She'd met up with barbed wire before. She gave the rotted rail a push with her foot and it loosened more, like a log falling in a fireplace. Always, she kept her eyes on the far field. Now the opening was big enough to get through. She went back, put the backpack together, took hold of the rope, and did not have to pull it hard before the donkey plodded along after her. Free of the cart and the heavy halter, the donkey could turn around and watch her.

The sunset was spectacular, a molten wash of red and orange. Had they meant to leave the donkey out here all night, the cart still hitched to him, the bags with their cumbersome burden, and no food, no water? Just his blind staring at whatever was out there on the road to help? She thought that the donkey had pulled himself to this corner to watch the road and hope that someone would stop. And someone had.

"So you were smart," she said, rubbing his back. "And you were lucky." —and steered the white moth thither in the night?

The line surprised her, coming unbidden as it did. It was a poem of Robert Frost's, something about a white spider. In her backpack she carried a small poetry anthology. "Steered the white moth thither in the night?" Why had she thought of this? It would come to her. She couldn't remember the line after that one, but that would come to her, too.

She led the donkey along the fence to the opening. He stopped at first, so she went ahead through it. She turned at the opening and gestured for him to come through. She did not pull on the rope; she waited. It was only a few seconds before he made up his mind and followed her.

The donkey stood patiently as she raised each hoof and looked at it. Walking didn't seem to hurt him, but who knew? They could not stop here because someone belonging to the farm might come to the field and start searching. But she bet no one would come until morning, if even then, and no one would search.

Now that his scabby wounds were taken care of, he seemed better. She liked to think he was more peaceful, clear now of the cart, though of course she didn't know. What they needed right away was water. She got out her bottled water; not much was left, only a few ounces. Any amount was better than none. She reached in the backpack for a plastic bowl she sometimes used for cereal, and poured the rest of the water into it. The donkey drank all of it and then pressed his nose against the bowl, first here, then there, wanting more.

As she'd been walking, she'd gotten glimpses of what must have been a stream or a river. Maybe it was a tributary of the Little Missouri. The light reflecting on the water was what caught her attention, distant though it was across a dry, burned-out field that backed onto a stand of trees. In and out of her line of vision was this dark green dazzle. Over there, nearer to the stream, would be a good place to go. They wouldn't be as exposed either.

After she'd shoved her arms into her backpack and wiggled it into the most comfortable position, she gave the rope around the donkey's neck a little tug. The donkey walked beside her to the road a short distance farther.

On this wider asphalt road, she could see for quite a distance in either direction. As they crossed it, she wondered if the road had once been the main highway, little used now, serving mainly as a local or frontage road. No, there was nothing to front.

They crossed it and crossed the dry field to the trees and the river or stream, which seemed like a different world from the field and the farm. She led the donkey to the stream, which moved slowly between the brown banks, and he bent his head and started drinking right away. She filled her plastic bottle. The donkey had put one foot into the water and now stepped in with all four feet. He just stood there. She bet it was relaxing. After removing her shoes and socks, she stood in it beside him. It was wonderfully cold. The donkey probably thought so, too. They stayed that way for a few minutes and then she got out and went to a tree to sit down in its shade. She knew she ought to have a plan, but how much can you plan ahead if you're with a donkey? And it was hard to plan if you weren't bound for anywhere. She yawned. She looked at the donkey still standing in the stream and wanted to think he felt a kind of bliss after however long he'd been stranded in the sun and dry air and dead grass.

She wondered, she was always wondering, what her home had been like when she'd had one. There was nothing in her mind, not a single image any earlier than the day she'd woken up in the Santa Fe bed-and-breakfast place eighteen months ago. What were her parents like? Had she any brothers or sisters? What was holding her to earth?

She yawned again and leaned back and closed her eyes and tried to think up a plan.

When she woke it was into pale light, the weak sun dappling the branches of the trees. She sat up with a lurch. It wasn't dusk, but dawn. Ten hours, she must have slept. The donkey was lying down nearby. She went to the stream and threw cold water on her face and felt more awake. She found her water bottle and filled it.

In that Santa Fe bed-and-breakfast, a man's things had been scattered about the room: clothes, watch, money. The money had come in handy. But she hated thinking about that morning. What had happened to her there might be the reason why she'd lost her memory. Although he put it down to the fire. "Daddy." That was her ironic reference to this man. "*Daddy, we're through.*" That was Sylvia Plath, she thought.

After she put the bottle of water in her backpack, she slipped the pack on and went to the donkey, who'd since stirred and was now nibbling the grass.

She had taken out and unfolded her map and tried to place herself. It was an ordnance map, so she could do this. The roads were all there. "There's a town not far up the road there. I guess once we get to it, we can figure what to do."

It was her way to talk to animals like that, as if they were going to be helpful, or at least willing to go where she went.

2

She knew the silence wasn't mysterious, that it was simply early morning quiet. Still, she couldn't help believing it was lost time, time that had broken off from the regular swing of the pendulum and stopped because things needed to be stopped.

She led the donkey along to the two-lane asphalt road. It wasn't far to the next town, only about a mile or a mile and a half, and there she might be able to find someone—a farmer, maybe—who could keep the donkey overnight.

The farm they had left behind was a mile back, and there was always the danger that someone from there might go by. Hearing a car in the distance, she looked over her shoulder and saw a pickup truck approaching. When the truck drew near, it slowed, and once abreast of her, it crawled. At first she thought it might be someone offering a lift, if they could put the donkey in the flatbed.

The driver, with a face as unformed as putty, and with his tattooed arm hanging out the window, called, "You got one hell of an ass there, girl!"

Now there'd be a lot of "ass" jokes, she knew. The one in the passenger seat leaned across and called, "Yeah, I got an ass, too. Wanna see it?" Comedians, both of them. The passenger had a bad case of acne even though he looked too old for it. The driver was chunky with a dark crew cut.

Go on by, she prayed.

But of course they didn't. They pulled the truck onto the shoulder and stopped. They both got out, laughing and walking back to where she was, slowly and with the ease of those who know they have complete control of a situation. For what could she do (they would be thinking), not only a defenseless girl but one with a donkey. Where could she run?

She was sick and tired of encounters with stupidity. Another useless confrontation with the cowardice of men who had to prove themselves by preying on weakness—or what they took to be weakness. What, she wondered, was the victory in that? It reminded her of the caged hunt she'd witnessed in Idaho—the remorseless shooting of a caged tiger. The shooter so pleased with himself.

That this was a road on which anyone might drive by didn't deter the two men. They had it all figured out; if anyone saw them, they'd just be two fellows helping a girl and her animal.

"Hey! You and me, we can have some fun with that ass!" They thought this supremely amusing, thought they were real stand-up comedians.

Shit, she thought. As they came toward her, she swung her backpack around so that she could reach into the outside pocket, and in one fluid motion pulled out a Smith & Wesson .38, shoved in a clip, and brought it up with both hands, steadying it. "Get back in your vehicle and drive."

They stopped dead. They looked at each other, big-eyed. The chunky one said, with a nervous laugh, "Ah, come on, you ain't goin' to shoot, girl—"

In the silence of the land the shot sounded like a big branch cracking. A cloud of dust blew up at their feet. That was what she had aimed at. "One. More. Step," she called out.

They would hate having to turn tail, hate that they were impotent to stop her from shooting, hate that they hadn't just gone bravely on toward her, overpowering her, knowing that she wouldn't actually shoot them—

Wrong. She brought the gun up again.

To themselves they could rationalize; to others they could lie. To the police—but she didn't think they'd be calling on the police; they wouldn't want police hearing her side of the story. And that donkey. No, it wouldn't hold much water that she attacked them, threatened them. "Sheriff, all we done was stop to help her!"

They had backed up to the truck and were nearly falling over each other in their haste to get back inside. When they did, since they now had the safety of the cab and the wheels to take them away, they both called back "Fuck you!" several times, and as the tires spewed up dust, the driver gave her the finger. It was the best they could do.

She took the clip out and stashed both the gun and the clip in the backpack. She was good with the gun. She had done a lot of sessions of target practice where she had her waitress job. Three or four times a week, she'd gone to the rifle range outside of Idaho Falls. That practice had made her a good shot, a very good shot. The gun she had found in the trunk of the Camaro the man had parked outside the bed-and-breakfast place. Under some rags in the rear: gun, clip, ammunition.

Those two were cowards, of course. If she'd had to, she would have shot them. One, at least. The other then would have run like hell. It seemed to her sometimes that it never ended, the meanness and cruelty of people. You could find it anywhere you looked. You could find it without looking.

She picked up the rope-lead and gave it a little twitch and they walked on. There were a few other cars and trucks that went by, but with no more reaction than a laugh and a wave.

It was almost nine in the morning when they got to the town, a black and white sign announcing it as KINGDOM. Someone had made a joke and whitewashed in "Come"—KINGDOM COME. The main street began as a mobile-home park on one side and a vegetable and fruit market on the other. She made sure no cars were coming and led the donkey over to the market. A woman was sitting by the bins, reading, and looked up surprised.

"Do you know anything about what donkeys eat?" The ignorance of the question made her blush.

The woman was further astonished, not only upon seeing a girl leading a donkey but also that the girl knew nothing about it. "Well . . . no, I don't guess I do. Wherever did you get him?"

"I found him."

This only added to the woman's surprise. "Found him?"

"Yes. I found him by the side of the road. He was by himself. I waited to see if anybody would come back but no one did."

The woman was standing now, examining the donkey for signs of really being lost. The girl didn't mind, as she didn't think the woman was doubting her word; she was showing concern.

"I gave him an apple and an orange and that didn't do him any harm."

The woman looked at the bins behind them. "Horses like carrots, don't they?"

"I guess so."

The woman thought for a bit, then said, "Why don't I call Jared? He'd know." She walked back behind the bins.

Who was Jared? The girl thought the market colorful. There were peppers in one bin—purple, orange, yellow, and green. A riot of colors.

Then the woman returned. "That fool of a Jared said hay and straw. Do I look like I'm selling hay and straw?" She held her arms wide. "Some people haven't got the sense they was born with. Finally, he told me apples and carrots. I've got both." She pulled some carrots from a crate behind the bins. "Real fresh, these are. Only you got to cut them so they don't stick in the donkey's throat. Lengthwise, he said; he was very particular about that. I've got a good, sharp knife."

The girl was so grateful for this small kindness she was afraid she might weep, which would have been foolish. This woman especially impressed her, following what had just happened. The two men had shaken her though she wouldn't show it. This woman with her bins of fruit and vegetables had come as if by edict to right things, smoothing life along so a person could stand it a little better.

She watched the woman hack one by one through a dozen carrots, saving the green tops. "I imagine he'll like this, too. It occurs to me"—and she stopped cutting the carrots while she said this—"if you're planning on staying in Kingdom overnight, I can ask Jared if he could put the donkey up. He boards some ponies. I'll bet he could take on this donkey. Give him a comfortable place to sleep." She went over to the donkey and looked him over. "Seems as if he's not been done very well by whoever owned him before you came along. You patched him up some, I see. That was real good of you. Not many would've bothered. No, not many." She put the carrots in a bag and took out another bag for the apples. "If you're fixing to stay, there's a real nice house that takes in guests right along the main street. It's not far from where Jared's place of business is."

"Good. Yes, I am kind of tired." Even though she'd slept all those hours last night, she had a sudden awareness of exhaustion. She thought it must have come from what happened back with the men in the truck. "Where is it?"

"You go right along Main Street for two stoplights until you get to Eucalyptus. It's the house on the corner, big white house. Victorian, I guess you'd say. You know what? Why don't I just call Jared about the donkey? Make sure he's there when you come. Why don't I do that?" She moved again to the telephone.

"I appreciate that."

The woman took down the receiver and dialed. "Now, what's your name, hon? Mine is Eula Bond."

It was as if Eula Bond didn't want to make her bear all the weight of name telling.

"My name's Andi. Andi Oliver."

It wasn't, but that was the best she could do.

3

She had made up the name from the initials on her backpack: "AO." She had been told eventually by the man who claimed to have found her that the letters stood for Alhambra Orphanage. It was not only that she did not know where or who her family was; neither did she know whether she'd been part of it. She could have been at the orphanage all of her life, given up by a mother who couldn't take care of a baby, or who didn't want to.

Finally, she'd started searching for this orphanage. She knew that if he'd picked her up and been driving from Idaho, going toward New Mexico, the Alhambra Orphanage would probably be in one of those states. In every town she'd stopped during the last year, she'd gone to the public library and researched it, never to be found.

He'd invented it. Even looking down the muzzle of a gun, he'd lied. There were people who thrived on others' misfortunes. Like vampires, they drink misery.

The second thing to research was the burning of the bus. That's when he said he'd found her—walking away, dazed, from the bus. She could find no accounting of such an accident, which was strange given the enormity of it. Every child on that bus had been burned to death, he'd said, except for her. One thing she did know was the approximate date on which this could have occurred—a day between the time he'd left Idaho and the day he—they—had arrived in Santa Fe. She'd scoured newspapers for a report of it and had found nothing.

So he'd lied about that, too. But here she'd been relieved. She had been thrown back on the emptiness of her past, the zero, the huge blank page, but at least she knew that when she finally remembered— for you do, don't you? Amnesia can't last forever, can it? When she remembered, there would be something worth remembering.

She was feeding the donkey the carrot tops and a carrot. She was afraid of overfeeding for he seemed very hungry and like he could go on eating forever.

"That's it, then," said Eula Bond. "Jared says yes, he can take your donkey overnight and charge ten dollars, which includes the hay and stuff. The stall's nice and clean."

"That's wonderful. Thanks."

Eula was stroking the donkey and making what she must have meant to be donkey sounds. "My goodness, but he is a patient old thing. Do you have a name for him?"

Andi shook her head. "No. I don't want to name him something that doesn't suit him."

Both stood looking at the donkey as if he should help with suitable names. Eula said, "Such meanness. How could a person just leave a poor animal on the road? I wonder if it's gypsies. I've heard how they mistreat their donkeys that do everything for them."

"Are there gypsies around?"

"No. None I've seen."

Andi had a small purse out that she used for daily expenses. Most of her money was stuffed down in the backpack. If she lost the backpack she'd be in real trouble. She had a few bills, figuring the apples and carrots weren't more than five dollars, and she handed that to Eula.

Eula held her hands out flat. "No, not one penny. If you can take on the care of him, least I can do is give a bit of food. Nope, your money's no good here."

"That's very nice of you, Eula." Andi put the purse away. "I wonder if he needs water."

"I got a rain barrel right around the side here." Andi and the donkey followed her.

While the donkey drank from the old barrel, Andi said, "People don't do this much anymore, do they? I can't recall ever seeing a rain barrel."

"There's a lot of things you don't see anymore," Eula said, breathing a sadness into the words.

It made Andi anxious; she didn't know why. It was as if something might be lost even as they stood there. "Well, I guess we better be going along to Jared's now."

Eula gave her directions, pretty much like the ones to the rooming house. "You turn left and walk till you're past the last house and you'll come to it. Looks like a big barn—well, that's what it is, right? 'Jared—Farrier,' it says on the sign. He shoes horses and things like that."

Andi thanked her and promised to come back again and left.

As they walked on the road, keeping close to the curb, Andi would stop once in a while to step to the sidewalk and look in a window. The donkey stood still while she did this. She liked the window of the haberdashery (a word she didn't know and found strange as meaning a store that sold men's clothes). There was a fine-looking dark suit in the window. It stood next to a dress shop, and that was next to a pharmacy. They were all old-fashioned and restful. The dresses looked as if they'd been worn decades ago—tiny floral prints and narrow belts and scooped necklines. Since she didn't remember, she didn't know how she could think "old-fashioned." On the deep window ledge behind the pharmacy window was a line of cobalt-blue bottles that seemed to have no particular purpose unless they had once held potions or were used to measure. Inside it looked as cool as a cave. The sun was very bright and hot now in the late morning.

The donkey waited in the street while she looked.

At the second stoplight they turned left and walked along until the houses gave way and Andi saw the barn. It was actually quite pretty, colorful, for it was painted blue and the sign brick red with JARED—FARRIER carved out in white. They stood in the barn door's big opening, the sun hot on her back as she peered through the gloom and her eyes adjusted after the brightness of the day.

Halfway in a man stood working on the upraised shoe of a white horse with what looked like a stiff-bristled brush. "Excuse me, but are you Jared?"

"Yeah, that's right."

Andi led the donkey up to him. The horse and donkey appeared interested in each other, touching muzzles and sniffing around.

"You must be who Eula called about. Andi, that right?" He was a big, heavyset man with a smile that caught a glimmer of gold somewhere in his teeth.

"Eula said you could keep my donkey overnight?"

He wiped his forehead on his shirtsleeve and adjusted his cap. "Sure can. That's a good-lookin' donkey you got." He stood inspecting the donkey and rubbing his back.

Andi smiled, thinking the donkey had probably got more attention in the last twenty-four hours than in the whole rest of his life. "He was just standing by the side of the road."

Jared said, "Farm back there, the Bailey place, had a donkey go missing. Lucas Bailey said it must've been stolen because the fence had been cut through. 'Who'd want an old donkey anyway?' he said. I said to him, 'Not everyone looks at animals the way you do.' But he didn't know what I meant." Jared's laugh was more of a snort. The donkey snorted, too.

Andi was delighted. "I think he took in what you said."

"Oh, I don't doubt it. Donkeys are smart. To me it's funny how folks think they're ornery and stubborn and that's all. You'd be stubborn, too, if you were made to pull a cart holding several cords of firewood day after day." Jared inspected the raw places Andi had medicated. "I'll say this: even if this was Bailey's donkey, well, he's never going to hear it from me, and that's a fact."

She felt relieved, and for no reason other than to prolong Jared's disdain for this Bailey, Andi asked, "What color was his donkey?"

"Brown, he says."

"My donkey's more silver, isn't he? A sort of silvery blue."

"Bailey says brown no matter if it's a donkey, a horse, a dog, or a pig."

She stopped herself before she actually giggled (surprised there was a giggle left in her). "Since when are pigs brown?"

"Since Bailey got hisself some. It only goes to show what credence he gives his animals. He'll probably be stopping by, usually does. That's his horse there." Jared gestured toward a horse on the opposite side of the barn from the empty stall.

She said, now worried, "If he can't tell the difference between one donkey and another, what's to keep him from claiming mine?"

"Me," said Jared, bringing the hammer down on the anvil in a terrible racket.

Somebody else on her side. First Eula, now Jared. It made her feel, and would have made the donkey feel, protected. Still, she wanted the donkey in his stall where he wouldn't be completely visible should this Bailey come along. She led him over to the empty stall and unlatched the little gate.

"There's hay in the hayrick, and that straw for his bed, that's fresh. Probably your donkey will eat that, too. What's his name?"

"I haven't given him one yet."

Jared straightened up from the anvil. "Give him a temporary one, then." He walked over to the stall where the donkey was chomping down hay. "Now, he looks like royalty to me, don't he to you?"

Andi nodded.

"So how about Duke?"

Andi started laughing; she couldn't help it.

"What's wrong with that? Duke's a good name."

She nodded, choking on a laugh. "Look at him looking at you."

The donkey was, too. He'd stopped eating after Jared said "Duke," and now seemed to be staring at him. Andi was about to say something when they both turned at the sound of another voice.

"Whose donkey would that be?"

The voice had a peculiar lack of timbre, as if it were speaking from another space. It was as thin as a razor.

"If it ain't Lucas Bailey, bright-eyed and bushy-tailed."

That was the last way Andi would have described this tall, gaunt man, thin as his own shadow, which, dressed all in black, he closely resembled. Far from being bright-eyed, his eyes were as light as still water and as narrow as knives.

"Nice-lookin' animal you got there; puts me in mind of the one missin' from my pasture."

Jared waved away his words. "Oh, for the Lord's sake. Is there anything in these parts you don't think belongs to you?" He was back to the anvil and shoe, placing himself between the man and Andi.

Lucas Bailey stuck his thumbs in his belt, hands holding back the long black coat. Was he dangerous or just dressed for danger? Probably the latter. But she was still afraid, for it looked as though he went to a lot of trouble to instill that feeling in people.

"Thing is," Bailey said, "Carl and Junior saw a girl and a donkey walking along the highway maybe a mile back. Description fits this young lady to a T."

Junior. She bet one of them in the truck hated that name.

Bailey went on. "That wouldn't have been you"—he aimed this at Andi—"I don't suppose?"

Jared brought down the hammer hard and said, "Junior and Carl, they'd lay claim to anything, just like you."

As Lucas Bailey moved up to the stall and Andi, he said, "Yeah, but there's somethin' else real peculiar. According to my boys, this girl they saw drew a gun on them when they'd stopped the truck to help her. Now, that is strange, don't you think?"

Andi said nothing; her expression didn't change.

"Oh, really? Now explain this to me, Lucas: if they stopped just to help her, then why did she have shooting them in mind?"

"Crazy, I guess."

"Or not. Maybe your boys had something else in mind besides just helping. As I recall, Carl got charged last year with assaulting a thirteen-year-old girl."

Bailey turned away from Andi. "He was acquitted. You know that."

"Oh, I know he was. That jury was made up pretty much of your friends."

"Hell, Jared. Just because you don't agree, that don't mean there was bribes and threats."

"I didn't say that; funny you should bring it up."

Lucas Bailey turned and walked to the stall. "Is this goddamned horse ready? I want to head home."

"Sure is." Jared opened the stall door and brought out the black horse.

It would be black, thought Andi.

"Where you from, then, little lady?" Bailey was saddling up the horse.

"New Mexico. Santa Fe." She always gave that answer since it was the first place she remembered in her life.

"Nice place, I hear, only it's a little out of the way, ain't it?"

Andi kept one hand on her donkey's silvery coat, as if he might be spirited away by this man if she didn't hold on to him somehow. "I travel a lot."

"With that donkey? He must slow you down some."

"I'm not in any hurry."

"Where you headed?"

"Alaska."

"Alaska? Good Lord, you got a way to go."

Irritated, Jared said, "Oh, for God's sakes, Bailey, stop givin' this poor girl the third degree."

Bailey had swung himself up on his horse. On that horse, and in his wide-brimmed black hat and his black clothes, Lucas Bailey probably felt he was a man of myth, an icon; he probably thought he looked like Johnny Cash. "What do I owe you, Jared?"

"Twenty dollars. I'll put it on your tab."

"Okay. Pay you next week."

Once he had gone, Andi moved away from the donkey. "Is he important in town?"

Jared laughed. "Hear him tell it, he's the only thing that is. He's a farmer. Has a pretty big spread two or three miles from here. Carl? His oldest boy? Biggest troublemaker around except for his other son, Junior. I'll tell you this, if some girl did pull out a gun, I wish to death I had a ringside seat. Oh, how I'd've loved that!"

Andi tried not to smile. "Why didn't they go to the police if some-one threatened them like that? I mean, did she hold them up and take their money or what?"

"Good question. Why didn't they go to the sheriff? Listen, would you kindly hold Seymour's reins. We only got this one last shoe. Don't worry, he's as gentle as can be." The horse had reared back a little. "Those boys didn't go to the police because Harry McKibbon would not have believed them. If there was a girl—any girl, wouldn't have to be as pretty as you—any poor girl, they'd've hassled her. If they told Harry she pulled a gun on them, he'd ask the same thing I did—why? He'd know it would only have been to protect herself. No, they don't come any meaner than the Baileys."

"Who's Harry McKibbon?"

"Sheriff. He knows everything that goes on in Kingdom and around. More important, he knows the people and the way they are. Especially the way the Baileys are. He's a good lawman."

"Does he investigate things like stolen donkeys?"

"I guess he would if someone made a formal complaint. I don't mean just mouthin' off about it. Bailey'd sure have to make one before Harry'd pay any attention to him. Harry can't stand the Baileys."

Andi said, "The thing is, you don't see a person walking down the road with a donkey very often. I mean, the sheriff would surely think I'm the one. It certainly looks that way."

Had she really thought no one would come after the donkey? No. The truth was she hadn't thought at all. Why hadn't she? She certainly wasn't a person who believed events would take care of themselves, that things would work out in the end. If anything she believed the exact opposite.

"Harry don't go by looks. He goes by evidence."

Andi smiled. "But it's evidence I'm talking about."

Jared ignored that and let the horse's leg down. "Fit as a fiddle, Seymour."

"Whose horse is Seymour?"

"Mine."

"I like the name Seymour."

"You see the way his ear twitched when you said his name? He likes hearing his name. Now, I suppose you'd want to go get you a room. Patty Englehart rents out rooms either overnight or long-term. Does meals, too, if you're a regular lodger. It's like one of them old-fashioned rooming houses. There ain't many of those around anymore."

"No, there aren't."

Actually, she'd rather have slept here in the barn near her donkey. And the horses.

"You seem kind of upset, Andi. Don't pay no attention to Bailey; he's a devil."

Andi was looking at her donkey, studying it. "I was thinking, maybe I'll call him Silver. His coat's kind of silvery, don't you think?"

Jared walked over to the stall. "That's a good name." He rubbed the donkey's muzzle.

"Maybe it's too fancy, though. I think I'll just call him Sam."

In Andi's mind there was a tiny starburst. It came and went in a flash—an image of a dog. Was it simply the one she'd invented, Jules? Why did it hit her like glare ice, so cold and bright she had to turn away?

"What's wrong?" asked Jared.

"Nothing. Just a memory."

He nodded and went back to Seymour. To Jared a memory was nothing or next to it. To her it was everything.

4

Mrs. Englehart said yes, indeed, she had a room, and for how long did she want it? It was twelve dollars a night but ten for more than one night, and for the week, just sixty. Andi said that was a very reasonable rate and she'd like it for two nights, at least. Maybe longer. She did not know why she said this; she hadn't planned on staying, but now, considering it as she followed Mrs. Englehart up the stairs, it seemed a good idea. At least the two nights.

The room was big and attractively furnished, not cheap castoffs or mismatched stuff from an attic or a yard sale. The four-poster bed and the ornately carved bureau and chair were dark and glossy with polish and rubbing.

Her reflection in the big mirror over the bureau gave her a start. She looked so travel-worn, just dull, as if she could use a good polishing herself. Her pale hair, lighter than any version of "blond," was pulled back in a ponytail. When had she last washed it?

Mrs. Englehart suggested the diner up the street for supper, saying that she often went there herself when she didn't feel like cooking. The bathroom, she said, was right next door.

Andi removed her shoes and lay down on the big bed, sank into it. She hadn't slept in anything but her sleeping bag since the motel in Medora. She closed her eyes and went back over these last two days. Was she crazy, taking the donkey? How did she think she would take care of him? What would she do if someone discovered where the donkey came from?

How strange. She was asking herself these questions that had already been answered. She *had* run into the owner.

Her eyes closed and she told herself not to fall asleep.

The next thing she knew, the window on the opposite wall looked out on dusk. She'd been asleep for hours and it was after seven o'clock.

Quickly, she rose and took a towel and soap from the bureau and went to the bathroom next door. Her hair didn't look too bad, she decided, and washed up.

Back in the room she got money from her backpack, enough for the two nights and for her dinner. She did not see Mrs. Englehart, so she put a twenty on the telephone table beside the stairs and anchored the bills with the telephone.

When she walked down the front stairs she felt a great sense of ease in knowing a place she was leaving was one she would come back to.

The walk in the dark along the main street was pleasant; after the heat of the day, the air had cooled off and was soft and carried the scent of some bloom she couldn't identify. She closed her eyes and breathed it in.

She glanced into the windows of the stores as she passed. Bonnie's Bouquet (artificial flowers in the window), the Dollar Store ("Everything for a buck!"), and the Unique Boutique, a place of "hot couture fashion" (or so the cursive writing in the window would have her believe), a bar called Two Dogs, and, farther along, another named the Plugged Nickel, which sounded rowdy. This was near a large square building that called itself "Begonia Apartments." She wanted to laugh. Whoever decided on that name she would like to meet. It was a brave name.

Ahead, the neon sign of the diner winked erratically, as if there were a short somewhere. The neon was blue and red and rather pretty, running vertically along the side near the door. It read MAY'S LONG GONE.

What a wonderful name, whatever it meant. Andi loved diners—diner food, diner waitresses, diner counters, diner booths. She thought about the one near the Idaho border that she'd eaten in with Mary Dark Hope. The waitress had sung, "Let's Get Away from It All."

In the window was a WAITRESS WANTED sign. She wondered if that had to do with May being gone. Probably not.

Sitting down, she realized it was already eight. She took one of the counter stools. There were four other customers at the counter, and three of the old Naugahyde booths were in use. People around here, a lot of farmers, she supposed, would have eaten supper much earlier. A group of teenagers sat in one booth, their bodies draped sloppily as if to make sure the other diners would see their response to the authority of the sign: PLEASE DON'T PUT YOUR FEET ON THE SEATS. Ones she took for married couples occupied two more booths, and a single man sat in the one behind her.

Andi plucked a menu from the space between the napkin dispenser and the bowl containing little sugar packets. She knew she had stirred up the interest of the other customers, as there weren't that many strange girls walking into town with a donkey, and she was sure everybody must have heard about the donkey. Hot roast beef sandwiches with mashed potatoes and gravy. She sighed, though she wouldn't eat meat anymore. She hadn't eaten a hot meal since that café in Medora. And she could not remember the last time she'd eaten a hot roast beef sandwich, but, then, she couldn't remember a lot of things.

She thought about it constantly, her blank and empty past. Once in a while, a piece of it would break away like ice from a glacier and sink and rise again, but this so seldom happened and was so out of context that it hardly helped.

"What'll it be, hon?"

Lost in the past she didn't even have, Andi hadn't seen the waitress approach. "Oh. I'll have a Coke, and a toasted cheese, and mashed potatoes and gravy—" She hesitated. "No, not gravy, butter." As if she were sharing a secret, she leaned toward the waitress, whose name—Mildred—was sewn across the pocket of her dress in blue thread.

"Could you make a little well, and put the butter in it?" She lowered her voice as she said this. It was such a childish request, she blushed.

But Mildred was matter-of-fact. "Yes, ma'am, I can do that." The waitress turned to slip the ticket order through the open window to the cook. Andi couldn't hear the words she spoke to the cook, but imagined it was probably the request about the butter.

She studied her place mat. Around its four sides were advertisements for the town's business establishments. There were quite a lot of them for a small town. Bonnie's Bouquet, the Dollar Store, the Unique Boutique. Her stainless-steel utensils were rolled in a paper napkin which she unwound, placing the napkin in her lap. She slid her eyes over the three men sitting along the length of the counter and quickly looked away. If she gave them any encouragement at all, one of them would strike up a conversation, and she didn't want to say two words to anyone except the waitress, who had set a Coke at her place.

Andi sat there, feeling ashamed and not knowing why. She felt this way often, as if she were supposed to do something but was too weak to do it. Or maybe it was something she was supposed to be, and was too cowardly to be it. Whatever it was, it was hazardous. That she knew.

"Now, ain't you the girl come into town on a donkey?" The man a few seats away at the counter smiled a ragged smile. His teeth needed seeing to.

Feeling trapped, Andi nodded. "More or less."

He looked down the counter at the other two men as if for support or encouragement. They smiled, too, all three watching Andi.

Not to answer would have made it worse, she knew. "I wasn't riding on it, though." She felt something in her chest clench, her heart perhaps. One of the men moved down the counter to sit next to the one who'd asked the question. They expected some entertainment from this exchange.

Mildred came along with her toasted cheese sandwich and gave the man a dirty look.

"Where'd you get that donkey at? Some sorry beast, I heard. Whatever's a girl like you mean to do with a donkey?"

She shrugged, feigning indifference. "I don't know exactly."

"What we heard is somebody stole a donkey off of the Bailey place."

Andi bit into her sandwich. Now she wasn't so hungry.

"That wouldn't be you, now, would it?"

She didn't answer. This sort of thing could drag on and on. She was too tired for it.

Behind her, a voice said, "Leave her alone."

She turned. It was the man who'd been sitting in the booth behind her. He was up now and moved to the counter beside her.

The first man threw up his hands, palms out. He was trying to make light of it. "Ah, come on, Jim, it was just an innocent question."

The man named Jim said, "People come in here to eat, Bobby, not to listen to you hone your conversational skills."

The second man looked abashed and went back to his original stool.

"We was only kidding around," the first one muttered.

Jim turned to her. "Don't mind them. They're harmless." He went back to his booth.

Andi was so surprised by this she didn't know what to say. She went back to eating her toasted cheese and mashed potatoes. The clenching inside her had relaxed and she was hungry again. When she'd finished, she put money down on her check, with enough for a big tip. She stood for just a moment looking at the man who'd come to her rescue, and when he glanced up, feeling her look, she said, "Thanks."

He smiled and brought two fingers to his forehead in a salute that reminded her of the Boy Scouts. "My pleasure."

Andi left the diner and walked back the way she had come. She felt the chill in the air, as if the season had changed while she was inside, and she zipped up her jacket.

Just past the Two Dogs, she looked down the road where Jared's barn sat. Somebody—no, some *bodies*—came thrashing out of a sunflower field and took off down the road. They were noisy, laughing.

She couldn't see them well, certainly not their faces, but it took her only two seconds to know it was the two who'd gotten out of the truck. Lucas Bailey's boys. She turned down the road and watched them run out of sight. Cowards. Only cowards prey on the vulnerable.

Andi did not have the gun with her. She knew just one move taught her by a tai chi master: knee to the groin of whomever's assaulting you. "Not only is it most painful," he had said, "but it conveys the idea that you know many more."

Moves, he meant.

Why would the Bailey brothers be here, anyway? No one knew she would veer off the main street onto this road. God, why couldn't she remember to always carry a flashlight? It was a deep dark, thick with darkness, the way night can get in these huge open places.

It came again, the sound of something in the sunflowers. In a threatening situation it was always best to own the threat. "*If your nerve deny you . . .*" Emily Dickinson. Poetry was her support. So she crossed the road, looked at the tall grass and low bushy trees. Someone, or something, was in there, she was sure. But of course it was most likely an animal; she should have supposed that at the outset. She walked into the grass, got the source of the sound again—it was Sam. What was he doing out here? Surely, Jared hadn't let him roam off. How could the donkey get both the stall door and the barn door open?

This, she guessed, was to have been her punishment. She had no doubt they had actually set the donkey down deeper into the field and he had, by dependable donkey-steerage, made his way back to the road this far.

"How did you manage it?" She rubbed his muzzle. "You are very, very smart." There was nothing to hold on to. They had taken off the blanket and the strap that had held it. But Sam came willingly when she put her hand on his side and pushed a little.

They were out of the field and onto the road and their steps fell gently as Andi made for Jared's barn.

Yes, it would have been her punishment, coming in the morning and finding the donkey gone. And because he would have been out the whole night and getting more and more confused about how to go, Sam might have been irrevocably gone. Why hadn't they taken him to their farm? Probably because they hadn't the transport to do it.

The padlock was still there on the barn doors, locked. They hadn't gotten in this way. She led Sam around to the back door, where she found the doors closed but not locked. Andi led Sam in and put him in his stall. She picked up the blanket and tossed it across his back and secured it with the strap lying in the hay. She put more hay in the hay-rick, then gave Sam a few reassuring pats. She stepped out of the stall and lugged the captain's chair over to the stall door. It wouldn't be the first time Andi had slept in a chair. She closed her eyes and wished she'd brought the gun.

When morning came, she hoped she still wouldn't be wishing that.

5

ndi formed instant attachments. She really liked Jared and she liked the barn; she liked the diner and her room at Mrs. Englehart's. She liked the man who had stood up for her. Had she been forced to leave this morning, she knew she would feel bereft, as if she had known this town all her life. Such instant attachment she knew would spell trouble.

She wondered if it came from her lack of roots. There wasn't time to make a study of things. There wasn't time for reason, only for intuition.

Jared had come in, surprised to see her there. She told him what had happened the night before.

"Oh, for God's sakes! Was it those damned Bailey guys?"

"I don't know. There were some men last night in the diner giving me a hard time. I think one was named Bobby. I didn't hear the others' names."

Disgusted, Jared took off his cap and brushed off his stool, then returned it to his head. "Yeah, I think I know who you mean. We got our share of idiots in this town."

"I think they were still in the diner, though. Probably it was the Baileys."

"I'm real sorry." He went to one of the stalls and led a handsome bay horse to where he could work on it.

"That's all right. If it's them, well, they were bound to do something sooner or later. It's all right. Listen, I was wondering—I don't guess you know of any jobs around here? There's a waitressing job at the diner, but that's too—" *Too public* is what she meant, but she didn't say it. She'd wind up putting up all day with men like the ones last night, to say nothing of the two she'd met up with out on the highway. "Too much indoors, you know?"

She wasn't desperate; she had enough money to tide her over for a couple of months, she figured, even more. Saving up was something she did extremely well. She went on, as if justifying why she wanted to stay. "And Sam here would probably like to just stay put. I think he's had a real hard life."

Jared let up on his shoeing and said, "Well, off the top of my head, I can't say I know of any jobs. Just give me some thinkin' room and maybe I'll come up with something." He went back to his work. "Where you headed, anyway?"

"Alaska."

He looked up sharply. "Alaska?" He laughed. "Sorry, I ain't laughing at you, but you're just a tad off course. I'd say Alaska's that way." He pointed west and then north. "You're heading east, aren't you? At least you must've been headed that way today."

Andi didn't know how to answer this, for she didn't know why she hadn't struck out for Canada first thing when she'd been in Idaho. She didn't even know why she wanted to go to Alaska, or why she'd said it. But she was saved from answering by someone who'd walked in just then behind her.

"Hey, Jared."

Andi recognized the voice and turned.

He brought a hand up to the brim of his hat, said, "Well, hello there."

It was the man who'd been seated in the booth behind her.

"Jim, by all that's holy!" Jared raised himself from his stool to shake hands.

"I don't know why you're so all-fired surprised to see me, since that's my horse you're shoeing. At least it looks like mine."

Jared laughed, and nodded toward Andi. "This here's Andi—what's your last name? I don't know if you said."

"Oliver. Andi Oliver." What she had really called herself was "Olivier" at the outset, but people always turned it into Oliver. Olivier—like the actor—had seemed so much more promising. The promise of what, she wasn't sure.

"I'm Jim Purley." He tipped his hat again. "Well, we kind of met in May's last night. They didn't give you any more trouble, did they?"

"Baileys," said Jared. "Being cute. You know them."

"Oh, hell, they've not got an ounce of sense between them."

"I think they're the ones that broke in," said Andi.

Jim raised his eyebrows, looked at Jared. "Broke in here?"

Jared opened his mouth to explain, but Andi answered. "Someone—or more than one—wanted to get at Sam—that's my donkey." She told him the rest of it. "They left Sam out in that sun-flower field. Or at least that's where I found him. If I hadn't found him . . ." Her voice trailed away.

"I'm truly sorry." Jim said this as if he were apologizing for the whole town. "You had trouble on the highway coming into town, too, I heard."

Jared said, "Trouble just dogs your footsteps, sounds like."

"No," said Jim. "People get afraid of what they don't understand."

"How's that?" Jared looked puzzled.

"How often do you see a young woman walking along the high-way with a donkey?"

"Never have, I guess."

Jim nodded toward the horse Jared was working on. "You finished up with Odds On?"

"Sure have." Jared patted the leg of the horse, then set it down. "Wait a minute, Jim. Don't I recall you saying something about need-ing help at your place?"

Jim pushed his hat back a little as if his eyes needed the light more. "I do, yeah. Why?"

Jared nodded toward Andi. "This young lady wants a job around here."

Andi stood up as if for inspection.

"I can tell you right now, this girl's got a lot of ingenuity and a lot of determination, too. Not what you're used to seeing around here. If I could use her here, I sure would."

Jim looked at Andi. "That's quite an endorsement. Jared here is nobody's fool."

Andi nodded. "I appreciate that. I really do." She did not want to seem to be pleading or needy. That could put a man right off.

He smiled. "Do you think you're determined, Andi?"

She frowned slightly. "I guess I never thought about it one way or another."

Jim laughed. "Then you most likely are. Anyway, the proof is standing right over there." He nodded toward Sam's stall. "You're certainly determined to take care of that donkey. I heard about what happened. What you're doing can't be easy."

She frowned slightly, not knowing how to answer.

He said, "If you'd like to take a ride to my place, I can explain what the work would be and that way you could see for yourself if you like it."

She smiled. "Oh, I don't have to like it to do it."

"It helps." He looked around at Jared. "Well, I expect there's room enough for your donkey to ride in the trailer. Think he'd get along with Odds On?"

Jim had, Andi thought, such a leisurely way of confronting potential problems that a person couldn't help but agree. Not that she needed help to do that. "I'm sure he would. Sam's not at all temperamental."

Odds On and Sam were herded into the trailer and Andi into the cab of Jim's truck. It looked fairly new and very clean.

He pulled the truck out, making a slow, wide turn.

"Do horses mind this? Do they lose their balance?"

"Well, they could I guess if you suddenly made a sharp turn too fast. As to minding traveling this way, probably they'd rather be in a pasture or maybe on a racetrack."

"Is Odds On a racehorse?"

"He thinks he is, yeah. But no, I've never entered him in a race. I think every once in a while of putting him in a claims race, but then somebody might up and buy him and good-bye, Odds On."

"Do you keep any racehorses?"

"Yes, a couple." His eyes left the road as he looked at Andi. "I hope you're not seeing glamour in this job. I'm not serious about horse racing; it's just kind of a diversion."

She felt just a tiny bit of a sting in this remark and said, "Do I look like somebody that's looking for glamour?"

He laughed. Hard. Shook his head. "Not from what I've heard."

Only, she was afraid she really might be, mostly from him, from the way he'd come to her rescue. Andi wasn't used to being rescued.

The country through which they drove was empty, but not bleak. Indeed it seemed to thrive on its emptiness. It was monochromatic, brown shading into gold, with long shadows cast by the sun. "Montana has roads like this. So straight for so long a time. There's no end in sight."

"Flat out," said Jim. "Dead-aimed."

She turned to look at him. "'Dead-aimed.' I like that description, but you make the road sound like a shotgun, kind of lethal."

They rode in silence for a few minutes. Jim asked, "What kind of work do you usually do?"

Andi turned her head to the passenger's window. "Waitress work, checkout clerk at Albertson's, but mostly a waitress. Here and there. You know."

Jim thought for a moment, then asked, "You have any experience with animals? Of taking care of them? I mean, besides that donkey you rescued."

A bright stripe of sunlight lanced the windshield and Andi squinted. "Well, not except for—" She stopped.

He waited. When she said nothing more, Jim asked, "Except for what?"

She was thinking about that winter in the Sandias and the trapped coyotes. But she did not want to go into that. It sounded suspicious; it sounded like a lie. She shook her head and told a lie anyway. "My family, we raised llamas. I've had a lot of experience with llamas." She doubted if Jim had. "And we had a few goats, too, but that was mostly a sideline."

"Your family does this for a living? I wouldn't think the market for llamas would be very big."

"No. My dad was—is—an investment banker." Why had she said that? If they had money, what was she doing out wandering from place to place, picking up odd jobs and trouble? "Until the market crashed." Had it? "I mean, his investments lost a ton of money."

"That's too bad. I'm sorry. Where are you from, Andi?"

"Santa Fe." She said that with assurance. That was, somehow or other, the gospel truth. Then, because the Hamptons sometimes got mixed in the telling, she added, "And New York."

"Santa Fe's a gorgeous place. Your family's still there?"

How should she answer that? "Some of it. A brother and a dog. The rest is in the Hamptons."

He was silent for a minute. "Do you keep in touch?"

"Oh, yes, of course." She had named one brother Swann. It sounded so exotic, like llamas. In a way, it was almost comforting to remember nothing before waking up in Santa Fe that morning. Because she couldn't remember a past, she could do anything with it that she wanted. Do anything, be anyone. She realized she was missing an opportunity here. "Oh, and one of my brothers is in Alaska." That could explain Alaska.

"Anchorage?"

"No." Why didn't she just say yes? "In Juneau. He has a small store that sells outerwear."

"You ever been to Alaska? Ever visited him?"

She shook her head. It wasn't so much that she was making this up to conceal the real reason she wanted to go; it was more that she didn't know what the real reason was. She didn't know why she needed to go to Alaska. She wished she did know. She wondered if anyone else could tell her. The wish must be rooted in something from the life she couldn't remember. And it wasn't really all that strong a wish, either. It was a wish easily deflected; indeed, that's probably what she was doing now, with Jim. Getting off a course that had never been particularly clear from the beginning.

"Well, Andi. You're not walking to Alaska, are you?"

That made her smile. Actually, she pretty much was. "It's why I want a job, you know, to get the money for airfare."

Jim thought for a moment. "It's none of my business, but why doesn't your brother get you a ticket?"

"I'd rather do it on my own. You know how that is."

"I guess. I've never been there. You been there before?"

"Once. It was gorgeous, and when you get out of the city, it looks untouched. It looks like this"—she nodded toward the land they were driving through—"only more so."

"The glaciers, that's what I'd like to see. Blue ice. They look so mysterious."

She nodded. "When a part breaks off and slides into the sea, it's like the beginning of the world. There aren't many places you can experience that. Maybe in Africa, maybe going down one of those rivers like the Congo." The sun was high in the sky, making the grass glisten, as hard as enamel. "Maybe we knew once how things really are; maybe we've forgotten everything; maybe we've blocked it all out and now what we're watching is just shadows." She was talking too much. It came, she supposed, from being alone all the time. "Sorry. Sometimes I just go on."

"You certainly think things through."

They were driving by some buildings situated in a depression, like a valley. The buildings were long, clean-looking, and brilliantly white.

"What's down there?"

"Those buildings? That's Klavan's." He slowed down. "It's a hog farm."

"One of those factory farms?"

"I guess. Only it's a pretty small one."

"Would you mind stopping just for a minute?"

Surprised, he stopped the truck. They had just passed the last of the long white buildings.

Andi got out, walked a little way back, and stood on the crown of the grassy shoulder, looking across the field.

Jim had never liked the place, had always turned his head away when he drove by. Indeed, had there been another way into Kingdom without having to drive some complicated route, he'd have done so.

"Why does it look so clean if they've got all of those pigs?"

For her, he thought, it was not a rhetorical question. "Sanitation's one reason. They've got to keep it all up to scratch for when the inspectors come around. State and USDA, I imagine."

"It looks so bright."

"Yeah, that's part of the whole thing, I guess."

She looked at him with a question in her eyes, as if he might be able to justify the operation.

Jim shut his eyes. "Girl, are you this intense about every damned fool thing you come across?"

Now she looked puzzled. "I didn't know I was being."

He gave a short laugh. "Come on, let's go." When she didn't move and appeared to have no thought of moving, he said again, "Come on. I got to get back." He didn't really, did he? His own pigs would be lolling in their pen.

She asked, "When do the sows get out?"

He had turned away and now turned back, trying to funnel the irritation off into some quiet place within him. After all, she wasn't some flighty, irksome teenager looking for an iPod and Easy Street.

"They don't get out."

"They don't?" She frowned at this. "Have you been inside?"

"No. People don't get inside."

She was looking at him, but, he thought, not seeing him. Then she turned back to the landscape and the bright, white, low buildings. It might have been some grand vista she was surveying—the Tetons or the Grand Canyon or the Black Hills. He thought she gave things too much meaning. At the same time, he knew she'd be good around the horses. She was a girl who did not give up easily.

Finally, she did turn to leave, and as she turned away, it was as if the air, pained, had torn.

It wasn't really a farm he had, as he wasn't interested in farming, at least not the kind where you tilled the soil and grew corn and wheat. Nor was it a livestock-producing business. The animals he had, he had just because he liked them.

"It's really pretty," she said, sitting high on the seat as they rounded the curve in the driveway. "It doesn't look as if you need anybody at all."

"Wrong. I go away some, like to Fargo, and the animals, they've got to be looked after."

They were out of the car and going around to the trailer. Andi said, nodding toward the house, painted a very pale blue, a blue sheared down to some unpigmented base, "It looks like Alaska, like blue ice, what you said before."

"I guess it does, come to think of it." Jim was leading the horse down the ramp, then went back for the donkey. "Here, you walk your donkey. See how he likes it."

Andi took the rope, smiling. It was as if Sam was viewing a room in a hotel to see if it was suitable.

As they walked to the barn, Andi ran her hand over the horse's flank. "Odds On, I like that name."

"There's another called Odds Against in there." Jim nodded toward the stables. "I tried to train him up to race in small races, but it was hopeless. Hopeless. I never could get him to keep a gallop for long."

They entered the dark, cool stable where Andi saw the other horses and one empty stall.

"Think this'll be good for Sam?" Jim opened the stall door and Andi led him in. Jim said, "He sure seemed to get on okay with Odds On. And the others look real interested in him."

Andi squinted, as if she could squint up an interest in the faces of the horses. She couldn't. She said, "For Sam, this should be donkey paradise." She undid the rope and closed the door.

"Well, if they don't take to one another . . ." Jim didn't finish that speculative comment. He said, "You ride, I'm hoping. I could use a good exercise boy. Girl, I mean."

Andi answered, "Oh, yes."

Oh, *no*. She had never ridden. But, then, how could she be sure of this, as her past was a blank. "I should say, I haven't done any riding in a long time. But we had horses, two of them." In her mind's eye she saw them, beautiful creatures much like these two, looking alertly over their stall doors. She really would have to stop making things up. She would trip herself up one day if she didn't stop. Yet, she had to have a past, didn't she? So she went on. "They were mostly show horses."

"Really? Then you're good at dressage?"

She wasn't sure what that meant, so she knew she'd better not lay claim to it. Another horse, looking over its stall door, gave her an excuse not to answer.

Once in his stall, Odds On bent his neck around to the horse in the other stall. The horse was a mahogany color, so dark it looked black. It was the color of the highly polished banister going up Mrs. Englehart's front stairs.

"They seem to be great friends."

"They are. This one's Dakota."

"Does Dakota get up to a gallop?"

"Yeah, when he feels like it. Won four out of seven starts as a two-year-old."

Andi was surprised. "You mean he's a racehorse?"

"Indeed." Jim stroked Dakota's muzzle. "Too bad I haven't got a show horse. We could put up the hurdles and you could put him through his paces."

"Too bad, yes." Andi felt her stomach lurch, as if she were on the unstoppable horse right then. The two horses in the next two stalls seemed interested in them. "Who is this?"

"That's Odds Against. Odds On and him are great friends." Jim moved to the next stall and a beautiful chestnut horse. "This is Palimpsest. I raced him a couple of times. He's okay."

"Palimpsest? That's a strange name."

"It means 'overwriting,' sort of. Maybe paper was so precious and expensive, you couldn't throw it away, so you erased what you could and wrote over it. That's Palimpsest. He's beautiful on the surface, but underneath is something more, as if instead of erasing or wiping it out, I just wrote over it. What was there once is still there, layer after layer of overwriting, but you still see what's underneath if you look hard enough. That horse is much more than what meets the naked eye; it's just a feeling I had about him, from a colt." He took off his cap and put it back on. He looked at the horse in the next stall. "This is Nelson. He's not spectacular, just a good old horse. Not temperamental, always ready to do what anyone wants of him."

They walked around behind the barn to the pigsty.

There were two pigs, the fattest she'd ever seen. One was rooting about, the other was sleeping on its side. They were comical.

"These here are Max and Hazel. I don't do any butchering any-more. I've had these two for years. Every time somebody stops by, Max and Hazel think it's time to eat. Hazel, especially. See this apple tree here? There never seem to be apples on the lowest branches."

The branches at the bottom, though leafy, were not hosting any apples. "What happens to them?"

"Pigs got 'em." Jim grinned. "You might ask how."

She looked up at the branches, down at Max and Hazel. "How could they?"

"It's a mystery."

"Well, what's the solution?" She smiled.

He shrugged. "You got me."

They stood, looking at Max and Hazel.

"Come on inside and we'll have coffee."

The invitation could have been for the pigs, the way they crowded the fence. She began to feel less burdened, or perhaps now he carried some of the burden, as if between them they would manage.

In the house, she sat down at a table covered in yellow and white checkered oilcloth. She ran her hand over its smoothness.

"I'll rustle up some lunch in a bit; meantime"—he set a cake stand on the table; underneath its plastic cover were a half dozen doughnuts, sugar and plain—"have one of these."

It occurred to her only then how hungry she was. She hadn't had any breakfast and it was nearly noon. But she would wait for him and the coffee.

He was standing at the counter, looking at the coffeemaker as if willing it to finish its cycle.

"Do you live here alone?" It was such a big house she would have expected a family, a number of children underfoot.

"Yep, I'm on my own. Wife died some years ago."

"I'm sorry." And she was, but at the same time it was comforting to hear that; someone besides herself was on his own.

The coffeemaker had finally sputtered out its last drop, and he filled the cups. "You worried what people will say?" He grinned, setting down coffee and a creamer. The sugar was already on the table. "I wouldn't think anyone who could walk into a strange town leading a donkey could care much for what other people think."

Propriety was something to which she hadn't given a thought. She smiled. "I guess so."

"Listen, Andi. Just what were you planning on doing with that donkey of yours?" He put down white cups and saucers and set the coffeepot between them.

"I'm not sure. I guess it was what you might call an impulse buy." She broke a sugar doughnut in half and rested half on her saucer. The other she dipped briefly in her coffee.

"That I can believe." Jim dunked his own doughnut.

Andi looked at him over the rim of her cup. "Do you know that man? The one who claims Sam belongs to him?"

"Lucas Bailey? Sure, I know him. Know his boys, too. They keep getting arrested and Lucas keeps springing them. Too bad you didn't just shoot them and put us all out of our misery." He drank his coffee. "You'd've saved the sheriff a lot of trouble."

"How did you know—"

Jim raised his eyebrows. "It was the Bailey boys that threatened you? My God, girl, everybody knew that before you hardly set foot in town."

"I really don't want the sheriff after me." Not after what happened in Idaho, she didn't. But that was more than a year ago, and whatever investigation there'd been seemed to have ended swiftly.

"Nor do I." He laughed. "Any particular reason?"

She didn't look up from her coffee and didn't answer him.

"I mean, if you don't want Harry McKibbon after you, it's probably best not to be packing a gun, to say nothing of taking donkeys. All that does is it attracts attention."

"How well do you know this Lucas Bailey?"

"Only to pass the time of day with. He's not much for conversation."

"Does he keep donkeys?"

"Horses, yes. I don't know about donkeys. The one he's after might be the only one."

Over Jim's shoulder, Andi saw a figure approaching. "Here's someone."

Jim turned. "Tom! Come on in! Didn't expect to see you today. Just brought Odds On back from Jared's. Look, this is Andi Oliver. We're hiring her. We could use a good hot walker. Andi, this is Tom Rio. We're in business together more or less."

"Mostly less." Tom reached his fingers up to his hat. "Pleased to meet you."

His eyes were hazel, his face angular—cheekbones, jaw—as if any extra flesh had been worn away by time and weather. He didn't look at all convinced they needed a new anything. He got himself a mug and sat down. Jim pushed the coffeepot toward him. "Andi's had experience with horses, but only show horses. That doesn't mean she couldn't do the little bit of riding for us . . ."

Oh, yes, it does, she thought. Why had she been so stupid as to say she knew anything about horses?

Tom pulled over the sugar bowl and dumped a couple of spoonfuls into his cup. "Show horses? That takes a lot of expertise; it's very precise, very measured."

"I'm not saying I know *much,* understand—"

Tom said, "Never mind. Since Quentin quit, we haven't got an exerciser except for Jesus, who's good, but overworked. Quentin wasn't much dependable anyway." He ate a doughnut slowly, almost meditatively, as if he had much on his mind. "You get yourself a donkey, Jim? Cause there's one standin' out there in the barn."

"Oh, that's Andi's. She came by it somehow."

Tom nodded, as if this were a fairly common occurrence, strangers wandering around with animals they'd just "come by."

Andi looked from one to the other, but neither man questioned the donkey's provenance.

Tom sat back and lit up a cigarette. "You the young lady that was accosted out on the road by the Bailey boys?"

"If that's who it was. I didn't know their names."

"I was just telling her," said Jim, "she'd have done us all a favor if she'd plugged them."

Tom snorted. "You got that right." He drew in on his cigarette, exhaled a thin stream of smoke. "But do you always pack a gun?"

"No. But maybe now I will. After that."

Jim shook his head. "I don't advise it, girl."

"I was only joking. You know." She hadn't been joking at all, given what her life had been like so far.

Tom looked over at Jim. "Wouldn't advise it why?"

"Hell, you know how liable a person is to shoot himself in his own foot."

"What would have happened, Jim, if she hadn't had that gun?"

"I admit, you're right there."

They sat as the afternoon melted away in one of those companionable silences, so rare in her experience. It was that poem she couldn't call up. The speaker in the poem would come back and find the swans flown away. It wasn't over, the ending, the loss.

"Something wrong, Andi?" Jim asked. "You look pale."

She shook her head and looked down at her empty cup. She was afraid that to say anything at all would sink her.

Jim got up. "Well, no wonder you're pale. She's not had a thing to eat except that doughnut and coffee. I'll make some eggs and sausage. You, Tom?"

"Thanks, but no. I'm just on my way to Fargo. I hope you hang around here," he said to Andi. "We could really use the help."

"Thanks." She watched him go, wished he would come back.

"I'll show you the room you'd have if you wanted," said Jim.

They climbed the pie-shaped back stairs to a landing and a hallway, off of which were several rooms. Jim opened the door to the first one, saying, "This one has its own bath. It's the nicest."

Andi would have been happy to sleep in the barn. But she'd certainly rather have this room, wide and spacious. It had two windows with sheer curtains that the breeze lifted and slatted blinds that threw stripes of sunlight on a big hooked rug. The wallpaper was printed with tiny blue and green flowers and leaves. The furniture was that no-nonsense mission style— bed, dresser, old rocker. The rocker's cushions were covered in a chintz that matched the wallpaper. Someone had gone to some trouble.

"It's a wonderful room. And it overlooks the barn." She liked being able to see if anything was going on there.

"Okay, if you want, it's yours."

As the car took the same route back to town, it passed the Klavan hog facility.

He saw her lifting herself part of the way out of her seat to get a better look. He didn't comment. It kind of worried him, this fastening on to what you couldn't do anything about. Jim believed there were just things in life you had to accept. One was that place.

Yeah, well, he could tell that to the marines, as far as she was concerned. When you're young you can afford to see life in black and white. For him, there was no way to throttle that sort of thing. Progress, that's what it was called.

"You don't much like that place, do you?" he said.

"Do you?"

6

'm sorry," Andi said to Mrs. Englehart, who was standing by the telephone table when she walked through the front door. "I'm sorry I didn't come back last night, but there was a kind of emergency with my donkey." Andi told her what had happened.

The woman shook her head, sadly. "Do they know who did it? That's a disgrace, treating a poor animal that way. The law ought to punish them, whoever it was."

"Yes, they should. Anyway, I found a job."

Mrs. Englehart was wiping her hands on her apron. "But that's wonderful. Where? I didn't know you were looking for one. Does it mean you'd be staying on?"

"It's at Jim Purley's farm. Helping to take care of things. Do chores. You know."

"Oh, well, Jim Purley is highly thought of around these parts. Yes, he's got some very fine horses, I've heard."

"That's right. And this way, I can see to it that Sam—that's the donkey—has a place, too. He'll be right in the barn with the horses."

"Well, that's grand. You won't be needing the room, then, after tonight?"

"No, I won't. But thanks for everything, Mrs. Englehart."

★   ★   ★

Up in her room, Andi opened the nightstand drawer and took out the Smith & Wesson. She had removed the clip and stuck it in a pocket of her backpack. This she'd done in the unlikely event that someone, a child, perhaps Mrs. Englehart's grandchild, might be in here looking around. She had no idea if Mrs. Englehart had a grandchild or if there were any children at all around.

But she did know that you had to prepare for just about any eventuality, anything that could happen, as nearly as possible. If you got careless (like leaving a loaded gun in an unlocked drawer) disaster would shortly follow. Not could, but *would*. Life was dangerous. The land mine in tall grass, the open well, the uncovered swimming pool, the crack in the iced-over lake. They were waiting right outside her door.

Andi knew she was paranoid, but she had ample reason to be and she'd rather be paranoid than dead.

The gun back in the drawer, she lay down on the tufted white bedspread and ran her fingertip over the initials on her backpack: AO. She still had no idea what the initials stood for, or whose they were.

It was what remained of a life she couldn't remember. Andi Olivier. A fiction. That the letters stood for Alhambra Orphanage was just another fiction. The entire story he had fed her of finding her walking the highway away from the flames of the bus, all of that could have been lies, probably all of it was.

If Harry Wine had lied about the burning bus and the orphanage, why had he done it? Was it because he was afraid the truth would get him killed? That, she thought, was really ironic.

Her life, then, was a fiction. She was just making it up as she went along. She had invented the name and the family. The Oliviers, now Oliver. Dressage. That had popped up from the well of spurious facts that she told people. But, of course, the Oliviers would have access to every luxury imaginable—tennis, riding, boating.

And she would have been proficient in dressage. She liked the word; she just wasn't sure what it meant, beyond its having to do with showing off horses. Show horses.

She lay there with her hands behind her head going over the day, which she thought must be one of the best days she had ever had, and now there was the prospect of living it over and over.

Andi sighed and closed her eyes.

7

She got up and washed her face before going to May's diner.

When she came to the pharmacy she stopped to get some toothpaste and noticed a rack of paperbacks by the magazine stand. She pulled out one with a gorgeous picture of a sunset, the silhouette of a cowboy against it, and across from him another silhouette, an Indian. Their outlines stood against a blazing sky. Westerns were something she couldn't ever remember reading, but she bought this one because of the cover.

In the diner, Andi decided to sit in a booth, thinking that a person sitting at the counter encouraged conversation. It was easier to pass the time of day at the counter than at a table. She slid into a shadowy booth, and when Mildred came along with a friendly grin, Andi ordered a grilled cheese sandwich, fries, coleslaw, and a Coke. Then she pulled out the paperback book and leafed through it.

Several of the customers who'd been here last night were here again. It was a hangout for the citizens of Kingdom, this diner and the bars down the street.

When she looked up from the book, she saw the two who'd stopped her on the highway and felt a rush of adrenaline. Andi wished she were not running scared so much of the time. Her defense against fear was not to show it. This probably made her seem cold or at least indifferent. But one of the points was just that, to put people off. As dangerous as that Smith & Wesson was, she was glad she carried it and glad she'd kept up target practice after leaving that cabin in the Sandias. An empty cabin, apparently used for only part of the year.

It wasn't poachers she meant to shoot, although thinking about that now, thinking about Harry Wine, she wondered if she would have shot a poacher. She had never seen them; she had only seen the traps they left behind and seen the animals struggling in them—coyotes and wolves and foxes. The pain must've been indescribable, like a human trying to saw off his own arm or leg. She had the gun with her in case she wasn't able to get the traps open; they were those steel-jaw leghold traps that had needed every ounce of strength to pry open. The kind an animal could get free from only by chewing off its leg. If she couldn't get the coyote free, she would have to shoot it. But she never had to. The first time she had found a trapped coyote, she tried again and again to get the trap open, but couldn't, and she trudged back and forth, back and forth, revolted by the prospect of having to kill something she would sooner save. She was sweating there in the dead of winter, pacing.

She wondered now whether she would have been able to shoot the coyote if she hadn't finally worked the trap loose. Maybe not.

It was easier to shoot a man.

When her sandwich and fries were set before her, she looked up, thanked Mildred, and let her glance drift to the jukebox, where the "boys" were lounging after shoving in coins to play some rap artist with enough attitude to blow up Kingdom.

The two of them leaned on the jukebox and stared at her.

Andi stared back. Hard. Their smiles flagged for a second or two. They looked at each other, as if they needed to exchange looks to muster courage. Andi saw that and smiled inwardly. A dead giveaway. Now they had to make a move of some kind, and so they moved over to her booth.

"If it ain't the little girl with the donkey. Hey, sweetheart," said Junior or Carl, same difference. "Dad wasn't altogether pleased with you stealin' his property. No, he wasn't."

Andi continued taking bites of her sandwich, looking at them as one might watch a boring TV program to have something to do while eating. The Baileys were there for one's passive entertainment. It was easy to see her lack of response was aggravating them. Carl (or Junior) drew back his fleece-lined jacket so that Andi could see the holstered gun.

Her expression was indifferent. Then she said, "Well, Carl, you and Junior here—"

This was the younger one and he didn't like being called that and clamped his jaw tight.

"—you better be a real quick draw because you'll never see me coming." She took another bite of grilled cheese and chewed slowly, eyes still moving from one Bailey to the other.

Junior moved his shoulders around as if he meant to do something with them, batter a door open, perhaps. He said, "You think you're pretty fuckin' good, don't you?"

She shook her head. "No. I don't think I'm good. I *know* I'm good. I've got the Academy citation to prove it."

Again the brothers exchanged an uncertain look. "Fuck's that?"

"You two don't know the Academy? Jesus." She shook her head in wonder at this ignorance and gave an abrupt laugh. "Citations for marksmanship." As she licked the grease off her fingers, she thought she might be overdoing it. Yet to judge from their expressions she could go even further. "Top one percent get citations. Top one percent of the Academy enrollees." She picked up a French fry and made an ambiguous gesture that could be taken—and was—as the good old American road gesture.

Both of them reddened like schoolboys.

Junior, bull-like, flared his nostrils as if readying himself for the charge. Everything about him looked mean, his narrow eyes, his heavy neck. The shoulders sloped away from that neck at too great an angle to give the impression of strength. Andi bet those slanting shoulders were a constant irritant. Every time he made the move to square them, he failed.

Carl said, "You best be careful, lady. You just try goin' up against the Baileys, you'll find your ass in a sling. We're big in this town."

Their father at least was a formidable presence and a man she wouldn't want to run into on a dead-end road. Andi continued eating her French fries and watching the window toward which their backs were turned. The county sheriff's cruiser had just pulled up outside.

This was luck hardly to be believed; good luck didn't often come her way. She wanted to laugh out loud. The sheriff was out of his car and walking toward the diner.

Andi said to Carl, "That gun you're carrying? Is it real or maybe something left over from the county fair?"

Swiftly, Carl pulled back his coat. "You'd better believe—"

When she saw the sheriff coming through the door, Andi jutted up from her seat and yelled, "Down everybody! He's got a gun!" She shoved her way between them and ran to the sheriff. Caught by surprise, they just stood there.

"They were threatening me, Sheriff!"

Sheriff McKibbon called out, "What's going on here, Carl? Junior? You acting like fools again?" He made his way to the booth. He had one of those rolling walks, like John Wayne.

The other customers, most of whom had risen and headed toward the door until the sheriff came through it, were gathered near the counter in a tight knot, watching.

"Which of you boys got the gun?"

With great reluctance, Carl pulled back his fleece jacket, having a hard time striking the note he wanted between belligerence and subservience. "I got me a license, Sheriff, as you know."

"Yeah, Carl, it ain't a license to flash that weapon by way of threatening another person." Sheriff McKibbon reached around to his back and pulled handcuffs from his belt.

Carl took a few steps backward. "Now, just you wait, Sheriff. I wasn't doin' nothin'—"

From behind the counter Mildred called over, "The hell you wasn't, Carl Bailey! You and your brother's been standing over that poor girl the last twenty minutes and I saw you—*saw* you, Carl Bailey—show her that gun before."

The sheriff turned to Andi. "That true, miss?"

"It is. Ever since I came to town—even before I came—they've been nipping at my heels like sled dogs."

Carl shouted, as if the sheriff were on the other side of the room instead of right there clamping the handcuff to his wrist, "Yeah? Well, what about her, then? She pulled a gun on us along the highway when all's we was trying to do was help—"

The little crowd dispersed, some with disparaging gestures and others—two women—giving Andi's arm an understanding squeeze as they reclaimed their seats.

The sheriff said, "We heard all about that, you and your brother running back to town with your tails between your legs . . . there!" Each of them wore one of the cuffs, so that they were cuffed together. They could, of course, both run at some point during this transport to jail, but it would be damned stupid.

Both of the Baileys looked at Andi as if killing her would be the first order of business once they'd gained their freedom.

"You just wait, you little—"

"Enough!" The sheriff got right up into their faces. "I'm tired of the both of you." He turned to Andi. "After they get out—doomsday, maybe—if they come within a hundred feet of you, they'll be right back in."

"Thanks. Thank you." The thanks was heartfelt. She hated to think she'd have to keep running into them. Although beginning tomorrow she'd have the protection of Jim Purley and Tom Rio. What a wonderful thought. She couldn't recall a time when she'd been under anyone's protection, except maybe Reuel, back in Salmon, Idaho. But she tried not to think about all that as she watched the sheriff herd Carl and Junior out the door at the same time another police car was driving in.

Andi sat down on one of the counter stools and faced the door.

"That was real good," said the man beside her. "The way you did that." He was smoking and flicked ash from his cigarette with his little finger into a tin tray.

"Did what?"

He smiled and sucked in on his Camel as if it were the source of oxygen. Everything about him was a little ragged—hair (earlobe length), mustache, that morning's bluish-gray beard, fingernails (bitten but not to the quick), denim jacket, faded brown and white checked shirt (or maybe red and white, once). Even the cigarette stubs in the tin ashtray looked mashed.

He didn't bother with the "Did what?" as the answer to that was obvious to both of them, but said, "You're the one brought that mule into town."

"Donkey." *Mule* made her unaccountably irritated. "People here talk as if Kingdom's a walled city. I mean, as if visitors are supposed to leave their belongings, including donkeys, at the door."

His laugh shook him because it was inside, barely registering a sound on the outside. "You got that right." His elbow was propped on the counter and that hand held his cigarette. He reached his other hand around and held it out. "I'm Norman."

She smiled. "I'm Andi Oliver."

"I gathered."

"Why?"

"Oh, please, such false modesty. You are the talk of this loose-lipped town."

"Well, then, nothing must happen here."

"'Nothing, like something, happens anywhere.'" He took a swig of lukewarm coffee, made a sign to Mildred for more.

Andi looked at him curiously. He seemed to be changing before her eyes, slowly morphing into another person. "That sounds like poetry."

"Probably because it is."

"Whose?"

"Forgot. So how'd you come by that donkey? Funny thing is, everyone's trying to figure out where you got it, overlooking what's much more important, which is why you got it."

Mildred came by with the coffee. "Leave the poor girl alone, Norman. She's had to put up with her share of crazies." Mildred walked off.

Norman smiled and lifted the hot coffee to his lips. He continued his line of talk. "Has the donkey been with you on your travels since the beginning? Or is it a recent acquisition?" He looked at her. She didn't answer. "Hm. Then let's proceed to the second interesting part of your arrival. You drew a gun on the Bailey brothers. That's almost as surprising as the donkey. I know you're going to make something up as an answer, if you answer at all."

"No, I'm not. The truth is—"

"Yeah."

"—I'm taking the donkey to a relative in Fargo. My grand-mother."

"Little Red Riding Hood told a similar story. Except Red wasn't going to Fargo."

"I'll tell you something if you don't already know. Last night some-body took Sam—that's my donkey—out of his stall down there at Jared's saddlery and left him out in that field of sunflowers near Jared's."

Norman frowned. "Who? The Baileys?"

"I'm guessing them, but I don't know. I don't know anybody in town. Who do you think would do that?"

He shook his head. "That's mean as hell. Is there anyone except for those brothers got a grudge against you?"

"How could they? I've only been here two days."

"Yes, well, forgive me for saying it, but other people's two days aren't exactly *your* two days." Norman caught Mildred's eye. He asked Andi, "You want some coffee?"

"No, thanks. My stomach feels a little peculiar."

"Nerves, that's all. No wonder."

Andi rested her chin on her cupped hand. "What do you do? I mean, what kind of work?"

"Write books. When I'm not sitting in here or at the Two Dogs bar talking."

She thought she had misheard. "Books? You're a writer?"

"Uh-huh. It isn't much, but it's a living."

Mildred had come down the counter with the coffeepot and had picked up on the tail end of the conversation. "This man is our one claim to fame. Can you imagine?" She rolled her eyes and walked off.

"You mean—you're a professional? You've been published?"

He nodded. "Yep. Twenty, twenty-one times."

Andi was dazzled. "What do you write? What kind of books?"

He drew in on his cigarette. "Westerns. Genre stuff. What you were reading there until Tweedledee and Tweedledum came in."

She pulled the book from her back pocket. "Like this? This kind of Western?"

"Actually, precisely that kind of Western. That's one of mine. I was delighted to see somebody actually reading it."

Andi looked from the book to him. "You're Norman X. Black?"

"I added the X in hopes that people would remember the name. I mean, Norman and Black are pretty common names."

"From what I could tell, these books are the old-fashioned kind."

"That's it. Nineteenth century, mostly 1880s."

Andi sighed. "It must be a wonderful life to lead, a writer—"

He laughed. "If you call Kingdom and eating in here wonderful."

"But you can go anywhere, that's one of the good things about being a writer."

He flicked a long ash from his cigarette. "No. I like it here all right. Got just about the right ratio of crazy to sane."

"Do you use Kingdom as a setting?"

"I'd be a sucker to pass it up." He laughed.

"Don't the people you use as characters mind?"

"Oh, they don't read. At least not my books."

"Surely some of them—"

Norman turned to look squarely at her. "I never heard anyone excepting Jared and Jim Purley ever say he was reading one of my books." He turned back to his coffee.

"But that's terrible . . . it's hateful. Why would you want to live among people who were that callous or indifferent? Or jealous, maybe. But how can an entire town be that deeply jealous?"

"You're the first person ever took my side," Norman said, smiling.

"Of course I'd take your side. That's because it's the only side there is." She looked at the Indian and the lone cowboy or whatever he was. "There's something almost comforting about this picture."

"Indian's a Sioux. The other one's my main character. He's known this guy for ten years. Maybe what's comforting to you is the conversation looks real intimate. You can tell they're friends. Indian and white man—one of the most contentious relationships in history. White man was at fault, but the Indians weren't great negotiators. They'd as soon take off the top of your head as talk."

"Irreconcilable differences. Like a bad marriage?" said Andi. "Sounds like maybe you had one."

He dropped the tight little knot of paper into his ashtray. "She wanted to move from here, called it the most sorrowful spot on earth. When I wouldn't—" He shrugged and said, "Just like you said, I could write anywhere. Only I couldn't. I seem to need this place, but I don't know why. It could be as simple as I've lived here all my life."

"That's understandable. It must be comforting to have that sort of connectedness."

"How about you?"

Her "life": there had been flashes of memory, but the images had always dissolved so quickly, she couldn't grasp them. "Santa Fe."

"Santa Fe? Well. So you hit the road, bored with its beauty?"

"You could say that." She smiled and looked at the big white face of the clock by the kitchen. "It's late, after nine. I think I'd better go."

"Nice talkin' to you, Andi. I'll see you again, I hope."

"Sure, you will."

Andi walked along Main Street, thinking Kingdom was the template for small plains towns. The Two Dogs, the Dollar Store, the Unique Boutique, Ernie's TV Sales and Repair—they were fossilized remains. No wonder Norman X. Black used this as backdrop. The town hadn't changed in decades. Not literally, of course, since a western town would hardly have had a dollar store—or might that not have been called a general store? And the Two Dogs could as easily have been Two Dogs Saloon.

Andi translated each store she passed. The boutique might have been Ladies' Furnishings—Ribbons and Materials. The barber shop and the Plugged Nickel she left alone. They were the same as they'd always been.

After she washed up and brushed her teeth—freshly grateful for the real charm of running water—she climbed into bed and lay there beneath the clean whiteness of the sheet, wondering, *What would life have been like back then? In the time of Norman's books?*

It was sentimental, she knew, to look at the past as good times, but seeing how her own past was zero, was nothing, how could she help but reach out for someone else's past?

Nothing, like something, happens anywhere.

8

At 8:50 Andi was standing on Mrs. Englehart's front porch with her backpack when Jim pulled up.

"Good morning," he said as she got in beside him. Between puffs on the cigar he was trying to get going, he said, "Harry McKibbon wants to know if you were really scared of the two assholes—that's how he put it—last night or if you just wanted to make sure he'd arrest them."

"Yes, I was scared. One of them had a gun, didn't he?"

"Yep. He did indeed." But she caught his sideways glance. "Of course, so did you."

Andi was exasperated. "Not *with* me. I don't carry it everywhere. At times I think everybody wants to blame me for what happened."

"No, that isn't it. I think it's more curiosity than anything. Trouble with a gun is, you use it once effectively—even if you don't shoot anyone—do that once, every tin horn upstart gun owner wants to prove he's better. I see you do not agree." He downshifted to make his way up the hill at the end of Main.

Andi had dropped her head in her hands. "You know what that sounds like? One of Norman X. Black's books. Do you know him?"

"The writer? Sure, I do, a little. I don't think anyone knows Norm but a little."

"Given he's written over twenty books, how's that possible?"

"Some folks keep themselves hidden beneath a lot of wraps. Then other folks can't penetrate all those coats and scarves, so to speak."

"You've read some of his books, haven't you?"

"Yeah, Jared gave me one. That's the only one I read, though. It's not to say it wasn't a good book. Good writing, too. I just don't like Westerns. Tom's read some of them."

"Well, Norman doesn't think *anyone* except Jared and you has read a word he's written."

"Maybe people are just in awe of him. Or maybe they just can't read. Or maybe they *have* read one or another and are afraid they'd sound stupid talking to Norman about it."

"Why can't they just say, 'Hey, Norman, I really liked that book!'"

"Because it takes confidence, Andi. There's always the possibility he'd ask what they liked about it."

"I don't think he'd do that."

Jim looked at her. "You're kind of argumentative."

"I am not."

They drove for a while in silence, Jim hoping he could get by Klavan's without her noticing, but there wasn't much hope of that. At the sign, she sat up straight in her seat, Norman X. Black temporarily forgotten. She did not ask him to stop this time, just sat up straighter in her seat and stared as he drove past.

Finally they were crunching along the gravel drive to Jim's house and Andi had the pleasant anticipation one connects with coming home.

"I'd like you to graze Dakota today. Take him out to the fields; he's been a bit testy."

"Sure," she said.

Jim pulled up in front of the barn, and a short, sturdy-looking fellow came out.

"Hello, Jesus. Where you been?"

"Flu or somethin'."

"This is Andi. Andi, Jesus Hernandez."

Jesus said hello, rather grudgingly, then asked, "You want me to breeze Dakota?"

"Nope. Dakota gets the day off. I told Andi to take him out in the field."

"You tell her about watching for holes and stuff?" Before Jim could answer, Jesus turned to Andi, said, "Don't let him out of your sight."

"Of course I won't." He seemed anxious for the horses, for their welfare.

Worried, he frowned. "You got to watch out he don't step in no holes or nothing."

"I'll look all out for anything remotely dangerous."

Jesus nodded, slightly mollified but still doubtful, as if measures to be taken regarding the horse's welfare were endless.

"Come on, Andi, let's get you up to your room."

After unpacking the backpack, Andi took off her boots and lay down on top of the white spread. It was some kind of downy stuff she simply dropped into, a relief after Mrs. Englehart's thin mattress. But that in itself had been a relief from the hard ground of the past weeks.

The room was restful, with its windows and their sheer curtains billowing inward, its faded, flowered wallpaper. The small intrusion of her belongings into this unalloyed and uncluttered space hardly left a mark.

Coming up from the kitchen was the woodsy smell of bacon. Bacon in the morning, spitting in its own fat, frizzled to thinness, was perhaps one of the purest pleasures there was for most people. She could understand how people couldn't resist it, lying in marbled strips in its tightly wrapped plastic container. Why would anyone think of Klavan's, and places like it?

Andi looked up at the ceiling, one corner festooned in delicate spider webs whose motion was like the curtains: lifting, falling. She wondered how it would feel to be held in something as delicate as that web, a hammock of light.

As if it were a film projector, her mind flashed an image for two seconds, three—a hammock swinging between trees, sun coming through the leaves, making a web of light.

She sat up. It was gone. Rogue memories, she called them, taking her by surprise, coming from nowhere, returning to nowhere.

"Hey, Andi! Bacon and eggs almost done."

It was Tom Rio's voice calling from the bottom of the back stairs.

She pulled on her boots, thinking of the long white buildings of Klavan's.

Jim said, "I thought you probably didn't even have breakfast and we should've gone to May's. This is better, though. Tom's making French toast, Jesus is on the omelets, and I'm doing the bacon."

Jesus actually smiled at her, as if the earlier admonitions had never been spoken. She smiled back, certain they'd come up again the minute she laid a hand on a horse.

"That's the most comfortable bed I ever had."

Tom said, "It's got one of those featherbed things on it."

Jesus turned with the big cast-iron pan and shook its contents. "This about ready."

"So's mine," said Tom.

"Bacon's done." Jim reached up to a shelf and took down four heavy white plates. "Let me just drain it." He flopped eight or ten slices onto paper towels, then onto the plates.

They were sitting around the table, enjoying the food, when Jim looked across Andi's shoulder to the window behind her. It faced the gravel drive. "Oh, Christ."

They turned to see a blue truck making its way toward the house.

"It's Lucas Bailey. He's got a nerve, just rolling in anytime he damned well pleases."

Andi was alarmed. "Why has he come?"

Jim said, "To disturb whoever's peace he can."

Jesus jumped up and was out the door as if he had the devil after him. Before anyone could say anything, he headed across the circle of driveway to the barn.

Silhouetted by the sun, Lucas Bailey stood at the screen door. He knocked against its frame.

"Come on in, Lucas."

He did, letting the door stutter closed behind him. He just looked around, betraying nothing in the look. He said hello to Tom and Andi. Even the simple word sounded scurrilous in his mouth.

"Sit down, why don't you?" Tom rose and hitched over a fifth chair, a tall ladder-back.

"You want something to eat?" said Jim. "There's French toast."

"No, thanks." Lucas slipped two fingers beneath the rim of his hat and pushed it back a half inch. He kept his coat on; it was one of those long ones, an ankle-length cowboy coat.

He did look sinister, but it wasn't the coat or the black brimmed hat. It was his face, deeply notched with runnels going from his nose to his mouth; that and his pale eyes.

"So what can I do for you, Lucas? Something on your mind?"

"Well, yes, there is, as you know. I've just come to pick up my property."

"What property's that?" said Jim.

"That donkey this girl stole." He looked at Andi, keeping his gaze on her as if pinning her to the chair.

"Come on. Have a cup of coffee and be sociable."

Andi wanted to laugh. She couldn't remember anyone less inclined to be sociable.

"All right, I think I will have a cup. Mind if I were to ask you a few questions?"

This was directed at Andi, who minded a lot. She hoped her voice would be steady. She said, "You already have."

Bailey ignored this. He said, "I'd like to know just where you got that donkey I guess you got stabled out there." He tilted his head backward, toward the barn.

"Lucas, leave it alone, for God's sakes. Leave the girl alone."

"No, Jim, I ain't going to. That donkey's mine."

Tom Rio reached around and plucked the coffeepot from the counter. He poured some into Bailey's cup and refilled his own. He said, "Thing is this, if Andi here is supposed to have stole him, how'd she ever manage to do it? Walk right into your barn and lead the donkey out?"

"Hell, no. He was out in the field. Out to graze."

"In *what* field? Did she have to walk your three hundred acres?"

"How in hell do I know what field?"

"All I'm saying," Tom went on, "is that your donkey would have to be visible from the highway for anybody to steal it. Now, as I recall, your land that edges the highway is damned far from the house and outbuildings. If this donkey was near the fence bordering the highway, it would be a long, long walk home. So you really didn't know where he was. You didn't know either if he was hungry or thirsty or sick or dying."

Jesus came in and sat down in his chair. "What you all talkin' about?"

"Bailey here is claiming that donkey belongs to him."

"What donkey?" Jesus started in eating his cold French toast.

Tom wanted to laugh and turned away, taking his plate to the sink.

Bailey said, "Don't give me that 'What donkey?' Mr. *Meh*-ee-co, you know damned well it's the one you got out there with the horses."

Jesus's frown deepened. "Me, I don' know what you talkin' about."

"Mind, then, if I go to your stables and have a look?"

The question appeared to be addressed to everyone, but they all looked at Jesus.

Jesus said, "I mind, yeah, I mind. I don' want you puttin' the voodoo spell on my horses."

Bailey, though, was already up and heading toward the door.

Jesus jumped up and followed.

"C'mon," said Tom. Jim and Andi rose and followed the other two.

They gathered at the door of the barn where Jesus was waving an arm, taking in the five stabled horses. The barn was, as always, immaculate, including Sam's stall, where no donkey stood. There was nothing in it to suggest any donkey had ever been there.

Bailey got his face down to Jesus's. "So where you keepin' him, *Hey-zous*? In *Meh*-ee-co?" He turned to Tom. "At Tom's?"

"Bailey," said Tom, "you don't really give a rat's ass about one old donkey. You probably never paid a nickel's worth attention to it anyway. Hell, you probably never even *saw* it. So back off."

"If it'll make you happier," Jim said, "I'll pay you for it."

"Why would you do that, Jim, if it's not my donkey?"

"Easy. To get you off my back."

Bailey's laugh was abrupt, cut off, as if he'd called it back. "No. I want my property returned, that's all." He turned toward his truck, walked off, and called back over his shoulder, "I'll get it, too."

Sam stood in the quiet of the trailer still hitched up to Jim's truck. He was waiting (or, she sadly thought, not waiting) for deliverance. Andi imagined he had gotten used to simply standing in some field or other. He was so docile it made her want to weep.

She hitched her fingers in the bridle Jesus had put on him—maybe afraid he'd bolt rather than go into the confines of the trailer. Andi could have told him Sam wouldn't resist. She led him back to the barn.

"Thanks, Jesus, for thinking of the trailer," said Jim.

"Damned clever," said Tom.

Jesus smiled and his neck reddened.

9

Andi had a lot of questions she didn't ask because she didn't want to parade her ignorance.

They had been standing for a while, looking at Palimpsest.

Tom said, "Now, this horse looks almost to be as big as Secretariat. If he could only run like Secretariat . . ."

"But is he fast?"

"Not that fast. Legs come down the same way though, like the spokes of a wheel. As even a gait as you'll ever see."

Tom took a toothpick from his shirt pocket and put it in his mouth, and rolled it around, thoughtful. His hands were stuck in his back jeans pockets. He looked down at Andi, who was watching him, and plucked another toothpick from his pocket. He handed it to her.

She stuck the toothpick in her mouth, same as he had, and found it rather comforting. She rolled it around and stuck her hands in her back pockets. "Well, is that what I'm supposed to do? Exercise the horses?"

"I don't know what Jim has in mind, but it'd be good if you could, once in a while. Jesus has too much work to do. But I think what Jim really needs is someone he can trust to watch over the ones that stay when we're taking one or the other to the track."

This surprised her. "Me? But you don't even know me. Neither does Jim. How do you know you can trust me?"

"It's obvious, I'd say." He smiled down at her, she with the tooth-pick and hands plunged in pockets. "He needs somebody with guts."

She was open-mouthed in surprise. "*Me?* I'm your original gut-less wonder." For some reason, the posture she'd assumed, which she noticed now was just like Tom's, made her a little braver.

"How about what happened out there on the highway? You saying that didn't take guts?"

"I had a gun, don't forget."

"Uh-huh. I'm wondering what happened to you along the way that made you carry the gun in the first place."

Andi kept on looking at Palimpsest, who was observing them and chewing a mouthful of hay. He seemed an awfully calm animal for a racehorse. She looked at Nelson in the next stall. "He's a beautiful horse." Nelson was caramel-colored, with a mane of gold and pinkish brown.

"Nelson? Yeah, he's a handsome horse. When he runs, gives off a kind of glow when the sun hits him, like a flutter of gold going around the track. Trouble is, he can't run worth a damn."

They moved to the other side, where Sam was installed. There were two horses on this side: the big bay, looking as if it had just been polished, and a smaller gray dappled horse with a white blaze running down its muzzle.

She said, "Odds On and Odds Against. I came here the first time with Odds On in the trailer." Yesterday seemed so long ago.

"They're great pals, almost inseparable. If we take one and not the other to the track, the one left behind just pines. I hope nothing hap-pens that they'd get separated for very long. Hope to hell one doesn't break a leg or something else bad." Tom ran his hand down the white blaze of the muzzle. "Looks like that one is pretty curious about your donkey." He nodded toward the next stall.

The big bay, Odds On, was stretching his neck as far as he could to get his head around the post between the stalls so as to get a better look at Sam, who wasn't paying attention to this quest for favor.

"Sam's so . . . well . . . so laid back, like he was when I found him out in—" *That field,* she'd been about to say, before realizing she had nearly admitted to stealing the donkey.

But Tom said nothing.

She went on: "I mean, he was in such bad shape and he looked as if he didn't ever expect things to get better."

"With saddle sores like he's got, can't say I blame him. What did you put on them?"

"Salve. It's supposed to be a painkiller. Arnica."

"We keep that here in the tack room. You carry a jar of this stuff wherever you go?"

"Yes. You never can tell what you might meet up with. I used it a lot on coyotes." She stopped, irritated with herself that she had said too much.

Tom fed Sam a carrot from a bag by the stall door. "Coyotes. We're not much bothered with coyotes around here."

"No. This was in New Mexico. In the Sandias. The Sandia Mountains."

"What were you doing there?" He moved the bag of carrots over to Odds On.

She had not wanted to talk about any of this, the past eighteen months, but here she had gone and done it, and now wondered what lies would accompany this narrative. Her brother Swann? No, say Frederick. "My brother Frederick and I were on vacation in Santa Fe a couple of years ago and we decided to rent this little cabin up in the Sandia Mountains. It's near the ski lift. That's Sandia Peak. He loves to ski. I don't. I liked walking in the woods, though, sometimes in snow-shoes. Going through the woods occasionally I would come across a coyote hurt from one of those leghold traps. So I'd use the salve on his sores." She shrugged. Simple as that.

"You're sayin' this coyote'd just sit still for you to salve up his leg?"

"Well, no, I'd have to give him a little bit of a tranquilizer to make him behave. Morphine, just a little. That quieted them."

"Morphine would quiet anything down, even the Baileys. So you just happened to have that around, too? Girl, you sure were prepared when you went snowshoeing."

This was just getting her in deeper and deeper. "No, it was my brother that had it. He had a bad back. Muscle spasms. That's what it was for." It would almost be easier to tell the truth. Lamely, she ended this story: "Anyway, that's how I came to have the salve with me."

Tom nodded. "That's very interesting about the coyotes, but—"

She was glad that Jim had come out to join them, because Tom wasn't about to leave the coyote rescues alone.

"Time Andi took one of these horses out, don't you think?" said Jim.

Tom nodded. "I was just thinking which horse to put her up on."

Andi looked from one to the other, anxiously. "Don't forget I haven't ridden in a long time."

Tom gave a dismissive wave of his hand. "It's like bicycling. You never forget. Let's go to the barn. Take Dakota out." He went to get the tack.

"This is one fine horse," said Jim. "Mild-mannered, too."

Looking at Dakota, she was sorry she'd eaten lunch. He had a look in his eye that didn't encourage trust.

Tom was back with the tack and slipped the bridle over Dakota's head and the saddle over his back. Andi just watched while he adjusted the girth. In the stall Dakota had looked almost comfortably sized. Out of it, he seemed to occupy the entire barn.

It was a small track, lozenge-shaped, with clumps of Junegrass in the middle. Jim said it was about three-fourths of a mile around.

Andi wondered, *How hard can it be?*

What she had gleaned from old Westerns was that you kind of turned your back, put your left foot in the stirrup, and hoisted yourself, in one fluid movement, over the horse's back. Now, how hard could that be?

The first attempt had her jump-jump-jumping up, failing to get high enough and coming down each time with a thud. If she hadn't been hanging on to the saddle horn she'd have landed on her ass. Using the fence rail as a boost, it took two more attempts before she landed in the saddle.

Neither Jim nor Tom said a word, which she supposed was nice of them. She gathered up the reins and made clicking sounds that seemed to mean nothing to Dakota.

"Just do a little trot around," Jim called over to her. "Nothing fast."

"Okay," she said, and gave a little flick of the reins and pressed her knees into Dakota's sides. Surprisingly, the horse started walking and then trotting. She thought it was a trot. Whatever it was, she felt she had no control whatsoever, not just over the horse but over her own body. She was jiggling up down up down up down when she knew she should be rising and falling in a rhythmic, even motion. If she made the horse go faster, she'd slide right out of the saddle.

By now they were on the other side of the track, where Jim and Tom couldn't see her as well, and she tried a few practice up-and-down movements. She thought she might just be getting the hang of it, and as she came around the bend, she waved to the two men. They were smiling as broadly as they would if she were about to sail across the finish line.

"You ever seen anyone look worse up on a horse?" said Jim.

"No, sir, I never have," Tom replied. "Well, I did see a white dog once at the circus riding atop a horse. I guess that old dog looked worse."

They were silent, watching her around the ring.

Tom said, "Changed my mind."

"Yeah?"

"Dog looked better."

They stood stock-still, their arms crossed over their chests. They were chewing gum, in rhythm. You could fall into that sort of beat when you knew someone for as long as they had known each other.

"So, Jim, think she'll be a help?"

"As an exerciser? No."

They both smiled and waved as Andi and Dakota came trotting by.

"You'd think that horse would've had her on the ground inside of two minutes."

"Give him time."

"Dakota doesn't suffer riders that don't know what they're doing."

"Nope. I recall the way he bucked and tossed Joey Chesny halfway across the paddock."

"And Joey's a good rider."

"Well, it was dumb of me, I guess, thinking she could do it. Exercise lads have a ton more of know-how than just getting up and riding."

They were silent again, watching Dakota trot by.

"You can tell she's pleased."

"As punch."

"Now she'll dismount and wonder if maybe she oughta be a jockey."

"Most likely."

Tom folded another stick of gum into his mouth and thumbed a stick out for Jim.

Jim took it. They both chewed.

"God, but does she look pleased with herself."

"She does. A born horsewoman."

"Uh-huh."

Andi—or at least the horse—had changed pace from a trot to a canter.

"Just as long as she doesn't gallop."

"The horse knows better."

"I expect you're right." Jim sighed. "I hate to be the one to tell her."

"Why tell her? You still think she'll take care of the place when we're gone to Fargo."

"Absolutely. I'll tell you, if she was bent on something, I wouldn't want to go up against her."

"No, sir."

"But by God, she sure is trying, I'll give her that."

"Hell, I'll give her marks for having the nerve to get up on the horse in the first place, with her not knowing a goddamned thing about how to do it. She's determined."

"Like I said, if she's bent on trotting a horse around or bringing a donkey into town, well, that's just what she's going to do."

When she slid down (smooth as cream, she thought) from Dakota's back, Andi felt exhilarated, almost felt like a new person, at least newish.

In such a short time, to have mastered—well, maybe not *mastered*, exactly—the art of riding, no, that was an exaggeration, she couldn't have done that in twenty minutes. To excel at such a skill as riding a horse for the first time, well, she must just have a natural talent for it. Given how little talent she had for other things—it had taken her a week of steady practice before she could shoot a gun right—perhaps riding was the thing that came to her most easily.

When she and the horse walked up to the two men, not waiting for encouragement, not bathing in compliments, she just dived right in and said, "I wonder what you have to do to be a jockey?" She frowned. "What? What's so funny?"

10

I'm supposed to take Dakota to graze."

"You take Sam along?" asked Jesus.

"Yes."

"You just remember what I told you." Jesus told her again as he moved from Odds On to Odds Against, replenishing the oats in their buckets.

"I'll be extra careful. But what is it you're most afraid of?"

Jesus was startled into putting the bucket of oats down. He looked very serious. "I dunno. Everything. No, most that maybe he'll disappear."

"Why? Why would the horse do that?"

Jesus ran his hand down Dakota's muzzle. "Dunno," he said again, "excep' maybe he too good to last." Embarrassed now, he turned his attention to the feed and picked up the tub of oats.

Andi looked at him, finding it strange that he should say such a thing, for Jesus's mind, she thought, held a strong element of magic. He believed in the sort of magic children believed in, in which things disappeared the minute the children turned their backs. People, things.

"I know what you mean, Jesus."

As Jesus slipped the bridle over Dakota's head, he said, "Take them to the north pasture. It's not so far." He opened the stall door and led

Dakota out. "That way." He pointed past the practice ring. "I take him there; he's used to it. There's a couple big cottonwoods. That's his favorite spot to browse. You'll see it."

She held Dakota's bridle and gave Sam a sign to follow, and the three of them walked across the forecourt, past the ring, and toward the rocks. The three of them. Andi breathed deeply. It felt like freedom. It felt like a new thing.

Dakota seemed to know where they were going. The field was full of Indian grass, some two feet high, foxtail barley, and big clumps of Junegrass for forage. The earth felt cool at their feet. The horse picked up the pace and walked a little faster, so she knew that up ahead was his favorite graze under the big trees.

She removed the bridle and her heart plunged when Dakota began to run. But then he came back. He ran for a while in a circle and then settled down to graze. For a moment she thought Sam would run after him, but the donkey merely stood watching.

Andi sat down in the shade of a cottonwood and watched the horse nibble on grass that looked as hard to chew as bone. Sam wandered off a few yards to find his own browse, although given the life he must have led she'd have thought he wouldn't be too particular. Dakota, though, just took what was to hand.

Maybe there was something beneath the dry growth that she hadn't seen or couldn't make out. Something written over, like the name Palimpsest. What was there once is still there, under layer after layer of overwriting, and you can still see what's underneath if you look hard enough.

If you look hard enough. She thought about what Jim had said, sitting with her chin on her drawn-up knees, watching the horse.

She looked off across the range and toward the rocks. It was the vastness of such places, the open range, that crippled one's ability to characterize them or even talk about them. It was like being asleep and dropped on the moon and waking and having nothing to look at except for that distended rock. The feeling was not unpleasant; it was as though the moon rock were embedded in one's consciousness, as if it were the real thing, and it had been written over by rawhide towns and tumultuous cities and everything that went with them, but it was still there, the real thing underneath.

Like a Smith & Wesson .38.

Andi could not have explained why she made that association. Her mind was ranging like Dakota and Sam searching out food.

Her life would always come back to the gun and the boiling white-water of the Salmon River. She should have gotten in touch with Mary Dark Hope or Reuel. She should have, but she was too ashamed to. She had run; she didn't know what else to do. She had tried to go back, but she had been too scared, too cowardly, too weak. The best she could do was to follow the story in the paper. There had been surprisingly little. It was dropped as less than newsworthy barely two weeks after she had left. Investigation into the death of Harry Wine had been suspended.

She seemed to have lost the ability to assign importance to what she did anymore. There was some kind of moral tilt to her, like cheating in a game of pinball by hitting the pinball machine to make the steel ball drop the way you wanted.

You're just a tad off course, Jared had said. She had meant to head due northwest toward Alaska, but instead had come east to the Dakotas. Why had she done this? She didn't know beyond thinking North Dakota must be the loneliest state in the country. Looking out over the plains, she thought this again.

For some reason, the nothingness exhausted her and she fell asleep.

She woke, alarmed, to the sound of thunder. Not seeing Dakota and Sam where she'd left them, she panicked, jumped up. But they had only gone around to the other side of the tree. Now, with ears pricked, both of them had lifted their heads to the sound or the sight of something, for they were watching the distance. She shaded her eyes, looked off toward the drumming sound, and realized something massed like a huge dust ball was moving toward them.

Dakota snorted. Every old piece of science fiction Andi had ever read or seen came to mind, ridiculous and infantile fears.

Wild horses. Dakota took a few tentative steps, snorted again. Sam stayed put.

She thought the horses had spooked Dakota, so she was quick to get the bridle back over his head, with him resisting, but she managed it and held on in case the horse was intent on getting away as soon as he could. But his training must have kept him there.

The wild horses—two dozen of them, at least—looked as if they were headed straight toward them, but as they drew closer, she could see they were taking a line a hundred yards or so away from them. Now she could see the wild horses were every color imaginable—black, white, gray, paint, copper. Where were they running to?

She draped an arm over Dakota's neck.

Who had the right to stop them?

11

The next morning was spent getting the van ready for the trip to Fargo. Jim left emergency phone numbers: two different vets, theirs and a backup. "But there won't be any emergency, don't worry."

That's all she'd be doing, worrying. They had gone to the Fargo racetrack, taking Palimpsest.

That afternoon, she was in the barn with Jesus, who was talking about the horse. "That filly, she real good. The only trouble is she likes to fall back. Gets in the lead then falls back like six, seven lengths, for no reason we can see. You know who like that? That American horse, Whirlaway. He won the Triple Crown in the States. Look like he was surely losing and then he started moving up. That's a long time ago, longer ago than me. Whirlaway, that horse was wacky. He was wild."

Andi smiled. She thought of the wild horses.

All the while he was talking, Jesus was sitting on a stool in Odds On's stall, using a nifty little pick to get dirt and grit out of the horse's shoes. Odds On didn't appear to mind having his leg pulled up and Jesus working on his shoe.

"It take a horse time, you know, to collect himself, like people say, 'pull yourself together.' You can feel it with a horse, all the pieces"—he brought his hands together, fingers interlocking—"like this. You can feel it, like a power surge." He picked up another leg and worked on the shoe. "All the good ones, the great ones, they do that. Maybe they all do it, even the not-so-good."

Odds On reached his head around and bumped Jesus's shoulder.

"Did I say you not so good? No, I didn't, so get outta my face, you horse."

Andi laughed and patted the horse's rump.

It must have been an automatic reflex; the hoof Jesus was working on pulled away from his hands and came up to strike him on the forehead. Jesus was pushed off his stool.

Andi was horrified. "Oh, my God!" She reached in and tried to pull him out by his shoulders in case the horse might be going for another kick.

Jesus waved her away. "It's okay, I'm okay."

"I'm so sorry, Jesus. Look, let me go and get some ice." He nodded and she ran off to the kitchen.

There she opened the freezer door, shook some ice cubes into a ziplock bag, let the screen door bump behind her.

Jesus was leaning against the stable door, a hand covering his forehead. He took the bag of ice cubes and crushed it against his forehead where a large welt was forming.

"I should have known better." Andi fretted.

Again he waved her words away. "No way you could. That left rear spot I think somebody, some goddamned fool, musta used to whip too much on that spot and made Odds On real sensitive there." Jesus sighed and said to the horse: "You big fool. Okay, come on." He turned Odds On so that the horse could see what was going on. "Don't worry Andi, hear. You worry Andi, you make dumb-ass moves, she'll run away, then you be sorry." Still holding the ice to his head, Jesus ran his hand down Odds On's muzzle and the horse tried to bump Jesus's chin.

"See, you sorry now, ain'tcha." Then to Andi, "I'm gonna have one hell of a headache. I think I'll go on home if it's okay with you, Andi."

It wasn't, really. She'd worry about the horses all night. "Of course it's okay, Jesus. Just tell me what else there is to do."

"Nothin' new. Just give them their oats as usual." He moved over to the board, picked up the ballpoint pen hanging by a string, and wrote his phone number on the "Reminder" pad. He tore it off and handed it to her. "Just call me, somethin' comes up. You've got the vet's number, too."

"Do you want me to drive you home? I'd be glad to. You might have a concussion."

She was a terrible driver. As far as she knew, her one driving experience was that trip with Mary Dark Hope from Santa Fe to Salmon. Neither of them had a license. Mary because she was too young, Andi because—why? She guessed she'd never learned.

But it was awful, Jesus having to drive himself home. People were supposed to take care of each other.

"No, no, Andi. You just go ahead and feed them. I'll be back in the morning, early. You don't worry, right? You do fine."

"Okay, Jesus. Take care."

He walked out to his truck, ice pack pressed to his head, and she wondered too late if she should have devised some sort of bandage-wrap so he'd have both hands free. He honked as he went down the drive, waved backward, and called her name, sounds lost in the dusk of early evening.

Andi experienced the wholly irrational fear that any hope of help today had just driven down the gravel drive.

Over the black griddle and pancake batter, she berated herself for such feelings of helplessness. She was not helpless, she had never been helpless, oh, shit, she still felt helpless.

She shoved a spatula under the foaming pancakes and turned them, at the same time shaking a pan with some imitation-sausage links. Breakfast for dinner. This took her mind off the horses, but that was no help, for now her thoughts turned to that complex of bright, white buildings miles away. She hated the way her mouth watered when she caught a whiff of bacon frying or steak grilling or pork chops, stuffed with celery and sage and bread crumbs, fattening up in the oven. Her senses went in one direction, her sentiments in the other.

She took down the bottle of maple syrup and let its thickness trickle around the pancakes, concentrating on the intricate, leafy design she was making. As she ate, she looked out the window over the sink to the purple twilight and the stables across the courtyard. With the kitchen door open, she could hear if one of the horses was complaining about something. She tried not to wonder if Jesus was all right or if the horses would be all right with just her there. She tried not to imagine an emergency, when she would have to call the vet. Maybe what she would do was not sleep. She would not go to sleep.

Nothing stirred as she ate her meal and dusk edged closer to dark. She lasted only as long as the meal—pancakes and fake sausage and coffee—before figuring that she had to check on them. She took the dishes to the sink and went out.

I2

ndi wanted to inspect all of the stalls to make sure there was enough hay and mash. She knew that Odds On could get through a tub of oats in a split-second. The only time she saw food in the tub was while she was pouring it. Right now it was empty and he was sleeping on his feet. She went from stall to stall, checking on the hayricks and saying good night.

Full dark had come while she was doing this, and Odds Against's white blaze was the only thing that showed in this darkness. Andi moved to the wall to flick the switch that turned on the caged light, but as her hand moved to it, Dakota whinnied and the others—at least Odds On and Odds Against—shuffled in their stalls. Her fingers drew away from the fixture and she moved to the stable door. It was dead dark inside the barn. Her eyes had not gotten used to the downward shifting light, which tossed long shadows from the lighted windows of the house across the outside of the barn. There was a spill of light from the kitchen window, and that luminance trailed nearly to the barn door. It was the blindness one feels walking into a dark auditorium, trying to orient oneself, seeing, for a few seconds, nothing at all.

Andi went to the door and peered out. It sounded like a car coming up the drive and she wouldn't have thought much of it, probably Jesus coming back, except that the headlights were off and it was moving very slowly up the gravel. Then it stopped. It sounded as if it had stopped halfway along the drive. There was the sound of car doors slamming. She ducked back inside the barn.

A slow drift of low voices, an undercurrent of words. She leaned her back against the wall and put her head far enough around it to see the driveway and the two figures coming along. Their faces weren't visible, but it didn't take much thinking to know they must be the Bailey brothers.

Andi hated herself in this moment, crouched in the blackness of the barn, frightened and alone and without her gun.

Why didn't she keep it with her? Probably because she wasn't planning on being assaulted every time she looked up. They were still a distance away, and Andi figured she had fifteen or twenty seconds to work out what to do. They were coming, she was sure, after Sam, or after her, or both.

If they went to the house, she would have more time. But why would they think they could get past Jim or Tom? The answer was simple: they knew Jim and Tom had gone to Fargo. Palimpsest was racing. Jim would have quite naturally talked about it in town. They assumed she'd be by herself, or if with someone, the someone would only be Jesus, a pretty small guy.

They passed through the light spilling out from the window, and she could see the brash faces of Carl and Junior. They went into the house through the door she'd left open, probably thinking she was inside and by herself. As for Sam, it had been bad enough their taking him into that field where he couldn't find his way out. Now it would be something worse.

After that meeting on the highway and again in May's diner two nights ago, they might both be carrying guns.

Had Tom left his rifle in here—rifle, shotgun, whatever—she wouldn't have hesitated to use it. But there was nothing. She closed her eyes hard into a squinty frown and balled her hands into fists. *Come on! Think!* She opened her eyes and looked at Dakota. She grabbed up the dark blanket that had been folded over the stable door, opened the door, threw the blanket over the horse's back, and led him out of the stall. He was being quiet. Then she noticed what she hadn't before—all

the horses were being uncannily quiet, as if word had spread about this
fix everyone was in.

She led Dakota to the rear of the barn, past the other stalls. There
she turned him, held up her hands in a gesture of "Stay," as if the horse
were a fractious puppy; but he did stand still, only a few flourishes of
head turnings to indicate his puzzlement or impatience at this
development.

Andi yanked a dark coat with a hood from its peg where Jesus had
left it and put it on. Then she pulled over the stool Jesus used and set
it beside Dakota. With an agility bred by fear, she jumped up onto his
back and slid back down, dragging the blanket with her. Dakota looked
around.

There was no time to saddle up. The saddles were in the tack room,
anyway. She tossed the blanket over him again, positioned herself on
the stool, and jumped. This time she managed to keep her seat. She
waited. All of this had taken her no more than three minutes.

In another five minutes the men were leaving the house; she could
hear them talking and laughing. In the porch light she could see them
clearly; it showed they had nothing in their hands, at least at the
moment. They walked toward the stables.

Andi felt Dakota gather himself beneath her as if he, too, were
tensing up. She wound the fingers of her right hand through his mane.
Having no idea what to say in command, she uttered an abrupt "*Go!*"
at the same time slapping his rump with her other hand in lieu of
a whip.

The horse shot forward and burst out of the barn, heading right
toward the Bailey boys.

She thought it must have been, for them, like walking along a deserted railroad track and suddenly looking back toward an oncoming
train.

They yelled; they ran. Down the driveway to the truck, with
Dakota on their heels. They vaulted into the truck.

"Fuck's that?" one of them yelled.

"Fuckin' horse!"

The truck accelerated and backed down the drive like a shot. Dakota was in pursuit, alone. He had dumped Andi halfway down the drive and she was lying in the dust and gravel laughing. She couldn't help it. Then she realized the horse might still be whipping along that road out there like the wind, galloping after the truck. Her side hurt, but it was only bruised; she could see to the end of the drive. The moon had come out from behind its cover and was pouring its diluted light over the land.

There was Dakota, across the road from the stone gate, interested more in a patch of grass he'd found than in any midnight thrill ride.

She crossed the road and went to him. There was no way to get back up on the horse, not that she wanted to, but she didn't know if she could get him back. She tugged at his mane, but he shook free of her hand as if really annoyed at such an upstart attempt at command. He lowered his head and went on browsing in the cold grass.

"Oh, come on!" She was tired. Her eyes went to the high rocks that sat way back from the road, ledges of red rock that made her think of the badlands. "Come *on*," she said to the horse.

Dakota raised his head and looked at her. Or through her. How did she know? Was this horse going to pay any attention to her? How was she going to get him back to the barn? Without a bridle, there was nothing to pull on. And she was afraid if she left him he'd just wander off, since nothing seemed to hold his attention for very long. Well, how could it, at night, in this field?

A car went by, and then another, light from headlights washing over her and the horse.

She checked out her clothes, wondering if the thin scarf she was wearing could stand in place of a bridle. She yanked it off and tossed it over the horse's neck. She tried to tie a knot tight enough to pull against the weight of the horse.

"Come on!" Andi gave his flank a slap and pulled on the scarf with one hand and his mane with the other. He didn't move an inch; he kept munching grass as he looked at her. She gave the scarf yoke another pull. No response.

She saw misty headlights a half mile down the road, tiny, like those of a toy car moving along the dead straight road, coming in her direction. Oh, God, don't let it be the Baileys come back for another try, angry this time because once again she'd foiled them. Whoever it was, she was afraid the car would spook Dakota, which might help if it spooked him back to the house, but she feared he'd go galloping off toward the rocks.

It was a pickup truck, not a car. She'd had her fill of pickup trucks, but at least (she saw as it slowed down) it was a stranger, not the Baileys.

The truck stopped, idled. "You need some help there, little lady?"

"*Little lady.*" She hated the condescension. "No, no. We were just out riding, that's all.

When the man started to get out of the truck, engine still on, ticking over, she knew there'd be trouble. "Well, you must be pretty good, then, you can ride bareback in the dark in that field."

As he came up to her she could smell the whiskey. But drunk or not, she knew he was bad news. It was that insinuating tone, that needling, raspy voice, as if he'd swallowed a cactus.

Dakota had looked up and kept on looking, as if he were turning over this new development in his mind. She got closer to the horse, her hand on his back, and the man just kept coming toward her. She drew in breath, smelling the liquor even stronger on his breath, and backed up until she was nearly behind the horse. Then she stepped back several paces, far enough to be out of Dakota's reach. But the man wasn't; he was directly behind Dakota, about to take another step toward her.

The leg came up like a lead pipe and caught him just above the neck. She heard a crunch. He barely had time to register either pain or surprise, his eyes widening, almost popping out of his head in the last vast moment of consciousness before he hit the ground.

Andi looked down at him. Undoubtedly, he was concussed if he wasn't dead. Had he been dead she wouldn't have cared a whit, except for the extra trouble that would cause for all of them. No, she could see his chest rising and falling. Not very strong, but enough to keep him alive for a while.

Dakota had gone back to a bush he'd been interested in. Again, Andi had no intention of leaving the horse here alone while she went to the house to call for help. There was the truck still idling by the side of the road. Maybe the man had a cell phone in there. She ran toward the truck and stopped. What would be the response of the police? Did the law treat horses that kicked the way it treated dogs that bit? What would happen? Would anyone believe the reason for the horse being over here in the first place? Why hadn't she called the police after she had chased those other two off the property, they would ask.

"Why didn't you just leave the horse in the field and go back home and call the police?"

"Because I didn't want to leave my horse alone."

"What harm could he come to? It's just a field. And look what happened because you didn't—"

"But look what could have happened if I hadn't been there! That man could have stolen my horse! Don't you understand?"

Andi went back to try again with Dakota. This time when she pulled on the scarf, as if he knew her limits, Dakota moved into step beside her. Maybe he felt the fun was over, so he might as well go home.

After she'd taken Dakota back to the barn, she called the police and told them there'd been an accident. She said, "I think he must've hit his head when he fell, on a rock maybe. My guess is he fell because he was drunk. I mean, this guy was seriously hammered. He probably won't even know what happened to him."

That was her story and she'd stick to it: she'd found the man in the field.

13

In the morning, Andi lay in bed thinking of what she would tell Jim and Tom. She was afraid that if she told them the truth, they would think—and they'd be right—that none of it would have happened if it hadn't been for her and that she must invite trouble.

They would of course hear about the drunk in the pickup truck, but she could tell the same story she'd told the police, who'd had no difficulty accepting it. No ambulance was available, so state troopers had taken him to a hospital.

"How is it you thought there was something wrong, miss?"

"It was the truck. I saw the lights. Then later, it was still there. I went down the drive to see."

It was perfectly plausible.

It occurred to her once she was downstairs and shrugging into her coat that the Baileys might have taken something. They hadn't come to thieve (except for taking Sam, she was sure), but they were so contrary, they just might have taken something.

Andi went through the living room, dining room, and office—especially the office because the Baileys would be the type to take away something they thought might have personal value to Jim. Not monetary value, but something he prized. Like a blue ribbon, or that little bronze statue of the mare and foal. Something like that. Maybe the framed photo of Jim and a jockey. When they came toward the barn, they hadn't been carrying anything, though; so if they did steal, if would have to have been something very small.

Wearily, Andi sat down in Jim's old swivel chair and looked around the room. But how would she know? She wasn't that familiar with the house or its contents.

She got up and went across to the barn and got the oats and maize mixture. The hay nets were still half-full. The buckets were empty and she filled them. Dakota had his nose in and out of his in five minutes.

"I guess last night was a real strain on you."

Dakota looked at her in a way she would have described as somber, even a little sad, but he was actually (she realized) indifferent to her musings and just wanted more oats. She filled the bucket only halfway and got one of Dakota's thankless looks before he buried his nose in it.

Andi had brought *People and Their Horses* along; she hadn't yet read it. The sketches in it were about celebrity horses and how they had bonded with their owners. She ran her hand down Dakota's muzzle and wondered, as he shook it off, if they were doing any bonding yet. They had certainly been through a lot together.

She should call Jesus, see how he was. Then she looked again at Dakota, whose bucket was already empty. She said, "You need exercise. After I eat breakfast, we'll go down to the track." Dakota shoved his muzzle into the empty bucket. Yes, they were definitely getting on better.

Eating pancakes again, she settled on keeping to the story she had told the police. Then a minute later, she changed her mind. And changed it back. Holding her coffee cup in both hands as if it were a chalice and as if engaged in some act of faith, she thought about the trouble she'd caused, and now she had the bad news coming to Jim's own doorstep.

Carrying the books she'd found on saddlery, she went to the tack room, took down the small saddle and a halter and bridle, and went into the stalls. She led Dakota—well, more pulled and pushed him—out of his stall, hoping the horse would stand still so she could saddle him, but of course he didn't. Andi opened the book to the instructions for getting the halter on, turned to get the saddle, and dropped the book. Dakota kicked the book away.

She managed to get the saddle on and adjusted the girth according to the instructions. Then came the halter, which was fairly easy. Taking up the rope attached to the halter, she clicked her tongue, flicked at the rope a couple of times, and Dakota stood resolutely still. The instructions said not to pull on the rope, but what options did she have after doing the clicking and flicking a half dozen times? So she pulled. Finally, the horse stopped being a dead weight and went along, walking ahead of her as if this had all been his idea.

The bridle would be tricky, she supposed, for that meant putting a bit in Dakota's mouth. When they got to the track, she tried to do all of this smoothly, fitting the bridle over his muzzle and neck and the bit in his mouth. It was very hard to do; she thought this was because Jesus and Tom were quite rough with this operation and the horse now was resisting because he had come to hate the bit. When Andi was done she stood back and surveyed the result, which had taken her twenty minutes to achieve as opposed to Jesus's two, but that didn't bother her; Dakota more than likely appreciated the extra effort. She was glad no one was there to watch her try to get into the saddle. She stood on a stump, which gave her a leg up, and failed three times. Jesus could do it in one try and from the ground.

But, finally, the reins firmly in hand and bit firmly in place, she squeezed with her legs. Dakota stood there, interested only in turning his head to see what she thought she was doing. After ten or fifteen minutes of this useless attempt to get going, she gave up.

It did not take much effort to lead him back to his stall. He fairly cantered there.

When had she become so uncertain? So ambivalent? Or was it plain fear? She was afraid of having to go on as she'd been going on before she'd met Jim. She liked comfort, the comfort of her room, of Sam's stall, of taking the horses out in the field. She liked routine. Routine said that you had a place where you were sure of putting your foot right today as well as yesterday, tomorrow as well as today. She pondered this, drinking her cold coffee.

And with her, there was no past to build on: you just made things like that up. Everyone lied, good as well as bad. Harry Wine had lied right through to the end. Even then he'd just gone right on lying; he'd gone out on a lie; he'd died lying. He was lying for no reason other than that he could. He was lying even while the blood curdled in his throat.

There was no bus going up in flames, a fire that she had been the only one to escape from. There was no picking her up by the side of the road as she ran from the fire. There was, in other words, nothing. No history she could claim, no beginning she could remember. All she'd been doing for the past year and a half was drift.

She went out, picked up Max and Hazel's bucket, and went along to the sty. She was late and Hazel was grunting as if she had something stuck in her throat, pacing beside the trough.

"Oh, for heaven's sake, cut the drama, I'm only a little late." She poured the food into the trough, and Hazel stuck her snout into it before Andi finished pouring. "Save some for Max." The pig looked up, chewing. Fat chance. "This is pig paradise, you know." She didn't mention the hog-farm operation a couple of miles away. She sat on an overturned bucket by the pigsty and watched Hazel vacuum up food and thought about Klavan's pig facility. She had never seen a factory farm. She had never wanted to. She didn't want to see this one, either. Who would?

Andi called up the ad she'd seen in the paper. Part-time positions. The "part-time" was their way of paying minimum wage, she was fairly certain.

No, Andi.

I was just curious, that's all.

No.

I don't have all that much to do—

No.

—here.

No.

Max had at last come out from under the anesthesia of sleep and was blinking as if he'd never seen daylight before, had no idea where he was or who Hazel was.

Andi stood there hanging over the fence, biting at a calloused place on her thumb, when she heard the truck and trailer crunching on the gravel drive. They were back, at least she hoped it was them and not Sheriff McKibbon, come to deliver her up to the law.

Jim was unloading Palimpsest, who made as graceful an exit down the ramp as any high-fashion model.

"She came in third."

"But that's great!" she said.

"Would've been greater if it had been first."

"Where's Tom?"

"Dropped him at his place." Jim had taken off his baseball cap and was scratching his neck. He was at the back of the van, folding the rack away. "Everything go all right?" he asked.

"Not exactly."

"Oh?" He looked at her, surprised.

Quickly, she held up her hands, palms out. "Nothing's happened to the horses."

"Well, okay, but has something happened to you?"

"Could we just go in and sit down and have some coffee? It's kind of a long story. I'll put Palimpsest in her stall." She turned and started away.

"Andi."

She stopped.

"This about Dakota again?"

She sighed. "Only partly, and no, nothing happened to him."

"Okay. I'll make the coffee."

The coffeemaker was just belching out its remaining coffee when Andi got to the kitchen.

Jim held up a white bag. "Doughnuts. Picked 'em up in town."

"Oh, good; I love those doughnuts."

Jim poured the coffee and put the doughnuts on a plate. He waited for her to pick one. She took up a sugar-raised, and he took the powdered sugar, which Andi knew was his favorite, and there had only been one.

"Okay, shoot. What happened?"

"It's the Baileys."

He fell back in his chair. "Christ, not again."

That was when a small chill lay across her heart like a hand; she was not worth this trouble.

"They came—Carl and Junior—last night. I'm sure they came for Sam." She supposed she always knew she'd have to tell the truth, and so she told it, including that she'd lied to the police. "See, I was afraid they'd take Dakota away—"

"And lock him up?" Jim raised his eyebrows.

"You know what I mean. It wasn't really lying; I just didn't correct their impression that the driver of the pickup hit his head on the rock."

"You hear anything today about him? How he is?"

She shook her head.

"Then he'll tell another story. Damned Baileys . . . I'm real sorry, Andi."

She said, "No, I'm the one who's sorry. The Baileys wouldn't be here bothering you if it wasn't for me."

"They're not bothering me. They're perfect little shits—pardon the language—and you took 'em down, and now they want to get even." He started laughing. "Christ, I wish I'd seen that, charging with Dakota." He went on laughing, slapping his hand on the table. "That almost makes up for only coming in third." His eyes teared up from laughing. He rubbed the back of his hand across them. "You listen, Andi: you're not causing trouble for me, but you sure are causing it for them. Good. Of course I suppose now we can expect Lucas Bailey around, asking what in hell you think you're doing, attacking his two innocent boys with a horse."

"But how could they make a complaint given what they came here for?"

"You don't expect 'em to admit it? They could just say they came here to make a friendly call."

"Who'd ever believe that? After what happened before? Would the sheriff?"

"Harry McKibbon believe them? Not likely. He knows they're scum."

She cut a doughnut in half and took one of the halves. "Well, I'll tell you, they're better off just keeping quiet."

"Of course, you could get the jump on them. You could put in the complaint yourself." Jim picked up the other half of the doughnut.

"But wouldn't the police wonder why I never said anything last night? I mean, it happened right before that man pulled up on the road."

Jim thought about that. "Yeah, you've got a point."

"And I never did go to the police about what happened on the highway."

"Those damn boys should be slapped with a restraining order. They'll try something again. I wouldn't want to come up against you in a dark alley, though." He grinned.

Andi thought about the restraining order. "Yes. I think I'll try and get a restraining order."

"Good. I'm calling Harry. Best not to leave it too long." He got up and went into his office.

Andi was in the stable when Harry McKibbon pulled up an hour later. She watched him walk to the side door. She wondered if she'd have to go before a judge, if there'd be a trial, or just lawyers would present the case to a judge. And if the Bailey brothers would have to appear, too.

"Why can't people leave people alone?" She was talking to Sam as she fed him pieces of rutabaga.

From the other end of the stalls came a loud whinny. Dakota, of course, wanting whatever food she might have around. She went down

to his stall. "I should be grateful, I guess, for you saving me from getting raped, but look at it this way: if you hadn't stopped over there
chomping grass, I never would have been there in the first place. Here."
She gave him a piece of rutabaga, after which he turned around.

She left to go to the house and see the sheriff.

14

"Sheriff," Andi said and held out her hand.

Harry McKibbon took it, smiling. "Nice to see you again."

"Where's Jim?" she asked.

Harry nodded. "In his office. He told me what happened, but I'd like you to go over it for me, since you were there."

"Sure." Andi told him the story in as much detail as she could muster; details were important to police.

Harry McKibbon said, "They knew Jim and Tom were gone?"

"I guess. He told people in town they were going to Fargo."

Harry was holding a mug of coffee and was standing by, rather than sitting at, the kitchen table. Andi felt he was a man with too much to do and he couldn't sit down until he'd done it.

He said to her, "Why did they go in the house?"

"I don't know. They were looking for me, I guess."

"How long you figure they were inside?"

She thought about this for the first time since it had happened. "I guess ten minutes."

"It would take two minutes to see you weren't there."

In other words, she was lying, and she wasn't. "Then they got interested in things inside, I guess."

"Were they after something? Jim said he doesn't keep money around."

"They were in his office, I think. I can only guess; I don't know the house that well, I mean, to know if something in particular was stolen."

"You're pretty sure they came to the barn to do something to your donkey?"

"Yes." Andi told him about Sam's having been taken away from his stall at Jared's on the evening of that day she'd come to town.

"Yeah, I heard about that." He smiled. "The Baileys don't take kindly to being bested." The smile broadened. "Tell me about your life, Andi."

"My life? Why?" She had sat down on one of the ladder-back chairs and he now sat down, too. As if both of them were giving way under a posture neither could support.

"It might be important," he said, clarifying nothing.

This baffled her; it also made her a little afraid of him. What was he after? "Look. Am I the suspicious stranger come to town and suddenly bad things start happening?" Which was pretty much what she'd been telling herself.

"No, of course not. I'd just like to hear a little about your life."

"I can't imagine why." In her mind she was quickly resurrecting the fiction she had told people before the Harry Wine part of her past had come along. She didn't even know how old she was. "Okay, originally I come from New York. My parents have a big house in the Hamptons. I have two brothers, Marcus, who's a painter, and Swann. And a sister, Sue. We had a badminton court and played a lot of that."

"Swimming pool?"

Andi didn't like that detail and rejected it. "No. We played a lot of badminton, though, as I said. I had a dog named Jules. He used to love to chase the badminton birds." She smiled at the look of this bogus memory. She left out the llamas.

"Sounds like your family's well-off."

"Yes, they are." She knew she'd be asked why was she knocking about, walking the highways like a tramp, bedding down—if she had the money—in rooming houses such as Mrs. Englehart's. She was prepared for this question.

And he asked it. "It can't be very pleasant, going from one place to another, even for someone who likes her freedom as you certainly seem to."

She looked at him. *No,* she wanted to say. *I do not like my freedom.* She thought of using the adventure-after-university-before-getting-a-job answer, but as he was a real sheriff, used to getting the truth out of suspects (not that she was one), possibly even by force, roughing them up and so forth, or leading them into verbal traps—

"What's wrong?"

"Wrong? Nothing's wrong. I was just thinking about whether I wanted to tell you . . . Oh, all right." That was smooth, the reluctance convincing, she thought, pleased with herself. "I had a fight with my parents. And my fiancé." She leaned toward him, wanting to appear earnest. "They wanted me to enroll in Harvard Law School, but I didn't want to."

"Pretty heavy-duty school, Harvard."

She placed her hand over her coffee cup as if refusing a refill. "What my parents did was threaten to disinherit me if I left to travel around the country. I said that's too bad, I could use the money. But I was going anyway." She sat back and crossed her arms almost protectively over her breasts and shrugged. Nonchalant.

"That's pretty rough for them to take that attitude. And your fiancé, what did he do?"

Andi had forgotten about him. "Him? Oh, well, I gave him back his ring." She would very much have liked to light up a cigarette and blow out the match and look at Harry McKibbon through a little curtain of smoke. That was always a grand gesture when Barbara Stanwyck did it.

"Why were you going to marry this damned fool, anyway?"

Why? She bit her lip. "I didn't know he was like that." *Damned fool,* he'd said. She frowned. "Why is he a damned fool?"

Harry gave a brief laugh. "Any man that'd give up on you, he'd have to be a fool."

She remembered only after five seconds to shut her mouth. Dear God, that had been a *compliment.* "Well . . . thank you."

"So what you're doing is just backpacking around."

Setting her chin in her fists, she looked at him. His eyes were marine blue. "That's right."

"Lucas Bailey might claim they'd just come here to get their donkey back—" He held his palm flat out like a traffic cop against what she might be going to say. "I'm not saying I agree with them, only what they might argue. Now, you told people you'd just found the donkey. Is that right?"

"Yes. I found him by the side of the road as if he didn't know where to go or which way. He was in very bad shape. I decided he'd been abandoned. Maybe by gypsies. Anyway, I'm getting tired of them saying Sam belongs to the Baileys. They don't really want Sam except to torment him."

Harry sat looking at her, his head cocked to one side, as if he were assessing this story.

"This is the third time they've come after me and Sam." She held up three fingers. "Three times."

He nodded. "So you want a restraining order to keep them away from you."

"Not me. To keep them away from Sam."

Harry blinked. "That's what you want it for? Your donkey?"

"Look at it this way: to get at me they'd do something to Sam like what they did do—took him out in a field and left him there. To them that's really fun."

"Andi, far as I know there's never been a restraining order for an animal. I never heard of one. Law doesn't do much to protect animals."

Andi's expression told him what she thought of that.

Jim had come back into the kitchen. "Never heard of what?"

"This restraining order. Andi wants it for the donkey, not for herself."

Jim laughed.

"It's what she says." Harry flipped his notebook shut.

Andi thought it was mostly doodles anyway he'd been scribbling.

"Judge Brown, she's not well-known for her sense of humor."

"Good, because it's not humorous," said Andi.

Harry thought for a moment, tapping his teeth with his pen. "What about for both of you? You and the donkey?"

"Well, that's fine."

"I'll run it by the judge." He set down his cup. "Where were you headed to, Andi? I mean, until you shipwrecked here?"

"Alaska," said Jim. "I told her she was going the wrong direction."

Andi was tired of this being a joke for everyone. But Harry McKibbon didn't laugh. "Where in Alaska?"

"Juneau."

"You got folks there, or what?"

She sat recalling what she'd said to Jim. "A brother."

"Thought they were in the Hamptons."

"Except for this one. He's more a half-brother."

Harry nodded. "Alaska's beautiful." He got up. "Okay, I'll see what I can do."

"Thanks, Harry," said Jim.

Andi rose and nodded. "I appreciate your trying."

He smiled. "They've got to let you alone, that's certain. They've got no business harassing you."

Harry said good-bye and walked out to his patrol car.

Jim opened the refrigerator, peering in while Andi gathered up the coffee mugs and took them to the sink. Then she said, "You know that hog farm's hiring part-time people?"

He had pulled out a beer and set it on the counter. "Yeah, they're probably always hiring." He turned to look at her. "Do not tell me you're thinking of getting a job at that place." He took bread and the rest of a pork loin from the refrigerator shelf.

"Besides working here, I don't do so much that I couldn't work there part-time. I need to save up some money to go to Alaska."

"What about your brother? He can put you up, can't he?"

"Yes, but I don't expect him to take care of me all the time I'm there."

He pulled out a jar of pickles and a tub of margarine. "You want a pork sandwich?"

"No, thanks."

"I figured not. The prospect of you working in a place where animals are born and raised to be slaughtered . . . I can't see you in such a place, Andi."

She watched him spread margarine on the bread. "What you want me to do here only takes about half of my day. If you want me to do more, of course I would. But I'm just saying, if you don't need me . . ."

"For one thing, how would you get there?"

"Walk. I can surely walk two miles, can't I?"

"If you say so, I'm sure you could. I think you could do just about anything you put your mind to."

What she put her mind to that afternoon was calling Klavan's and applying for the job, whatever it might be. The pay wasn't all that good, only a few dollars over minimum wage, but she didn't care. The man she talked to was named Jake Cade, and he told her to come around in the morning.

15

Tom drove her to the hog farm the next morning. He'd come back in a couple of hours, he said. "I figure someone'll be showing you around all those buildings."

Inside the frame building that served as the office, someone handed her a form to fill out. It was a simple questionnaire: name, address, age, "general" state of health. *"Are you given to respiratory infections?"*

Was this a high-risk environment? No, that question was for the sake of the pigs, not her. She looked out the office window where three of the white buildings were lined up, the other two off to one side.

When Jake Cade took the paper she'd filled out, she asked if there were others who'd answered the ad, and he said not so far. He told her she'd have to speak to Mr. Klavan and showed her his office.

Mr. Klavan's comments were largely grunts and he spent most of the ten minutes observing her breasts. He had a nasty temper, she could tell. The only full sentence he spoke was "Abramson can show you around."

"Farrow to finish," said Lionel Abramson. "That's what we do here. Farrow to finish. Get 'em up to market weight, then to the market, if you know what I mean." He fluttered his eyebrows at her, as if what he'd said was clever. "Some has charge of the farrowing sheds, some the baby pigs, others the feeders."

He was a small bald man, so completely bald that Andi could have put a finger in each ear and rolled him down an alley toward the pins.

"Yep, farrow to finish."

It might have been a mantra, for he never tired of saying it.

They were wearing white coveralls. Andi had donned hers after she'd gone through a disinfection process, necessary to keep from tracking in something that could infect the hogs.

He sailed a hand up through the air like a kite as they walked toward one of the buildings that he referred to as huts.

"Here is a place where everything runs right along, smooth, you know, like clockwork. Synchronicity, they say. Everything's covered, everything's accounted for, no surprises. No, ma'am, we're always prepared for any event-u-ality! Come rain, come sleet, come snow."

"What about pigs getting sick? There's that awful swine disease— TGE, is it?"

"It is, and we got it covered."

"But an outbreak of that is nearly impossible to stop."

"You've had experience along these lines, I see. Good. But *impossible* is not a word I care for. No ma'am. We got it covered."

"What about these animal welfare groups?"

Abramson laughed and slapped his leg. "Now, that's really amusing. In the first place, they'd never get in. And in the end, well, what could they do? Open one of the huts and say 'You're free!' And let out a thousand hogs?" He spread his arms wide. "Where'd they go, little lady? Where in Hades would they go? They wouldn't know what to do, would they?"

"I get your point. But you know the way they are about animal abuse."

He gave her a hard look. "Do you see them being abused?"

"No, not at all. I'm not talking about me. Or here," she added.

"Terrorists, that's what they are. What gives them the right to go around setting fires and exploding bombs?"

"They think, I imagine, that they do it because animals can't defend themselves."

"Ha! You ever try and have a conversation with a cougar?"

"No, and I've never seen a cougar with a gun, either. I've never seen a coyote setting a leghold trap—" *Shut up!* she told herself. Talk like that and Mr. Abramson would take her for one of the terrorists.

"That's real smart talk, young lady. You always so sassy?" He made a circle with his hand and directed Andi to follow him.

Actually, it was really dumb talk. "How long have you worked here, Mr. Abramson?"

"About fifteen years, give a day."

"Do you like your job?"

"Like it?" He turned, surprised, as if it had never occurred to him to like it. "That's not the point, no, that is not the point." He smiled then, having settled this to his satisfaction.

They started walking again while he said, "You ask a lot of questions. If I were you I'd be more careful."

"Of what?"

Exasperated, Abramson stopped, hands on hips. "There you go again. Questions."

"I'm just making conversation, I guess."

"Well, don't make it around me."

As they picked up their pace, Andi was silent.

"Here's one of the swine huts." The structure they entered was massive.

When he opened the door, there was a huge rustling—not the full-throated noise she would have expected from so many animals caged together. But they rushed forward; she was sure that at times they must push one another down, must trample some in their hurry to reach a possible source of attention.

"Now, down that way"—he pointed to the other end of the shed— "are the buckets that you load up. Come on." He made that wide circle with his hand again, as if spiriting the troops along. "You got your feed bin outside, and you turn this"—he pulled a kind of metal bar around— "and the feed drops into these buckets. Then you take your buckets along and distribute the feed to each. Come on." This time his movement came from his shoulder, as if he were rowing.

The next building, he told her, was the farrowing shed, overseen by Vernon Whipple. "Some of us care for the baby pigs; we move a thousand baby pigs a year, about. It takes six months for your average pig to reach his market weight."

Row upon row of pigs lay or stood in their separate, tubular steel stalls that didn't look even two feet wide, wide enough only for the nursing pigs to lie down in, but not wide enough for them to turn around in. Their snouts were poked evenly over the end of the stall, waiting, she supposed, for food. Or something. They were all pointed toward their feeders. It all made for minimal movement.

He told her to follow him on a wooden walkway that led between the rows of pigs. "As you can see, this floor is built so that manure can fall through. It's slatted. The pit down there gets pumped out three or four times a year. Be glad you're wearing your mask. Again, the feed comes in from an outside bin and you fill it just so. But you're gonna be on the cleaning end more than the feeding end."

What astonished her was their uniformity, all with the same pinkish hide. "They're all the same. What breed are they?"

He thought that was an amusing question. "Breed? You talking about Yorkshire or Berkshire or Chester White? One of those? No, that's pretty much history, young lady, excepting for your small-farm operation, where they think they can afford to be picky. What we want now is uniformity so the packers know exactly what they're getting and what they'll be selling. No breeds; that's all past."

"But that's sad," she said. "We picture all of those different pigs— brown and white, red, dun-colored—out in the fields. All different. If you had your choice, wouldn't you rather see all of those different breeds?"

"Why? It'd just confuse the issue."

Andi was silent for a moment, then said, "They live only for six months before they're slaughtered?"

"Six months and they're off to the packer."

"You mean the slaughterhouse."

He sighed. "If you prefer." Abramson just looked at her, shaking his head again. "It's people think like you that'd have us back in the days before the Internet and cell phones . . . as I speak!"

His cell had rung with a bit of some song Andi had heard but couldn't identify. He spoke briefly and snapped the phone shut. "Mr. Abramson, what's that music on your cell phone?"

"'Tumbling Tumbleweed.' Great song: 'Here on the range I belo-ong, drifting along with the tumbling tumbleweed.'"

Andi didn't know whether to laugh or cry. "But that's the old West."

"Hopalong Cassidy. I bet you never heard of him. Famous movie cowboy." He walked along humming.

Andi looked again at the rows of pigs and the nursing piglets. They were as uniform and as transparent as teardrops.

16

When Andi got back to the office area, she found Tom Rio waiting in the truck. He reached across the front seat and opened the door for her.

"Have you been waiting long?" She climbed in and pulled the door closed after her.

"Nah," he said as he turned over the engine. "Five, ten minutes is all. Did you get the job? You look more like you'd lost one."

"Oh. Yes, I got it. I'm supposed to work afternoons, one to five. I hope that's okay with Jim. I can do all the chores in the morning, which is really what I have been doing. I can get up early and take the horses out—"

"Sure, it'll be okay." They pulled out onto the main road. "So what's it like? How many hogs they got in there, anyway?"

"Five thousand."

He whistled.

"One of the men told me that for a pig operation, that's not many. You have to wear a respirator sometimes when the stink is just too much. I'm to be working in the farrowing shed mostly, keeping that clean."

"That's where they keep the sows, is it?"

Andi nodded. "Where the piglets are born, only—"

He glanced at her. "Only what?"

"There's no room for them, the sows, to make a nest. There's no straw or anything. The concrete is bad for the piglets; they get a lot of broken bones that way. And they can only be around the mother for five weeks before they're weaned and they're taken away to the shed where they keep the feeder pigs."

"I dunno. It's the usual amount of time on any farm."

"It is?" Andi felt a little relieved. It was as if she wanted to hear anything that would show Klavan's in a better light.

"Yeah. That's about as long as Hazel ever held on to hers. Of course, there's other things to be considered beyond just nursing. Pigs are social animals, and there's a whole social structure to teach the piglets. If they're not involved in that, too, it's real hard for them."

They drove along in silence for a while. Andi said, "I feel sometimes I'm boxed in."

He looked at her as he was trying to light a cigarette. "That don't sound very pleasant. You don't have to work there; is it the money, then?"

"Not altogether." She looked out of her window.

"Why?"

"I don't know."

"I won't be able to drive you every day, but—"

"I could ride Dakota. It'd be good exercise for him. He's gotten used to me now. What do you think?"

Tom cleared his throat. "Would Dakota put up with hanging around all afternoon? That's four hours you're talking about."

She frowned. "Yes, of course, you're right. Stupid of me."

"I don't know as how you'd want to take on something else new along with the job."

"Dakota's not new."

"No, but using him as regular transport would be. Dakota can be ornery; we had a real time getting him broke, let me tell you."

"I haven't noticed he's ornery. He's certainly determined, though."

"Same thing, really."

Andi was silent, turning this over in her mind.

Tom said, "Dakota had a hard life. Jim got him off one of those farms. PMU farms. That stands for pregnant mare's urine. They collect it. That means the mares got to be tethered in small stalls while the collection process goes on. Which is most of the year."

"You're saying Dakota was the foal of a mare they were taking this urine from? What happened? Did the mare die?"

"No. She was bred again. That's how they do it. The object is to keep 'em pregnant because of something in the urine—estrogen, maybe. It's used for a drug that helps women going through menopause. Hot flashes, that sort of stuff. My wife took it. Premarin, I think's the name. Now, if the foal is female, they might keep her so she can be used the same way, maybe to take the mother's place. If it's a male, like Dakota, they auction them off."

"Are there a lot of them, a lot of mares?"

Tom pulled into the gravel drive. "As many horses as you saw pigs today. As many foals, too, would be my guess. And as there's no use for the males, they go to the packing plants."

"They're slaughtered, you mean."

"That's right." Tom opened the driver's door and waited. "You getting out or are you gonna sit there all afternoon thinking about this?"

Prepared for any eventuality—that was Mr. Abramson's belief in the workings of Klavan's. "I got that covered."

"What?"

"Getting out," said Andi.

17

Andi stood in front of Dakota's stall, doubting that a horse could sigh. Yet the sound he'd made was not exactly a whinny or nicker, but more of a long-suffering release of breath.

She crossed her arms and rubbed at her elbows and frowned. This horse definitely didn't know how lucky he'd been. Which was, she realized, a shallow thought. A number of things that should never have happened to him happened anyway and could not add up to luck. If you lost a thousand dollars at the roulette table, would you consider it good luck to win back a hundred? If one of the Bailey brothers was bearing down on her by the side of the road, was it good luck she had a gun? Anyway, the bad was so determined and deliberately chosen, it could hardly be called luck.

She ran her hand down Dakota's muzzle. The horse tossed its head. Then she went to Sam's stall. He hadn't had any exercise since yesterday morning. The others had probably been walked or taken down to the track.

It was always a wonder to her how Sam made no noise beyond hooves falling on hay or earth or stone. She would not say "You should be grateful" any more than she'd say it to Dakota. They shouldn't need to be grateful; they should have been taken care of.

Andi wondered about Sam's silence, whether this was a donkey characteristic, or whether it was just Sam. She opened the stall door and Sam shuffled out. He didn't really need a lead; Sam just went where he saw her going. She walked around the barn to the pigsty, Sam following.

Hazel and Max were out of their shed. Andi rested her forearms on the top of the dilapidated fence, and Sam stuck his head over it. They stood that way for quite a long time—far too long if the grunts coming from Hazel were any measure of it. Max preferred to sit in a patch of cool mud and stare up at Sam, who stared down. Hazel didn't think anyone would come to the pigsty without filling the trough. With her bandy legs, Hazel kicked at it as if kicking would make the sky rain down food.

Andi's experience with pigs was perhaps too narrow—only here with Hazel and Max or out there with the great crowd of them in the Klavan buildings. Those were fed exactly the right amount of grain. "Phase-feeding," Mr. Abramson had called one kind of feeding of the gilts and barrows, which were fed precisely one-quarter to one-half a bucket at certain times. Nothing was left to chance. *We've got it covered.*

Hazel walked up to the fence and made a series of snout noises, then back to the trough in case Andi doubted her message. Max sat and looked up at Sam. Tom had said pigs were social animals; they needed to interact with others. Andi imagined all of those pigs at Klavan's turned out in the surrounding meadows and fields. Would they know immediately what they were meant to do? Could you miss what you'd never experienced? Maybe some things are bred in the bone: the sky and the fields, sunlight and moonlight.

When Hazel had her litter, she would have moved straw from outside to inside the lean-to, or maybe Tom or Jim or even Jesus had forked in some fresh straw and Hazel had taken it into the lean-to for making a nest.

Max sat ruminating, maybe meditating on humans or donkeys, for he was still studying Sam.

She looked behind her at the apple tree. If the tree's bottom limbs had still held apples she would have given them to the pigs. The bottom limbs—the ones she could have reached—were shorn of fruit.

"*Pigs got 'em,*" Jim had said.

The branches hung just over the fence, perhaps a foot or two over. But if Hazel and Max couldn't get to the top of the fence, how had they managed to get hold of those apples?

Jim smiled. "*It's a mystery.*"

The wind, maybe? The wind had blown the branches hard enough to set those apples sailing—oh, but that was only a poetic happening. The apples pushed by wind would have fallen to the ground; they would have been windfall fruit, then.

"*Pigs got 'em.*" Andi smiled, loving this little mystery.

Sam stood, content to spend all of the dusky day here, beneath the overhanging branches of the apple tree. . . . Was that the answer, then? Had one of the horses, like Dakota, pulled the apples from the branches and lobbed them over the fence?

Andi wondered, *Is this the stupidest idea anyone ever had?* She blushed for no one in particular.

Andi still liked the image: Dakota pulling down apples and sailing them somehow into the sty. It was pleasant to think they all helped one another out, which, of course, they didn't and wouldn't.

But in her mind's eye, the apples sailed about and she thought of Robert Frost. In her poetry book was that poem of his about apple picking. It was actually about death. Most poems were. She had nearly memorized some of these poems, she read them so often.

And this was joined by the image, again, of all of those pigs in the white buildings confined, crowded together, and she thought that boy or man on his ladder in the poem could have seen the fields and meadows and streams stretching away to the horizon, full of pigs that had come from the white buildings and were now grazing, moving slowly about in the dying sun, their smooth pink skins luminous.

18

er first job was to clean the farrowing hut and feed the sows. She hoped the job of scraping caked manure off cement and boards would be offset a little by seeing the piglets.

She went to the supply room to get herself a respirator, but they'd all been taken that morning. She'd just have to make do without it. She did have a mask, though. Apparently, the detox she'd had to go through the first time she came was pretty much for show and was now in abeyance.

When she opened the door, the smell was bad enough that she pulled the neck of her T-shirt over her mask as an additional filter. The pigs must suffer with it, too, she thought, even though they were its cause. You could shit and still not want to stand in a roomful of it.

The sows couldn't rush toward the food because they could hardly move at all. Even so, it was almost as if their energy, itself unconfined, rushed forward and pressed against her.

Cleaning might be her main job (as Mr. Abramson had said) but she was pretty soon into feeding. She filled two buckets but decided to carry only one at a time because the boards where she walked were slippery. She would have to go back and forth and the sows in the last crates would have to wait. Maybe next time she'd begin down there. She could alternate where she started. It was only as she was finishing this task that she noticed the venting fans in the ceiling. She could only imagine what the smell would have been like without them.

In the fourth crate the sow was poking at one of the baby pigs as if it were trying to nose it up or roll it over. Then Andi saw that nearly half the litter was dead, or certainly looked dead. The sow went from one to the other; the litter had been twelve, and five were dead.

Andi wondered if she should rush out and tell someone, but then when she looked in the next crate, the piglets were all right. It wasn't, then, some disease, or the others down the line would have been sick, too. No, it was what Mr. Abramson had simply called "collateral damage."

One piglet had its leg caught between the boards. That happened often. She dislodged the leg and picked it up and put it inside her coat for company. She named it Oscar.

When Vernon, who was in charge of the farrowing hut, came in, she showed him the dead piglets.

"Yeah, that happens. They're too damned crowded for it *not* to happen." He gathered up the dead piglets.

When his head was turned away she quickly took out Oscar and set him carefully back beside the sow. "Where are you taking them?"

"Dead pile, out near the lagoon. Come on."

There were dead pigs in Dumpsters, with another pile outside that the Dumpster couldn't accommodate. The stink off the lagoon, the huge pool into which the animal waste ran, was something beyond words.

She said, "This isn't a lagoon, Vernon, it's a cesspool. It's got to be messing up your groundwater. You couldn't do this with human waste; why can you do it with animal?"

"There are other ways to do it," Vernon said, "but they cost money."

"So does a coffin."

"Girl, you're gonna be burned out by the time you're twenty if you keep railing away like this."

"I *am* twenty. Twenty-one, to be exact."

"Well, come on, Twenty-one, I'm taking this feed to Hut Three; you can help."

"What about the smell, I mean, for people who live nearby, like the ones who have to put up with that runoff from the cesspit?"

"Grab hold of this, will you?"

Andi held the tub on one side, Vernon on the other, until he had it better balanced. "I do know there's been a lot of complaints of people getting sick by smelling this stuff," said Vernon. "Real sick. Especially kids."

They walked the cement path to the third building.

"Who do they complain to?"

"Here. Klavan. But that's not to say it gets 'em anywhere. Next they go to the county and that don't get 'em anywhere, neither."

"Why am I not surprised? And what about those dead hogs piled up over behind the first hut? Don't tell me that's not illegal."

He laughed. "That's because the rendering truck didn't come when it was supposed to."

She could see it in her mind's eye and wished she couldn't. Hogs tossed one on top of the other, a small mountain of the dead. "It's what I just can't understand: how sterile these buildings look, yet with that cesspit and those dead pigs out there . . . it just doesn't compute."

"Hell yes, it computes. It's money that's the computer, babe. It pays off. It all pays off. If they could double their profits by treating that cesspit and making sure the dead hogs were right away taken, well, they'd do it. Nothing hard to understand. Profit." Vernon banged open the door and they carried the tub in.

Each time Andi looked at those pigs, nearly a thousand of them in this one building, she couldn't take it in, the perfect symmetry of the rows, the pigs, all looking like copies of one another, the same pale pinkish-brown hide, clean, and looking flash-frozen. It made her think of those paper chains kids scissor into a design that shows the same figure over and over, in perfect replica.

Only here in this place the chain of figures diminished to a vanishing point where the last one in the line was all but invisible; it made one think the line was endless and might stretch to the end of the world. And she could not say whether, for her, this vantage point was frightening or consoling, that the pigs would always, even out of sight, be imprisoned, or whether, out of sight, they could break loose and forage in bright fields or vegetable gardens or sun themselves in meadows and pastures, also out of sight.

Whatever it was, she had no power to alter or change it; she could only witness it as a driver on a freeway might slow down to see the end of an accident, cars crumpled like paper and burning out.

"Give me a hand here. Ain't no one paying you to stand around thinking." Vernon had come up to her now. "Swear to God, you are the broodiest person I ever come across. Your life must be one sad affair."

His voice grew as he came closer and diminished as she turned away. Had she not known better (but what did she really know?) and because a pig's snout was formed in such a way it looked to be perpetually smiling, she would have thought the pig nearest to her had turned its head and smiled.

Beyond the cesspit and that mountain of dead pigs, she continued to help with Vernon's feeding chores. She watched the pigs snuffle up their grain as if it were the only action they could take, which it was, and their last meal, which it soon would be.

19

J im was wrestling the cork from a bottle of wine when Andi walked into the kitchen.

"What are we celebrating?"

"First day on the job." The cork came out with enough force to knock Jim back against the counter.

"That's nice of you. I'm not sure it's much to celebrate, though."

"Sure, it is. The mere fact you got through it is." He poured wine into thin-stemmed glasses.

Andi took one, thanked him, and sat down. "What kind of wine is this?"

"White." Jim picked up a knife and chopped up some onions. "I'm not serving pork for dinner, please note."

"I do note."

"Which isn't to say I'm giving it up forever."

"Understood." The kitchen was redolent with a pleasing odor. "Smells good."

Jim grunted. "McKibbon was here before."

"Again? What for?"

"It's about the restraining order. The judge apparently got quite a kick out of it being for the donkey. 'That's original,' she said. As you can imagine, we don't get a lot of originality in our legal proceedings around here."

"The judge is a woman?"

He nodded. "Harry told her he thought you should be included in this order; that is, the Bailey brothers weren't to come on the property for any reason. It doesn't cover Lucas, though, unfortunately."

"That's too bad. He'll probably turn up on general principles, won't he?"

"To save face. I told Harry I never saw anyone so damned intent on getting an animal back—it's just pride. And he didn't take too well to this restraining order for his sons, as you can imagine."

"It's already been served?"

"It has."

"Good. Will they pay any attention to it?"

"They damned well better. They'd have to be a lot stealthier than they were the other night if they mean to come on this property anytime soon." He picked up chopping again, this time, peppers. "Did you know that Harry worked in Idaho a year or two ago?"

Andi sat up, alert. "No, I didn't."

"Weren't you there around that time?"

She nodded. "Why was the sheriff there?"

Jim put down the knife and scraped the onions and peppers into a pan. "Helping out a friend that got sick. Harry took a few weeks' leave, went there to work with this friend. He let the deputy here pick up his duties. It wasn't all that long. Anyway, he said something real peculiar happened there. This was around Salmon? Harry said there was a drowning on the Salmon River, white-water rafting these people were doing. Worse, a murder. They never did catch him, whoever did it. You want some hot peppers in this?"

"What is it?"

"My Mexican dish."

"If you do, yes. Did the police have any ideas about it?"

"What? Oh, in Idaho? Well, police always got ideas. McKibbon thought it was highly personal."

"I suppose shooting someone is always highly personal," she said, drily.

"I didn't say shooting. You read about it?" He looked at her, curious.

She shrugged. "Must've." Her facility with lies sometimes depressed her.

"No, I mean—well, Harry means—it wasn't cold-blooded, you know, like a hit man–type thing. That it was vengeance taken to an extreme, though in the case of this victim, it couldn't be too extreme. Did we decide on hot peppers or not? Do you want some more wine? Just help yourself there."

"Was Sheriff McKibbon actually there?"

"Harry? No, I think it must've happened after he left. But I think it was real soon after he left. Anyway, I invited him to supper. You can ask him yourself if you want. I'm putting in the hot pepper."

Andi stared at the third place setting with a kind of dread. She wished she hadn't shown any interest in the sheriff's story; now it could take up most of the dinnertime conversation. She picked up the bottle of wine—Sancerre, it was called—and poured some into her glass, then got up and replenished Jim's.

"So do you recall any of this?" he asked.

"No, I don't. Do we want salad? I can make it."

"Oh. Sure, that's a good idea."

Andi retrieved lettuce, onion, and tomatoes from the refrigerator and got the big wooden bowl from a cupboard. Over the tearing up of lettuce leaves and the quartering of tomatoes she talked about Hazel and Max.

"They're lazy as grass growing," said Jim. "You putting hot peppers in that salad?"

"This," said Harry McKibbon, holding up his whiskey, "is real good, I mean real good. He turned the bottle of Scotch so that he could look at the label. "Glenfiddich. I don't think I've ever had that—hell, I know I've never had it before. Where'd you get it, Jim?"

"Scotland."

Harry looked up from the bottle. "When were you ever in Scotland?"

"Back awhile. Before you came here."

"I've been here for sixteen years."

"Well, it was more like nineteen or twenty years ago." He stopped tossing the salad to have a drink of Scotch himself. "Um. That is smooooth!"

Jim went back to the salad that Andi had already tossed. He was never satisfied with others' work in the kitchen.

Andi smiled and drank her wine.

Jim brought the salad over to the table with three smaller wooden bowls. "This can just rest here until we're finished with our drinks. I'm having more of this Scotch in the meantime."

"Count me in on that." Harry slid his glass over. "You're saying that you've kept this Scotch for twenty years? I don't think I could keep it for twenty days without breaking the seal."

"That's right."

Andi said, "Why did you open it this evening? And don't say to celebrate my job."

Jim looked off through the window. "I don't know. Funny, but it just seemed time to drink it."

"Time? That's peculiar. What's changed?" asked Harry.

"Nothing I can think of." Jim held up his glass; there was a thick squat white candle on the table; its flame magnified and the candle looked as if it were sitting in the whiskey. He shrugged. "Just time."

"That sounds ominous," said Andi.

Harry quoted, " 'A time to be born and a time to die.' You know, I've never thought that part of Ecclesiastes to be very—edifying, you could say."

"I was just telling Andi about that murder over in Salmon, Idaho, when you were there. Andi was working—"

Andi's stomach took a dive. Quickly, she interrupted. "I wasn't there when it happened."

"Police or state troopers, they never solved that case, did they?" said Jim.

"They never tried very hard. Guy was a solid-gold son of a bitch. No one much liked him but a lot of people really hated him. They thought it was done by somebody from out of town."

"Why's that?"

Harry smiled. "Because they didn't want to think it was from any-body in town, most especially his long-suffering wife, who had plenty of reason to want him dead. He'd been beating on her for years. Cops knew it; cops liked her, everybody liked her, just as they didn't like him." He looked at Andi. "You were in Salmon?"

"Yes, I was."

Harry was looking at her speculatively.

If a person could be flash-frozen, Andi was, in an instant.

"You okay, Andi? You've gone pale," said Jim.

What Andi fervently wished was that her body, in all of its hectic echoes, would stop giving her away. She felt like weeping. Would the long arm of the past keep reaching out except in the one way she wanted: her memory restored? "I wasn't in Salmon for very long; I was visiting with a friend. So all this must have happened after I left." She picked at her food, no longer hungry, as if Jim had set before her a plate of ashes.

But Harry went on remembering. "You know, I might've seen you in that coffee shop Jack and I went to. Popular spot. Were you with another girl? Younger, real dark hair?"

How was this possible, that he should remember details like this in a scene of no intrinsic interest; whereas she could not even remember her own family? What misstep of consciousness was this? "Mary, that's her name, Mary." Mary Dark Hope had been years younger yet much older in the way of good sense. Andi hadn't much good sense.

"Those were some days," Harry said, shutting down the discussion all of a sudden.

She went on looking at her plate, dragging her fork through Jim's Mexican dish and trying to make it appear she was eating.

"So what did you do in Fish and Game?" asked Andi, shifting the subject a little further afield.

"Helping out a friend with Fish and Game. Jack Kite. Went on calls with him. Weird, sometimes. I mean the calls, not Jack. It made being your local sheriff pretty tame. I mean, around here I don't get many calls about a bear in my garden 'eating my cabbages,' as one old woman claimed."

Jim chimed in. "Hell she did!"

Harry said it was absolutely true. "Bears like to prowl around at the edges of civilization."

Andi said, to get them out of Idaho and into Dakota, "How long is this restraining order in effect?"

"Long as you want; it's pretty much a closed-end deal; we can keep them from bothering you as long as you're here."

"But what if they manage to sneak in here anyway, like the other night?"

"They do that and they're caught, they both go to prison for a long, long time. It's serious business, going against a restraining order."

She said, "They can't stand it that a girl got the best of them."

"Oh, that's for sure."

Maybe it's time I moved on, she thought, hating the thought. It wouldn't be easy to find another place like this. It wouldn't be easy at all. The likelihood of doing that was nil. And there were the pigs now, too. Why did danger lurk around her? Why were there so many pitfalls? Why did she attract trouble? She looked at her much-read paperback of poetry, lying carelessly among cookbooks and horse books. She thought of A. E. Housman, a poem about how people so foolishly and wantonly had only fleeting thoughts of love and fame. It was trouble one should put his mind to, for trouble was bound to come. It made her smile. God, no wonder some people loved poetry. For the poets had all gotten there ahead of you.

"What are you smiling about?"

"Oh, just one of the poems in this book." She pulled it over and went to one of the dog-eared pages and read part of that Housman poem. "'Mine were of trouble,/And mine were steady,/So I was ready/When trouble came.'"

She closed the book. "I love that poem." Again, she smiled; she really smiled, and it was clearly a corker of a smile from the way they smiled back.

"To think this girl is lost among the pigs," said Jim.

Later, she lay in bed thinking of Frost and Housman and Emily Dickinson. How did they know what they knew? How did they know what *she* knew, only better? She would like to be a poet; she could think of nothing nobler than to be that. But why did she want to be noble? She sighed and guessed she didn't and rolled over on her side. Anyway, poetry wasn't about that. It was more about making you either see things you hadn't or, if you had known them and forgotten, remember them. Or maybe to get you to understand the person in the poem—the apple-picking boy and man were really you. No matter how strange, or far from your experience, the person in the poem was really you. It was you who must set aside dreams of love and fame, and you who must be ready for trouble.

She thought about the pigs that she saw in her mind's eye, covering farms and fields. Released from the bright white blistering buildings and that unnatural silence. She thought about herself, something she didn't like to do because she was disappointed in herself. Now, though, she realized, odd as it was to her, that she wasn't one of those whose thoughts were on ephemeral things like beauty and money and fame. No, she really was the speaker in that poem. Her thoughts lay low, but she kept them on trouble. There was always trouble like she knew that truck was going to be; she knew those boys would do something and she had been ready.

She didn't have to be anything. She didn't have to be smart, brave, cunning, heroic, courageous. She only had to be there, that was all. Courage (she was surprised to realize) wasn't the point. It had never been the point. Which was a relief, since she had so little of it. But blindness was; blindness was the point. Of blindness, she had plenty.

20

It was nearly eight AM when she got up and dressed and went down to the kitchen. The chores of the last hour had been performed by the others. She apologized and drank her mug of coffee while standing at the counter. Tom was eating the French toast that she craved.

"Sit down," Jim said. "I'll make you some."

Feeling the need to make up for her slackness, she said, no, she had to go to the barn.

"They already been fed," said Tom. "You don't have to. Thanks." This was to Jim, who'd just slid another piece of French toast onto Tom's plate. It looked an inch thick.

She said, "I thought I'd take Dakota down to the track and ride her a little."

They nodded and looked at each other and, as soon as the screen had clattered back behind her, shook their heads.

Dakota saw her coming and turned toward Sam's stall and rested his muzzle on top of the side that divided the stalls.

"Morning," said Andi to Sam, and rubbed his neck and held out a sugar cube.

"Morning," she said to Dakota. She couldn't reach his neck the way he was standing and he didn't so much as blink when she extended the hand with the sugar cube as far in as she could reach. "I bet you're the only horse in the state that doesn't like sugar." Andi thought that was interesting.

She went into the tack room and returned with saddle and bridle. She opened the stall door and waited. Dakota didn't move. He seemed to be paralyzed. She went into the stall with the bridle. "You feeling okay? Probably you're still anxious after what happened the other night." He was as far back in the stall as he could push himself, so he couldn't avoid the bridle that she was putting over his head.

Andi pulled him out of the barn. Then he stopped dead.

Tom and Jim were watching from the kitchen window.

"There she goes," said Jim.

"And there he stays," said Tom.

"You're being really stubborn," said Andi. "More than usual. Well, if you're determined to stand there, okay. I'll just saddle you up." She tossed the blanket over his back, then raised the saddle. Dakota was gone like a shot out from under her hand to stand under a tree. Andi shook her head and walked over to the tree.

"Need some help there?" Jim called out.

Jim and Tom walked toward her. Tom got his fingers in the bridle and Dakota went with him.

"He's the most determined animal," said Andi.

"Oh, they get that way," said Jim, and all of them rambled on toward the track, Dakota as easy and nice as pie.

At the track fence, Tom saddled the horse, who gave him a look (as Tom said later, "like the one Washington must have given Benedict Arnold") as he gave Andi a leg up.

"Thanks," she said. She made that clicking sound with her tongue and waited for Dakota to move onto the track. He didn't.

Tom said, "Ornery beast," and slapped his rump.

Dakota moved out onto the track and then shot like a bullet, nearly dumping his rider by the fence from the force of the start and again when he stopped suddenly.

"That damned horse can stop like a Porsche braking," said Tom.

"On a dime," said Jim.

They stood by the fence, side-by-side, feet up on the bottom rung, waiting. Both were chewing Teaberry gum.

"Think they'll ever be of one mind about anything?"

"Nope," said Jim.

The first stop-on-a-dime brake didn't do it so—

"Christ, there he goes again."

—the second one did.

"Jesus, right into the fence, poor child."

Jim gave a snuffling laugh. "We gotta stop joking around like this. Poor girl could get hurt."

But Andi was up and brushing earth and grass from her clothes. Dakota stood nearby, moved to the grassy verge to nibble away.

Andi was bawling him out. They could tell this from that hands-on-hips posture.

"Damned horse couldn't care less. Looks like he's yawning."

Jim had his baseball cap off and was scratching his head. "Horses don't yawn."

"They get bored, don't they?"

"Maybe," said Jim.

Keeping to her hands-on-hips posture, she went on talking. Dakota raised his head with his mouth full of grass that he'd rummaged for under the fence. He looked at her and chewed.

"What I can't understand to save me is how a girl with such earnest feelings for animals can't seem to read that horse."

Tom frowned. "I grant you, that is a puzzle."

"It's all those incarcerated hogs. I don't believe her when she says it's to save up money to go to Alaska....There she goes trying to get up on him again."

Andi had chosen the rails of the fence to give her a leg up.

"You want some help there, Andi?" Jim called to her. She yelled back no.

She threw her leg over, shoving hard against the fence, and finally managed to get back on the horse.

Dakota permitted that, and as soon as she had settled herself in the saddle and gathered up the reins, the horse shot forward and forced her backward. The girl hung on.

Tom raised his binoculars and watched the horse and rider on the back field and coming around the curve. "What I fail to understand," he said, lowering the glasses, "is how, since she's been practicing—as she calls it—ever since she's been here—"

"Yeah?" said Jim.

"Then how could she be worse?"

Jim laughed.

"Christ almighty, she might as well be in a rodeo breakin' wild horses. Dakota thinks it's a game."

"What? Horses don't think that way, Tom."

"This one sure does. Got any more of that gum?"

Jim fingered the pack of Teaberry out of the shirt pocket where he usually stashed cigarettes. He was trying to stop and not having much luck. He handed the gum to Tom.

Tom said, "Here they come again. At least he's not at the gallop. Somebody should give her a talking to about that horse, you know, so she doesn't get hurt."

"Yeah." Jim nodded. "You ought to do that."

"Me? No. I mean, it's your horse, after all."

Jim nodded again. "Well, I'm not talking to her."

"I just don't see how any man, woman, or child can look that bad in the saddle."

They both watched her go by, bumping around as if the horse were an SUV on rocky terrain.

"Hey, Andi! Dakota's looking kinda tired."

Andi waved and rode into the curve. They watched as Dakota slowed to a trot. When they paused again, Jim complimented her on handling the reins.

"I'm not really handling—"

To demonstrate the truth of that, Dakota took off again.

They both shook their heads. "You say you think she wants that job because she feels sorry for those pigs?"

"That's my guess."

"Like she felt sorry for the donkey?"

"That's what I'd say, yes."

"God almighty."

21

She had done more than a full day's work and it was after five and the sun went sulking off. The weather, she found, was temperamental. She was in the second farrowing building, scraping manure off the slatted floors; it was crusted and the hose wouldn't move it. She was on the center walkway. A few of the pigs watched her out of hollow eyes, as if the eyes had pulled themselves back so far into the sockets they had vanished, only the pale gray sockets remaining. Andi found it somehow heroic that they could still show interest in surroundings that seemed deliberately engineered to ensure suffering. The piglets, though, were enthusiastic about whatever this was she was doing, and crowded up against the bars.

She was on her knees when Nat and Hutch swaggered in. They went down the line, opening the gates, and driving, or trying to drive, the sows out, not all of them, just some. How could they expect these sows to move freely, the way they'd been crated up for so long.

Andi watched, stone-faced. The sows that didn't move as fast as they wanted them to got whipped or prodded. Nat used a whip and Hutch a prod. The two of them moved almost in unison. A lot of the pigs were either lame or sick and wouldn't move at all. Nat lashed them until they did.

"Where you taking them?" She asked this in her careful, neutral tone. If she showed any pity, she knew they'd just beat the pigs harder.

"Truck," said Hutch.

Be careful, she told herself. "What truck's that?"

"Over to Sweetland farm."

"Why?"

"Christ, don't you ever stop asking questions?" One of the hogs, sick with a tumor as big as a basketball underneath its stomach, resisted. "Come on, you pile of shit." Hutch whacked the pig across the back and it slumped on the waste-slick boards. Nat gave it a couple of licks with the prod, but it still didn't get up.

Andi saw what was wrong. "Its foot's caught between the boards."

It was one of the last three—the others had to clamber over or step on the downed one. "Goddamn it." Hutch tried to yank the pig up but its leg was wedged in tight. It could only squeal when Nat laid the prod across its back. "Damn it, we got to get going."

Andi said, "Listen, you two have got better things to do, so just go on ahead. I'll get its leg out of there. It can go later." She held to that stony expression she'd put on from the start. They were both looking at her and she knew she had to be careful.

They herded the remaining sows outside and she could hear their hooves rattle on the metal incline, and their squeals about not wanting to get up it in the first place. Nat stuck his head back in and said in his bullhorn voice, "We'll be back in a half hour or so to pick up some more."

"Yeah. Sure." She thought she knew now what they were doing: selling pigs to Sweetland and pocketing the money. It would be possible to do this; there were so many pigs in the first place, and some dying or near dead and thrown on the dead pile. What would Sweetland do with the pigs? What was there to do?

She waited until the truck pulled away. Then she took off her down vest and wedged it under the pig's head. "That'll help." She looked at the boards where the foot was stuck. "We got thirty minutes. You got any notion as to how you can keep out of this truck? Think, think."

She needed something like a ball-peen hammer. That or maybe a saw. Usually, there were a few tools in the huts, and she went up to the door area to see. No hammer. There was the awl Nat used sometimes. It might do. If she couldn't find a tool to come down hard on the board, then maybe she could use this to get some leverage and loosen it. She went back to the pig. Using the awl, she pried up the board. It was old wood and splintered badly. She cleared the pig's leg and set it level with the rest of her. What was left was twenty-five minutes to figure out what to do and how to do it. Though she doubted they'd be back that soon; they'd spend time jawing with their buddies over at Sweetland.

There was the van, the white one that just about everyone used to go back and forth from the office to the various huts. She could get the pig into that—well, theoretically she could, since it weighed probably three hundred pounds and she didn't see how she could move it. *Cross that bridge*, she told herself.

It never ceased to amaze her, the lack of traffic around these buildings, the absence of people, even though she knew people were around, for there was the occasional figure moving through the silence. On the outside there was always the silence. It wasn't the muffled silence of snow. It was the silence of absence.

Andi looked up for a moment at the blank sky. This was all that was over her or around her—the blankness, the whiteness, and the suffering. And that was it: a white spider, a white whale, and that was God.

The van had a loading platform, she remembered, stashed in the back. She would need to get the pig up that. She couldn't lift her. She had kept her hand on her back, feeling a little silly to be petting her, but what did it matter?

"I'll be right back." She left the hut.

The van was parked by the end hut, keys in it like always. The thought of stealing a van from this place struck her as deeply absurd. Anyone was allowed to use the van, but she still would have to have a story ready in case someone stopped her. She didn't have one.

Andi was an awful driver. She'd driven all the way from Santa Fe to Idaho and she was just as bad at the end of it as she'd been at the beginning. She was glad she could ride a horse better.

She turned the key and the engine sputtered to life. There was gas, but not much. She reversed on the wide path—not really a road—connecting the various buildings. The van bucked, but she got it heading in the right direction.

The van bumped along the path. Finally she pulled it up to the back of the building, and when she went back in, the pig was standing; the leg would not cripple her, then. The pig regarded Andi out of her small, pale eyes. She was doing, the eyes seemed to say, the best she could.

"We've got to get out of here." She gave her a push from the rear. The pig still had its head turned to look at her. She pushed harder; the pig wouldn't budge. She turned and leaned her back and all her weight against her rump and suddenly she moved forward and sent Andi sprawling; she sat down heavily on the boards.

The sow pricked her ears and looked around. Quickly, Andi got up and put her hand on her back and kind of steered her along and out the door. The back door of the van was open and only a few feet away.

She wouldn't like this, Andi thought. But the pig made no trouble about walking up the metal plank. She hopped in after her and thought of throwing the tarp over the pig in case anyone stopped her. That wouldn't be very smart, though; if anyone looked in the back, they'd know she was hiding something.

She jumped down, went around to the driver's seat, and started up the engine. There was no truck in sight and it had been more than a half hour. Probably Hutch and Nat were warming their behinds on a couple of bar stools.

It was well after closing time, the sky going to gray. There was no one in sight as she drove around to pass the office—the only exit—but then she saw someone come out and stop, looking at the approaching van.

It was only Jake, thank the Lord. He signed for her to stop and she did, bringing the van to a halt on the gravel parking lot. All of the cars had left by now.

She smiled. "Hi, Jake."

"Oh, it's you. What's with the van?"

"I'm transporting this pig to where Nat took the truck."

"Sweetland's?"

"They didn't tell me why they were taking them."

"That's kind of extreme for just one pig, going all the way there."

Andi heaved a sigh. "Well, okay, but it's what I should do." He was looking at her. She didn't think he believed her.

But he just smiled and said, "Okay," and slapped the van. "You go, girl."

She started up the engine again and he said, "Just bring the damned thing back. Knowing you it could be halfway to Alaska before anyone ever found out."

She laughed. "I'm not that much of an idiot."

"Sure, you are. You'd probably try anything you'd a mind to."

"No." She thought for a moment. "Look, since the place is closed and no one wants this van, do you think I could keep it overnight? I mean, it would be nice if I could just drive home afterward. It'd save someone the trouble of coming to get me."

Jake folded his arms and smiled at her. "Don't see why not. Only if you promise to get it back first thing in the morning."

"I will. I promise not to drive to Alaska."

She put the van in gear and bumped off, watching in the rearview mirror as he grew small in the distance, all the while watching the van as it disappeared.

Jake. He was a nice guy.

It was going for dark and the dull gray sky settled lower on the horizon. She slid open the narrow window between the front and back seats so that she could hear if the pig was okay; presumably she would give off distress signals.

Now, driving, she took time to wonder how Jim (and Tom) would greet the news of another pig—a stolen pig. They already had a stolen donkey. It was one thing to get herself into trouble with the sheriff;

it was another to get Jim in trouble. And she hadn't (of course she hadn't) worked up a story for tomorrow to cover today.

The lies were endless. She wished she could go somewhere and settle down and stay and never tell another lie.

The van bumped over stony soil and she could hear the pig shift around, the clicking of her feet on metal. The road was winding and cluttered with rocks. On top of her terrible driving.

There were a few dim stars out and a misty-looking moon when she drove up to the house. She passed it and parked the van right by the sty. She wanted to get the pig in there, settled, if that was possible (and it probably wasn't), before she told Jim about it.

She had a lot of nerve, in the worst sense of the word. She was counting on the fact that no one would miss the pig. It wasn't the same as taking Sam, for Sam had been a working donkey. Well, a forgotten working donkey. So it was the same, wasn't it? This was a sick pig, and, she assumed, a forgotten sick pig. But if someone guessed and reported it to the sheriff's office, well, Harry McKibbon would be right there at Jim's. The sheriff would really have to stretch belief to think she wasn't the one who'd taken this old sow. Donkey and pig.

When she opened the back of the van the pig turned around and stood looking at her. The sow did not seem disturbed by the sudden alteration in her life, but, then, how could she know?

Andi rested the metal plank on the edge of the door and gave the pig a little push. She moved without any coaxing or shoving and stepped to the ground.

Max and Hazel were rooting in the dirt, turning up an old corncob, a piece of rag, a lettuce leaf. The new pig stood inside the fence, watching. Andi felt sorry for her; she'd never had a taste of freedom, or knew there was such a thing, and here she was. It's what she'd heard about prisoners. She pictured a convict on his day of release, standing outside a prison, a suitcase in hand, waiting. Not for a bus or a ride, but for something to be explained.

After a few moments Hazel came over to investigate. The new pig backed up a step or two. Andi laid her hand on her back. Max moved away from the trough; seeing no harm was coming to Hazel, he went to stand by her. The new pig backed up several more steps until her butt hit the gate. There was grunting from all three, and Andi wondered what sort of communication was taking place.

She didn't want her pig to feel trapped, so she opened the gate and let the pig back out and then she put her into the fenced-off part of the sty. Maybe, she thought, she should leave her there overnight. It would be less stressful. Stressful? This pig had been living in hell all of her life, one litter after another, until her system was too exhausted to keep it up and she was, therefore, useless to Klavan's. Meeting Hazel and Max would hardly count for stress.

The pigs stopped vocalizing and were quiet again. She looked again at the tumor. It was awful, almost frightening. Tomorrow she'd get the vet to see to it. She wondered if it was painful. This reminded her that if the pig was missed at the farm, it wouldn't be hard to identify it. If the tumor was removed, it would look like anybody's pig.

A light came on in the kitchen. There was Jim. And Tom. There was no way she could not tell them the truth.

The kitchen opened and she heard her name. "Andi!" Jim called in the distance.

She closed the gate, left the three regarding one another through the fence. Max and Hazel did not seem to mind the new pig; they were only curious.

She walked across the gravel to the kitchen door, held open by Jim. "What's the van for?"

"It's just a spare one they use at the place to transport stuff around the huts. I'm driving it back in the morning. Hey, Tom," she added, smiling with a brightness she didn't feel.

Tom looked up from his plate of ribs. "You look whipped, young lady. Whatcha been transporting? Or should I ask?"

She turned at the sink to wash her hands.

"I take it you'd sooner not have any of these?" Jim held up a serving platter of ribs.

"No, thanks." Why did he keep on doing that? She got down one of the thick white cowboy plates and sat down between them. She forked a baked potato up from a plate and decided to just go ahead with saying it. "I transported a pig and he's out in the sty with Hazel and Max."

Tom slowed down chewing.

Jim said, "A pig. Well, why'd they give you a pig?" He paused. "Something's wrong with it, isn't it?"

"Yes. It's got a tumor on its side and I thought maybe the vet could help."

"Never heard that place was so all-fired generous, no, not even with a sick animal. Downers, sick animals, they go ahead and slaughter anyway, though it's against the law, of course."

"That's for sure," said Andi, watching a rivulet of butter wander down the side of her potato.

The two of them went on gnawing at the barbecued ribs. Andi relaxed a little and cut into her potato.

"Sheriff was here," said Tom, looking cross-eyed at the rib between his fingers.

Andi stopped relaxing. "Why?"

"At the behest of the Baileys."

"Really? Well, I was nearly raped at the behest of the Baileys."

Jim nodded. "Harry's aware. But Lucas Bailey wants you charged with assault."

"I didn't assault anyone. Dakota did, so charge him. Good God! I haven't got time for the law."

Jim chuckled and wiped his hands and said to Tom, "Let's go see this pig."

They had agreed the pig should have the tumor seen to and Andi had insisted on paying for the doctor.

Now she lay in bed trying to invent a story to give out if anyone—especially Nat and Hutch—asked her what happened. Would she tell them that it had just got away? That it had died? What could she have done with the corpse, then? And what about what she'd told Jake? She wished she hadn't, but what else could she have done?

On the way to the farm the pig died so I had to get rid of it. I guess it was that tumor. I didn't know what to do, so I took it back to Jim's farm and let them take care of the carcass.

But why do you care? It was always meant to die.

22

She was hosing down the boards the following morning when Abramson walked into the hut, carrying his clipboard. "Not supposed to do too much of that." He nodded toward the hose.

"It stinks to high heaven in here."

He smiled. "Supposed to stink. Place is full of pigs, ain't it?"

"There's stink and there's *stink*. Write that down." She pointed at his clipboard. "What *do* you write down?"

"Notes. Keepin' tabs."

"On me?"

He laughed. "Hey, it ain't all about you, you know."

"I'm glad."

"Did you get that old pig taken care of?"

She nodded and fiddled with the spout of the hose to keep from looking at him. "You could say so. It died on the way. So I just drove the van to Jim Purley's, where I'm staying. He took care of it. Buried it maybe."

"You should've brought it back here. Seeing it's Klavan's property."

Andi put the hose back on its hook. "Why? They couldn't have done anything with it. It was so sick."

Abramson nodded. "Just in the future, if a situation develops like that, just remember, it's Klavan's property."

Raising her eyebrows, she said, "Now, what kind of situation could develop like that? I mean, how many times in my life am I going to be driving a vehicle a pig dies in?"

"Just be careful."

"Has anyone said anything about the missing pig? In a crowd of five thousand of them, I wouldn't think it'd be much missed."

"Pig, no. Van, yes. Nat and Hutch couldn't figure why you'd be following them. Said they didn't tell you to."

"I never said they did; I thought I *should* go after them, that's all."

Abramson still kept looking at her as he slowly chewed his gum. He was making her nervous. "What?"

"Like I said, be careful."

She shrugged. "I always am."

Midafternoon, she was giving the pigs extra rations. The runovers that weren't confined to their separate cages crowded up to the bars as if there weren't enough food in the whole wide world to feed them. No wonder people got fat. Misery, pain, emptiness—what could you do but eat? No wonder they called it "comfort food."

Andi carried a bucket of feed, kneeling sometimes to give hand- fuls of it to the pigs mashed to the ground. When what she had of the food was gone, she leaned into the pen and picked up Oscar and carried him around as she did the chores, staying alert to the sound of someone coming. When she heard the voices she put Oscar back in the pen, too quickly, so that his leg tore a tiny hole in her vest. It would probably only be another week before Oscar was put in with the feeder pigs, fed up to his market weight, which would be around fifty pounds. An even shorter time to live than his mother had.

In walked Nat and Hutch.

"So what the fuck were you doin', girl? Abramson says you took it in a van to your place."

"It died on me. It died in the van. What was I supposed to do, bury it? I couldn't even roll it out of the van. And everybody was gone from here."

Hutch was tossing corn into the chute. Nat said, "Question is, why the fuck was it in the van in the first place?"

Andi let the bucket drop. "Look. I explained all that to Mr. Abramson and Jake."

"Yeah, that you said we told you to bring it to Sweethand."

"That's *not* what I said. I said I thought I *should* try and get it there." In spite of Abramson's instructions, Andi started in hosing down the floor. She kept her head down and focused on waste, that and its smell. She didn't have a mask; the stink might have been overpowering had she not by now grown fairly used to it.

"So where'd you take the pig?"

She heaved a sigh. "I took the pig home to get help disposing of it."

"You live at Jim Purley's place, don't you?"

She nodded, said nothing.

Hutch had finished filling the bin. Now the two of them kept staring at her, both with arms crossed, their hands stuck in their armpits.

"Why are you making such a big deal of this? The damned pig was sick here; you know that. So it died." She picked up a broom and started sweeping off water.

Nat put on his thin-lipped, disbelieving smile. "Thing is, we don't believe this cock-and-bullshit story."

"Oh, *really*?" She brushed hair off her forehead.

"Uh-huh. What we think is you stole that old pig."

Her heart was thudding, but she kept that to herself. Instead she dropped the hose and moved toward Nat until she was right in his face. He even took a step back. "What in *hell* would I want with a sick pig?"

Hutch said, "You're the one took that donkey, that's all."

She turned to Hutch. "You know how dumb that sounds? I took a donkey so I must have taken a sick pig. God!" Andi went back to the broom. "If you want me fired, go tell Jake or Mr. Klavan or whoever." Klavan probably would fire her, too. Meanness, she'd heard, ran through the man like an electrical charge.

"No one's lookin' to get you fired. But you shouldn't be taking that van for your own personal use."

"If you call *transporting a pig* personal use." The word *transport* had taken on a different and unpleasant meaning. "It was for the pig that I was *transporting*."

"Oh, yeah." Nat snorted.

"Anyway, both of you use it all the time to go hang out at Two Dogs. That's a lot more personal than transporting a pig. I apologize for going joyriding."

Hutch said, "You know, we can't figure you out, girl."

"Did someone tell you that you had to?"

"What the hell were you doing bringing that donkey into town?"

"That was like six weeks ago. You're still worried about that? Excuse me." With the empty bucket, she shouldered her way past them, and they both had to bend backward. The walkway wasn't wide enough for two abreast, much less three. "I'd like to stand around and chat with you, but I've got a lot of work to do."

23

When Jim asked her how things were going at work, Andi did not tell him about the pile of dead hogs or the lagoon because he would ask her (still again) why she didn't quit such a depressing job; nor did she tell him about her reverie, for she didn't want him telling her she was too sentimental or romantic. She could not get the picture of all those hogs stuck behind bars or lying in that pile out of her mind.

"We don't all seem to be—" What? Living in the same world? She said that.

At least he didn't want to explore the meaning of that. He just said she had some strange ideas. He said he needed to go into town and run some errands. She would like to go into town, she said. And thought that having no one else—not Jim, not Tom—to tell such things to, she would tell Dakota about it. Hadn't he had experiences like those pigs? Herded up to auction with the other foals, terrified, none of them with any other place to go except the slaughterhouse?

They were driving past Klavan's, and Andi thought once again how its whiteness made her think of absolution, and how utterly at odds this was with its real purpose.

"Do you think horses understand what you're saying to them?"

Jim thought a bit, whether out of respect for her or horses she didn't know.

"Depends what you're communicating. Some direction to go or to stop—"

"Not just that. I mean . . . you know, just talk."

Again, Jim grew thoughtful. "Well, now, you know you have a kind of hard time with Dakota."

"I'm not saying about riding him. I think he likes to hear me talk to him, though. I believe it's soothing for him." She turned to watch the road. "At least, that's what I think."

When they drove past the vegetable stand, Andi waved to Eula, who was sitting in her chair. Andi asked Jim to let her out so that she could talk to her. Jim stopped and said he'd probably have to drive back not too much later, forty-five minutes or so, and would that be long enough for her to do what she wanted? She probably wanted to go to the stores.

It amused her the way Jim would tell her what she'd like and what she wouldn't. "That's okay. I'll just take a cab back."

Jim nodded. "Well, I'll see you later, then. You be back by suppertime?"

Andi said probably she would, that she'd call him. Jim sketched her a little salute and drove off.

How strange it was: she'd only been here for weeks and it felt almost like home would feel if she'd had one. How quickly people and places laid claim to her. She waved Jim off and said good-bye to the empty air. Right away she felt the bleakness of one who has seen a person go for the last time. For a few seconds, before she turned to walk back to the vegetable stand, desolation swamped her; she did not know why. Was her life so precarious, so moment-to-moment, that the ground could open and swallow her?

And it always made her wonder what she'd been like then, back before the person she was now. She thought she might have made up that story about the Olivier family not so much to tell others as to tell herself.

"Hey, hon," said Eula. "How's that old donkey doin'?"

"He's swell. I really got lucky with meeting Jim."

"Seems to me you were deserving of a little luck. Jim's one fine man."

Andi thought her voice was wistful and wondered if Eula had feelings about Jim. Then she wondered why Jim and Tom Rio, too, weren't married. Jim, she knew, was a widower, but what about Tom?

"I wonder why they aren't married."

Eula said, "Oh, you don't know that story? They were married once and their wives were good friends. The women were driving in the old truck to Fargo and a tire blew; it wouldn't have been so bad if the road hadn't been slick with black ice and a guardrail had already been hit in an accident just before. The truck went into it and over the side of a hill and they were both killed."

Andi felt helpless listening to this.

"I guess it's a terrible thing to say, but I remember being glad those two women had each other, that it wasn't one of them alone having to go over that hill. I just imagine how terrifying it would be happening anyway, but to be alone when it happened . . . how much worse."

"I had no idea," said Andi. "No idea at all."

Eula had tears in her voice in the telling of this story.

"No, they're not ones for talking about troubles. But they're best friends now, and I doubt either one of them'll get married again. They never had any children, either. Isn't it strange the way some people's lives run parallel to each other?"

Andi nodded, not knowing at all about a life running parallel to her own. She said, "I know what you mean about the wives not being alone. I had a brother who would almost always have the same thing happen to him as happened to me. Like we both got sick at the same time, both broke an arm at the same time, and both broke up with our boyfriend and girlfriend at the same time. It was consoling to have someone there who knew just how I felt."

"Well, you've been gone from home for quite a while, haven't you, traveling around on your own?"

"Yes, I have." Andi was looking at a cardboard container of carrots.

"I'll bet your brother misses you."

"He does, I know." She held out the carrots. "These look so fresh; I'll take some for Sam and the horses."

Eula snapped a brown bag open and Andi dropped the carrots in, a couple of pounds' worth. Eula made change in her old cash register, the kind with the numbered totals popping along the top, with the pinging of the cash drawer.

"There you go." Eula handed back Andi's change. "Those horses, they'll be happy."

Andi nodded and smiled and said she was going to look around town for a while. They said good-bye.

There was Mrs. Englehart's big Victorian house on the corner, but no sign of Mrs. Englehart on the porch. Over the road, set in its solitary half-acre, the Dairy Queen and the Donut Delite had one customer apiece. She wondered how they stayed in business.

Andi crossed the street to the Dollar Store to see what you could possibly get anymore for a dollar. Actually, you could get a lot. As she walked up and down the aisles, she picked up a few things: a wiry scrubber for pots and pans, a dish towel, and a nail brush in the shape of a pig.

After the Dollar Store, she passed the Plugged Nickel, where voices were raised, as usual. Something shattered, bottle or glass. She stopped in at the pharmacy to buy another Norman X. Black novel. By now she'd read four of them and thought the writing pretty high-class for a Western. But, then, hadn't Walter Van Tilburg Clark written "Westerns"?

How did she know that name? Amnesia was a strange condition. Apparently, still stored in a person's mind were things like how to drive a car, how to ride a horse. Well, she wasn't very good at either, but there they were.

When she went to May's a little later, she hoped Norman would be at his stool. The idea that here was a writer, a professional writer, who'd written more than twenty books, simply dazzled her. First, though, she wanted to go to the saddlery and talk to Jared.

A distance away on the dirt road she could hear that clanging of metal on metal. Shoeing a horse, she supposed. She went inside the big barn and said, "Jared."

He turned from the forge and smiled at her. "Look who's here! How're you doing?"

"Fine. I really like it at Jim's."

"Well, good." He toed off a cat that was slithering around the foreleg of the horse he was shoeing.

"Do horses usually put up with cats doing that?"

"Depends. The cat picks up and the horse picks up." *Clang* went the hammer.

"Picks up what?"

Jared stopped and pondered. "Thoughts, brain waves, stuff like that."

"You mean they communicate, is that what you're saying?"

Jared just gave her a look. "Naturally. You think animals spend their whole day just inside their own heads?"

"Don't humans?"

Clang. "I don't think so. Half the time we're trying to get inside the other guy's, God knows why."

Andi was perched on a bale of hay. "That's what I've been wondering about. Do you think people and animals communicate?"

"Sure. People train dogs, don't they? People ride horses."

"No, that's not what I mean. Those things are habits. I mean, do they know how each other feels?"

"You got Sam in mind?"

"Well, him, yes. But especially Dakota, that horse of Jim's."

"Oh. Dakota." Jared gave a sniffing sort of laugh through his nose. "Dakota's a strong-minded horse. But he's easy at the same time. Nice as pie if he likes you. It's kind of strange."

"How does he act if he doesn't like you?" Her heart sank a little.

"No way. He ignores you. When he's been in for shoeing and people come in and go round the stalls, Dakota ignores them all over the place." There came that nose-snort of a laugh again, as if Jared thought Dakota a rare treat.

Well, he certainly didn't ignore *her*, Andi thought, relieved.

★   ★   ★

In the diner, Norman Black was hunched over his coffee, as if he were guarding it.

Andi slid onto the stool beside him. "Hey, Norman." She pulled out the menu, ran her eyes over it.

"Andi." He grinned.

"Doesn't May ever change the menu?"

"Nah, anyway, there's no May. I mean no real one."

"What are you talking about? That's her right down there." She nodded toward the blonde at the end of the counter, talking to one of the other waitresses and a truck driver. "I remember."

"The girls just take turns. That one, she's actually Estelle."

"Norman, what are you talking about? They take *turns*?"

"Yeah. You've been here how long? A month, six weeks? And Estelle's been May for all that time. In another little bit, in about a month or so, Estelle, she'll stop being May, and Carly, the brunette, she'll be May. And then Mildred will be. 'May's Walked Out'—that's what the diner used to be called."

She laughed. "Why did they ever change it to 'Long Gone'?"

"According to Carly, people driving through town couldn't figure out this was an eating place, despite those big pie signs in the window. Transients got confused."

"Norman, how can the one name be any more confusing than the other? Anyway, how many transients can this town get?"

"Oh, you'd be surprised."

May had come over and was standing before Andi with her order pad and a smile. "Hey, dear. What're you having?"

"I don't know. Maybe a grilled cheese and fries and slaw?" As the waitress wrote this down, Andi said, "Is your name really Estelle?"

"Estelle? No, it's May. I own the diner. Together with my no-account son-in-law. Why?"

Andi looked at Norman, who said, "Don't expect her to admit it. It's a big secret, like the Masons, sort of."

May had one hand firmly planted on a hip. "Norman Black, what have you been telling her?" She turned to Andi. "Don't believe a word this man says. He thinks the whole world is all made up. I'll go get your grilled cheese." As she left, she gave Norman a *humpf!* and a dirty look.

"You're making it up, aren't you?"

He brushed crumbs from the counter. "No, I am not."

"Why would she lie? And how come you know it if it's such a secret?"

"Carly told me. For a few months there, Carly and I were an item."

"*Item?* You've got to be kidding!"

"You don't think a good-looking woman'd give me the time of day?"

"Of course she would. I'm laughing at the *word* being used in Kingdom. So Carly told you about May's Long Gone?"

"That's right."

"Norman, you are *so* putting me on." She held up the paperback she'd just bought. "The cover looks kind of lonely. The faded colors, the empty land—they look sad."

Norman took the book from her hand. "It is, kinda. The story's sad, too; yeah, I guess it is sad. Come to think of it, maybe most of them are sad." He thumbed through the first few pages and then looked at his list of books. He said, "I never noticed this before, but I can't recall a happy ending in the lot. People want happy endings."

"That's pretty sad in itself."

"Maybe I've used up my emotional capital; maybe I can't think up a happy ending anymore."

"Emotional capital?"

"You know. It's F. Scott Fitzgerald's notion that we begin with a certain amount of emotional capital, then we draw on it, some too much, some too soon, and when it's gone, it's gone. *Pffft*, good-bye."

"That's strange. Do you believe it?"

"No."

Andi laughed.

"Have you cornered the Baileys lately?"

"Not since they favored me with a visit last month."

"So how's the restraining order been doing?"

"So far, okay. I never told you the whole story, though." Andi looked around to see who might be within hearing distance, saw nobody. "About the man in the truck?"

"One that fell and knocked himself in the head?"

"It didn't exactly happen that way."

"Funny, but I never thought it did."

"We went back—Dakota and me, I mean—back to the house and I called the police. I'd pushed the body so the head was nearer to a rock, so that was the story of the accident I told the troopers who came. That he fell and must've hit his head. I wasn't going to tell the police what really happened; they might claim that Dakota was a danger and had to be put down. And, Norman, this is strictly between us, okay?"

"Absolutely." He chuckled. "You should hire out as a bodyguard."

She laughed. "Not hardly."

"That horse must really like you."

"He doesn't seem so awful eager to have me ride him. Do you think animals and humans can communicate?"

"Hell, yes. It's on a whole other plane; it's not words, at least not words we know."

Norman offered his cigarettes, which, for some reason, she was tempted to take and wondered why. She shook her head.

"How's work?"

Andi lowered her voice and told him about the pig. "This is in the strictest confidence, now."

"Everything you tell me's that. These lips are sealed. I wonder what Harry McKibbon would say or what punishment the court might mete out about a pig infraction. Considering you only took it to help it and not for personal gain. Did they believe you at Klavan's?"

"I don't think most knew about it. And why would they care? What's one pig out of thousands?" Andi looked inside the cheese sandwich May had set before her to see if there was pickle relish on it.

There was, and she bit into it. She ate for a moment, then said, "There's Jake, too."

"Who's Jake?"

"One of the managers."

Norman made a wide sweep with a match he brought up to his cigarette. He blew a smoke ring. "It must be hard on you working there. You know, maybe that's what you should do with your life. Study veterinary medicine. You'd make a good vet."

"And just where would I study this?"

He shrugged. "State university, for one place."

"Norman, does that sound real to you? Even if I had the aptitude, what would I use for money?"

"Scholarship, maybe?"

"That would mean I'd have to produce some record of my high school performance."

"So? All you have to do is get it. Your dad could get that for you, surely."

"*Your dad could*" . . . It seemed so strange to hear such words on the lips of another, spoken with the clear understanding that everyone at least had a dad, no matter if it was only a memory of one. No matter whether they were on speaking terms, or had grown apart, or seldom seen. He might be a traveling salesman or a journalist or an explorer. Or something as mundane and unexceptional as an accountant or a teacher. She smiled at this ordinariness; it appealed to her.

Even if he hadn't come to her aid when she fell off her bicycle or hadn't come to the grade school pageant or the play she had starred in in high school; even if he had missed her graduation. Even if he had failed her miserably and in every way possible, even then she could call him up. *"Dad, I need my high school record."*

Even if she couldn't call him or write to him because his old address was no longer valid; even if she couldn't call him because he had abandoned her, at least she would have a knowledge of that instead of what she had now, which was nothing. Even for all of this she could forgive him, if just to know there was someone somewhere to forgive.

"Maybe it's something else that keeps you working there. You thinking, maybe, of torching the place?"

"If I did that, they'd all burn."

"Like Jake?"

"No. The pigs." Like Oscar.

24

ndi couldn't remember the last time she'd bought something new to wear. She stopped into the Unique Boutique, where she was the only customer. The proprietor was probably in the back behind the curtained alcove.

The clothes were nice, despite being a little dated. She tried on a jean jacket, a red wool coat (which she found too startling), and a gray quilted vest, and another in light blue.

She had decided on the blue vest when a woman in a flowered dress (old-fashioned, like the ones on the rack) came through the curtain and apologized, asking her if she had found things all right. The woman was middle-aged and her skin was fine and heavily powdered, like back when women used loose powder and rouge. Andi wondered why she thought that, since "back when" was a useless concept to her.

On her flowered dress, the owner wore a big old-fashioned silver brooch of a cat, a dog, and a pig looking at the moon above a little lake. The detail was intricate and told a little story for whoever took the time to fashion it. The shop also had a case of costume jewelry and Andi wondered if this brooch had once lain there.

"I'll take this." Andi handed over the vest and said, "I really like that pin you're wearing."

The woman twisted her chin to look down at it as if she might have forgotten, then said, "Yes, isn't it sweet? My husband got it on one of his trips."

Andi liked to imagine the husband's trip had been to this lake or bay where he'd found the real cat, dog, and pig. She could have stood there fantasizing all evening about this trip and others she would make up for him.

"That'll be $43.50, please."

Andi handed over two twenties and a five, collected her change, and said good-bye and thanks.

"Sorry, hon," said Alma, the Kingdom Kabs dispatcher, "but Bub's out on a long run, had to go to Beulah, and Ernie's out sick."

First time Andi had ever heard of Ernie, sick or well. "How long'll he be?"

"Oh, probably another couple of hours."

Andi thought about this. It was Saturday night and she didn't have to go to Klavan's tomorrow. "You know, I think I'll just go over to Englehart's tonight."

"Why, that sounds like a real good idea. And Bub can drive you home first thing in the morning. I'll tell him."

Andi smiled. Everyone seemed to know just what she'd be doing, or should be. "Fine. May I use your phone to call Englehart's?"

Her old room was available, Mrs. Englehart reported with vigor.

Andi liked the idea that it was referred to as her old room. "Just for the one night, Mrs. Englehart. I decided to stay in town."

Now Andi lay on the still-made bed, on the tufted white spread, hands clasped behind her head, thinking about her spent $43.50. Then of Fitzgerald's notion of emotional capital. If the emotional capital was spent, then this had to work in the person's favor as well as against her, didn't it? If feelings were gone, they were gone, both good and bad, happy and sad.

She would no longer care about finding her father, or about donkeys left alone by a fence, or about sick pigs, or about Oscar, or about the wild horses. Or about shooting a man back there in Salmon so many times he seemed to dissolve right in front of her, the air a mist of blood. No, and she would no longer care about caring—

There was a knock on her door and she sat up.

"Andi?" Mrs. Englehart opened the door a crack.

"Yes?"

"Sorry, I hope I didn't wake you. Oh, you're still dressed. Sheriff McKibbon phoned up and asked for you. Said he'd like you to just step over to the station."

That surprised her. "Oh. Okay. How did he know I was here?"

"Said he was driving by and saw you come in."

"He didn't say what he wanted to see me about?" It could be about the restraining order, but she didn't think so. She pulled on one shoe and was rooting with her foot for the other under the bed.

"No, he didn't, dear." The door closed.

Before she left her room, she had a look at her face and hair in the mirror, lipsticked one, smoothed the other, descended the stairs.

"Sheriff?"

Harry McKibbon looked up from some paperwork, mouth hinting at a smile, but trying to be serious. "Andi. Come on in. Just shut the door, will you?"

Quietly, she did this. She saw he wasn't wearing his dark Ray-Bans, and she was struck by the intense blue of his eyes. She waited.

He nodded toward one of the straight-backed wooden chairs on the other side of the metal desk. "Sit down, why don't you?"

She could think of several reasons why, but she sat down anyway, trying not to do it on the edge of the chair. The chair was not built for comfort.

He'd been filling out a form and tossed the paper in his out-box. "I got a complaint from Klavan's, reporting a missing pig that they're saying you drove off with a couple nights ago. Also, you were driving one of their vehicles that no one had given you leave to drive."

She sighed. "This isn't about that stupid van, surely." But he'd just said it was. She strapped her chest with her arms, as if the arms were a straitjacket and she the offended one, the victim of someone's foolishness. "Don't tell me they really care."

"About the pig? I imagine you're right. It's you that's got them in a lather. Anyway, Ben Klavan claims you said the pig died on you while you were driving the van to the Sweetland farm."

"Yes. I didn't know what to do. I mean, I couldn't get the pig out of the van, as it was too heavy, so I went back to Jim's and—" She stopped.

"Go on."

"And I buried it."

"*You* did?"

She nodded.

"But how'd you get it out of the van?"

How stupid could she be? Hadn't she just said the pig was too heavy? But she didn't want to implicate Jim and Tom. She'd done this all wrong. "Well, the pig wasn't as heavy as I thought; I just . . . rolled it out."

"Uh-huh. Into an open grave. See, I've come from Jim's place, where I had a look at his livestock. Now, what I recalled from before was Jim had these two pigs, same ones he's had for years. Only now there's three pigs, one looking like it had some kind of surgery recently. Could have been to remove a tumor, or something like that."

Andi chewed at the inside of her lip. "What did Jim say?"

"Jim didn't. I didn't take it up with Jim. I thought maybe I'd just ask you, for starters."

Even though he might be going to toss her in the county jail, she couldn't help but like him. More now because he was trying to keep Jim out of it, which is what she should have done and didn't. "Can the pig be identified? Is there anything on it that tells where it came from?"

"Nope. The pig doesn't have a driver's license. At least not on him."

"So I guess you're thinking this pig I had in the van didn't actually die?"

Harry had drawn his foot up over his other knee and was rubbing his ankle, thoughtfully. "That's pretty much it, yes. Didn't actually die.

Maybe somehow looked dead or maybe pretended to be dead. Without, you know, actually being dead."

"So what you're thinking is I stole that pig and ran away in the van up to Jim's place?"

"Along those lines, yeah."

Andi looked at him, trying to muster a hardness she didn't feel. "I guess that's what you'll have to think, then, because I'd never be able to change your mind, since you think that old sow herself is living proof you're right." She slid a little closer to the edge of her chair. "But don't you feel at all silly having a pig investigation to do when what must've been on your mind for weeks is the Bailey brothers, who nearly assaulted me out on the road, then broke into Jared's and took Sam into a field, *then* broke into Jim's house and were coming to the barn to steal Sam or hurt him? Maybe kill him? Or has the fate of this pig driven everything else out of your mind?"

"No. But I expect *you* will, what with donkeys and pigs being un-accounted for. Pretty soon farmers around here will be keeping their cows and sheep in their living rooms. So you're saying that pig at Jim's is not from Klavan's."

"No, I'm saying nothing until I get myself a lawyer. Of course, you could get your forensic team over to Jim's pigsty and see what they pick up. But for that you'd need a warrant. I'd love to see that judge signing off on gathering pigsty evidence."

Harry had to bite off a smile. He rose and said, "Okay, I guess that's all for now."

Andi had gotten up with him. "I'm sorry you have to waste your time on this, Sheriff."

Hands on hips, one over the leather holster, he said, "Why don't you quit that place?" He appeared to be pondering this. Harry stood looking down at her with what seemed to be real commiseration. "Someone that feels the way you do? How do you stand it? I can't see how you stand it."

Maybe it was because she *could* quit; she was free to go or stay. Her foot wasn't trapped between the warped boards. She was free to leave a place that was a misery. She was free to turn around and walk away. *We all were.*

They crowded her mind as they did their crates and cages, hundreds of them pushed up against the bars, watching her out of doomed eyes. Why were they forced to live in a world different from hers? Why did they end up as corpses tossed in a heap by a dead lagoon or under the sticker's knife? And why did they sink down to chops and cutlets pressed under slick plastic wrap while she could walk away from the cold void of the marketplace?

She looked up at the sheriff and answered, "Some things you've just got to stand, Sheriff."

For a few moments he looked at her, then nodded and opened the door for her to go. No question, no arguments, just the look and the nod.

She almost wished he'd call her back.

Back at the rooming house she was knocking the dirt off her shoes when Mrs. Englehart came out from the rear of the house with her bathrobe on, her hair in a braid down her back. "Andi, I completely forgot to tell you about your friend who called here—"

"You mean Alma? Is it about the cab ride in the morning?"

"No, no, I mean came here. This was a man. Said he was a friend of yours and were you here. I told him you were over to the police. He didn't come in while you were there?"

"No," she said. She stepped off the mat, moved closer to Mrs. Englehart, hoping for some word, some nuance, some unexpressed image that would recast the stranger in a better light—an old acquaintance, perhaps, wanting her to go out for a drink. But she didn't have old acquaintances. "What else did he say?"

"Only just what I told you. He was a friend who was passing through and just dropped by to say hello."

"What did he look like?"

Mrs. Englehart seemed to be trying to dredge up words to describe the magnetic appeal of the man, but couldn't. "He was well spoken, tall, dark-eyed, dark hair." Her finger poked in her cheek, she looked like some old cartoon depiction of a person thinking.

"Did he say if he'd be back?" Of course he would.

"No, nothing except 'Tell her I'll catch her later.' "

Andi stood there, her breathing shallow. "Thanks." She turned on the stair. "But if he should turn up, tell him I'm still out. I'm just kind of tired."

She was more than tired now, she was drained. She was scared.

Still in her clothes, she lay on her bed.

Was there always someone you couldn't shake off? He might have been a friend of Harry Wine, but she doubted Harry had the kind of friends who'd be set on vengeance.

No, this was someone who went back further in her life than that, and if that was the case there was no sense in trying to work out who he was.

The past, weightless at one moment, would turn leaden at another. She fantasized sometimes that she had simply fallen out of the sky.

That cabin in the Sandias where she'd taken refuge, the sense that someone else had come there, looking. Harry Wine had said he had. *"I was there once."* She had believed it then, but later wondered. Harry Wine was a liar, and it had been more than once that Andi had sensed someone had gone into the cabin in her absence.

She would have thought this mystery man was a product of her overactive imaginative had it not been that others had seen him.

"Tall guy, dark hair, was here asking after you."

That had been Janine talking while she was clearing off a table in the Opal Bar and Grille. Andi and Janine worked the late shift. It was usually midnight before they got off.

Andi had asked what he wanted and what his name was. And Janine had said she didn't know either answer.

"What'd you tell him?"

"Me? Told him nothin'."

"But did he say he'd be back?"

Janine shook her head. "Didn't say. How many mystery men do you have in your past?" She laughed.

Ruefully, Andi smiled, although she didn't feel in a smiling mood. "None. But I wouldn't know, would I? They being mysteries?"

That night back then, lying in bed, she feared it might be the Idaho police—some state trooper, maybe. But that was ridiculous; a policeman would have been dressed in a uniform and Janine would have said so. A homicide detective, maybe? He would have been wearing regular street clothes, yes, but wouldn't he have to show a badge? Some sort of ID? A private investigator was a possibility. She didn't think they had to announce themselves.

But why would anyone hire a private detective to come after her?

The shooting had made headlines in the lesser papers back then, but was relegated to the inside pages of the bigger ones, like the *Post Register*. Stuck on the inside even though it had been a violent crime; you would have thought it rained down blood in that motel room.

You would have thought, too, the police presence would have been a little more intense and the investigation taken a more dedicated turn than it did; it had been staged in a kind of halfhearted way.

It had been nearly a month between that event and putting glasses on a tray in the Opal Bar and Grille that midnight outside of Idaho Falls. It wasn't two weeks before Harry's murder had stopped being any kind of news at all.

Four months after Idaho Falls he turned up in a fairly nice restaurant in Billings, Montana. Same thing happened, and again she hadn't been there; it was her day off. It was the hostess he spoke to that time, who later told Andi a tall man in black had wanted to see her. No name, nothing about his business with her. Nothing about his coming back, either.

A few months between that restaurant and another on the other side of the state in Miles City, he came again.

Now, a few months between Montana and Dakota and here he was *again*.

She could have called it stalking, only how can you make that charge against someone who turns up once every several months, turns up when you change jobs? What enemies had she made to drag this out for a year and a half? It was more mysterious than the usual case of stalking; that happened over and over in the same place, the same city. But this man had traveled across three states to see her.

Or not see her. She wondered why he always turned up when she was gone. He must want her to know he was there and able to catch up with her no matter how far she went.

She fell back onto her pillow, weary with thinking about it.

25

In the morning she went across to the cab office and found Ernie, recovered from whatever illness he'd suffered, ready to drive her. Ernie turned out to be a nontalker, for which she was grateful.

When they got to Jim's, she decided she could turn away from all of last night's worry by leading Dakota out to the exercise ring after feeding him half of an apple (keeping half for a future bribe).

She looked back toward the house, hoping nobody was watching. By now, she really should have mastered the art of mounting a horse; it was basic. But every time she tried to get her foot into the stirrup and swing her right leg over the saddle, Dakota would take a quick step forward or backward and she'd wind up sliding down his side.

After several aborted attempts, she wound up giving him the second apple half. That did nothing; she still couldn't mount.

She tried putting him up against the fence so that the saddle was even with the top of the fence and she could just slide from the top rung right onto the horse's back. She tried this maneuver several times. Dakota would be perfectly still until she lurched for the saddle, when he would step away from the fence and leave her dangling.

What was wrong with this horse? He acted like he was spooked. But there was nothing around to spook him.

★   ★   ★

Jim and Tom had driven over to Tom's house and Andi was alone, washing lettuce for a salad.

What brought her to the window and then the door was the sight of a truck pulling slowly up the drive, one she didn't recognize, a Ford Bronco or one of those other trucks that really weren't.

And a man getting out, tall and wearing black jeans and shirt and big-brimmed hat. He shut the door of the truck and then stood and looked around.

The outer door was open; Andi stood behind the screen door. Trepidation, that's what she felt watching the stranger come up the walk. Men in black clothes automatically looked a little intimidating, which was probably why men like Lucas Bailey wore them. The adrenaline that flooded her system was the same that had twisted her stomach when the Bailey boys had stopped their truck on the shoulder of the road. She knew who this man was.

He was taking his own sweet time drawing close to the house. He saw her, of course, on the other side of the screen door. He saw her, looked at her for a moment. Beneath the broad-brimmed black hat that shaded his forehead, he smiled. It was a slight smile; it was proprietary; it was a smile meant to be shared or at least understood.

"Ma'am." He was touching the hat brim with thumb and forefinger, a small salute. He was waiting.

Even though it wasn't much of a shield, she made sure she kept the screen door between them. "Did you want something?"

"Only information." He said no more, as if she would know the information he sought.

"Well?" She stiffened. "Are you lost or something?"

His full smile added no more happiness to his face than the stingy one. "No, ma'am. But I'm looking for one who is."

One who is. What a peculiar way of putting it. It sounded almost mythical. Biblical, full of fate. Someone lost, she supposed.

And it made Andi think she had best be getting on to a new place. That unreasoning thought came unbidden. It was awful. She waited, arms crossed, guarded only by the flimsy screen door. "I don't know anything. I mean, I haven't seen anyone strange around."

They were both ignoring—or, rather, she was, for only he knew his purpose—the obvious question of what he was doing here at this house. She could understand him pulling up at the sheriff's office or even sitting down in May's, showing Mildred the snapshot and maybe even passing it along the counter to Norman and the others. Or maybe stopping at Eula's produce stand and asking. That all made sense. This didn't. He'd made the effort of pulling his car into Jim's drive and getting out as if there were some particular reason.

"I don't understand why you're stopping here, though."

"Just the chance somebody'd know, I guess. Blind chance."

He moved his eyes from her face to see beyond her, but couldn't, not through the backdrop of darkness. "Anyone else here that might help?"

Jim and Tom had left only a little while ago, fifteen or twenty minutes, and she bet he had been somewhere, parked somewhere, hidden, waiting for them to leave.

Vigorously, she shook her head. "No one." Then she realized how stupid she was being, letting him know she had no protection. "They'll be back any moment."

He looked around, his eyes traveling over the drive and the barn and back. "Nice place you got here. Nice country. Wouldn't mind living here myself. Passed a fine-looking farm a mile down the road. Looked deserted, though. Sturdy house, sturdy barns."

Then he was fishing something out of his wallet that turned out to be a smudged snapshot, which he flattened against the screen. It showed a family, or at least she thought it was a family. A man, a woman, a girl. It was hard to tell if the girl resembled either of them the way they were all squinting, sun-blind. The girl was probably eleven or twelve, the parents poor and disagreeable-looking, like the house behind them.

"You remember them." It wasn't a question. Now it had changed; now he had come to talk to her, not just anyone.

She shook her head. "No."

His looked sharpened as if he'd cut the memory out of her. "You saying you don't remember Alice?"

She looked again at the girl. She shook her head.

He stood there hard and silent, a dark carving, without a thing worth moving for.

She was also motionless.

Now he pushed the hat back off his forehead as if he meant to go on shooting the breeze. "I thought maybe you would."

That was no answer. She rubbed at her forearm, said, "I've got things to do, I'm sorry. Wish you luck finding her. It must be really sad for you." She could extend that bit of sympathy.

He puffed out his cheeks, blew out breath, as if to say, *"I'll huff and puff and blow your house down."*

Andi felt a cold finger touch her spine.

He pulled the hat forward, made a leaving gesture in a little bow, and turned and started to walk off, then turned and said, "I find it hard to believe you don't remember."

She shook her head, not wanting to say a word that might prolong his visit.

Not long after he left, after he swung himself up into the cab of his truck and turned on the gravel circle and seemed to wrench the gravel and shale loose from the earth, Jim and Tom pulled in.

"Hey, Andi."

"Hey, girl."

They said this as they came up to the door, where she was still standing. "You watching for us?"

She smiled and opened the door and said hello to them and went into the kitchen to finish making the salad for dinner.

"That old sow out there appears to be settling in," said Tom over his baby back ribs.

Andi was eating spaghetti with tomato sauce.

Jim said, "People in May's were saying Klavan was loaded for bear because someone was making off with his stock."

Andi looked up from her plate sharply. "Now, how on earth would he know with all the pigs they've got there? And he's sure not out there working."

Tom said, "I don't understand it either. It was one of their prize sows."

"Prize? Prize? Didn't you see the tumor on the poor thing? There's no prize anything over there. They treat all of them the same: awful."

"I'm with you there. I was just saying what I heard Klavan said."

Andi rolled spaghetti around her fork, concentrating. She could not comment further on the pig—and the fate it was bound for. She marveled at Klavan's hypocrisy and all the others' before going back to thinking about her black-garbed visitor.

"There was somebody came here while you were gone. Maybe you passed his truck on the way? A black Ford truck?"

They shook their heads. Jim said, "What'd he want?"

"He said he was looking for a girl named Alice. It sounded like a daughter, as far as I could understand." But that wasn't right, was it? The girl was standing with her mother and father in the snapshot, surely. "He's one of those people who likes to talk everything into a mystery." She repeated most of the conversation.

"That's damn peculiar," said Jim. And he said exactly what she had: why had this fellow driven up and stopped at this house?

Tom said, "Makes no sense. He wanted something. Describe him again."

Andi did. It was harder to convey his manner. "You've probably met someone like that: they make you feel they've got a trick up their sleeves, that they know a lot more than they're telling and a lot more than you do."

"Maybe we should let McKibbon in on this. Harry knows everybody around."

"Oh, but this man isn't 'around.' "

She wanted to tell them, to have some comforting exchange about the likelihood of this stranger's being on her trail, stalking her. She put this thought away to bring out later, alone.

"I made bread pudding," she said, "for dessert."

"Good."

"Great."

"With rum sauce."

"Even better," said Tom. "But I'll tell you what." He reached around to the sideboard, which was behind his chair, and grabbed the bottle of Myers's rum by the neck. "Here's the best sauce there is. Just bring on the pudding."

They laughed.

Later, she was lying in bed with her forearm flung across her forehead in a stagy gesture that made her wonder if what she wanted in her life was drama, if drama explained it all: the black-clothed man, the donkey Sam, the pig. The danger.

Was it just her need for drama? Did she really care what happened to the sow, to all of the Klavan pigs? Or any of it? With a sigh—she made it a deep and histrionic one—she took her arm from her forehead and sat up a little. She became intensely aware of the objects in her room: the green wastebasket with the puppies painted on it; the hairbrush and comb and old mirror on the bureau; the slant of moonlight that allowed her to see these things.

The little family group of dispirited-looking people staring into the sun in that dumbfounded way people do bore not one ounce of resemblance to the Oliviers, nor did the house behind them look anything like the Oliviers' house, although she had not imagined that house in all of its detail. There was the tennis court, and the dog Jules chasing the badminton bird (feathers mangled, feathers flying).

There were the Olivier children, not really children, more adults, five of them altogether, older than she, younger. Swann was the oldest. The other three . . . Marcus and . . . how could she have forgotten their names? How easily things passed away if you weren't careful to tend them.

The little group of people looking as if they'd sooner be back in the house.

This was the first time the man had shown himself to her; those other times in Idaho Falls and the restaurants outside of Billings and again in Miles City in Montana, he'd only inquired about her. It was hard to believe that in this obscure place he'd found her more easily.

Maybe she was wrong. Maybe the man in those other places wasn't this one and it was all her imagination

She picked up her paperback collection of poetry from the night-stand by her bed. It was cracked and so dog-eared she couldn't find her place.

There was a poem by Wallace Stevens about a woman sitting with coffee and oranges and thinking of the deer who walked the mountains, the berries ripening in the wilderness, and, most of all, a flight of pigeons whose wings made "ambiguous undulations" when they flew downward.

The sound of those two words coming together was wonderful. But why "ambiguous"? Because one couldn't tell exactly their direction? Why?

The lines were so perfect, they hurt. That's what beauty does: it hurts.

For she wanted what she couldn't have. She wanted the deer and the flight of the birds. She wanted not the physical objects themselves, but what lay behind them.

At least all of this thought about poetry had allowed her to forget the stranger for a few minutes.

Tomorrow, when she got off work, she would go and see Sheriff McKibbon again.

26

She met up with Jake on the walk to Hut 3. He was coming from the office with papers in his hand.

Andi thought it would be the perfect opportunity for Jake to go into the pig theft, but all he did was to stop and gaze up at the sky and comment on its enamel blue.

Andi looked up, too. "Where you going?"

"To give this to Vernon. Transport."

"To the slaughterhouse."

"Yeah. So?"

"Do you ever put yourself in their place?"

He returned to looking at the sky. "Not a chance, no." He looked back at her. "But I guess you do or else you wouldn't be asking."

She shrugged. "Sometimes."

"Why?"

She hadn't thought to be questioned on this. "Well, if I were going to be slaughtered, I think it would make it easier if somebody was trying to feel what I felt."

Jake chewed his gum reflectively. "We ain't pigs, Andi."

We don't have to be, she wanted to say, but she merely watched him walk away.

★   ★   ★

Vernon was hosing down. Andi thought all the water in the world couldn't wash out that smell. He was holding the papers Jake had brought.

Vernon had his favorite chaw going in his mouth and he was arcing the brown spit across the rails. He was pretty good at it, if that was something to be proud of. It was such a dark brown it was almost black, the color of his eyes.

"You want me to do that?" she asked.

Vernon turned, surprised. "Oh, hey, girl. Yeah, I do, if you don't mind. I need a coffee." He handed over the hose. He stood with his thermos, looking at the papers. "Shit."

"What's wrong?"

He shrugged. "I just don't like what they got me down for here. They oughtn't've put me down twice in a row for transport. That one's always the last to get out."

"You're talking about the slaughterhouse?"

"Yeah." He spit, forgetting the artistry of it.

Andi swallowed what felt like a rock in her throat. "Well, maybe I could do it for you. Take your place, I mean."

At that, Vernon stood open-mouthed. "*You?*"

She shrugged as if she were used to transporting pigs. "Why not, I mean, there's two drivers, right? So I wouldn't be the main one, right?"

"I appreciate the offer, but, look, it's more'n just drivin'. You ever done worked at deliverin' animals for slaughter? Or worked at a slaughterhouse? I seriously doubt it."

"Is it so hard?"

"No. But it's mean work."

"Mean how?" Was Vernon here another sympathetic soul? But the "meanness" she imagined was all for his own discomfort.

"Well, 'cause I gotta stand there outside the chute and whack the little bastards into it. They don't want to move."

"Because they know what's coming."

Vernon was about to answer her when his cell phone blurted out some nonsense tune and he answered. "Yeah, okay. I said okay, didn't I?

Keep your shirt on." Then he turned and walked out without any further comment on the "meanness" of the job.

There was the usual commotion when she went into the swine building, the rush to the bars without the room to rush the bars. You weren't supposed to go into the pens; it was disruptive, whatever that meant; it was dangerous.

"*Insurance, it costs me an arm and a leg,*" she'd heard Klavan say. *There* was meanness. He was mean and he was cheap.

She had brought the leftover bread pudding and the remaining plain wheat bread. She unlatched the gate and went in and was immediately surrounded, but she just started breaking up pieces of bread and handing them out. She could get killed probably if they all pushed at her at once.

But look at them. They had bitten one another, bitten off ears and tails out of the craziness of being penned up. That and hopelessness. There was sham chewing, literally chewing air, because they hadn't anything else to chew. But they didn't push at her much. She could not figure out how to get to the ones in back, and so she moved toward the back, the pigs closing up the seam of her walking, like water. It kind of scared her, this lack of exit if suddenly she needed it. It was like swimming too far from the shore.

Andi handed out all she had and some had to go without. She pushed back through to the front of the pen, surprised when she was through the gate that they hadn't crushed her.

Later, this afternoon or maybe next week, they'd be herded out the door and then crammed onto trucks so tightly packed they'd be unable to move. Then at the other end, the process would be repeated the other way around, except the end of this line would not be a barn, but something like a chute where a bolt would be driven into their brains to knock them unconscious. She didn't know exactly what the process was after this and was afraid to know. She didn't know if Vernon was about to take her up on her offer to sub for him, and she had to admit she almost wished he wouldn't.

"What in the hell you doing there, girl?"

She turned quickly. It was Regis Watts. Thank the Lord he hadn't caught her in the cage or she'd be fired then and there.

"These pigs," she said, trying to call up a high-and-mighty tone, saying by it that she had every right to be doing what she did, "are the ones going for slaughter and there's some that aren't fit to."

"Ain't *fit* to? Whoever gave you authority to oversee the operation? Where in hell's Vernon? He was to meet me right outside."

Compared to Regis Watts, Vernon was almost saintly. "He wasn't feeling good. Thinks maybe he's coming down with flu. He went up to the office, I think. Why? What do you want? Maybe I can do it."

Regis was coming toward her and she had to make an effort not to shrink back. No, she held her ground. Andi wondered if that's what life was really all about: holding your ground.

He was up to her now with that assertive posture of his and a sour smile. "You mean, help out like you did with that old sow? Me, if I was Klavan, I'd a fired your sorry ass outta here. Damn but I never knew anybody to meddle so much."

He was right. "I was bringing that sow to Sweetland like Hutch said. I'll tell you, though, I don't see how anybody would've offered money for her with that tumor ballooned on her side. I know the Agriculture Department wouldn't have passed on her. No way." She knew nothing of the sort. The inspectors were probably eating out of Klavan's hand. Just as bad as the rest of them.

Regis fake-laughed. "So now you're a meat inspector, is that it? Where the hell you ever come from, girl? You shouldn't be workin' in a place like this. You're just too fine and fancy for it."

How she wanted to laugh at that. "Fancy? Where do you get that?" He didn't know why he'd chosen those words, she bet. What he meant was that she wasn't like the rest of them and, therefore, suspect. Andi pictured Klavan's former pig in the yard with Max and Hazel and smiled. She walked toward the door.

"You know what? You know *what*?" Regis called to her. "You just think you're holier than thou, don't you?"

Over her shoulder she said, "I guess that depends on who the 'thou' is."

★   ★   ★

Al Cully, who was going to the Two Dogs, gave her a ride in "the rig," as he called his ancient pickup. Al spent a lot of time in the Two Dogs and the Plugged Nickel, as he would be the first to admit.

"Home away from home," he said with an air of jubilance more likely to attend a meeting with a long-lost lover. "Or maybe just home, period. Buy you a drink? Or will they card you?" He snuffled up a laugh.

"Did you ever see the Two Dogs card anybody? I bet not."

"What d'you do for fun around here? I mean, except shootin' up the Bailey boys?"

"I don't know what you're talking about."

"Ah, now, come on. We know you had a gun and drew on them. Your only mistake was missing." The snuffle-laugh came again.

"Where'd you hear that?"

"In the Two Dogs, a course. We all know ever'thing that comes down the pike. Sometimes before it happens."

Andi just shook her head; she was tired of denying she shot anybody and figured that in a town like Kingdom, even *her* coming along was an event.

"That old man of theirs, Lucas? I never could stand him. He is one mean old bastard. It's one reason them boys is so wild."

She watched the parched land slide by, the great level distance of thirsty wheat that even in its blighted gold was still beautiful. "The land needs rain."

"Hell's bells, land always needs rain here. If we'd stop pointin' that out, it probably would rain."

They reached the edge of town, the sign that always made Andi smile. KINGDOM with the word "Come" added in whitewash. Why didn't they wash it off? she wondered. There was probably a war going on, some citizens wanting it back the way it was and some old Bible thumpers liking the change and wanting to leave it with the extra word. So they left up the stricken sign.

"Where do you want to be set down?"

"I want to see Sheriff McKibbon, so the station, I guess." Then she wished she'd said May's diner.

"What you want with the sheriff's office? Something else happen to you? My word. Since you come along, girl, more's happened in a month than's happened in Kingdom in a decade!"

"I'll take that"—and she said it again with a smile—"as a compliment."

"Yes, *ma'am*, you ought. Things have really livened up."

Cully stopped in front of the sheriff's office and Andi thanked him and climbed down.

27

The deputy, Leroy Lambreseau, was alone in the office. Deputy Lambreseau had once shortened his name to Lamb—Leroy Lamb—but then took back the other part as he thought having such a distinguished French name worked in his favor. Nothing else did.

"Andi. You in trouble again?"

"I was never in trouble before, so I guess I'm not again. Where's Sheriff McKibbon?"

"He's over to Golden Valley. They got a mad dog terrorizing people."

"That's too bad."

"You bet. There's a lot of people keeping themselves in their homes."

"I mean it's too bad for the dog, not for the people."

Leroy flapped his hand at her in dismissal. "Donkeys, pigs, pretty soon everybody's gonna be keeping their cats and dogs inside."

"Since we killed all the cougars off, I don't see why they're worried."

"Hell, you're as bad as any cougar."

She smiled at that and said, for the second time, "I'll take that as a compliment."

Leroy had risen and was adjusting his Sam Browne belt. "Wasn't meant as one." Then he went out the door as the sheriff's car pulled in. They were talking to each other when Andi peered through the window in the door. They parted and she went back to her seat against the wall.

Harry McKibbon came in. "Andi."

His smile, to her, seemed blinding in the absence of them all day long. He hung his jacket on the back of his chair.

"What happened with the dog, Sheriff?"

He sat down. "Well, we had to shoot it, unfortunately."

"You did, you mean."

He nodded.

She said, "There's not much choice, is there, when it comes to rabid animals? Do you wonder what's going on in their minds? They look mad, don't they? I mean, not crazy-mad but angry. But, then, I guess their poor brains do go crazy."

He sighed and said, "It's no wonder you got the weight of the world on your shoulders. You always been like this?"

"Maybe." Then she came out with it: "I'm being stalked."

Harry's eyes widened. "What?" He leaned back in his old swivel chair. "Life doesn't give you much peace, does it? Who—you're not talking about one of the Baileys, I hope."

"No."

"Do you know him, this stalker?"

"Why would a stalker let you know who he is?"

Harry looked surprised by the question. "Because that's half the pleasure. Remember Jodie Foster? Hinckley was obsessed. He wanted her to know who it was that was going to all this trouble, shooting the president. Testimony as to how much he loved her."

"I guess if you're Jodie Foster—" she said, looking down at hands that clearly weren't Jodie's, red and bitten as they were, "—you can get police attention."

"I'm police. You've got my attention."

She looked up quickly to see if he was covering up a laugh, but he looked dead serious.

He motioned for her to come closer, to take the chair beside his desk instead of sitting where she was, against the wall. She moved.

"I guess you think I'm making this up." God, did she have to sound so childish? As if she were pouting?

"Why would I think that? Anyway, you haven't told me enough to make me think anything yet."

"I guess it just makes me so nervous." Her sweater sleeves were pulled down so far they covered her hands, whose redness she was now trying to hide.

"I expect so. Now, can you think of anybody who'd do this?"

She shook her head. "No, sir."

The sheriff pulled over a yellow legal pad and plucked a ballpoint pen from a jar. He wrote something down. Andi saw he was left-handed, the pen held at what seemed an impossible angle.

"Okay, when did you first come into contact—where did you first notice this person?"

"It was more becoming aware of him for a long time. It was other people who actually saw him."

Harry frowned. "Where was this?"

"I was waitressing in a place in Idaho Falls and one of the other waitresses told me a man came by looking for me. She told him I'd be there in a couple of hours and for him to come back, only he didn't."

"Did she tell him where you lived?"

"No. She said he was a stranger—at least to her—and so she didn't think I'd want that."

"Good for her. When did this happen?"

Andi thought. "Over a year ago."

"Then what?"

"The second time was in Montana, in Billings. I was working in a restaurant, same thing, as a waitress, only the tips were a lot better. This woman, who was the hostess in the evening, told me a man came in and asked about me. Said he was an old friend."

Again, Harry frowned. "You were expecting he'd come again?"

She swallowed. "I guess so. After Idaho, I decided to use another name, but it didn't help much."

"What name did you use?"

"Amy Olds. I thought I should keep the initials, see, since there's an *A.O.* on my backpack." Those initials had been pushing her around for a year and a half.

"And did he turn up at the restaurant later?"

"No. But after a few months working in Billings, I started walking again, walking and hitching rides. Then I got a job in Miles City at a diner. The same thing happened. That was seven or eight months ago. This was the third time."

"And that time—"

"Same thing. Then yesterday he turned up at Jim's."

Surprised, he put down the pad. "Jim's? You mean he just walked up to the door—?"

She nodded. "Yes."

"How do you know it was the same man?"

"He fit the description and he was being really cagey. You know, the way a person talks, but you know he's saying something underneath the words. Almost as if they're talking in code."

"Tell me what was said." Harry pulled over the legal pad again. "He didn't go to Klavan's, looking for you?"

"If he did, nobody told me. Which means he didn't; they're all such gossips there."

Harry smiled. "I know. Go ahead."

Andi repeated the conversation almost word for word. The words had burrowed so deeply into her consciousness, his words and he himself.

"What he's saying this time is that he's not looking—no, turn it around—is that he's looking for a girl named Alice and thought you knew her? Would remember her? Why?"

"I don't know." Andi leaned toward him. "He wasn't pleased when I told him I didn't remember her or anything about the people in the picture."

Harry McKibbon put down his pen and thought for a moment, leaning back in his chair, which creaked beneath his weight. "It's a strange thing for a stalker to do. He's not acting like your classic stalker, if you'll forgive the phrase; he seems to have in mind not you so much as whoever was in this photo. You know, it sounds to me like this fella means to unnerve you instead of do you actual harm. But, of course, I'm going on not much information. Tell me: in these other places, can you think of anything you'd done that's like what you've done here?"

Andi looked at him, puzzled. "What have I done here?"

"Well, you take a lot of interest in animals." Harry rubbed his thumbnail over his brow. "There's a lot of people perceive kindness as an insult to them. It's like you're saying to them, you should've done this yourself."

"I'm not saying that."

"No, but people get defensive. Anyway, that's what I'm talking about. Could you have done something perfectly all right, but made someone furious by doing it? Think."

Andi did. There'd been that poor dog in Idaho Falls that was always chained up. "Well, I did call Animal Control once about a mistreated dog. Is that what you're talking about?"

He nodded. "Only bigger. Like a mistreated person."

To Andi, that wasn't bigger. She shook her head.

Harry leaned back in his swivel chair, elbow on the arm, his head against his fist.

She just sat there, thinking it was of course impossible to expect him to figure this out when the only things she could recall about her past she didn't want to tell him. But she figured she had to, at least part of it. "There's something. . . . Nearly two years ago. I was in New Mexico. In Santa Fe. I woke up one morning in a bed-and-breakfast place and didn't know how I got there. A man's clothes were strewn about the room and there was money in the pocket of some jeans. I'm pretty sure, given how I felt—I hurt so much—I knew I was raped."

Harry McKibbon dumped his chair forward and himself in it. "My God."

Andi told him the rest, or most of it. Not the most important part at the end, though.

"That story you told me, then, was fiction? You can't remember anything about your past before that Santa Fe bed-and-breakfast? Did you say anything to them, the owners?"

"No, I didn't tell her. I talked to her a little to try and get information, but since I couldn't ask her directly—"

"Why? Why didn't you go to the police? There was probably a report of a bus on fire—"

"Because I couldn't even remember my name. I figured this man could talk his way out of things. What I wanted wasn't to report him; it was to get away from him."

Harry sat silent for a moment, then said, "You think this stalker has something to do with this? That maybe he was the man in the bed-and-breakfast?"

"Or maybe a friend of the man."

There was something in the sheriff's eyes, some hint of disbelief, that made Andi anxious. The trouble was that if you tallied up the things that had happened to her in Kingdom—Sam, the donkey; the Baileys and their attempts to scare her or worse—all of that was strange enough without adding to it amnesia and rape and a stalker. And perhaps her delivery was too restrained to be convincing. But that was the only way she could handle things without breaking down.

Or had she become so inured to trouble that she no longer felt much of anything?

Harry said, "Why would this man who you say raped you—"

(But she caught the "you say," the doubt it implied.)

"—have a friend go after you? Did you take something that he wants back? You said there was money, but if he was carrying it in his pocket it couldn't have been worth tracking you down—"

She cut him off. "No. I didn't take anything except the money. Three hundred dollars. I didn't take anything else." Except the gun. Better leave that out.

But Harry was following his own line. "Something you didn't know was valuable to him?"

Again she shook her head. "No."

"Why wouldn't this guy be going after you himself?"

She kept her eyes on his face, her gaze steady. Because he was dead. Instead of that, she said, "It must be someone unconnected to all that. He found me three times before. I get the feeling he can get at me anytime he wants. If his purpose is to kill me, then I don't understand because he's had plenty of opportunities." She thought the sheriff was looking at her and perhaps not seeing her. "You think it's all my imagination?" But she said this almost with hope, as if she'd rather be a little crazy than have this man after her.

"No, not unless you imagined the other women imagined him, too." Harry smiled. "That's not likely."

"What should I do? I mean, what can I do?"

She had never quite believed those descriptions in novels about a character's eyes: how expressive they were, how indicative of all sorts of subtle variations. But Harry McKibbon's eyes were such a vivid blue and expressed so much emotion, looking at him made her wonder if she was using up too much emotional capital. She said, "I guess I'll go." She made to get up but didn't.

"Listen, Andi, all I can do is keep a sharp lookout for this man, which I certainly will. Please let me know right away if anything happens. He does not seem bent on staying hidden. His behavior doesn't follow any pattern I'm used to." He pulled over his pad and pen. "Give me the names of the women who saw him where you worked."

"It's been so long. One was Janine Westwood—that was at the Opal Bar and Grille in Idaho Falls; then there was Irene Jones in Billings; and Esther Mack in Miles City. Then in Billings, there was my landlady, Mrs. Negley. She saw him, too."

Harry wrote all of this down. "I'll start with Mrs. Englehart."

"I think she told me everything she knew about him."

"There might be something she left out unintentionally. Usually people focus on one thing, face or voice or clothes, but see other things peripherally. Why are you squinting?"

"Trying to see everything."

"About me?"

"Uh-huh."

"Thankless job."

"What happened about Jodie Foster? Did he get out of jail?"

"No. He's still inside."

"I wonder if he'd do it again."

"He'd be crazy to try."

"But he was crazy in the first place."

Harry had risen and now Andi got to her feet. "Yes, you're right." Andi sighed. "I wish I was."

"What?"

"Jodie Foster."

"I don't."

Walking past the field of sunflowers, Andi thought about that, what he'd meant. He'd rather have her around than Jodie Foster? That was hard to believe. He was just exceptionally nice.

She looked at the field where the Baileys had stranded Sam as surely as pushing a poor swimmer off a dock into the sea. It would have been a beautiful and comical scene, Sam in the sunflowers, if he hadn't been planted there by the devil.

Jared was working at shoeing a big horse. She stood in the open gates of the barn and said his name.

"Hey, Andi." He kept the horse's foreleg up as he considered the fit of the shoe.

Andi loved the way the scene resembled a shoe store, with Jared the shoe clerk, fitting a fancy shoe on a customer.

"Come on in, don't pay no attention to Mooney here; he's too good for this place, so he seems to think."

Andi peered into the shadowed back of the barn. "Isn't that Nelson back there?"

"Oh, yeah. Jim brought him in earlier."

"Well, then, is he ready to go?"

"Uh-huh." Nail in his mouth, Jared nodded.

"I don't have a ride, so I could ride Nelson back."

Jared let the nail drop in his hand. "Oh, Jim's coming to get him. I was just talking to him before you came."

Andi wondered why Jared seemed anxious. "If I can borrow your phone, I'll call him."

"Yeah, okay, help yourself."

Receiver pressed to her ear, she pursed her lips while the ringing went on at the other end. She said hello and that she was at Jared's and could ride Nelson back. "But it's not that far."

She clasped the receiver against her jacket. "He says to ask you if that far a ride would be bad for Nelson."

"Yes. Yes, I'd say so." Jared grabbed the receiver from her. "I advise against this, Jim."

She watched him as he listened. He kept saying um, um, um before he hung up. "Jim'll come with the horse box and get Nelson. You'll have a ride then."

She sat on an old orange crate and watched Jared finish with the horse, Mooney. She said, "Do you know anything about jockeys and if there are limits on height?"

He looked up. "I expect so. Jockeys are small people. Has to do with how much weight a horse carries."

"So it's the weight that makes the difference and the only reason jockeys are so short is that if they were tall, they'd weigh more?"

"Could be. Why? You thinking about being a jockey?"

Andi nodded. "Right now I weigh one hundred twenty."

"That's prob'ly twenty pounds too much."

"A few jockeys have weighed a hundred and ten, a hundred fifteen."

The horse snorted (as if registering his opinion) and Jared rubbed Mooney's neck. "Very few, I bet."

"I looked it up in one of Jim's books."

"How tall are you?" Jared gave the horse a friendly slap on its flank.

"Five feet six and a half inches."

"That's about five inches taller'n your average jockey."

Andi was exasperated by this. Anyway, she was sure it was a sex thing, that he didn't think women should be setting foot in this male enclave. "But that's my point, isn't it? It's not height, it's weight."

Jared led the horse back to a stall, saying over his shoulder, "Even so, if you lost twenty pounds you'd be skin and bone. You'd hardly be able to get up the stairs much less get up on a horse. You'd be thin as some of them Paris models that's so thin you can almost see through them."

"Oh, that's *such* an exaggeration, Jared."

"Well, anyway." He walked back to his tools.

"I would love to ride Dakota on that track in Fargo."

"The Fargo *racetrack*? Now, I don't mean to discourage you, but that's about as likely as Mooney here growing wings and flying around that track. Don't you know how much *experience* it takes to be a jockey? My Lord, it takes tons of riding hours; it takes years and years of all sorts of different jobs related to racing."

Unscathed, Andi said, "But maybe I'm a natural."

His jaw unhinged itself, not at his bidding. He gaped. "*Natural?* Now, how long've you been riding over at Jim's? Well, it surely ain't been more than six or seven weeks."

She felt herself redden. "I'm not talking about the next race, for heaven's sakes! I just mean, sometime . . . you know. And anyway, how do you know I'm *not* a natural at it? You've never seen me ride."

"I'll tell you what you're a natural at: stubbornness. No, I don't mean that as a bad thing. Let's say you're a natural when it comes to determination. You're the most determined person I ever did meet. Hell, you could probably stay the course by just grabbing on to that mane and refusing to let go." Jared laughed a hawking laugh. The image amused him. "You are most definitely a natural for getting the job done, that's what you're a natural at."

She wanted to clap her ears shut with her hands. She wished she'd never used the word. "I guess I'll go over to May's for some coffee until Jim comes. He could pick me up there. Just tell him, will you?"

Jared was fighting laughter. "Be pleased to." He was off-and-on laughing as she walked out. He even got hiccups.

28

Tom pulled over the big platter of ribs and forked some onto his plate. He looked at Andi, who was watching, and said, "You must hate it that we eat ribs and steak, yet you never say anything; you never object."

To her, he looked saddened, not by her but by his fork, still stuck in the ribs, as if it and not his taste were the culprit. She didn't like him looking mournful, and smiled. "You've been eating that way all your life. Why would I object?"

"It takes some forbearance," said Jim.

Andi shook her head. "I don't have that, for sure." Then she asked, "Can you drive me to work earlier tomorrow? At seven?"

Jim nodded. "How come?"

"Pigs are going to be trucked to slaughter in the morning. Those trucks are huge. They say they can get two hundred fifty pigs in one of them." She felt really tired, wondering about this transport.

"Where are they taking them? Where's the plant?"

"Preston. Northeast of here."

Jim shook his head. "I want some coffee." Andi started to get up, but he waved her down. "No, I'll get it."

Tom said, "You have to be there early to do what? Herd them onto the trucks? You shouldn't have to do that."

"Not that. One of the guys can't go so I'm taking his place." She didn't expect them to let this pass without comment.

Jim turned from the kitchen counter, holding the coffeepot. "You're going to this processing plant in one of those trucks? *You?* For God's sakes, why?"

"Like I said, this fellow Vernon had something come up and can't go."

"Yeah, well, you're going to have something come up and it'll be this dinner."

Andi fake-laughed. "Oh, come on. I've never been to a processing plant."

"Well, I've never been to a public hanging or a Ku Klux Klan meeting in the woods and don't mind missing out on them, either," said Jim, plunking a mug of coffee down in front of her, and then the Procter-Silex pot. "That's crazy. You shouldn't go." He looked at Tom, who raised his eyebrows.

She drank some coffee.

"Who's driving this rig?"

"I don't know who."

Tom pulled over the pot of coffee and poured. "Come on, Andi, if there's anyone should stay away from a slaughterhouse, it's you. The way you feel about animals?" Tom levered himself halfway across the table, locking eyes with her. "What's this going to accomplish, you going in that truck? You're not going to spell this guy with driving, I hope? You're an awful driver."

"I'm not going to drive, of course not."

"There isn't a thing in the world you could do for those pigs. You can't do anything about their fate. You can't pick up those two hundred fifty pigs and carry 'em away to some nice green pasture. You can't keep 'em from getting slaughtered." He leaned closer and spoke with rising intensity. "It's going to happen with you or without you. All you're doing is setting yourself up to be miserable. I mean really freaked-out misery. I've been in slaughterhouses. You want no part of it, believe me. What I'd like to know is what you need to be miserable *for.*"

Andi looked at him. "I don't know what you mean."

"I mean it sounds like maybe you feel guilty for some reason."

She worked the edge of her napkin, rubbing the cloth back and forth. She felt befuddled.

"And all this"—Tom hooked his thumb back over his shoulder in the direction, she supposed, of the pig farm—"is recompense."

She had no comeback for this. She couldn't think of a single thing except to go back over the eighteen months she'd been given to remember for some clue that would save her from thinking all of this was punishment for Harry Wine. There were the coyotes she'd rescued from steel-jaw traps, the fox family, the starving dog—but this all preceded the second meeting with Harry Wine.

"Thing is," Jim put in, "if you're on some mission—and I don't think you're that naïve—well, it's hopeless, like Tom said." He spread his hands, his arms, to encompass the hopelessness of it. He had risen and gone to the kitchen sink and turned on the water. "Don't you know it don't make a particle of difference your making this trip? There's nothing you can do that'd help those pigs." Jim let water rush into the sink, unaware. "It's still going to be the same." He hooked his thumb over his shoulder toward the pigsty. "You got your one pig, which is good for the pig, but how much can you do just saving one?"

"It's always one," she said, looking down at the table.

Jim frowned. "I'm not sure I know what you mean there, but anyhow, those pigs going to slaughter, they'll go down the line, and believe me, you don't want to know about the line."

"I know they're stunned."

Tom said from his chair, "If they're lucky."

She looked at him, but didn't pursue the subject. She was sorry she'd said anything.

Jim had a pot in the sink that he was scrubbing hard. "Pretty soon you'll be saying slaughtering those pigs is as bad as the slaughter of six million Jews in the war."

"No, I won't."

Jim snorted. "That's something, at least."

"It's worse."

Jim turned, red-faced. Tom looked shocked. "Now, I just can't believe you mean that."

"I do. I can give you a dozen reasons for believing it."

They looked away, blood suffusing their faces. "I guess that's enough on the subject," Jim said.

But it apparently wasn't, for he went on, "You've got to get over the idea you're personally responsible for what happens to those pigs."

Andi got up, holding her mug. "Are you?"

"Am I what?"

"Responsible?"

"God's sakes, of course not."

She looked at Tom. "Are you?"

He frowned. "No."

"Well, if you're not responsible, and *you're* not responsible, and *I'm* not responsible—who is?" She left the table. "Good night."

She lay in bed, wondering why they objected to her going, why the whole thing made them angry. But she didn't want to ask herself why. She feared the question more than she feared the answer. The question made a wedge in her mind, an opening that could get wider and wider until the *Why?* engulfed her.

Andi rolled over in bed and dragged the blanket up to her chin. She couldn't sleep, so she turned on the light and picked up her poetry book from the floor.

"Sunday Morning." Wallace Stevens. Inscrutable. This was fine with her; the denser, the more ambiguous, the better. She didn't want to understand. She wanted the words to slide off her mind and leave no impression at all. The words could fall and break like little plates on the floor around her bed.

Sleepless, she lay there. Finally she got out of bed and went to the north-facing window, the one that gave a view of the outcropping of rocks. The whitewashed moon made the rocks, the fields, look pale and sickly. In the white silence of those huts, the pigs would not be sleeping, but waiting. They would not be certain of what was coming, but would grow more suspicious, more and more afraid, the closer they got to the end.

Andi was up and dressed by dawn. She went down to the kitchen and got out a saucepan and heated up the cold coffee from last night's dinner. She drank it standing at the sink and looking across at the barn that seemed to float toward her out of the ground mist. She had the strange and far from happy thought that from now on there would be signs. She dismissed this as fanciful nonsense.

Signs. For her? Of what? Dumping the bitter coffee into the sink, she pulled on her jean jacket and went outside to the barn.

Andi gave Sam's neck a rub, then turned to Dakota, who was facing the other way, nosing around at the hayrick.

"It's empty," she said.

Dakota kept at it. "Sometimes I wonder just how smart you really are. I get tired of talking to your rump. I'd like to take you out for a ride but I don't have time this morning."

Dakota turned then to face her.

"But when I'm back, we'll have a good ride."

Dakota turned away again, hindquarters squarely toward her.

Slow getting up, Jim almost made her late, slower yet getting his breakfast. He insisted on frying up bacon and would even have made waffles if she hadn't urged him not to.

"Jim, the truck will leave without me."

"Oh. Okay, no waffles." He went back to turning the bacon with a fork, humming "Camptown Races" and keeping time with his foot.

"You're coming right back here after you drop me off. A cooked breakfast could wait till then, couldn't it?"

"Could, but I'm hungry enough to gnaw through a fence post. How about you? You eat? You should, as I imagine there's not going to be much stopping along the way." He went back to pushing the bacon and humming.

Andi groaned and sat down.

"Okay, okay. Here, I'll just make a sandwich." He grabbed the toast out of the toaster and slathered it with butter. Then he dropped the four slices of bacon between the two pieces of toast. Holding the sandwich in one hand, he went for his keys, said brightly, "Don't have my keys. Now, where—?"

Andi smiled and held them up. "I have them." She almost laughed at his expression. *Foiled.*

HELL AND GONE

29

The truck, three tiers in its bed, was pulled up to the third hut. Nat and Hutch were having a fair time pushing the pigs up the ramp, Hutch with a prod. She hoped only that it wasn't one of them replacing Vernon. She really didn't think she could take it.

But she was in luck—if luck was any more than a rumor around here. Jake, who'd been on the other side of the truck, came around and told Hutch to stop with the prod.

"It ain't a game, man." Andi heard him add as he walked over to where she stood, *"Sadistic motherfucker."*

The pigs weren't cooperating. The bottom tier was full and the second one nearly. There was no room to move; they huddled together, pressed hard against the slats, some half-lying on others. Cries and grunts. Snout to snout and rump to rump.

"Jake, there's too many."

He looked down at her with a slight smile, an ironic one. "Am I going to be listening to you complain for the rest of the day?"

"Are *you* driving?"

He looked at her, shaking his head. "Why in the hell did you sign on to do this? It ain't your scene, believe me."

She accepted that for a moment, watching the pigs trying to get their snouts through the bars, watching them trying to back out and getting whacked for their troubles. "Yes, it is."

"Jesus, girl, what planet do you come from?"

"Same as they do." She nodded toward the truck.

"Well, Klavan says there's to be as many as we can get in, and two hundred six is what we can get in. I agree it's too many, but if you turn out to be a whistle-blower, I'll deny I ever said that. Or are you one of those undercover animal activists? You got a camera hid on you somewhere?"

"Don't be ridiculous."

"Listen: I been working at Klavan's for nine years. Before that I worked at some places that make all this look like heaven. It's good pay here and good perks and I prefer to keep it that way."

He walked over to the truck, moved along it. He was putting weight against the bars, seeing that they'd hold. He rubbed at a couple of snouts and ears. Jake, thought Andi, was basically a kind man. He didn't like his job, but he had to live.

Finished loading, they pulled the ramp back. She moved to the truck and, as Jake had done (and because he'd done it), she rubbed the head or snout or ears of any pig she could reach. She felt especially bad for the ones on the upper tier, for they were exposed to the elements. The sun could get really hot. She'd seen no one take on water or food.

Jake was calling, motioning for her to come on.

"Where's the water? They have to have water. And food."

He shook his head. "They'll be okay. I've done this before. I swear, though . . . are you going to give me trouble?"

Vigorously, she shook her head. "No, no. I just thought maybe we'd forgotten to load it."

"Let's move out, then." As he climbed into the driver's seat, she went around to the passenger's door.

She was surprised at how high they sat above the road, how the truck must dwarf the ordinary vehicles on the highway. She wondered if it gave a truck driver a sense of power, and if they were more aggressive because of this. "Do you feel more powerful driving this?"

He had a map open, was running a finger along a line. "Yeah, sure. I feel I could fly these pigs right over the Grand Canyon. We could be Thelma and Louise, lucky us."

"I only mean, truck drivers can act like they own the road."

"They wouldn't if they had you in the front seat." He folded up the map.

Andi ignored that and said, "But the water—animals have to have water. Don't they get any until we stop and let them out?"

He turned to her, his expression somewhere between a frown and a smile, disbelieving he'd heard her correctly. "We what?"

"We're supposed to let livestock"—she didn't want to sound as if she were just a mouthpiece for pigs—"out of the truck every eight hours or so, so they can have food and water and so they don't get too stressed out. I think there's something called the Humane Transport Act?"

Jake looked from her to the windshield and back again, as if he couldn't decide which view was worse. "Well, if stressed out is the chief worry, I think maybe we should get one of the pigs to drive and I can just go back with the others. The trip doesn't take eight hours—thank the Lord, or you'd never shut up. But anyway, you just keep your eye out for some nice, green meadow so we can let 'em out for a frolic." This time he reached across her and took hold of the door handle on her side. "Now, get out."

Andi was astonished. "Why? What'd I do?"

"You're going to drive me nuts. I'm not listening to you all the way across the state. So, vamoose."

"Come on, Jake. I won't talk about food and water, even though we're supposed to provide—"

They both jumped at the slap against the window. Abramson was doing a rolling motion with his hand.

Jake rolled down the window.

"My friends, you planning on sitting here till the goddamned sun goes down?" A false smile. "You got to get there this afternoon."

"Just reading the map is all."

A change in Abramson's falsely solicitous tone: "Move these here animals!"

Jake nodded, turned the ignition, accelerated. The truck butted like a bull and bumped along the dirt road before it reached the asphalt.

"You just try and keep your mouth shut this trip, will you? I don't relish the idea of listening to you bellyache." He pulled his hat down on his forehead as if he meant to shut out her and her talk and the road ahead.

30

They drove north to State Road 200, which took them through Beulah and Hazen, then made a sharp turn north to Pick City and Lake Sakakawea, where the state rode set them down on U.S. 83. That was the route north to Minot.

The fields rolled past, bordered in late-summer yellow and purple coneflowers and goldenrod. Hills carpeted in grass rolled one into the other like waves, and in one place the shadow was so intensely blue that Andi mistook it for a lake, like the one near Pick City.

Andi heard nothing from the truck bed, the silence making her feel worse than all the noise in the world. She thought of telling Jake she'd rather have her eardrums crack than to have the pigs be quiet as they moved toward death. It would have helped to be able to talk, but Jake wasn't in a mood for her point of view. She nevertheless found it hard to believe that he was completely inured to this job and to Klavan's. He was too nice.

They passed a farm with a barn nearly sunk to the ground, its roof grazing it and a few outbuildings and nearby a few cows, some sheep, heads bent nibbling short grass. *That,* she thought, *is what we see. That's what we know. Not the other. People in passing cars flick a glance at the truck and turn away.*

As the farm shrank in the rearview mirror, she said, "I guess small farms like that one are having a hard time."

"Yeah. It's too bad. Outfits like Klavan's are pretty much putting them out of business."

They drove in silence for another hour and Andi asked him, "You've been inside a slaughterhouse, haven't you?"

"Used to work in one. It's no place for man nor beast. I was there five years, don't know how."

"What did you do there?"

He was quiet for a minute, then said, "I was a sticker."

"That's how you kill them, right? You stab them or something."

"Or something."

"But they're stunned first, aren't they? They're not conscious."

"Supposed not to be."

She looked over at him, but said nothing. For some reason, that made her think of her grim stalker. Maybe it was the air of menace. He leaves, but the menace stays, like a calling card or a package left on the doorsill.

Jake made a stop for gas at a truck stop with a small eatery flanked on one side by a scattering of houses up a narrow dirt road. He said he'd get some coffee for them.

The first of the houses down the dirt road, she could tell from the outbuildings, was a small farm. She sat for a moment, thinking. She took a key from the glove compartment and went around behind the truck.

It was parked with its rear wheels facing onto the fields and dirt roads. She was shielded from view, but he'd be back any moment. She unlocked the panel and let it fall down. She could reach the first tier all right and, amid squeals and grunts, tried to pull out the smallest pig she saw; she knew there were a few under market weight that Klavan's was going to try to unload, but even the one she pulled out must've weighed almost two hundred pounds, too much for her to pick up and carry. She was afraid it would run around, but it was so used to confinement, it just stood there, maybe dumbstruck by a world utterly new. That was her romantic bent. Probably it was just waiting for whatever came next.

It could hardly walk, but Andi managed to herd it to the fence that surrounded this part of the property. She pushed the pig through. The pig stood looking at her and she reached her hand out and petted it. It might get shot, it might starve to death; Andi wasn't expecting deliverance or pig heaven. She was only trying to save it from pig hell. Nothing that could happen to this pig roaming free could possibly be as bad as what would happen if it stayed on that truck.

Through the café window she saw Jake paying for his purchases and went quickly back to the truck, checked the lock, checked that everything was as it had been, put back the keys.

He came out with chips, a coffee, a Coke and a six-pack of beer he stowed in a foam cooler behind the seat. She took the Coke and a bag of chips from this awkward load.

"I got the coffee," he said, "to help me stay awake, seeing as how I get no help with the driving. You drove that van pretty much like a dodgem car. I got the beer for later to put me to sleep after spending a whole day and night with you."

"I'm sorry about the driving."

"Well, come on and get your sorry self up here."

She hurried around and hoisted herself up to the front seat.

He gunned the ignition and nosed the truck out and around the pumps then out to the road.

They'd driven barely two miles when smoke started seeping out from under the hood. "Oh, good God," Jake said. "Now what?" He slowed and looked at the engine gauge running hot. He stuck his head out the window as if some answer would come back to him on the wind, then pulled his head back in again. "Radiator, I'll bet. Or coolant. We'll just have to stop, that's all."

They were a few feet from one of the crossroads and Andi saw a motel over to the right. "You can just pull in there, can't you?"

Jake turned right, drove up to the place, and inched the truck into the motel parking lot. "Owner won't like this but what the hell." He switched off the engine and smoke ballooned out from the hood.

They both slipped down from the cab after Jake pulled some rags from behind his seat. Now he went around and opened the hood and hung back from the steam. He let it die down before he looked. "Well, the hose seems okay, so I'm guessing coolant. Couldn't've happened back there at the stop, of course. Hell."

A tall thin boy came out of the small motel office and joined them in looking at the complicated insides of the truck.

"Hi," said Jake. "Don't suppose you'd have any radiator coolant in there, would you?"

The boy shook his head. "Sorry." Then he looked up at the sky as if a new radiator might drop down from it. "Nearest you might get that's maybe in Garrison or Minot."

Jake shook his head. "No, there's a truck stop back there, but it's a couple miles and I can't really take the time from this trip to walk it."

The thin fellow was inspecting the pigs. "How many you got here?"

"Two hundred," said Andi.

"Kinda smell, don't they?"

"They're pigs."

He nodded his head patiently, as if this conundrum were finally solved.

"Look," said Jake, "there wouldn't be one of the motel's cars I could borrow, would there? I'd be only too happy to pay for its use."

"Well, you could take mine. It ain't no prize, though."

"Thanks, that'd be a lifesaver."

"That old Toyota, there." He nodded toward a once-silver-colored car near the office, reached in his back pocket, and got out the key, which he handed to Jake.

"Be back in a little bit." Jake jogged over to the car, backed out, and drove it off the lot.

Andi was looking at one of the pigs whose ear looked nearly bitten through, then at another who was bleeding from an eye. Of course they would fight; they were agitated. She saw a number of wounded ones. And their wounds would go unattended. Some would die before they got to where they were going; some had likely already died. She couldn't see them all.

"My name's Andi; what's yours?"

"Oh, Eddie. Eddie Crane. Glad to meetcha."

"Eddie, is there a hose around here?"

He frowned. "Yeah, I guess."

"Two, maybe?"

"Hoses?"

"Un-huh. Could we use them while Jake's gone?"

"'We'? For what?"

"Watering the pigs. I mean, giving them a drink. They've been traveling for hours in the sun with nothing to drink. Let's just do this thing; I don't think only one person could get to all of them."

He nodded. "Well, okay, I guess."

"Good! Thanks!"

"I'll hook 'em up." He went off toward some supply room and Andi went to the truck.

Soon, Eddie was coming from around the building with the circled hoses draped over his shoulders. "Over here's one of the hookups." He set one hose down, took the other, and went to a point in the wall near the truck. "Hoses is fifty feet and that'll do it," he said as he fitted the hose over the fixture. He picked up the second hose and took it some thirty feet down the walk. "I'm turning it on," he called over his shoulder, "so step away for a moment and tell me if water's coming out."

She did. Water snaked through the length of the hose and came out in a spray. "It's okay." She picked up the hose and fiddled with it to change the spray to a stream.

He'd gone to the second hose and turned it on. He hauled it along to the truck. "Now what?" He looked uneasily at the snouts of pigs pressing against the bars on the side.

"Just try and spray it on them. No, better, try and give them a stream of water to drink. Maybe you can take one side, and I'll take the other. That way the ones in back won't try to crawl over the ones in front because the water'll be coming from both directions. Look." She shoved the mouth of the hose toward one of the pigs' mouths. The pig nearly bit off the nozzle to get to the water, but then just drank. They would never get to all of them. The top level, she was afraid, would miss out completely.

The pigs were pushing as hard as they could toward the water, and Andi called over to Eddie, "You getting them okay?"

"Hell, yes. Got three or four going at the hose at once. Just put your finger half-over the end of the hose and you can spray several at a time. I always thought pigs was stupid. They just look stupid, is all. I'm up to the second story now."

"How'd you get up there?"

"Via this RV. It's got a ladder on the side of it. All I had to do was climb up and hold on."

"Can you reach up to the third level?"

"Yep. I just give 'em a good squirt."

Andi smiled. "You're a genius, Eddie."

"Been called a lot of things, but never that."

Andi levered herself up to the hood of the pickup parked beside the truck, then to the top of its cab. To her joy she found she could reach both the second and third levels. She tried using the hose the way Eddie was doing and it worked; it was more efficient than getting at the pigs one at a time. Sometimes she put her finger over the nozzle and sprayed them down. She figured any moisture was welcome.

"Stick the hose between the bars," Eddie called out helpfully. "They'll fight over it but they'll get water. You'd a thought someone would've figured out how to put some kind of water receptacle on a truck, right?"

"They don't care." Andi worked the hose in between the bars and the pigs crowded over to it.

She climbed down and went around to Eddie's side. He was up on the ladder belonging to the RV, hosing down the pigs that were mashed up against the bar like beggars with bowls.

They turned the hoses off and climbed down. Eddie went to the wall to turn the water off. "I'll stash 'em," he said, "if you just roll yours up."

While she waited, Eddie took the hoses back to wherever he'd gotten them. By the time he came back, Jake was pulling the Toyota in. He got out with his can of coolant.

"You get it?"

"Yeah, thank God." He looked at the asphalt. "What the hell? It rain around here?" He didn't wait for an answer, just went ahead and unscrewed the cap and poured in coolant. When he finished, he banged down the hood.

Looking down at the still-dripping water and the pools of it on the ground, Jake said, "What the hell you been doing?" He looked from one to the other.

"Nothing," Andi said.

"Nothin'," Eddie echoed.

Jake looked at Andi. "In the time I was gone you'd have had plenty of time to brainwash our friend here."

"He's Eddie."

"Pleased to meet you, Eddie, and I do thank you for the car." Jake reached out the Toyota's keys, and then pulled out his wallet.

"No, no. Honest, that's all right." A half-moon smile broke his face in two. "It was a lot of fun, actually." He turned the smile on Andi.

Jake looked at them. "I can just imagine. Time to go, I guess." He went around to the driver's seat.

Andi said to Eddie, "Thanks."

"I sure hope you come back this way," said Eddie.

"Maybe we will. Jake chooses the route. But I know we'll see each other again. We're bound to." Hesitating for a moment to see if Jake was in the driver's seat, she hugged Eddie. "Thanks. Really. Thanks."

"Anytime."

After she'd climbed up to her seat, Jake pulled away from the curb, away from the stones that marked the margins of each parking place and always put Andi in mind of gravestones. She leaned out and waved to Eddie, who was standing where he'd stood. He waved back. She watched him in the long mirror outside her window. He still stood there and was gone only when the truck turned onto 83 and the mirror could no longer hold him.

31

They stopped to eat some lunch in a little town off U.S. 83 on the other side of Minot. There was one business street, which had a bank and post office on one side and a feed supply store on the other. Beside the feed store was a plant shop with boxes of nasturtiums and geraniums sitting outside, sunning themselves. There were a few other stores, and a restaurant, where she and Jake ate stacks of blueberry pancakes and talked about one thing or another, being careful (she thought) not to step on each other's toes.

Beneath the give-and-take about North Dakota and crops and weather, Andi was trying hard to put herself in his place, but she couldn't, and that bothered her. She wanted to feel for a moment his resolve to deliver animals to this place; she wanted to feel where he was coming from. Jake and Jim and Tom: she saw this in all of them. They were good men. She did ask him about that period in his life. The slaughterhouse: here were the soul's dregs.

"You quit the slaughterhouse—"

"Andi." His look stopped her cold.

"Sorry." She looked down at her nearly empty plate. She had eaten a stack of pancakes; she could order more if she wanted; she could eat until she was drenched in syrup, until she was sick of eating. Yet the pigs got nothing. Got nothing and again nothing and could do nothing about it. She pushed the plate away.

"Can't we get them something to eat?"

He looked at his bacon and chewed more slowly, as if he, too, would push his plate away. "Don't see how we'd feed them. It's not practical."

"One at a time." Arms folded on the table, she leaned toward him. "Come on, Jake, we could find food—"

Suddenly angry, he pointed his fork toward her, his eyes now hot on her face. "I don't know what your story is, girl, but don't try writing me into it. I done paid my dues a lot of years ago. I ain't going down that road. You're free to take any road you have a mind to, is my guess. You act like a person with nothing to lose. Me, I got plenty to lose. I lost it all once, and I'm goddamned if I will again. I'm not killing these animals; I'm only driving 'em. You don't see any difference in that. You think it's as good as killing. You see people eating pork chops and ribs and you sure don't put them in my category, and Lord knows not in the same category as a man with a bolt driver. But all I can say is, if all of you stop eating 'em, then I'll stop driving 'em and BigSun'll stop killing 'em."

He stopped as suddenly as a truck braking on a downward slope, dangerous.

Andi let a full minute pass, watching him eat his pancakes, and then said, "I have money. We passed a feed store right back there."

Jake dropped his fork and dropped his head in his hands. "Sweet *mercy*, you *never* heard a single word I said."

"I did, too, Jake, every word, and you're right. You're right. Except all of what you said has nothing to do with that feed store. It'll only take ten or fifteen minutes and I've got plenty of money." She pulled out some bills and showed him.

He sat back, slowly shaking his head. He flipped back the top of his Zippo and rasped up a tiny flame for his cigarette, flouting the sign with a red circle around a cigarette, diagonal bar running through it. "Tell you what: you pay this check and then see what's left over."

Andi grinned as the waitress bore down on their table. "Sir. This is a no-smoking environment."

Jake smiled. "Oh, we pretty much set our own rules." He slid across the booth. "The young lady here, she'll take care of that check while I go seek another environment."

He walked out, smoke spiraling thinly upward.

"He's just a great kidder, that's all."

The waitress shrugged as she handed Andi the check, which Andi covered with a twenty. "Keep the change. The pancakes were really good."

The waitress smiled her thanks.

It felt like Christmas in the feed store, all of those bags of meal, corn, oats, and fancy mixtures. Jake looked over the garden tools and household tools that had nothing to do with feed—he was making his position clear, Andi supposed. Or maybe men just did this automatically whenever they got around new tools; they needed to look at them carefully, weigh them as Jake was now testing the weight of a wrench.

The owner, a nice old man named Timms, made his recommendations. Putting his hand on a sack, he said, "We got your corn, oats, and so forth, but we also got your developer feed that's got your BMD mixed in. That's nice, not having to mix it yourself. Now, how old are your pigs? This is good for growth, see."

"Well, they've pretty much done their growing."

"Okay, then you might want to stick with stuff like this meal—"

Jake was sticking his wrist out, pointing at his watch.

She bickered with Mr. Timms in a pleasant, not aggressive, way about discounting prices, as they were buying several bags. He reduced the prices a little.

They carried the bags out. She turned down Mr. Timms's offer to help because she didn't want him to see the truck.

"Now, just how do you plan to administer this food? Toss it by the handful as if the pigs was pigeons?" said Jake.

Andi had her eye on the plant store next door, on the geraniums and other flowers sitting in long green plastic boxes. "I'm buying some of those." She started toward the plants.

Leaning against the truck, Jake called after her, "Flowers for the table? That's real thoughtful."

She was back in a minute with nine of the plastic planters. "We fill these up and put three on each level. That'll spread the food out enough they won't be killing each other to get to it."

"Who's going up top? Not me, so I guess that leaves you."

"Lift me up as far as you can and I'll get myself over the rail." Shoeless, she stood on his shoulders and pulled herself over the bars.

The pigs sent up a wall of noise. Noise, to say nothing of excrement. It was awful. The smell was bad enough just from being near the truck, but actually being in it was almost insupportable. Her eyes stung with the ammonia smell. She leaned over the top. "Hand me up the planters. You filled them, didn't you?"

"Yes, boss." Jake handed up a trough full of corn, then another of meal, and a third of more corn. The pigs would have stampeded if they'd had the room to do it. As it was, the snouts nearest were the ones that got first crack. Soon, others shoved their way in.

Andy got out, her socks slimy with excrement, and into the second level, where they repeated the process.

Then she was on the ground.

"Jesus, you smell like shit, and I mean that literal."

She took off her socks, tossed them in a big drum of trash. "I need to wash."

"The rest of you could stand it, too, but there's no time for you to take a shower. Try the ladies' in the pancake place."

"I'll only be five minutes."

"I know, long as you don't meet up with a pig."

Andi took off and Jake climbed into the cab of the truck, and when he looked again she was gone.

Jake thought she was the strangest girl he had ever met. Girl? Person. Man, woman, child. And he'd known some doozies. He didn't mean "strange" in any negative way, no; he meant it in the sense of interesting. More than interesting—otherworldly, if such can be said. He wanted to get her right, to explain her to himself. Come out of nowhere, said she'd come from Miles City, Montana, walking—*walking*. What the hell was she doing, walking across Montana?

She could not be turned. That amazed him, her determination. Unconditional, unnegotiable, take-no-prisoners Andi Oliver. If she tried to go into the packing plant he'd tie her to a tree. Gag her, naturally. He did seriously wonder if she was one of those activists who get into places like circuses and factory farms undercover.

He pushed his hat back, saw her coming, running along the sidewalk, sort of skip-running. Five minutes on the nose. *What are you about, Andi Oliver?* It was like taking care of these damned pigs was her only purpose in life.

And she would not be turned from it.

Andi made a quick survey of the pigs before piling into her seat. "Thanks for waiting."

"Uh-huh. We're like over an hour off our schedule. But I didn't plan on the truck breaking down."

As Jake drove, Andi slid down in her seat and watched the pastures go by. It was a day of brilliant sun and brittle air. She pulled her parka closer around her neck. It was beautiful October.

Jake had lit a cigarette and hung his arm out the window that let in the smell of pig waste.

"How much farther is it?"

"Two, three hours. Hundred and fifty miles."

"Do the pigs get fed when we get there?"

Jake slapped his forehead. "Girl, in case you haven't noticed, this is not a Hilton we're going to, where the hungry travelers go first thing to the dining room."

"They don't, then." She shrugged. "We've got enough."

Again, he hit his head in mock disbelief. "So you think the line will wait while you hand out corn and oats and that other goddamned special diet you bought for a small fortune?" Now his voice rose, and not in the earlier mock-anger. His fingers whitened with his fierce grip on the steering wheel: "These pigs aren't going on vacation. *They're going to slaughter!* Can't you keep that in mind?"

Andi stared straight ahead. Unprovoked, she said, "It's always in mind. So your idea is if animals are going to slaughter, everything else drops away, goes by the board. In a way, these animals are untouchables. We're not supposed to do anything for them; we're supposed to forget about them. They don't exist. I wonder why that is. And why are you so mad about it?"

Jake didn't answer; he just drove faster.

32

They got into Preston in midafternoon. The truck rattled along the road into the huge yard, where a couple of dozen trucks were already parked, unloading animals—cows, pigs, sheep, calves—by the hundreds. There were outfits that accounted for more than one truck; Klavan's, by comparison, was one of the smaller facilities.

All of these animals stretched away as far as she could see; then it didn't look so much like hundreds, but thousands. They swept away almost to the horizon. The noise was a roar, the sounds of lowing, squealing, screaming, as they were herded into holding pens.

Workers, handlers, whoever they were, moved among the animals, and would sometimes yank a pig or sheep out of the crowd and toss it to the side. They were culling the dead and the ones who couldn't move as fast as the handlers wanted them to—too sick or weak or injured to act on their own. *Downers*, Andi thought. There was a law against forcing downers into the slaughterhouse, but it was a law that was forgotten here.

Jake stepped down from the cab and stood by her side. "Used to work here. BigSun is the place I was talking about."

Andi looked at him as if it hurt her eyes to do it.

"It's the world, Andi."

But which one? She imagined at this moment Jim and Tom eating and joking, eating their baby back ribs, a description she'd not actually thought of until right now, watching the trucks crowded with piglets. They were bred to a certain standard, one that would make them all as nearly the same as possible.

Crates were being unloaded, dumped, really, let fall and whatever was inside let fall with them. The handlers were moving calves along with rakes or prods or any other instrument they could find to hurry them on. But they'd been raised in crates, they'd never exercised, they'd never moved their legs, and so were clumsy. A lot of them fell down; a number of them were tossed down, dead or immobile. No, they weren't all dead, for she could tell the ones underneath were trying to get out, but with their weak limbs they could get no purchase, and so stayed and were smothered. They had no strength in their limbs, no strength at all.

Weakness was bred into them; weakness was good for the quality of the veal; devoid of muscle, the meat would be tender. They were of course anemic; that kept the flesh pale.

Andi knew all of this; she'd never seen it in action before.

They were hurried and harried, poked and prodded. The calves were always falling down. Jake came around the truck. "We got to get the truck up closer."

He was about to hoist himself up when a barrel-chested man called out to him, "Jake, goddamn it! Where the hell you been? What the fuck?" They slapped hands, handshaking seemingly inadequate for all of that muscle.

Jake seemed less than enthusiastic. "Bud. How you been?"

Bud jiggled his eyebrows. "At what, man?" He laughed fit to kill and enough for both of them, which was just as well, since Jake didn't laugh at all.

Bud looked Andi up and down, the dirtiest she'd ever been looked at, even by the Bailey brothers. He said, "My Lord, a shame to waste all that on a bunch of hogs! Yes, ma'am, I'd show you any old ropes you want to see. I—"

Shut up, shut up. In the background she heard the most terrible bellowing, as if the sky were lowing. She looked behind the two men at the cattle being driven from the pens through the alley. Her eyes were still on the cattle being harried; being shoved, pushed, or prodded into line, one at a time, and then moved forward to the tunnel-like enclosure that she knew must go into the killing area.

"What's the tunnel?" she asked.

"Tunnel o' love. Care to join me in one of them little cars?" Bud laced his fingers behind his head and did a few pelvic gyrations.

She opened her mouth.

Jake said, knowing she'd say something no one here would want to hear, "Come on, let's move the truck."

Bud said, "Just take 'er on down there behind Snow's."

Andi was up and in before Jake.

He said, "Let's not start in on the Humane Slaughter Act. They've been violating that six ways from Sunday and every other law ever passed like it, and been doing it forever."

"Well, why doesn't the Department of Agriculture stop it, then?"

"Two reasons is my guess. One is whenever an inspector's slated to pay a visit, management gets word of it, and goes in there like hell on wheels"—he nodded toward the plant—"and makes the workers clean up their act—not knocking right or dropping pigs in the blood pit before they're dead, not making sure animals are dead before they're skinned, stuff like that."

Andi stared at him. "Funny, I'm sitting here trying and I can't think of *any* 'stuff like that.' "

"Chrissakes," he muttered.

"What's the second reason?"

He was looking back over his shoulder, slotting the truck into an empty space. There were a lot of trucks sitting around. "Plus, some of them have likely got a vested interest in the whole operation." He stopped the truck, braked, said, "We gotta get 'em out, get 'em counted."

The pigs counted. Andi thought for a moment. "I'll do it."

He shook his head. "We don't do the counting. Stockyard does it."

Say it's a miscount. . . . Say the missing pig wasn't ever there. Mistake was made at the other end.

"Warren!" Jake waved his arm, motioned for a thin man with glasses to come this way. He was wearing a dark blue feed cap.

"Hey, Jake, how you doing? You want a job? They need a decent sticker in there. One they got now don't know from nothin'. Ma'am." He looked at Andi, touched his fingers to his cap.

Andi opened her mouth and saw the warning in Jake's eyes, and said only, "Hi. I'm Andi."

Again he touched the bill of his cap. "Well, you'll want to stay clear of the plant, there." He studied his clipboard and repeated it: "You wouldn't want to go in there."

"We got to unload these hogs and get on back."

"Right." Warren wrote something on the yellow notebook in his clipboard. He was still hung up on Andi. "You work at Klavan's?"

Andi nodded. "I just started a couple of months ago."

"You like it?"

Again she nodded. "More or less."

The pigs were coming down the ramp of the truck, moving skittishly into one of the pens. A lot of them slipped because of the steep angle; some tumbled and knocked over others.

The trip here was probably their first experience of the outside world, and they would find this world infinitely worse.

The top level was empty now and Jake called over to Warren, "How many you got there?"

Warren looked at his notebook. "I count seventy right now. How many you bring altogether?"

"Two hundred and six." Jake was opening the gate for the ones on the second tier.

Warren nodded, then said to Andi, "Reason I asked is there's a lot of jobs on offer here. There's a big turnover."

"Why's that?" Andi was running her hand over every back she could reach as the pigs came drunkenly down the ramp.

"Hard work and not very pleasant."

"What kind of job you talking about?"

"End-of-line ones, like organ collection."

"What about on the line?"

"Well, yeah, but you want to steer clear of that. Yes, steer clear."

Andi hauled up a sow that had slipped in manure, steaming in the sun now. She managed to get the sow to her feet. "But those jobs are the ones that pay best, aren't they?"

Warren looked up. "Yeah, that's because they're the worst."

"Like a sticker?"

"I'd say so. Don't tell me that's what you want?"

Andi didn't answer.

"Warren," called Jake, "you can't count and talk to her at the same time."

Warren laughed. "I can do anything and count at the same time."

"There's seven dead. Surprised there's not more; usually, there's more."

Andi said, "Is there a hose around here, Warren?"

"Yeah. One right over there. They wash things down end of day."

Andi walked over to the hose plugged into a faucet jerry-rigged to a pipe. It was beside one of the cattle pens, cows waiting their long wait. Two turned their heads and looked at her, nailing her to the spot. Better a tornado or tidal wave, she thought, or the eruption of Mount Vesuvius. Better drown under water or lava. Better anything than what was going to happen to these cows.

She looked at them and felt a complete failure of nerve, a total want of courage, a loss for words. It was a disappointment in herself so devastating she felt she was losing her balance.

She turned on the water and dragged the hose back to the pen. Without word or question, she turned the water on the pigs. Some opened their mouths and she poured it in. There was a piglet that had got in with the sows that could hardly stand. With Warren and Jake busy at the back of the truck, she picked it up, shoved it inside her vest, and went around the front of the truck to the cab. She set the piglet on the floor of the passenger's seat and put her vest over it. Then she went back to the hose, still splashing out water.

Warren called to Jake, "That all of 'em?"

"That's all."

Warren raised his thumb from the sheet—as if he were keeping his information secret—and said, "You said two hundred six? Taking off the seven dead, that'd be one hundred ninety-nine. There's a hundred ninety-eight, Jake. One missing."

Jake hopped down from the truck bed. "Something's wrong. I helped load 'em up." He looked at Warren's sheet.

"Well, it's only one, Jake."

"You know what Klavan's like. It might as well be a hundred."

"Could the both of us do the count again?"

"Sure."

"Andi, Chrissakes, stop with the hose."

"Why? You can't count with water running?" But she pulled the hose away, let water pool at her feet and run in under the fence of the pen where a half dozen pigs lapped it up.

She looked along the pens to the slaughterhouse. There were three stories, and each was dedicated to a different species: sheep, cattle, hogs. The animals were pushed down the drive alley, where the drivers prodded and pushed with whatever they could find, the cattle bellowing. One of the workers was using a cattle prod on a bull, who was resisting with all his force, then shocked into bellowing from the electric prod rammed down his throat.

Andi was sure that they knew where they were going. How far away do you have to be to catch the scent of blood?

Behind her the two men had finished their counting and come up with the same number: 198.

Jake was trying the truck's railings, but they were sturdy enough. "How could it have got away?"

Warren said, "Jake, I've seen animals escape from ever'thing you could name. I even saw an old sow escape from there"—he pointed his clipboard at the plant—"right off the killin' floor. Animals, you wouldn't believe how much they want to live. It's my opinion there's a mistake on your end. Hell, I've counted wrong and I'm the most reliable there is."

"Yeah. And you're probably right; it's just Klavan....You know what an asshole he is."

"So how much are they worth? How much do you get per pig?" Andi asked.

"Four dollars."

"That's *all*?" She was scratching behind the ears of one in the pen. They hadn't moved yet. Four dollars for this great pig; she couldn't believe it. That's all the value put on them: about the cost of a large latte at Starbucks. She said to Jake, "I'll pay it."

"Oh, the four bucks, that's not important. I just don't want to listen to old man Klavan go on about it. He's the biggest penny-pincher I ever did see."

She took up the hose and coiled it and walked it back to where she'd gotten it from. The cows in this pen were filing out to the driving alley. She watched them. Some held back, some simply stopped, immobile. The driver decided the cure for this was the electric prod. A cow bawled.

Jake had gone to the office to collect his money for the pigs. Warren was still standing there with his notebook.

"Of course, I'd have to see the place," said Andi. "I mean, if I was deciding to work here. I'd have to see the line."

Warren looked very doubtful.

She cocked her head. "Warren, are you saying people take these jobs on without seeing what they have to do?"

"Experienced, they know."

"Well, they're not all experienced. Not even trained is my bet. If they were, maybe they could figure out a way to make those cows move"—she pointed off to the cattle in the drive alley—"without sticking an electric prod down their throats or up their asses. No training is why you get so many incompetents, right?"

Warren stuck his clipboard under his arm. "You seem to know a lot about it for someone's never worked in a slaughterhouse."

"Jake talks about it—" She looked over her shoulder in case Jake was returning from the office. No.

Now Warren did the cocked-head gesture. With a bit of a smile, he said, "You wouldn't for instance be one of them undercover people from PETA or some humane farming bunch, now, would you?"

She sighed, stagily. "Warren. No, of course not. I work for Klavan's, have you forgotten?" Where she could be undercover as well as anyplace else. But he didn't appear to be connecting any dots.

He went on, " 'Cause we had one of them in here took pictures with a hidden camera. Hell, but management wanted to kill him over that!" He laughed, perhaps not liking management much. "Tuttle almost pissed his pants, pardon my French."

"Who's Tuttle?"

"Manager. Cheap little bastard, worse than Klavan."

"Look." She stepped nearer to him. "It'd only take ten minutes, Warren, and I'd rather Jake didn't know I was looking for another job. So couldn't we, you know, just do it now?"

Warren sucked at his lower lip, considering. "We don't let people inside there. Liability, you know. Let me check with someone."

Liability, hell. As if BigSun cared who got hurt. Andi nodded, watched Warren plug in numbers on his cell. It was a BlackBerry. She didn't know whether to laugh or cry. Fellow working in a slaughterhouse and he's got a four-hundred-dollar phone. The world's gone mad, is all.

Warren made his contact and stepped away from Andi. Spoke. Listened. Said, "Okay. Let's go. Only Jake's gonna wonder . . ."

"So let him wonder."

Warren shrugged. "You say so."

They had to walk past pen after pen, going toward the plant. Pen after pen of terrified, grieving animals. For that's how it struck her; it also struck her that she hadn't enough breath in her body to take the thought further, to think of it longer, or it would stop her dead. She could sit right down on this stink-soaked ground and not get up again.

A sea of grieving animals. Not for their old life, but for any life at all. She knew there were so many more than were penned in here, not just thousands, but millions, even *billions*, a concept so staggering that it was impossible to take seriously.

And this was all before she saw it.

33

Warren had told her when they walked in to stay beside him in case she attracted attention.

"Of course, I'll stay by you." She meant this sincerely; she was afraid to be separated in this place.

"Pigs is on the first floor so let's go there."

There was a sort of balcony walk that stretched around all four sides, probably for whoever needed it to be able to see how slaughters were proceeding. She asked Warren.

"It's to see who's holding up the line. It's all the line. One person don't do his job fast enough, then the next can't do his, nor the next his. Guy with the stunner misses, or gets sloppy, the shackler and sticker gets their animal conscious and that makes what they do tons harder. And dangerous."

Andi shut her eyes. *Pardon me for not caring about the sticker,* she thought, now with her eyes on the next pig coming into the restrainer. It was grabbed by the stunner, who ran the bolt into the pig's head.

"Now, that," said Warren, "was a good'un. That must've knocked it out. You never know."

The pig was passed along to the next person, who clamped a chain on its leg and hauled it up, head down. Now it went to the sticker, who slashed its throat and left it to bleed out. The sticker pit was pretty deep in blood.

"That fellow—his name's Hank Dew and he's real good. He can do four hundred hogs an hour."

Andi's mouth dropped. "Four hundred an *hour*? But that would mean a pig goes through every ten *seconds*!"

"Get a good line going, yeah, that's about right. Lookie there, though." Warren was pointing at a pig that was being stunned two, three, four times on the head and was kicking wildly when the shackler tried to get the shackle on its leg. The pig's flailing leg hit the man in the chest. The shackler picked up a piece of metal pipe and thrashed the pig until its body ran with blood. The pig screamed before it was beaten into silence. Then there seemed to be an argument between that worker and the sticker.

The pig, shackled and beaten but still not dead, tried to raise itself up, its face a bloody pulp. Hanging, it was passed to the sticker, the pig still trying to raise its head. It bellowed and was grabbed by the sticker, and its throat slit and left to bleed.

"Don't know how there could be any blood left in it," said Warren. "God*damn*, that pig wanted to live."

Andi said nothing; her mouth was frozen.

"See, that's the kind of thing that's the trouble. When the stunner don't do it right and then beats them, that holds up the line and the quota ain't met. That's what the sticker was mad about—you got to stun, shackle, stick"—with each word bringing his small fist down on the railing; he had quite small hands.

Andi listened to him. He talked of it as an event demanding the precision of a platoon of soldiers on a parade ground, or a ballet, or a blackjack dealer. The rhythm must be maintained. They might have been assembling cars; they might have been canning peas. In her mind's eye, she saw Warren's fisted hand thumping down, punctuating his points.

She was suddenly afraid of him. Not that she felt in any danger. He wasn't as fearsome, anyway, as those men down there. It was that she had so misread him, the other Warren; she would have thought him incapable of this cheering-section behavior.

"Warren." She couldn't help herself putting it into words. But she needed to hear it. "You like watching this, don't you?"

The old Warren then asserted himself. He had been leaning with his forearms on the wooden rail and righted himself. "What? Hell, no, I don't; it's real awful." There was another sheer scream, as clear as a pane of glass, if one would just look through it. "Couldn't get me down there for all the tea in China, no, ma'am."

"What's that big vat over there?" It was a long metal trowel-like piece of equipment that the pigs were passed through as they hung head down, like laundry on a line.

"That's the scalding tank. They get submerged in it so's to soften up their hair. Makes it easier to skin 'em."

"But they're not conscious when they go in it." This was something she was telling herself rather than asking him.

"Mostly not. No, not if everybody's done his job."

A pig had gotten free of its shackle and was running loose in the blood pit, the sticker trying to grab it. Some of the blood was the pig's own, most of it from others before him. The pig was painted with it.

It seemed almost to be reaching its snout up to the sticker in search of something it would never get, something impossible from the moment the pig set its feet down in the stockyard. If it was mercy, that had long ago been expunged.

Yet with its bloody face, its torn eye socket, it seemed to sense some remnant, some possibility that Andi couldn't fathom. She turned her back as the sticker grabbed the pig that had been supplicating him and slashed its throat.

There are circumstances so bizarre, so dreadful, and even so beautiful that the mind is ludicrously ill-equipped to deal with them. Unimaginable, unspeakable, inexpressible.

She shook her head to try to shake away the sounds coming from the floor—the angry yells of the men on the line, the screaming of the pigs. The din beat her back. She leaned against the wall.

Warren looked around over his shoulder. "You okay?"

No, she would have answered if Jake hadn't right then come bursting through the door.

"What the *hell* do you think you're doing, bringing her in here?" Jake tore at Warren's arm, would have had it pulled out of the socket like a burned-out lightbulb if Warren hadn't managed to squeeze himself out of Jake's grip.

Andi said, "No, Jake. I asked him to. He never wanted—"

"*Shut up, Andi!* Just you shut your mouth for once." He turned to Warren again.

Warren was rubbing at his upper arm. "Goddamn, Jake! I ain't no fucking babysitter, you hear? She said she maybe would like to work here but she had to see first what went on—"

Jake got right up into his face. "She was lying, Warren. It's what the girl does. To get what she wants she'd say anything."

Andi was looking below. Not one of the men seemed to notice there was a ruckus going on up here, in spite of Jake's ferocious voice. It didn't stop the line.

"Come on!" Jake pulled at her shoulder. She twisted away, but still followed him out of the building.

"Why are you so *mad*?" Andi called to Jake, who was now stomping off. They were passing the pens; the ones vacated by those animals inside were now filled up again. Trucks came in, went out, again in that kind of awful rhythm she'd noticed in the slaughterhouse.

Jake strode on ahead, and she stopped by a pen filled with cattle. She held out her hand to what she was almost sure was a pregnant cow, the belly bloated to twice its normal size. She put her hand against the cow's side. Jake was back beside her. He yanked at her hand and pulled her away. "I must've been crazy letting you come along. What were you planning in there?" He bent his head in the direction of the slaughterhouse. "Blowing the place up?"

"No, but it's not a bad idea."

He wheeled. "Don't talk smart. Don't fucking talk." He put out a finger at her.

She almost laughed. "You're not my father, to teach me what I can and can't do." Now her own voice was rising.

He had been turning away and now turned back. "Long as you're with me and on Klavan business, yes, ma'am, I can tell you what to do. Not that it does any good. You are really the most devious person I ever knew."

She ran back to the truck to see where the piglet was. Its head was poking out from under the vest.

"Get in," said Jake, who went around to his side and hoisted himself into the driver's seat. He looked down at the small face.

Without saying anything, she looked at Jake.

"Hell, what's one more piece of fraud or misuse of company funds or plain old theft?" When she got in, he slammed his door. He put the truck in reverse, his arm across the back of the seat, maneuvering around half a dozen other rigs, most with the animals as yet unloaded. Sheep, cows, more pigs.

Jake pulled out on the road, and the sun would have limned the sky with the color of blood, only blood was brighter.

34

arren should never have let you into that place."

"I did make him, you know."

"Oh, I'm sure you wheedled and connived. But Warren knows better. Remember I told you I worked that line for five years. It's nothing you need to see. There are things in this world you shouldn't see and that's one of them." He honked at a Fiat that was crowding the passing lane.

Andi didn't want him to think she was arguing, so she waited several beats before she said, "But if you don't see it, Jake, then you don't know it's happening, and you can't do anything about it."

His eyes left the road and turned to her. They looked hot. "That's just the point; there's nothing you *can* do about it. It's the world, Andi. Nothing anyone can do because people have got to have their morning bacon."

"You worked there for five years as a sticker. I can't see you doing that for five minutes. You're too kind."

That brought on a guffaw. "First time I've ever been called that."

"You are." She was thinking back on his anger. "You really hate it, don't you? You hate that place."

"Yeah, I do."

"So it had just the opposite effect on you as on those men on the floor. For you it got worse and worse; for them, they went lower and lower. Now they like it or part of them does."

"Stop talking as if you know all about it. None of them likes it. I've known decent men drink themselves blind or go home after a day in that infernal place and beat up their wives and kids. Which is what I did. Which is why I quit, only I quit too late."

She was once more surprised. "I didn't know you had kids. Or a wife, for that matter."

"No more, I don't. She divorced me and I can hardly blame her. She has the kids. Boy and girl. Johnny and Jeanette."

"Where are they? When do you see them?"

"I don't, at least not for the last couple years."

"Where are they?" she asked again.

He shook his head. "Don't know. She up and moved to somewhere else and didn't tell me."

Stunned, Andi twisted around in her seat. "How could she do that? That's illegal, isn't it? You can't do that to a parent. Did you go to a lawyer?"

"I did. Said I could take her to court. Only thing is, I'd have to find her first, and I can't find her."

"Couldn't a private detective?"

"One I hired didn't have much luck. Of course, he wasn't exactly Sam Spade. He was all I could afford. Amazing how a woman with two little kids can just drop out of sight."

"I'm really sorry. You must miss them a lot."

Jake nodded. His right hand was doing most of the steering; he had his elbow out the window and the back of his hand against his mouth.

To Andi it looked as if he wanted to cry. She said, "I haven't seen my family for a long time, either. It's hard; I know it's hard."

He pulled his hand away and rested it on the steering wheel, two fingers, teasing the wheel. "How come? You all have a big difference of opinion?"

Andi smiled at the way he put it, saving her some kind of embarrassment in case the "difference" had got her thrown out. "I guess so." How she wished it had been a difference of opinion instead of this blankness.

They were driving through a blitz of neon that washed the wet road, skimming blue and green and red over puddles.

"Rained here," he said. "That air smells good, don't it?"

"It does. Where'll we eat? McDonald's?"

"You want to?"

"I hate McDonald's."

"Me, too. There's a Conoco Truck Stop other side of Minot. Hard parking this big rig except at one of them."

It was an Econostop. Jake rolled the truck across the parking lot past a dozen trucks, slotted into spaces that fit like Lego pieces.

They got out and Jake came around to pick up the pig. "There's plenty of food in the back. Enough to feed you for the rest of your life." Once stowed and with a little feed on a tin plate Jake produced from behind the seat, the pig rooted around in the feed.

"Well, don't expect us to bring you out a T-bone."

"I'll bring him out some milk."

On the way to the restaurant door, Jake asked, "What're you planning on doing with him?"

"Keep him at Jim's, I guess."

"Lord, your friend Jim can start planning for an ark, the way you bring 'em on."

"He won't mind. He was fine about the other pig—" It was out before she realized it. Uncertainly she looked at Jake, who was holding the door for her.

"What pig?"

She smiled and they went in.

Jake forewent the double-sized sirloin and settled on the same thing Andi did: pecan pancakes and fried eggs.

The waitress looked from one to the other. "Bacon? Sausage?"

They both shook their heads.

The waitress was named Mabel and she looked like she'd been taking orders from truckers for a good long time, crevices running from her nose to her mouth like tire tracks, but a sweet expression, nevertheless.

"We got our Happy Trails Special on tonight; that's real popular. Beside the pancakes there's a slice of French toast, three eggs scrambled or otherwise, rib-eye steak, and hash brown and biscuits, too. Or a corn muffin, you want it. We make 'em here."

"Can a person really eat all of that?" asked Andi.

Mabel laughed. "You better believe it. Some go for seconds."

"Okay," said Jake. "I'll have that, only hold the steak."

"You don't like steak?" Mabel's thin eyebrows hovered.

"Not tonight. And coffee, don't forget the coffee."

"As if I could." Mabel turned to Andi.

Andi said she'd just stick to her pancakes.

Then Mabel was back to Jake: "What about a corn muffin?"

"Sure."

Mabel stowed her pencil behind her ear, picked up the menus and turned on her rubber heel, and walked off toward counter and kitchen.

"You didn't have to do that, I mean, not have the steak because of me."

"Who said it's because of you? Not everything's because of you. I just can't eat all that."

"Only the pancakes, three eggs, French toast, hash browns, and a corn muffin."

"Hey, you should do some waitressing with a memory like that."

"Yeah, well, I did do some. A lot, really. It's the kind of work easiest to get."

"Where did you do it?"

"One place was Idaho Falls. Then in Billings and Miles City. You know, Montana. That was for nearly a year. Idaho City, I was there for a little while, too."

Jake frowned. "Any life before that?"

It was odd the way he put it, as if he himself were acquainted with lives beginning only a couple of years back.

"Sure, but it's dull."

"So you're doing this walk across the Great Plains for the hell of it? Permit me to say you don't give the impression of someone struck with wanderlust."

"Why wouldn't I be struck by it?"

He smiled. "Mind if I smoke?"

"Mind if I mind?"

"No."

Mabel was back with a coffeepot that was so hot, steam was clouding the air. She set down two white mugs, poured the coffee, dumped little plastic tubs of half-and-half on the table.

"You got a smoking section?" Jake asked her.

"You're sitting in it."

He nodded and lit up.

Andi clamped her hands around the mug and took a deep breath. That was coffee.

"Why wouldn't I be a wanderer?" she asked again.

Jake stripped two of the plastic containers of their tops and dumped the milk into his mug, then sugar, and stirred, thoughtfully. "Well, you strike me as a person likes to settle. Doesn't like to leave a place once you stay for a while. You like the fit, I'll bet, of every place you've been for more than a week." He sipped his coffee, held the mug up between his hands. "Or the people. It's probably more the people."

They sat in silence for some minutes while Andi thought about this. She was surprised by his knowing it, and felt, oddly, she'd failed, but she couldn't say at what. And how did he know this? She looked into her own coffee, brought it up, hiding part of her face. "You're probably right, there. But you could feel that way and still be a wanderer. Those two things are not mutually exclusive." She said this tartly and precisely. She was glad Mabel was a step away with their food. "Wow!" she said. "That's got to be the biggest plate I've ever seen."

It covered Jake's half of the table, nearly.

Andi's plate was more conventional, but still stacked with a lot of pancakes.

"You need your strength," Mabel observed, and went away with her heels squeaking.

Andi wanted to turn the conversation away from her past. She said, "Why did you say to Warren that lying is what I do best?"

"Because it is. You're one of the most accomplished liars I ever did meet."

She took in a mouthful of pancakes drenched with maple syrup. They were the most puffed-up pancakes she'd ever seen and there were three kinds of syrup.

They finished and paid and walked back to the truck. Andi stopped. "You saw me with the van."

"What d'you mean?"

"You knew I took the pig from Klavan's to Jim's; you saw me in the van. You knew right from the beginning I could drive."

"Saints above us, you mean you lied? If you call that driving, yeah, I knew."

"I guess I do lie a lot."

He looked in at the pig. "Truth be told, I wouldn't be surprised if your name's not Andi Oliver."

Andi was glad he was looking not at her but at the pig, and that the night seemed to crowd them, revealing nothing.

35

They were back on 83, heading south.

Andi asked Jake, "Where were they, your family, the last time you were with them?"

"South Dakota, same house as when I moved out."

"That was the last time you ever saw them?"

"No. It was months later when I saw them at the state fair. I took my little nephew, Davy; he wanted to go so bad and his mom—my sister, Sis, I always called her—she had to work. So I took him. That's when I saw her. Them."

He went on. "At the Ferris wheel. Davy really loves those and I kind of do, too. So we were getting in line and I saw my little girl, Jeanette, up there in the line, a lot of people ahead of us. She was holding on to some guy's hand and for a minute I thought I was wrong, you know—why would she be with this man?"

Andi let this story wash over her, for once not her own story, not a story she was telling herself. It was dark, a comforting darkness, the headlights coming toward them shimmering with a soft firelight glow. A little rain, more mist than rain, collected and was removed from the windshield with one swipe of the blades. The moon looked watery, as if it were reflected in a pond. It wasn't cold, even with the window half-down. The air was sweet. It was nothing like the trip going the other way, which felt as if it had happened long ago.

"I was scared for a minute that maybe Jeanette had been abducted—kidnapped. It was just a flash of fear. Then on the other side of this guy, I saw Dawn and Johnny. She was laughing, had her mouth wide open laughing."

"I bet that was hard, seeing your kids with some strange guy."

"I could hardly stand it, and that's the truth."

"What did you do?"

"Nothing right then. I had Davy with me. I wanted to march up to her, deck the guy holding my little girl's hand, then yank Dawn out of the line and give her holy hell for running off with the kids.

"But that wouldn't have done me any good, so I cooled down. It wouldn't have got me what I needed. I needed to find out where they were living and tell my lawyer so he could get the cops after her. That meant waiting around until they left and following them. My nephew was getting tired and I couldn't make him hang out for God knew how long, so I didn't know what to do. Then I realized, of course, stupid, get Sis to come to the fair and take him home. She hated Dawn's guts almost as much as I did. I knew Sis'd be off work in a little while. That's what I did." He wiped his hand down over his face, hit the steering wheel, made a Volvo in the next lane over swerve a little. "God, but I wanted to murder the both of them."

"Me, too."

"Thanks."

"So your sister showed up—"

"Sis got there in another half hour. Because I had to keep Dawn and them in view, she'd figured to call me to see exactly where I was. Which was, at that moment, at one of those duck shoots, you know, you pay for how many shots you want to take. From the way this dude held that fake rifle I just knew he had to be a hunter. He was even dressed for it: the heavy checked shirt, the cap—"

"Tell me where he is and I'll shoot him for you."

Jake laughed. "You'd only take that chance for a pig."

"Come on. You're as good as a pig."

He laughed again. "I bet that's the biggest compliment I'll ever receive in my life."

"Probably. So go on."

"Sis took Davy, but it was all she could do to keep from going after Dawn. It was hard to keep myself in line, watching them. They didn't stay much longer. There was only one parking area and a lot of people had already left, so I was able to keep them in view and get in my car and pull out right after they piled in theirs. An SUV, yeah, like that damned one in front of us that keeps switching lanes." He nodded toward the black Land Rover, driving as if every other vehicle were holding him up, even though there was very little traffic.

"Then what'd you do?"

"Started to follow them and then wondered what the hell was the use. And what was so strange about the woman finding a new man? Happens all the time. I turned around and went home."

Andi was surprised. "But, then, you didn't find out where they were living."

"I know. Don't ask me why I did what I did."

So Andi didn't. In another mile or two, she saw what was up ahead. "There's Eddie's motel. The Stardust. I never even noticed the sign. Can we stop?"

"Uh-huh." Jake slowed and gauged the turn into the Stardust Motel. "He must be your buddy, the way he got down with the pigs. He was all over that scene—or all over you, but I think the pigs got to him."

Andi slipped down from the truck. When she entered the office, it wasn't Eddie who was sitting with his nose in a magazine, but a woman watching a small television. She was old, probably over sixty, maybe seventy, with a face pitted from a childhood bout with a serious disease. She was wearing a gray cardigan over a flowered dress and dark carpet slippers. She managed to convey the impression that Andi had interrupted her in her own home.

"Where's Eddie?"

"Gone." The woman sat back down in her old rocker, turned toward the television, and crossed her flaccid arms across her chest.

"You mean he's out? See, we were here this morning—"

"Well, he ain't here this night and good riddance." She delivered this news without taking her eyes from the television.

"What happened?"

"Got fired. By yours truly."

"Why?"

The woman turned then and regarded Andi. "You sure ask a lot of questions. How come?" Her narrowed eyes hinted at more good riddance of Andi herself.

"Nothing. I just met him today and he was very helpful."

"Him? Well, he ain't to me. He left the office for must've been a whole hour that I tried to get hold of him. Maybe you was the reason."

Her suggestive smile angered Andi. "Yes, I was. Our truck had trouble with its radiator and Eddie helped out. He even let the driver borrow his car so he could get to the station. So if it's anyone's fault it's ours, not his."

The woman sat with her cigarette close to her mouth and her mouth working as if she meant to nibble the end. She was wearing bright red nail polish, which only made her heavily veined hands look old.

"You the kind always takes the blame if a thing goes wrong?"

The question, so unexpected, blotted out any answer Andi could think of.

"You may have asked him for help, but that don't mean he had to give it." This was hardly said for comfort. "And that was my car, not his, you was using."

Andi said, "You fired him just because of that? You didn't lose any business. We were right there on the other side of the lot with the office in sight. No one came."

The woman's eyes slitted against the smoke of her cigarette. "You just get along now. Your friend must wonder where you are."

Andi stomped out. Like a kid. But she hardly cared.

She swung up into the truck and slammed the door.

"Somethin' wrong?" Jake looked concerned.

"Jake, that woman in there, she fired Eddie! Fired him only because he wasn't in the office when she phoned this morning. I told her Eddie was only helping us out with the radiator parts. And she just sat there smoking and smirking."

Jake gave a chuckle. She felt it kind of moving up from his waist. He said, "She's jealous, is all. That's her problem."

"Jealous? Wherever did you get that?"

"She's how old? In her sixties maybe. I caught a look at her through the window. Then you go waltzing in, a pretty girl, wily and smart. Eddie broke her law because he was helping *you*. Well, dear Lord, you're just bowling men over right and left. Tut-tut." He reached around and pulled a couple of beers out of the cooler. "Be back." He hopped down from the cab and went to the office.

Andi tried to get a view of them, but couldn't, so she just waited.

In another twenty minutes he was back without the beer.

"I told her," he said, after climbing up to his seat, "that I thought she'd maybe want to hire him back—Eddie—since for the reason he'd left his post was because we needed him to help with the truck and that he did, but kept on saying how he had to get back to the office, because Mrs. Orbison—that's her name—was depending on him. 'Eddie really thinks the world of you,' I told her." He smiled and put the truck in reverse and backed out.

"You didn't." She laughed.

"Of course I did. I, too, can be devious if the situation calls for it. "'You know his mom passed long ago,' I said, 'and he kind of looks to you—well, you know what I mean.'"

"Are you saying that poor woman fell for that line?"

They were back on the road again, heading west.

"Oh, yeah. Well, look at her life. Husband dead, kids gone off and never looked back, relations she never sees because they live out east." Jake shrugged and chewed on a biscuit. "Pretty lonesome life, I'd say." He sounded like one who was only too well aware of lonesome lives.

"So you think she really will hire him back?"

Jake turned to her. "Oh, I think so."

"That was really nice of you."

"It was nothing. We had a beer together; it's amazing what a drink with a person will do."

36

They drove the truck back to Klavan's and got there a little before ten o'clock. Jake gave her a ride home in his old car he said came with a can opener, in case you got trapped.

Andi held the piglet as they rolled into the circular drive. Jake refused the offer of food. "But thanks." Andi took the piglet over to the sty, put it in by Hazel, and watched to see nobody stepped on it. Jake drove off, and she went to the house.

Jim and Tom were sitting in the kitchen, smoking and drinking Glenfiddich. They were glad she was back.

Andi took a plate from the sideboard and sat down. She was still hungry after the truck-stop food. She dug a fork into the beans and told them about BigSun.

"Told you that you shouldn't go," said Jim, with some satisfaction.

"Is that all?" she said.

"All what?"

"Just that you're glad you were right about me going?"

Tom and Jim looked at each other.

"Because you weren't right. Going is what needed to be done." She reached for the salad bowl.

Tom shook his head. "You're being kind of self-righteous about it, aren't you?"

"I'd rather not be, but whether I am or not doesn't change any-thing, does it?"

She looked from one to the other.

Jim said, "What do you mean? I don't know what you mean a lot of the time."

"I just mean that if I stopped being self-righteous—and I'm sure I should—would that help the pigs and cattle and sheep down there at BigSun?"

Jim sighed. "There's no talking to you, girl."

Tom said, "What I can't understand is why Klavan let you go."

"It was really up to Jake."

"Jake Cade?" asked Tom.

Andi nodded, aware of a note of disapproval in Tom's voice.

"Listen, don't you go getting tied up to Jake Cade."

"'Tied up'? What do you mean? Why? What's wrong with him? He was perfectly nice to me."

"Harry McKibbon had to run him in on more than one occasion." Tom paused and took a serious drink of his whiskey. "For disturbing the peace. You recall that, don't you, Jim?"

Jim's forehead creased in his attempt to call up the memory. "Vaguely."

Andi said, "What peace did he disturb?"

"In the Two Dogs. Broke up some furniture as I recall."

"There's no peace in the Two Dogs. They're always breaking up furniture in there. Who was he fighting with? I assume he was and ob-viously drinking to boot."

"Never mind. Just take it that man has one awful temper."

"I know." Andi pictured Jake coming into that slaughterhouse where she stood with Warren. "But maybe his temper's justified some-times."

"It's dangerous is what it is." Tom gave his undivided attention to the whiskey for a moment, then tilted back in his chair. "There was a man murdered over in Killdeer. Harry's sure it was Jake Cade shot him, but never could prove it."

"Why does he think Jake did it?"

Tom shrugged. "Don't know. Harry didn't say."

"That's all pretty vague, Tom. So why do you believe it?"

"Good question!" said Jim, largely to his whiskey glass.

Andi wanted to laugh. "You guys are drunk."

"No, not a bit," said Jim, tilting back in his chair. "What were you doing at the pigsty?"

"Nothing much." Andi took her plate to the sink and hoped to get out before this line of questioning drew on.

"I've known you to do a lot of things, but 'nothing much' isn't one of them," said Jim.

Tom pounded his glass on the table, laughing. "Oh, you got that right."

Jim went on. "So will I be getting any surprises when I go out there in the morning?"

Andi sighed. "It's only a pig."

Both of them brought their chairs down fast.

"Ex-*cuse* me?" said Jim, holding his hand behind his ear.

"Yeah. Excuse me, too." Tom copied the gesture except he stabbed his ear with his index finger.

Andi looked at the two of them and shook her head. "A *piglet,* is all, but it's nothing compared to the both of you being funny."

They laughed uproariously and pounded their glasses on the table.

How childish. Well, it just made her job easier. She'd been nervous about the piglet, so at least now she'd told them. "I'm going to bed. See you in the morning."

As she was leaving the kitchen, Tom, sobering up for the moment, looked at her with that level gaze of his, as though he could impart a fact of profound importance. "Your friend Jake Cade: I guess you know he was a pig sticker for years at that very same plant you went to. I guess you don't like that much."

"I guess the pigs didn't either. Good night."

She couldn't sleep. She lay in bed thinking of the cow and its sad eyes, of the pig looking up at the sticker. Her mind burned with such images.

It was no good telling herself to forget it for she knew that she had to remember, but she did not want to. If she lingered over these images too often or too long, she felt they would smother her. Yet she couldn't look away.

But what in God's name could be done about it? Rank comparison showed that Klavan's was not as bad as the slaughter plant—except, of course, BigSun wouldn't be in business were it not for the likes of Klavan.

She had rescued only that piglet. What was that to the hundreds that had been marooned in the pens?

It's always one. She had said this to Jim and Tom. She should follow her own advice. *It's always one.*

She thought about BigSun. All she could come up with was either rescue or dynamite. It was all she could think of.

37

Where'd you find this one?" Dr. Jenner had turned up early while Andi was in the stables feeding the horses. He was looking the piglet over. "Where you found the others?"

Andi frowned. "What others?"

He looked at her and merely raised his eyebrows.

"He's just an orphan I found by the side of the road."

"Was he hitching a ride?"

"Very funny."

After inspecting him, the veterinarian said, "She's not in good shape, but nothing I can't fix. Dehydrated, obviously; could have a virus. You never know what's lying around out there beside U.S. 83, do you?" He closed up his bag. "Anything else? Any Tasmanian devils? Rare red-ruffed lemurs? Australian bilbies?"

Andi cocked her head. "I can't help it if an animal crosses my path."

Dr. Jenner sucked in a lungful of air and looked at the roof as if he were thinking hard. "Some people just let it get to the other side. You, on the other hand, stick out a foot and trip it."

Andi broke out a big smile. "Thanks for coming on such short notice."

"All of your notices are short. Your life isn't really a life; it's an emergency. Bye."

★ ★ ★

Dakota watched Dr. Jenner depart and gave a big snuffling sigh.

"Sometimes I think you're jealous. You must have missed our early morning ride."

Dakota shook his head in wide sweeps.

"What's wrong with your neck?" She unlatched the gate, draped the reins over his head, and Dakota dropped his head as if too weak or tired to keep it lifted.

"Come on; I've got time for a couple of turns around the track before work." She gave the lead a little shake.

Dakota refused to budge. She coaxed, wheedled, implored, inveighed, promised treats. When she looked around she saw they were all staring at her—Odds On, Odds Against, Palimpsest, Nelson, even Sam. "What are you all looking at? I'm not putting on a show here!"

Right on cue, they all looked away. "Oh, for heaven's sakes . . ." She jerked off the bridle and hung it on a peg. "Don't expect to see me anytime soon."

And with those dire words, she left.

They were sharing Jake's thermos of coffee in the farrowing hut. Andi didn't want to meet him in his office because she was keeping her eye on some piglets whose legs had a way of slipping through the grill and getting stuck. They were talking about BigSun.

"What would you do about that place? It's a hellhole."

"Me? Easy. Nothing, which is what anyone with any sense would do."

"I feel as if I've got to do something."

"Listen to me, Andi: this single-handed saving of the whole damned animal world has got to stop. One big reason is that it can't be done, anyway."

"Am I talking about the whole world? Why do people have to exaggerate to make a case?"

"With you, I'm not so sure it *is* an exaggeration. You come on with both guns blazing." He poured the dregs of his coffee between the metal grill and the dirt floor.

Andi made a half-turn away from him. "Oh, that is *so* overstated."

"Yeah, and that's another thing. Even if you could put one out of business, there's always another. A worse one, too."

"It's always one."

"Well, 'one' doesn't do it for me. Listen: that one-day trip we just made, that's not a patch on how far these rigs usually travel, or how many hours it takes for one trip. Seventy-two hours is common. Seventy-two hours for animals without food, going down to Mexico, and you can imagine the rules governing slaughter *there*. There are none. So our trip was damn near a mercy trip if you compare them."

"But this is what happens when you do compare. Things that were dreadful turn out good when you do what you just did. And 'mercy trip'? Let's say we go back to the blood pit and tell the pigs hanging there and passing rivers of blood that this was a mercy trip."

Jake picked up his thermos, said, "I gotta go; I got things to do." He turned and made for the door, slipping on the waste-slick, water-slick metal.

Andi watched him go, feeling that maybe she was leaning on him too hard. But why was he so angry? Her ideas made *everybody* angry.

She reached down and pulled a piglet's leg free of the metal grid. How old were they now? Four weeks, five? In another week they'd be taken from their mother and put in another crate in another hut. The sow had given birth nine or ten times in the last few years and was so weary, she was reaching the end of her usefulness. Andi knew she'd join the other sows on the dead truck or the road to hell-and-gone. She reached in and patted her head. The sow looked up at her wearily. She was positioned lying on her side for the piglets to suckle. Was this the one nearly bright spot for the sows?

Probably not.

38

ndi stood on the wooden walkway that went from front to rear of the sows' hut, watching Dewey Petty drag a sow with a broken pelvis from her crate toward the door. The only way the sow could move herself was by using her front legs to pull herself forward. That wasn't fast enough for Dewey, so he'd put a metal snare around her ear and was dragging her by the chain attached to it. The sow was screaming.

Andi watched this, feeling as if she were floating under a thick sheet of ice, looking up with frozen eyes. It was where she had put herself so that the screams were muffled. She came out of this fugue-like state, knowing she would have to try something.

"Hey, Dewey, where are you going with that old sow?"

"Cull truck."

This was where they tossed the injured hogs, making a mountain of them, flung one atop another. A mountain of death to be picked up and trucked somewhere to be rendered into animal feed or cosmetics or something. *If* hogs were condemned. Too often, they weren't, though they should have been. Too often they were taken to the slaughterhouse; almost all were downers.

"You should see yourself, Dewey. You look like you're going to a dance." She forced a laugh.

"Shut up!" Dewey dropped the chain and the sow collapsed in a trail of her own blood. Some of the hide had been scraped off by the friction of dragging.

The taunt infuriated him. He and all the other workers here could not stand to be seen as weak. But most of them were, as far as Andi was concerned. Maybe the job attracted them for that reason—that they could assert themselves; that they had power. They could show others how manly they were by beating up the hogs. Dewey would go at them with chains and pipes, the same treatment as at the slaughterhouse.

Andi said, "Why, it looks like you and that old sow are—"

"Shut your goddamned mouth! You think you're so damned smart, you do it, then." As he was going out the door, he turned and gave her the finger, and yelled back, "I owe you one, lady!"

She waited until he was out of sight before she went over to the sow. She used the small towel she always carried in her back pocket to wipe the blood from the sow's face. This sow could have no more litters; her system was exhausted. She'd been at it God only knew how many years, litter after litter, always in the crate. That's what had done it to her legs. Now she was useless to Klavan's.

The way the chain pulled on the metal snare had nearly torn the ear off. Andi balled up the towel, now bloody, and pressed it against the ear to stop the hemorrhaging of blood. Her hands were covered in it.

Lady Macbeth, she thought, the blood on her hands so awful that if she dipped one into the sea it would turn the green sea red. *Incarnadine*, that was the word.

No, Andi didn't think she was Lady Macbeth. She wasn't that bad and she wasn't that interesting.

Tired of squatting, she sat back on her heels, the towel by now a clot of blood. There was nothing to wipe her hands with so she wiped them down the legs of her jeans. She unbuttoned her heavy wool shirt, removed it, then took off her T-shirt. Both of them were now stained with blood. She put the wool shirt back on and balled up the T-shirt, which she then put in the towel's place. The bleeding was not so heavy now.

All around her, Andi became aware of the quiet. Two hundred plus sows in their crates, and the quiet was penetrated only by the occasional grunt or small rustling movements of the piglets.

It had started to rain. It beat heavily on the roof.

She would have to move the pig but knew she was too heavy to lift. She looked for something and saw nothing to help her. At one end of the hut there was a shelf and some pegs used for tools and buckets. On one of the pegs hung a jacket and underneath it a thin blanket. She took the blanket back to where the pig lay, thinking it might work as a makeshift harness; it was all there was.

She fitted it around the sow's middle and tied it as tightly as she could. Then she got in front and ran the blanket over her shoulder and pulled and felt the weight move behind her. She looked back to see that the blanket hadn't slipped up to the sow's neck. Satisfied, she turned and pulled again. This time, the weight wasn't nearly so heavy and moved more easily. She pulled it farther.

Andi looked back to see the sow was helping by using her front legs to push her weight. This was what she had been doing before Dewey used the chain and the snare.

Andi smiled. She almost expected the sow to smile back. In this way they got themselves to the door, where the cull truck would be picking up the sows.

At least today there was not a pile of hogs, a little mountain of them. They were lying down, separately, in the mud and the rainwater collected in puddles. It was like a lake of pigs, washed by rain. Some, like Andi's sow, with a broken pelvis, some with broken legs, head injuries, open wounds, running sores. All of them in every manner of distress. One of them, clearly dead, had its front legs stuck up in the air, in rigor. The pig must have been lying here for hours if the rigor was that advanced.

They would all, at the end, be condemned for human consumption. But the ones least injured would still go down the line at the slaughterhouse unless an inspector forbade it, which might or might not happen. The pig with its legs in the air looked to Andi like a drowning child, unsavable. No one would swim that hard or that far.

39

S he got a ride into Kingdom with a woman named Betty Sue, one of the many Andi hadn't even seen until now, that invisible body of workers. Betty Sue dropped her off at the diner.

It was crowded, for once. She asked Norman Black if Kingdom had ever attracted tourists.

"You bet," he said. "May's is one of those destination restaurants."

Andi slid over a menu. "What's that?"

"You are seriously out of the loop. It's a restaurant you travel to that's an end in itself. You said it was the best grilled cheese you'd ever eaten." He smiled. "Hear you helped transport a load of pigs to that slaughterhouse up in Preston." His head was turned to the cake stand on the counter before him. It was a coconut cream cake.

"Does nothing ever happen around here that people don't know about almost immediately?" She closed the menu, finding that she wasn't really hungry. Just thinking about BigSun pretty much ruined her appetite. When May came along, Andi asked for coffee and a Danish.

"We got cherry, raisin, cheese, strawberry—"

Andi stopped her. "Cherry's fine." Did everything in life require a decision?

"It doesn't exactly go together, you know. Slaughterhouses and you. Ever since you came here, I've been trying to figure you out."

May set coffee and a Danish before Andi and said, "Norman, not everybody's a novel." She walked away.

Andi choked a little on her pastry, laughing, and had to take a drink of water. "You know, you've got the imagination, Norman. Say you were to write a novel about one of these factory farms. How would you go about it?"

Norman swirled the dregs in his cup. "Well, I can't see doing it on the inside, say, by messing with the machinery. Only maybe whistle-blowing would work. I guess I'd try that. Nothing very original."

"Or effective. Blow the whistle on who? State agriculture? The USDA inspectors? They let a lot go by without even inspecting it. Or let contaminated meat get stamped. But there are the good ones. Jake told me that one inspector he knew would secretly, *secretly*, take meat out so he could inspect it properly; he couldn't do it when he was on the line because it slowed things down and the guys would get furious. They beat one inspector nearly to death, he said. There's this meat called head meat, pretty clearly not your top cut. It gets really bad, pus-filled, and it still goes through. I think some fast-food chains use that kind for their burgers."

"Remind me never to eat fast food again."

"They don't know they're getting contaminated meat or how it gets that way. The floors in BigSun's were filthy—"

Norman lit up one of his cigarillos. "Tell 'em."

Andi paused, cup halfway to her mouth. "Tell who?"

"The chains." He puffed. "I'd have a character go to the corporate headquarters."

Andi cocked her head. "And?"

"He can take one of those heads in a portable freezer with him." He looked at her apologetically. "He'll be kind of crazy, naturally."

"He'd have to be to get into one of those corporate headquarters."

Norman didn't speak to that. He said, "Maybe he could actually work at a fast-food store. Be a manager or something. He'd be one of the little guys, you know, in this great American saga of the little guy against corporate structure—"

"But it's actually not the corporations doing this; I mean, they don't know about the meat."

"Right. He's trying to get *the fast-food company* to blow the whistle on the slaughter industry. Now, *that's* a twist!"

"But how's he ever going to get into the headquarters?"

"How do I know?" Norman said, irritably. "I'd have to write the damn book first."

A brief silence as each thought about the problem.

Then Andi asked, "Where'd he get the head from?"

Norman shrugged and tapped ash into the dented metal tray. "You're the one that was there, not me."

"Yes, but I didn't see that particular—" She stopped when she saw the Baileys come in, the brothers and their father, Lucas, as thin as a shadow. Andi looked away.

Norman didn't see them and wouldn't have cared, in any event. He was still talking about the cow's head. "How would he get it through security?"

"I don't know. But you've got to work out how he came by the head." She turned in such a way as to shut off any view of the Baileys, leaned her elbow on the counter, her head in her hand. "Go on."

He cleared his throat, scratched his neck. "Thing is this: as far as I can see, there's no way of getting the animals out, so the next thing is to shut down the line. There's your unions, but obviously, they'd only strike because of the hellish conditions *they* had to work under."

To Andi's mind came images of the killing floor: the pig flinging itself out of the scalding tank; another one hanging upside down, eyes seeking, trying to right itself, thrashing to raise itself; another running around the blood pit, bathed in red, screaming. When Andi looked at the drunk and happy party down at the end of the counter, she tried to fit these two experiences together—the carefree drinkers and the stuck and screaming pigs. She couldn't do it. She couldn't even fit herself and Norman into the frame.

"—and you don't look happy, either."

Norman had been speaking and Andi hadn't heard him. "Sorry, I missed that." She knew she could substitute a number of things in place of the pigs. There was any manner of atrocity: genocide in Africa; little children running, screaming, from men with knives and guns.

"Tell you what," said Norman. "There's a woman named Odile Nekoma used to work there. She took pictures. When she was there, they hanged pigs."

"*What?*"

"Yeah. Strung 'em up."

"Dear God, why?"

Norman shrugged.

She started to speak again when she sensed someone standing behind her and an arm shot between herself and Norman to collect the three bottles of Heineken that May had set down while she got glasses.

The arm was Lucas Bailey's, who, in mock-politeness, tipped his hat. "Evenin'."

Norman said, "Hey, Lucas. Do me a favor, won't you? Stop sneaking up behind people."

"I'm only tryin' to get these beers." He touched the brim of his hat again and took his leave. May looked after him and put back the glasses.

Several customers vacated their booths, went to the register, and walked out. Cold air replaced them, along with Sheriff McKibbon, who just then entered. He looked the room over and his eye fell on Andi and then lit on the Baileys. Harry stood there for a moment before he walked along the aisle to the Baileys' booth.

"Stand up, both of you, stand up."

Carl and Junior looked astonished as they worked their way out of the booth.

"Now, Sheriff—" began Carl.

But he didn't finish.

"Shut up," said Harry McKibbon. He swung Junior around and clapped handcuffs on him, then did the same with his brother.

"What the fuck—?"

"And watch your mouth!" said Harry. "You're not to get within a hundred yards of Andi Oliver and that's her sitting not more than ten feet away."

"Now, just a damn minute there," said Lucas. "These boys ain't done one blessed thing for you to arrest 'em. If I remember correctly, we was here at this table *before* this girl walked in—"

Norman set down his coffee and said, "Well, your memory, then, is faulty because she was sitting here beside me when you all arrived."

There were confirming head nods up and down the counter in agreement with Norman's statement.

Andi wondered why Lucas had lied about something so easily checked up on.

"Even if that were so it wouldn't make any difference. You saw her, so you should have left and gone somewhere else. And you knew it. Come on, let's go, boys."

"You takin' these boys to jail? Is that it?"

The sheriff didn't bother with an answer.

"My lawyer'll have 'em out in two shakes, you wait."

Awkwardly and red-faced, the Baileys went through the door of the diner; the sheriff followed.

Lucas pulled money from a vest pocket, threw a bill on the table, and went off muttering aspersions.

Andi always felt clearer and cleaner for being around the sheriff. She swiveled on her stool. "It's nice to have somebody watching out for you, isn't it?" she said to Norman.

"You're not used to that, I take it."

She shook her head.

"I don't think I've ever heard you talk about yourself."

"That's only because there's not much to tell." *That* was quite literally true. "And what there is isn't very interesting."

Norman grinned. "Now, why don't I believe that? I guess because you walked into Kingdom and there's all sorts of things got stirred up. Why'd you decide to stop here anyway? This just doesn't strike me as a very exciting place for an eighteen- or nineteen-year-old."

"Twenty," she corrected him.

"Okay, twenty."

"I'm not looking for excitement."

May was filling the coffee mugs and heard this. "You come to the right place, hon."

Andi smiled, drank her coffee, and slipped off the counter stool. "I've got to get home, Norman. Thanks."

Before he could ask for what, she was out the door.

40

It was a long ride for a cab, but she went to the Kingdom Kabs dispatch office anyway. She didn't want to bother Jim or Tom to come and get her.

She didn't much care for Bub and hoped one of the other drivers would be available, but Bub was the one in the office at that time besides Alma, the dispatcher.

Alma said, "Somebody in here awhile ago lookin' for you." She pushed back her two-way mike.

Andi froze. "Who? When?"

"Name of . . . Wayne, maybe? You recall, Bub? That man lookin' for Andi?"

Bub was reading the paper. "Hell, I don't know. I got too much to do to be filing away names of strangers." He turned a page of the paper. "Oh, yeah . . . I'm not sure he even gave a name. Tall fella, not bad-lookin' if a little hard, you could say."

"When was he here?"

"Well, let's see. Day before yesterday, it was."

"Not longer ago?" Two days would have made it after he'd been to Jim's; *after* he knew where she lived.

"No. I remember because it was the day I took Juney in for a flu shot. It was Tuesday, I recall."

Juney was her boy, a little hellion. Probably she would remember exactly when she took Juney to the doctor.

But why was this man looking for her after he'd already found her? She just stood there until Bub put down his paper and got up. "Okay, Miss America, let's us go." He rolled his pelvis a couple of times in case Andi didn't get it.

Andi didn't want any of it. Bub was a good forty pounds over-weight, mostly belly fat. He was short and Andi would have said he had a pig's eyes except she had too much respect for a pig. She thanked Alma and left with Bub.

After he'd revved up the engine of the cab as if he were in a stock-car race, he turned and said, "How you tonight, pretty girl?"

"Fine." She cut this as short as she could. Anything else he'd take for conversation.

He did anyway. "How's your mule?"

"Donkey."

"Same thing."

She didn't comment.

"Ain't it? Mule, donkey, burro? Four legs and no brains." This he thought extremely witty and laughed and slapped the steering wheel. They were just outside of Kingdom now, heading for the state road.

She said, "I guess that's better than two legs and no brains."

Silence. Then he said, "What's that supposed to mean?"

"You tell me." She turned her face to the unlit fields and the wind making dark ripples in the corn.

"Well, I just asked you, din't I?"

"It means some animals are a lot smarter than some people."

Silence again. Then he said, "If you mean me you better watch your step."

"Really."

"Yeah. You don't want to get on my bad side."

"I thought I already was."

He struggled with this, getting the sense of it. "You're bein' funny, right?"

"Yep."

The rest of the trip was made in blessed silence, or would have been blessed had it not given her awhile to think of the man in the black hat. There was some hideous irony in all of this, that his search somehow mirrored her own, and she couldn't understand this, as if the two of them were interchangeable. This thought even frightened her, for if that were true, what did that make her?

She had made so much of the family she'd invented, those people she'd described when she couldn't steer clear of questions about her family—she'd almost convinced herself they were real.

The lights of the farm shone up ahead, a patch of light in a field of darkness.

"Here y'are," said Bub.

Andi dug into her small purse and handed him the fare. "Keep the change." She walked quickly away from the cab.

It was dinnertime, but she detected no cooking smells. From the office came voices.

Jim had his back to the door, but heard her come in, for he turned, still with the receiver against his ear. He said good-bye, dropped the receiver into the cradle.

Tom was standing by the office window, looking out on darkness.

"What's wrong?" Andi asked. "You're both dead white."

"It's Dakota," said Jim.

Andi stiffened, felt adrenaline squeeze through her. "No. Is he sick?"

"No. Gone."

"Wait," said Tom. "Jim doesn't mean he's dead. Literally, Dakota's gone."

"Where?"

"We don't know. Last time he was seen, Jesus said, was in the field like always. Sam was okay except he was walking around as if he was looking for Dakota. We're thinking it had to be the goddamned Bailey boys."

Andi shook her head. "No. Sam was still there. The Baileys would've taken him."

"Well, maybe it was only one of them."

Again, Andi shook her head. "They're too cowardly to work alone. Someone came through the fields up there and none of you saw anything?"

"We went to Bismarck. There was only Jesus and he would have been busy in the stables."

Andi looked at the floor, then picked up the strong lantern and went out the back door.

Three feet from the tree in the field the hard earth was saturated with hoofprints, Dakota's and Sam's, she assumed. She had started at the tree and was working outward, finding hoofprints less dense and joined by boot or shoe prints. Some would be Jesus's. She and Jesus were the only ones to take the horses out here, so she doubted any were hers as she hadn't been here in at least four days.

Andi was on her knees, the lantern held up or down as her eyes traced the damaged pattern of prints. A small boot: Jesus's? He had small feet. Then there were bigger ones. Tom's or Jim's. No, they hadn't been out here. It was a little island of prints, horse and human, pretty much messed about, only she was almost certain that of the boot prints there were two different sizes.

She gathered up the lantern and walked back to the house.

"There were a lot of prints. I think you should call Jared to see if he'll come and look."

"Jared? Why?"

"He knows prints. I think he'll be able to make something out that's helpful."

Jim shrugged and picked up the phone.

While he was calling, Andi went out to the barn. She looked into Sam's eyes as if to see printed there the mystery of what had happened. She went around the stables checking on all of them, then sat down. She stayed with the horses until she heard a truck rumbling up the drive.

"Dakota," said Jared. "Hell. And your guy didn't see nothing?"

"No."

"Horses aren't stupid. They been known to find a way back."

If only humans could, she thought. She said, "I wish you'd look at the prints out there."

"Well, sure. But I kind of doubt I'll be all that much help."

Andi smiled faintly, for his tone said he bet he'd be a hell of a lot of help; after all, he was a first-rate farrier, and there weren't too many of them around.

She picked up the lantern. "By daylight I was afraid they might be blown away."

As they walked, she wondered if that's what had happened to her. All of her prints had been blown away. Nothing was so deeply embedded that it couldn't be blown away in an instant.

She held the lantern as Jared directed, a cold wind now pulling at their jackets. He was on the ground squinting over the particular patch of cross-hatched boot prints. "There's two different sizes of boot prints here, you probably noticed."

"I did."

"One's smaller; the other's your average size. The bigger boot looks like it's over the smaller one. So that it looks like the bigger came after."

"After Jesus. I'm pretty sure the smaller ones are his." She got down beside Jared, holding the lantern up. "Do you see more than two sets of boot prints?"

"Just the two."

"What about hoofprints? I can't tell if there were any more than Dakota's and Sam's. Sometimes wild horses come through here but I've never known them to get this close."

"Well, I can sure tell you these prints"—he rubbed the dirt around—"aren't one of Jim's horses, easy. This hoof's not shod; it's bare. All of Jim's wear shoes. You can see here where the wall is beginning to wear, and the water line, that ain't giving enough support. Yeah, the hoof's bare, but it shouldn't be."

"So we've got two sets of animal prints and two sets of human. Boots."

"You think it was Lucas Bailey?" Jared shook his head. "That horse he rides, I've worked on. It's got shoes."

"Jim thinks it was the boys, but I don't because they didn't take Sam."

"Yeah, I do remember they took Sam that night. Pure meanness, that was. I can't account for their horses."

"Anyway, I don't think the dad would bother to do something like horse thieving."

"You think he's not low enough?"

"Oh, he's low enough. I just don't think he'd go to the trouble. He's one of those people who gets off on just trying to make you *think* he's going to do something."

Jared hunched his shoulders against another chill wind. "Maybe it's just a plain horse thief."

"How many horses around Kingdom get stolen?"

"Not many, but it's not an unheard-of crime." Jared had risen and dusted off his pants. He said, "That other boot print, size ten or eleven. There's a lot of it, and it makes me think there was ruckus."

"What do you mean?"

"A fight, which would happen, wouldn't it, if the horse is resisting? And he would have been, I bet." Jared found a cigarette in a crumpled pack, clicked his lighter open, and lit it. He shoved the pack toward Andi, who declined. "But I tend to agree with you, that it's something more personal than your regular horse thief."

Dewey. He'd told her he'd get back at her. Dewey was a little squirt of a guy who, like so many short men, thought an attitude would make him taller.

She must have said it aloud, for Jared asked if she meant Dewey Petty.

Andi nodded. "He didn't like something I did at Klavan's and said he owed me one. Stuck his middle finger in the air as he was leaving. A really original mind."

"Yeah." Jared chuckled. "Know what you mean. I know Dewey Petty. He's a no-account SOB. Workin' in that place I think dulls your feelings so you can look at all those animals and know what's in store for them and go on workin' as if nothin's wrong." He took a drag on his cigarette, which had been burning down to ash.

"But I hardly know him and I wouldn't think he'd know about out here." She swept her arm to take in the land.

"What're you thinking of doing?"

"I don't know."

"Some people around here, well, you gotta be careful."

"Thanks. Thanks for coming out here at night; I really appreciate it."

"Oh, that's all right." Jared took his hat off, wiped his arm over his forehead, readjusted his hat. "I'm glad to be of help. All them pigs at Klavan's: they were not dealt a fair hand. It's nice having someone trying to even the score."

Andi felt grateful for his saying this.

They walked back to the house, Andi's hands shoved deep in her pockets. "You know where Dewey lives?" she asked Jared.

"The Petty place? Yeah. He lives out this way, somewheres. Lives with his uncle. It's rumored the mother ran off with a fireplace-insert salesman and the husband followed after them and neither's been heard from since."

"Fireplace insert. What's that?"

"Like a cast-iron stove."

"Where out here do they live?"

"I don't know the address. If you find it, I'd think it would be better not to go alone, if that's what you're thinking of doing."

"I'm not." She was.

They were by his truck now. It smelled permanently of horse, she imagined.

"You say good-bye to them for me. I got to get back to a shoeing job."

"I will. Thanks, Jared."

He nodded and started up an engine that didn't want to and that had to choke itself into action. Jared waved as he went down the drive.

Andi looked after him, frowning in thought. She went through the side door where Jim and Tom were sitting in front of the fire, legs stretched out. They were still tossing around notions and hadn't hit on one they liked yet. At least that's what they said. Their only good idea was to call Harry McKibbon. They told her this.

"He's coming over tonight."

"That's good," said Andi. "But I'm surprised he's got time to investigate a horse theft. Why doesn't he have that deputy do it?"

"Leroy's dumb."

Andi had the phone book out and was turning pages. There were several Pettys and she didn't know the uncle's name. If he was the brother of the disappeared father, then his name would be Petty, too. But there weren't many who lived out this way. Beulah Road. There was one Petty there named Drew. It was worth a shot. She'd been on that road; it was only a mile south.

"Can I borrow the car?"

"For what?" said Jim, pouring another finger of bourbon into Tom's glass.

"To go talk to someone about Dakota." Why hadn't she given more thought to this? Probably because she was too upset to think. She was raging inside, but held on to a cool exterior.

Jim said, "Well, wait and talk to Harry McKibbon."

"The both of you are doing that. I thought I'd go to see Jake."

Jim shook his head. "Now, Andi, I don't think that's too good an idea. Nor do I see how he can help."

"Because he's smart. And he knows what goes on."

"You never told us what Jared said."

She told them.

"Well, hon, I think you might stay here and tell the sheriff about that."

"So I can't borrow the car?"

Tom's legs were stretched out, his feet on the fireplace fender. "You learned to drive, did you?"

Hands on hips, Andi glared.

"Then I guess I'll go for a walk." It was only a mile; given she'd walked hundreds and hundreds of them, that was nothing. "I'll be back to talk to the sheriff."

Upstairs, she put on better shoes for walking, looked at herself in the mirror over her dresser, wondered why she was looking at herself, then reached into her bedside table and got her gun.

41

She passed sunflowers that looked silvery and alien in the darkness. Gathered there, they might have been watching her. The night sky seemed to be full of the moon, the stars pushed off to one side. And Beulah Road was right up ahead and there was a house at the crossroads. She could see all the lights, if not the shape of it. It turned out to be quite small and very old—a frame house, white-washed. Or, in this night, moon-washed. A mailbox made of a metal tube pocked with rust stood by the road. The house was a good way back from it. There was a narrow gravel and cinder path to the porch.

From somewhere close came the sound of wind chimes which she located at the end of the porch. She did not immediately go to the door; instead, she went around back, keeping herself in shadow, which wasn't hard, for the place was full of shadows. She saw the barn and started toward it, but then turned back.

She walked around and up to the front door and knocked and heard the wind chimes again. There was a deep silence until the door was opened and an elderly man, thin and spare, squinted into the dark.

"Yes?"

"My name's Andi Oliver. I work with Dewey at Klavan's. I was wondering if he's here."

"He's here. What did you say your name was?"

She told him.

"Come on in." He held the door wide. "I'm Dewey's uncle; Uncle Drew, folks call me, as if it's my only claim to fame, being an uncle."

Andi smiled. "Thank you."

The house smelled of apples and age. It was very clean and orderly, probably owing to the care of the uncle.

"Come on back to the kitchen."

She followed him into another tidy room, painted a weak shade of yellow, with a yellow-checkered oilcloth-covered table and two yellow chairs. Fussily, he removed newspapers from one of them and swiped the seat with a dish towel.

"I'm having tea. Would you like a cup?"

He wasn't eager, apparently, to find Dewey.

She thought it would be a little mean to refuse. For she had the idea that Uncle Drew didn't often get to play host. "That would be really nice."

He talked while he opened one of the cherry cabinets and clattered down a cup and saucer. "You work at Klavan's, too? Yeah, Dewey's been there a good while. There's lots of Pettys worked there." He set the cup and saucer before her. The floral print of hers was different from the one already on the table. She couldn't remember the last time she'd seen a saucer. It was all mugs now.

She had a flash of memory. People around a table in a garden or on a lawn. It must have been summer, for no one wore a coat. They were drinking tea in fragile cups. She sat very still, so still she might have been holding a house of gauze that a careless breath could topple. Then it was gone—house and teacups—and she was left to wonder who those people were. Had they been family? Had they been real? Why here and now?

She looked at Uncle Drew Petty, who was carefully tilting the teapot over her cup, pouring through a little strainer, and then wiping the spout, as if it were a Communion cup. He pushed the sugar bowl toward her and sat down and picked up his own cup.

He seemed to expect nothing of her or of himself. After a minute or two of silence he said, "Dewey's out in the barn. You want me to go get him?"

She smiled. It was as if Dewey were an afterthought and not why she had come. Why she had come was tea. "Oh, that's okay. I'll just go on out to the barn."

He nodded. "He's with a new horse he just got." He drank his tea.

"Oh? Where did he get it?"

"Over from Tompkins's feed store, he said. But I can't say where they'd have a horse around there. Funny to me Tompkins'd even sell feed, as he don't much care for animals." He set his cup carefully in his saucer.

"That *is* funny."

Uncle Drew sat back and clasped his hands behind his neck. "He went kinda crazy in the head after his wife up and left."

"It seems to me a lot of wives run off around here."

Uncle Drew frowned a little and scuffed his cheek with his hand, as if polishing it. "That's so." He dropped his hand.

Andi said, "Well, I'll go out to the barn now. Thanks for the tea, Uncle Drew."

The horse was a chestnut bay and quite beautiful, more elegant than Dakota, and too elegant for Dewey.

He'd been wiping her flank and jumped when he caught sight of Andi. "What the holy hell you doin' around here?"

"Looking for a horse."

Dewey snapped the rag he was holding. "What horse?"

"A black one. He's disappeared from the range out behind the farm. We can't figure out how he could have gotten away."

Dewey slapped the rag over his shoulder. "I get it. You think I stole him."

"No, I don't." At least not now. "I'm just asking everyone around if they might have seen him."

"Well, I ain't." Dewey returned to rubbing down the bay.

"He's really beautiful, your horse."

Dewey stepped back as if he hadn't noticed until Andi mentioned it. "Yeah, he is. Got him over at Tompkins's place."

"Your uncle Drew said he was surprised Tompkins had a horse because he didn't like animals."

"Uncle Drew been shootin' off his mouth again?"

"No. I can't imagine him shooting off his mouth, ever. He's a calming sort of person."

"He's all right. You talk like you know him."

"I feel like he reminds me of someone." But that wasn't it. It wasn't just the uncle, it was an entire aggregation of things. "I guess . . . is that your only horse?"

"Nope. I got another. Now, you just wait a minute. You think maybe I got *yours* hid away somewheres."

"It was just an idle question."

"Yeah. One thing about you I know is you never ask idle questions. Any question you ask, it has fifteen different questions layered on."

"Well, I could stand here and peel the layers one by one, but I've got to get back. Thanks."

Dewey nodded and turned again to his horse.

Andi walked back to the kitchen where Uncle Drew was still sitting with his cup and saucer. The teapot had been replaced by a thick white pitcher. And there was a second cup and saucer, the cup turned over in the saucer, waiting to be put to use.

"Want some cocoa? I just heatèd it up. I've got marshmallows, too."

Again Andi was taken with Uncle Drew's solicitude and didn't want simply to leave him there with his pitcher of cocoa unshared.

"Thank you. I love cocoa with marshmallows." She sat down across from him as he turned over the cup and poured from the pitcher.

He said, "Now, you just go ahead with the marshmallows. I only like one, but a lot of people prefer two or even three."

Andi piled in two.

"Did you find Dewey?"

As if in the sprawling landscape, Dewey might have proved too distant to pin down or even been rendered invisible. "He was in the barn, like you said."

Uncle Drew nodded emphatically. "Thought he might be." He sipped his cocoa.

"This is really good cocoa," she said, with a marshmallow rim over her lip. She wiped it away with one of the paper napkins neatly stacked on the table.

"Glad you like it." He was patting his pockets like someone searching for cigarettes, and, finding none, wasn't bothered by the lack. "Did you find out what you wanted to?"

"No, I didn't."

"Oh. That's too bad."

"You see, a horse of ours is missing. I'm just going around asking people if they've seen it. His name's Dakota."

"Well, now, I'm sorry. Did he run off or was he stole?"

"We think he was taken."

"Bad business that. Bad business. Why would someone take him?"

"Revenge."

Uncle Drew didn't seem to think this an odd answer, rather that this might be something one would expect. He took it in, thought about it. "Of course, that would likely be somebody you know. You can't know too many people that'd have it in for you. There could be someone you didn't *know* you'd given cause to get back at you."

"I didn't think of that, really." That was true. Had she offended someone and not known it? She shook her head. "If what I did made them mad enough to walk onto somebody's property and steal an animal—" She stopped. She was back to the Baileys again, and this time with herself in the wrong. She *had* taken Sam from the Bailey place. "If that happened, I surely would remember it, don't you think?"

"Yeah, I reckon. Only you're not takin' into account the person might just be plum crazy, blowing up some little thing to huge proportions."

Andi rested her elbows on the table and, chin in hands, looked over at him. He was really a very clear thinker. And it seemed to go with his meticulous attention to the minutiae of life—the cups and saucers, the pitcher, marshmallows neat on a little plate. And the spotless kitchen.

"Thing is," he went on, "we go rushing around and miss a good half of the things in our path. So maybe there's somebody's shoes you stepped on and didn't know it. Then—" He brushed something from his vest, imaginary ash from an imaginary cigarette, perhaps. "Then there's your practical joker with malicious intent."

He seemed to be chewing something Andi hadn't observed him putting into his mouth. Tobacco? Gum? Air?

"Then o' course there's your kidnapper."

"But—we're not rich."

"It ain't only money, neither." He spoke as one who'd had a wide experience in hostage negotiating. "There's lots of reasons for kidnapping."

A clock chimed somewhere in the front of the house. It was a delicate music, and suited him. Andi looked at her watch. She'd been gone more than an hour. "Oh, dear, I really have to go. There's company coming."

"Don't hurry yourself. They'll wait awhile."

Andi was up, drinking down the rest of her cocoa. "I know people say this just to be saying something, but you really have been helpful, Uncle Drew. I'd like to come back sometime and talk some more."

He was up and moving slowly toward the front of the house. "Well, I'm glad I could be of use."

They walked through the living room, and he held the front door open for her. "I sure do hope you get your horse back. You know there's lots of wild horses around and they like to pick up the domestic ones and all run off."

This image struck her as comical and poignant together.

Uncle Drew continued, "It ain't a bad life for a horse, running wild. And if it's so, you'll see him again. So just watch careful what runs by you."

She put out her hand. "I'll be watching."

They shook hands and he shut the door.

She looked at the shut door and felt sad.

42

The sheriff's car was parked in the driveway, and she was glad she hadn't missed him. She went in through the kitchen and was sorry not to see him at the table there, relaxed and drinking coffee.

Voices were coming from the office, where she'd left Jim and Tom earlier.

"Andi," Jim said, "where've you been?"

"I'm sorry. I went to see someone who might know something about Dakota. Hello, Sheriff."

"I'm sorry about Dakota."

She nodded and leaned against the wall, by the gun rack, as if she wanted to have one handy in case trouble came.

Harry McKibbon said, "We don't get many horses go missing. Leaving out all the personal motivations—"

"You mean like the Baileys," she said.

"Right. But apart from them, Dakota could have been taken to sell or even to stud, but you don't have his pedigree."

Tom said, "He's from one of those pee farms; that's what they're called. PMU farms. This one's up north, right along the Canadian border. Foals, if they're male, they go to the slaughterhouse. They're useless to them. It's that hormone-replacement drug made from mares' urine. I know because my wife used to take it before we all knew how the stuff was made. Terrible to treat a horse that way just so a middle-aged woman can stop a hot flash. That's what I told her." He smiled. "She asked me if I ever had a hot flash." The smile broadened, then faded, as he remembered.

Harry waited a little, and finding Tom was through talking, went on. "Thing is, to take the chance of stealing him right out of the field, the motivation must have been strong."

Andi said, "Dakota's a good runner. But I think hurting us is the real motive."

"Jim says you don't think it was the Bailey brothers. Anyway, they're cooling their heels in a cell."

"Besides, there were only two sets of boot prints and one of them must have been Jesus's. Jared came out and looked at the area around the tree. The scuff marks he was certain about. And more than certain one pair of hoofprints was from an unshod horse. So not one of Jim's."

Harry said, "I think the first person to look hard at is Lucas Bailey. Assuming somebody did take the horse, with him it'd be payback for you stealing his donkey."

"Allegedly stealing," Andi said.

"Allegedly, right. Except for Lucas there's no 'allegedly' about it. Whether you did or didn't, in fact, he's sure you did."

"Well, I disagree," said Tom, "that it was Lucas. Hell, yeah, he'd have reason, but you're leaving out the kind of man Bailey is. In the first place, he's bone-lazy; second place, he doesn't plot, probably because of what's in first place. He waits for things to come his way because he won't go out of his way. He might instead send the boys to do it, whatever it is.

"Anyway, what would he do with Dakota after he'd taken him? He sure as hell wouldn't want the expense of another horse. So he'd sell him, only how? Not around here, that's certain. People would know about Dakota being hijacked, so he'd have to sell him at auction somewhere else.

"Now, all that's too damned much *trouble* for Lucas Bailey. And he isn't the kind of person to wait and wait and then take action. He'd've done something before now. I mean, besides harassing Andi, which he sure enjoys doing. As to the boys, I agree: they'd not do anything except together. They're cowards. Any man that'd stop a woman on the road is a double-dyed coward, as far as I'm concerned.

"And kidnapping? In spite of Dakota's being a great little horse, he's not Seabiscuit or Nashua or one of them. At least not yet. So how many thousands of dollars would Jim pay to get Dakota back? No, this thing wasn't done for money. And it's not like a crime of opportunity. This wasn't like someone passing a mistreated donkey and taking it—"

"Allegedly," said Andi. She'd never heard Tom Rio talk at such length. And she agreed with every word.

Tom just gave her a look. "It surely wasn't someone strolling around out there in the middle of nowhere looking for a place to have a picnic. This was definitely premeditated."

"It couldn't have been a couple of schoolkids?" said Jim.

"I guess that's possible," Harry said. "It just doesn't seem probable."

"Who are we left with if it's not the Baileys?"

"We're assuming too much," Tom said. "It's not Lucas or his kids, I agree. But I still think it's premeditated."

Just then, as if on cue, the phone rang. Jim picked it up, said, "Yeah? Hello."

The men were all smoking and Andi looked up at the canopy of smoke that had formed over them.

The chair Jim had started to lean back on he now brought thudding forward. "What?" He listened, receiver pressed tight to his ear, but the call must have gone cold because he pulled it away and looked at it as if the voice might still be hidden inside. "He hung up."

"Who?" Harry and Tom asked at the same time.

Jim stared at them. "It was premeditated, all right. That was the one who took Dakota."

43

They certainly didn't all start talking at once. There was an anxious silence.

Finally, Harry said, "Jim?"

"The guy who took Dakota. He sounded real pleased with himself." Jim stopped, shaking his head.

"What does he want?" asked Tom.

Jim frowned. "Not much, when it comes to the money. Five hundred's what he's asking for. But I don't think the ransom's the point. I think the delivery is." He looked at Andi, who frowned.

"What do you mean?" Harry said.

"He wants Andi to bring it."

Her hand fell away from a rifle stock. *"Me?"* Then she wondered how she could have been so unerringly stupid. He should have been the first person she suspected and he hadn't come into their theorizing at all. There was no question as to the danger. He was brash about it. He could turn up on people's doorsteps, turn up out of nowhere, no bother about hiding his face, defying anyone to challenge him.

"And Dakota?"

"We'll get him back when the exchange is made."

"What will happen otherwise?" said Andi.

"He'll shoot Dakota. Or drive him off."

Andi thought, ludicrously, of Uncle Drew's comment about wild horses.

"But who the hell *is* it?" Harry asked.

Jim shook his head. "Name's Waylans."

Like Wayne, thought Andi. Alma at Kingdom Kabs had said that.

"Who is he?" He seemed to be asking Andi.

Andi didn't answer. Fear shut down her voice. She cleared her throat. It was like starting a stalled engine. "Three days ago, that's the first time I ever saw him. He came here; remember the one I told you about?" Her glance took in all three of them.

"The stalker," said Harry.

She nodded.

Jim sat forward, eyes intent upon her. "What stalker? You never said anything about a stalker. You mean you knew him?"

"No. I never actually *saw* him before." Weren't they *listening*? She felt like shaking all of them into the same awful wakefulness she inhabited. "I didn't say anything because it wouldn't have done any good. There's nothing you or Tom could have done. The man's like a ghost."

"Where's this ransom to be delivered?" Harry asked Jim.

"He never said. He told me I'd hear from him again."

"That's to make you nervous. Let it sink in, let you try and bring sense to something with no sense to it." Harry, who'd been leaning against the desk, moved and sank into a club chair beside it.

Jim said, "I can get the money easy enough. That's no problem."

Andi heard an utter lack of blame in his voice. The lack of ambivalence, the lack of question. She had brought the trouble with her; all of it was a part of her baggage, just as Sam had been.

"So what do we do, then?" asked Jim.

"What he says," said Andi. "Exactly what he says."

"You? There's no way you're taking that money to him."

Andi was silent, turned on the window seat looking across to the barn, trying to make out its shape in the dark.

"One of us'll go, me or Tom," said Jim.

Andi turned back and said, "That won't work. It's me that's got to be there. I'm the whole *point*. Not that I find that particularly flattering."

Harry said, "I'm afraid she's right." He sounded glum. He sat, bent over, studying his shoes, as if he felt ashamed, him being the law, that he couldn't come up with some plan that would not endanger her.

Jim said, "Well, that's it, then." He let his hands drop to his thighs. "We'll just have to wait and see if he'll let the horse go."

"No," said Andi. "We don't wait and see. He'll kill that horse in the blink of an eye. And who's to say but that he might take one of the others if he doesn't get what he wants?"

"We don't *know* what he wants," said Jim.

"Yes, we do: he wants Andi to deliver the money," said Tom.

"I have no memory of this man. None. I have no idea why he's following me."

Harry said, "It sounds as if the stalking is an end in itself. He's had plenty of opportunity to get at you, but he hasn't, so maybe the object is to keep you afraid.

"Except this time," Harry went on, "this time he's doing something different. Why?" He stood up. "I've got to get back. When he calls—and I bet he waits for a day or two—I want to know. I want to know where he wants this exchange to be made. My guess is somewhere open, big, and flat, without much cover for surveillance."

"Then you can't," said Andi. "Which is good because he'd know if you were watching."

"I said without much cover. Not without any."

Andi sighed. "Look, I appreciate—"

"No, you don't," said Harry, walking right up to her, getting in her face. "You can't appreciate what you don't understand and there's a lot to this you don't. It looks straightforward to you, doesn't it? It isn't. There's a hundred things that could backfire; you have no idea. And as we don't know why this guy is doing this—it sure isn't for five hundred bucks—we have even less control, but what little we do have I'm taking advantage of, and you're *not* going out into this thing on your own. Understand?"

"No. *You* don't understand."

Harry swore under his breath. "I don't want you going off half-cocked, hear? I want you to promise you won't."

She sighed. If it made him feel better. "Okay."

"You just remember that, Andi. Good night, then. Jim. Tom." He headed out.

The three sat there for a moment, until Andi said, "Where's he staying? Where could he keep a horse without attracting attention?"

"You said he came in a car. Maybe he's sleeping in that."

"A truck." Andi frowned. "But the horse—"

"It could be tethered, couldn't it?"

They sat there together, the three of them, discussing the likelihood of harm coming to Andi. The men agreed that she was probably right; if the man wanted to harm her, he would already have done so.

"What he wants is information; he wants to know something. He's not going to shoot me. And if he wanted to kidnap me, well, he could've done that already."

Tom finally rose, saying, "I'll head on home." He shook his head. "Bad business." He put his hand on Andi's shoulder. "Child, you live a life would knock the stilts out from under most of us." He smiled at her. " 'Night."

Tom's smile was always comforting.

"Good night, Tom."

After he left, Jim crossed his arms and declared he was sitting up awhile. "Just in case. You go on to bed."

"Thanks, Jim. But he won't come around."

"Probably. Go to bed."

Andi figured since this Waylans had reason to keep the horse alive and no reason to kill him, then Dakota was okay, at least physically. How much animals could suffer from displacement and being in the hands of a stranger, she didn't know. The stories she'd read about remarkable journeys to get home certainly suggested an animal knew where home wasn't.

She leaned up, punched her pillow a few times, lay back down.

Where in hell was he, this man who was so driven to follow her? He could not be too far. He had that truck, but no horse box, at least he hadn't when she saw him. Why had he come to see her that day? Had he wanted her to know what he looked like? Or had he wanted her to know he knew her story about her past was a lie, by pretending he was searching for his girl? Alice: had she known someone by that name? It was a kind of torture, which was exactly what he meant it to be.

Had he said anything at all that day on the porch that would serve as a clue to finding him right now, this minute? And just as important, had he *meant* something he had said as a clue?

He'd found her several times, and that he hadn't actually confronted her on those occasions was puzzling.

She covered her eyes with her forearm as if to help herself to more of the dark.

He probably figured the more he talked about nothing, the more fearful she'd get about something. There was something very scary about an evil person engaging in talk about nothing: weather, the country, houses, barns—

Barns.

The Custis farm, standing there empty. That had been the one he'd been talking about.

Andi swung her legs out of bed, stood, and moved to the window. It was a mile and a half away driving; crossing the fields it would be less. She might have been able to glimpse it had the Custis family been there, for there would be lights. But over in that direction, it was all dead dark.

There were two barns. One would certainly hold a truck, if need be, and the other, a horse. No one would think anything of a vehicle going or coming. Probably even if they knew the family, they'd think it was one or the other of them. But people around here didn't pay much attention to their neighbors because neighbors were so distant.

She threw on her flannel robe and opened the door to go down and phone the sheriff. Then she remembered what he had said:

"*I don't want you going off half-cocked. You've got to promise . . .*"

She had promised, since he apparently put stock in such things, and even more absurdly thought she did, too.

No, Harry McKibbon would take this in hand and go to the Custis farm, and end up with nothing except maybe a dead horse. The man after her was smart enough to evade police; if there was a hint of police presence on that property, he would have some story at hand, or else he'd be gone.

"I don't want you going off half-cocked . . ."

Why not? The whole world was half-cocked.

Andi lay down again, tired with the effort of thinking about this Waylans and what he could possibly want of her. Assuming he wasn't after her just for the fun of it, then what he wanted must be awfully important to him, if it meant keeping tabs on her for more than a year.

She hated having to deal with him at a time like this, when Klavan's and BigSun were uppermost in her mind.

Did they stop the killing come five or six o'clock? Did the men on the line clock out then? Did they know what was happening to them, how such bloody killing made them thoughtless, even casual, by its sheer numbers?

But maybe that was the one possibility, the one hope: that they weren't comfortable at all with it. Then she felt stupid. It was their job. They had to earn a living, and this was the living, bad as it was. Comfort or no.

She imagined dramatic scenarios. Fire bloomed in her mind, fire following a huge explosion, not only the slaughterhouse, but the holding pens, the fences, the offices—all going up in flames. Or she imagined herself like the border patrol, stopping every rig transporting farm animals, stopping them at gunpoint . . .

She pulled out the drawer of the bedside table and got the gun. She took out the cartridges, sighted along the barrel. Then she reloaded it and returned it to the drawer. What did she think she was doing?

Maybe he was waiting for her to lead him to lost treasure. Yes, she was the last of them in the Gang of Fools who had held up banks and jewelry stores, and she had stashed the money or the diamonds some-where; he couldn't kill her until she led him to it.

Then it would be showdown time where they'd meet on some dirt road or other dusty venue and—Pow! After watching his blood pool beneath him . . .

She yawned. God, would she never grow up? What was wrong with her? Hidden treasure, money, jewels. Or a safe cracked. Maybe only she had the number. A code only she could break—

Andi sat up. That must be it. It must be.

It was the reason he kept on following her.

He wanted her memory.

44

They watched her stride across the gravel drive and head toward the field and sensed something bad. What?

The moon was low and for the moments she was silhouetted against it, it was hard to tell them apart, she with her moon-colored hair and pale skin.

Odds On and Odds Against were hanging their heads over each side of the empty stall, sometimes looking in and sometimes looking out, wondering where that other one was that used to be here, each expecting the other to explain.

Hazel looked up from a midnight snack at the trough and watched her walk across the courtyard. Ruminatively, she chewed and followed her progress to the field. What? she wondered, and made a deep sound in her throat, bringing the others over to join her. They made a fat cluster against the fence, all thinking, what?

Andi looked around at the house, the barn, the pigsty, and felt she was being watched. She burrowed a little more deeply into her jacket. The air was so clear and cold it was hard.

Each time Andi told her story, she would embellish it, adorn it with more detail. Indeed, she had entered into a fantasy so greatly detailed she was beginning to believe in the Oliviers herself and their power to save one another and that they would save her if they knew of her predicament.

But the basic storyline remained the same—the brothers; the sister; even the dog, Jules—they all turned up every time she told it. It was a comfort, the constancy of the Oliviers, the unchanging character of their house and gardens. And that house, those gardens, were doubly imaginary, for the setting was not original at all, as she'd borrowed it from a film.

Thus in what she now had to think of as her real past—the past she couldn't remember—this man must have figured. Perhaps not as relative or friend or even foe, but as someone to whom she was important because she knew the combination to the safe (to put it one way) whose contents he wanted.

Over the past eighteen months—or even longer, how was she to know?—he had found out where she was and gone there. He had gone to where she was, but how did he know when she left one job and one town and went on to another? Again, her coworkers, after she'd left. Andi always gave notice.

What in heaven's name did she know? Had she actually known *him*? Could it have been something she witnessed? Some crime?

Or was it the other way around and he had witnessed her in a crime? And that went right on back to Harry Wine: she'd considered before that this man had been a friend of Harry Wine, and that only brought her back around to the question—if the man following her wanted to avenge his friend, why not do it a year ago?

But if he wanted something from her, if he was waiting for her to remember, would that explain his presence on the porch that day? Perhaps he was tired of waiting for her to remember on her own, and he had presented himself to jog her memory, thinking that seeing him in the flesh would give her memory a jolt.

Only it hadn't, and now what was he planning?

As she walked through the field she thought it must be true. This is the way he had come, walking or on horseback. Another horse could have helped make that blur of hoofprints. Yes, this was the way. It was all so logical, the more she thought about it, to hole up at the Custis place, Dakota out in the barn, and to sleep in the barn or the house.

Was she playing into his hands? Was she making it easier for him? No, she didn't think so, for he wanted a meeting at his bidding, not hers. That might be important. He had to be the one in control.

Andi walked for another fifteen minutes, with only the moon for light. The night was as black as the gun in her pocket.

Then she saw the Custis farm. No light came from it—lantern light, candlelight—but that told her nothing. The house was tall and narrow, so tall it might have stood on stilts. It was one of those houses kids loved to pretend was haunted. Maybe it was. Maybe that was why the family had left.

Ridiculous. It was just a fantasy to take her mind off something worse. She would welcome a ghost, or two. She felt, even though this meeting would be one-on-one, outnumbered.

She had brought a flashlight, but although it gave off only a pencil-thin beam, she was afraid to use it. There was the house to her right, two barns to her left, and between them spikes of Indian grass, foxtail barley, and Junegrass almost covering the path and the unkempt dirt yard.

Andi didn't know what to do at this point, so she sat down in the unshorn grass and waited for a sound, a movement, an idea. Minutes ticked over. She lowered her head and wondered what she thought she was doing here in this abandoned place with a loaded gun. Did she really think she could shoot him if he didn't give up Dakota?

Yes, she could.

A threshing sound came from the nearest barn and she jerked her head up. Nothing outside moved. The sound of bales of hay or boxes or boards being moved around came from inside the other barn. Andi took the gun from her pocket. She rose and as quietly as she could moved toward the barn. Along the way, there was a hedge high enough to conceal her and she had just crouched behind it when she heard a nickering sound and froze. What she felt was a combination of relief and fear—there were horses, but that meant he must be close by.

Or not. It was possible he kept Dakota here, but he himself was elsewhere. Not only possible, but even probable. After all, the problem he would have was what to do with the horse, not himself. He could easily keep Dakota fed and watered for a day without putting in an appearance afterward.

Andi lowered the gun to her side, but still held it as she neared the barn door, which was open, most likely because it couldn't be closed. Holding the gun in both hands and pointed down to the ground, she stepped inside.

It was dark, nearly black, and the horse melted into it.

She knew it was Dakota.

Now she thumbed on the little flashlight and played the beam over his face. He whinnied and backed away.

"Dakota, it's me," she whispered. "It's me. Calm down." She moved over to the stall; there were three stalls, each fitted with a Dutch door that had begun to splinter and warp with age and lack of care. She rubbed his nose when he finally came close enough for her to do so. She looked around. There was enough water, enough hay. But it badly needed mucking out. She was looking for something she could use to ride the horse home.

On a hook fastened to one of the posts was an old bridle; it looked as if it had been there for years. It would do.

As she took it down she heard a vehicle moving very slowly up the road. There were no headlights; that must be the reason for the tentative movement and also the reason she froze, bridle in hand. The car or truck could only belong to the man who had taken Dakota; why would anyone else have to cut his headlights?

The truck stopped. Then there was a silence. The silence was worse than the sound preceding it. A door slammed.

Andi stood motionless between the post and the side of the stall, and then finally shook off the paralysis and lowered herself by the stall. She pulled out the .38.

Now the footsteps that had been coming toward them receded and a door opened and a spectral light washed over the dirt floor. He had returned to the vehicle and was using the headlights for illumination. The light spread like an apron, but didn't reach the horse stall or her.

Holding the gun in both hands, one anchoring the other, she slowly rose. "Stop right there." She was surprised that her voice was anything but quivering reeds.

The dark shape took another step and she nicked the safety off. With a full clip this gun would fire fourteen times before it emptied. "No farther," she said.

He was backlit, caught in the headlights like some uncertain animal, deer or raccoon. It would have given her pleasure to run him down.

He laughed briefly. "You wouldn't—"

The bullet hissed into the dirt near his foot. He jumped.

"Wouldn't what?" she said.

He jutted out his arm, palm flat toward her. "Okay, okay!"

Andi stepped closer but kept a good dozen feet between them. "Toss your gun out."

"What gun? What the hell—?"

"The one you were carrying when you came to the house." As he hesitated, she yelled, "Do it! And slowly."

His right hand moved toward his left shoulder.

"Uh-uh. No. Use your left hand."

"I can't get at it—"

"Yes, you can." God, but she was dying to shoot him where he stood.

Awkwardly, he maneuvered his left hand toward his left side and pulled the gun out of a shoulder holster.

"Drop it and kick it over here." No wonder people loved guns. The sense of power was breathtaking. Here she was, up against the man who had followed her for more than a year, and she could order him to do whatever she wanted.

He kicked the revolver through the dirt.

Andi kept her own gun steady as she pulled it toward her. "Who are you?"

"I'm who I said I was when I was standing on your porch."

"You never said. Did you know Harry Wine?"

"Who? No. Never met the man."

"Why are you following me?"

"I ain't, girl." Calmly, he spat something out of the side of his mouth, tobacco juice maybe. He'd been chewing something. "What in hell gave you that notion?"

"You gave me the notion. You've been following me for over a year, first in Idaho; then Billings, Montana; then Miles City. Why?"

"Well, now—" He threw up his hands in a dramatic gesture and then two things happened in quick succession. His raised hand seemed to pluck a second gun right out of the air as if this were a magic act. The second thing was Dakota rearing back on his hind legs and nearly battering the stall door down.

The shot went wide and missed Andi, who fired and missed his shoulder but grazed his right arm and saw the gun drop from his fingers. She covered the distance quickly between herself and the gun and picked it up, all the while keeping her eyes on him. "Now we're getting in your truck. You're driving to Kingdom."

"Oh, I don't think so." Blood leaked from the wound on his upper arm, which he was grasping. "What I'm figurin' is we could strike a bargain."

"With you? I don't see what we could possibly do for each other."

"Oh, I bet there's some service I could provide."

"Such as?"

"Well, you tell me. Let's say I ain't got any particular problem with the law."

Frowning, she said, "Meaning what? You're not on the wrong side of it?"

His laugh wasn't pleasant. "At the moment, no. But what I meant is the law don't mean much to me, nor to you, neither, I'd bet."

Andi lowered the gun, genuinely confused. "Why in God's name would you think that?"

He shrugged. "You sure ain't got any permit for that piece you got there."

She raised it again. "Of course I do." Of course she didn't.

He made a derisive sound and looked away, then back at Dakota, standing, watching, eating hay. "See, my guess is if it ever came to shooting me or your horse, it'd be me."

Andi snorted. "That's no contest."

"Thing is, the law favors me. Not the horse. All I'm saying is you wouldn't mind the law there."

"What about you taking the horse? What about the ransom? Why would that make me want to enter into any bargain with you?"

"That was only to get you to pay attention."

"It's a pretty stupid way to do it."

He spread his arms. "Why? You're paying attention, ain't you?" His chuckle sounded as if there were nothing living behind it. "Far as I'm concerned, one way's good as another. You can take your horse. Nice animal."

"I intend to. So what's my part of this bargain?"

"You got the Information."

She heard it, oddly, with a capital *I*, as if it were somehow the essence of the thing. "What 'information'? I don't know what you're talking about. I don't remember anything."

"Yeah, you know. You maybe don't want to remember. Maybe that's what's turned you into a vagabond." His smile this time was more tired than sinister. "Ain't got much choice, though. Mostly, that's what life is, I guess: not much choice." He grinned. "Well, look: ain't much point in this if you're going to keep stonewalling. So I'll be around when you're ready to talk." His gun still lay in the dirt between them. "I'll just take my weapon back, you don't mind." He saw her arm stiffen. "Look: you know I ain't gonna shoot you—"

"You just tried to."

"That was hardly a try. If I'd tried, I'd've done it. And you won't shoot me in the back, either." He smiled, picked up his gun, and touched the brim of his hat in some kind of salute. He turned and walked toward the opening of the barn. "So stop thinkin' about it, girl." He threw those words over his shoulder.

Then he turned. "Oh, yeah. The name's Waylans. If that means anything to you."

She did not know what to say, so she said, "Your horse? The one in the other barn. You should get him shod."

He turned. "Maybe. Only, he ain't my horse." Then he walked on into the dark.

She didn't see him get into his truck. She heard its door open, close, an engine turn over, tires spitting gravel. Then a slow descent along the drive to the road beneath. Then nothing.

Andi emptied the Smith & Wesson of the magazine and stowed the gun in her jacket pocket again. Then she stood for a moment, baffled.

Waylans.

Dakota was still ruminatively eating hay. He suffered her putting her arms around his neck and then laying her head there. Then she picked up the old bridle, which he, still chewing, tried to throw off. But Andi was getting good at this and she managed to fit it and tighten the strap.

No saddle around that she could see, but she did see a blanket and a belt. Maybe she'd be able to ride him with that on, and the bridle. So she threw the blanket over his back, then the belt, which she tightened. The trouble was she had no stirrups to help her up.

She dragged over a crate, which she used to give her a step up to one of the wooden slats of the stable, which she then maneuvered one foot into. This gave her enough of a leg up that she could throw the other leg over. What she had was too much momentum and fell over the other side of the horse.

With far more patience than he was used to exercising around her, Dakota stood still and waited. She swore, went back around, hoisted herself up, carefully calibrated the force it would take, made her move, and slid back down.

Dakota blew through his nose.

This is rescue?

45

Andi got a ride into Kingdom with a stony-faced woman named Willa, who offered to take her along if she paid three dollars for fare. "Cheaper than a cab, ain't it?" Andi handed over the three dollars, not especially surprised by the greed or the smallness of mind.

But Andi was depressed and wanted to go to May's for a grilled cheese before she went to see Harry McKibbon, a visit she was ambivalent about at best. At worst? She wanted to run.

She found Norman Black sitting in his usual seat at May's.

He said, "Now, correct me if I'm wrong—"

"You bet," she said, opening the menu, even though she knew what she would have. "But shouldn't you be home writing a book? I can't think how you could've published twenty of them because you're always in here."

Mildred came down the counter to take Andi's sandwich order and set a glass of water before her, then stuck her pad back in her pocket and went off.

Andi sipped the water. "Have you ever been in a slaughterhouse?"

"Once. You couldn't pay me to go back."

"You'd think someone would come up with some other way. I mean, why not just shoot them?"

"Waste of money. Read about a man working at some animal shelter used to chase dogs off cliffs. Someone asked him why he didn't shoot them. Bullet costs five cents. Cliff costs nothing."

Andi leaned her head in her hand. Now there would be another image she couldn't get rid of. "I wish you hadn't told me that."

"Sorry. It doesn't make a nice picture."

"Why'd you go to a slaughterhouse anyway?"

"Research. Was going to have a scene in my book take place there, but I decided not to. Folks don't want to read stuff like that."

"Do you get any animal activists around here?"

"Animal rights people? Once, I recall. Yeah, one of those groups did investigate that facility up north that collects urine from mares. 'Pee farm' is what they call it, which is bad because it makes it all a joke."

Mildred came along, placed Andi's grilled cheese before her and refilled Norman's mug, and sailed off again.

"That's where Jim got Dakota." She picked up the sandwich, took a bite, put it down. "The farm has no use for male foals so they auction them off. Most go to slaughter. Dakota—" Why wasn't she telling Norman about last night?

Norman nodded. "Poor things." He went on. "The thing is, it never used to be this bad like forty or fifty years ago, before agribusinesses got a head of steam going. They can raise so much cattle and hogs and chickens that it's mind-boggling."

"How would you stop it? I mean aside from whistle-blowing?"

The spoon clattered in the mug as Norman set it down. "I don't know, sue 'em, maybe? I expect these animal welfare people must try that sometimes. They got lawyers."

"Are there any around here?"

Norman's laugh was a little exhausted, as if he'd used up what he had for the day. "You're the most suggestible person I ever met. All I do is say 'lawyer' and you're out there looking. Probably, you could find one in Bismarck, but I don't know any. Never had cause."

Andi picked up the sandwich again, but just held it there. "This is cause."

Norman chuckled. "Next, it's going to be torching it."

"I already thought of that."

46

You should have called me last night." Harry McKibbon was angry. "I'm surprised Jim didn't—"

"No. He was going to call, but I stopped him. It was two AM."

"You think people only need the sheriff's office between nine and five? I've been out more two AMs than you've ever slept through." He sat back. "This fellow drove up to the Custises' barn, correct?"

"Yes. I didn't get the plate number."

"I wouldn't have expected you to." He leaned forward again. Andi was on the other side of his desk. "Andi, what was he talking about? The 'information'? What do you think that means?"

"It sounds like at one time in the past, I found out something. Say, the combination to a safe. Or maybe I saw a crime being committed."

Harry shook his head. "His name's Waylans, right?"

She nodded. "First or last, I don't know."

The swivel chair creaked as Harry leaned back, looking hard at Andi. "Does he know about the amnesia?"

"How could he? And still think I knew something that happened in the past? How could he know I'm living a made-up life?" She looked down at her hands in her lap.

Smiling slightly, Harry said, "What's it like, your made-up life?"

She shook her head. "Just things about my family and where we lived. He thinks I'm just refusing to tell him what he wants, just stonewalling."

They were silent for a moment.

Harry said, "I don't get this guy. He seems to be *enjoying* what he's doing. He must have thought taking your horse was a lark. Calling Jim, demanding money." Harry shook his head. "Did he say anything at all about where he was going? Staying?"

"No. I'd have told you."

Harry tapped a worn-out pencil on his legal pad and after a while said, "What if it's not this 'information' that he wants? What if he's just tossing that out, but what he really wants is something else?" His smile was wan. "Just to confuse matters?"

"It certainly does. If it *could* get any more confusing."

"Let's backtrack a little: when he came to Jim's house that day, he claimed to be looking for someone."

She paused, bemused. "He showed me a picture of a family—I guess a family: man, woman, girl of maybe eleven or twelve. He assumed I must remember them." She looked across at the sheriff, and quickly looked away, as if she anticipated what he might say.

"You're saying they didn't look at all familiar."

She nodded. "I never saw them before."

"The girl—"

She cut this off. "He was looking for a girl. Alice. Whether she was his daughter or . . . no, no. She wouldn't have been. The man in the snapshot wasn't Waylans."

"That doesn't say she couldn't have been, though. The man could have been anyone—uncle, some other relative, or a friend—"

"You think I'm the girl?"

He held his palm out, as if stopping the thought. "For Lord's sake, no. Why would I think that? Simply because he's been after you all this time? Of course not. If you were, he would hardly be acting as he's acting."

"He didn't actually say 'daughter'; he said 'Alice.' He was surprised I didn't recall . . ." She sat forward. "No, he was more angry than surprised when I said I didn't *remember* her. He didn't think I have amnesia; he thought I was lying."

Harry's look at Andi was keen.

"Don't even say it!" She held up her hand, as he had done, as if to push away the words he hadn't spoken. "He is *not* my father. Not *him*."

Harry shut his eyes, impatient. "Of course I don't think that. But I am wondering: is it possible Waylans is not the man who's been following you all of this time? Could the man your friends saw in Idaho and Montana be somebody else?"

Andi looked at him almost in disbelief. "Sheriff. Are you really suggesting that it's a *coincidence*? Are you saying that Waylans just turned up here out of the blue and came to the house, and then went to Mrs. Englehart's and then to Kingdom Kabs?" She got up wearily and started for the door.

He rose, too. "Andi—"

She walked out.

47

Lawyer?" said Tom, who had shoved the sausages he was cooking out of sight when Andi came through the back door with her question. "Lawyer? What did Klavan do? Hit you with a legal suit when he caught you pettin' a pig?" He laughed and turned back to cutting pieces of bread in half for French toast.

"You know what they do to piglets that have something wrong with them? Throw them against the wall or swing them against it by their tails. 'Thumpers' is what they call them."

Tom watched water droplets bounce on the griddle. "Come on, Andi."

"They do. It's no wonder people don't believe it. You know what excuse they give? It's industry practice. She took off her quilted vest and hitched it around a kitchen chair. "Where's Jim?"

"Over in Bismarck. He should be back about now. I was just making supper. I hope you don't mind French toast."

"I love it; you're a better cook than Jim, but don't tell him I said it. What about lawyers?"

"No, I didn't invite any of them."

"Funny. I mean do you *know* any. Have you used any?"

"Yes, of course. No one gets to a certain age without a lawyer. They're counting on it. One I used is in Fargo. I think Jim's is in Bismarck. They've got a lot of lawyers in Bismarck." He turned from dipping halves of thick bread into an egg mixture. "May I inquire as to why you need a lawyer?"

"I was thinking of maybe suing the Department of Agriculture—"

"That's real good. That's a corker," he said, turning back to the stove. "Then I'm just glad the word *maybe* crept into your calculations." He let a piece of bread soak up the liquid and moved over to the table and picked up his coffee mug. "Where did you ever get this fool idea?"

Andi squinted up at him, as if his brightness burned her eyes. "From the thumpers being played like baseballs."

He pulled out a chair and sat down. "Andi—"

"Just the way you said my name means you're going to be really condescending."

"No, I am not. I'm only wondering if you've *thought* about what's involved here."

"No, I didn't spare a moment thinking about it."

"Stop being sarcastic." He rose and went back to the bread. He tossed a limp piece into the sink.

"Stop being condescending. I take it you're not a big fan of this move? Well, if you hadn't interrupted, you'd know I decided not to sue the DOA."

Tom pulled back the sausage pan, lit the stove again. "Thank God for that."

"I'm suing BigSun and Klavan's."

"That's crazy," said Jim, who'd come in as they'd started eating. He stared at Andi over his forkful of French toast. "What gave you such a screwy idea as that?"

In a pretense of considering his question, Andi squinted at the ceiling. "What was it? Maybe—yes, I think it was watching them slit the throats of pigs that were still conscious."

Jim shook his head vigorously. "That's a meat-processing plant, BigSun. That's not Klavan's."

Andi brought her gaze down from the ceiling. "I said both of them, didn't I? And you're really distinguishing between the two?"

"Well, of course."

"Klavan's is no better. You should have seen Dewey Petty dragging a crippled sow along by her ear."

"Andi, you've got to cut this stuff out. You can't seem to understand there are things that go on in this world that you cannot do anything about, and here is number one: Klavan's. Or any of these factory farms and agribusinesses. Like it or not, they are here to stay."

"I'm not talking about getting rid of factory farms, although I'd like to. I'm talking about this one. You've never been inside it. You've only seen it from the road, Jim. You've only seen that pristine whiteness."

"Whether I have or haven't isn't the point!"

"It isn't?"

Jim was getting in a real temper. There it was again. Andi wondered why people got so mad.

"Trying to actually sue this place and put them out of business is a fool's errand. Next you'll be talking about blowing the damned place up!"

Tom sat back and picked up his coffee cup. "I kind of wish you hadn't said that."

Jim stopped and had to laugh.

Andi stepped into the new mood. "So do you know a lawyer?"

She had, with some coaxing, managed to get the name of his attorney out of Jim. It was Bobby Del Ray, and his practice was in Bismarck.

"Is he good when it comes to trials? And juries?"

"That's what he's best at. He's a performer."

"Would he do a good job with my case?"

"No, but that wouldn't be his fault. No lawyer would."

"You talk as if no one has ever done this before. Plenty of people have gone up against factory farms that break the law."

"Yeah, but not a nineteen-year-old without a shred of hard evidence."

"Twenty-year-old," she said with disdain.

★   ★   ★

Out in the barn, she handed out turnips and thought about evidence. Dakota turned his back only *after* he'd received his turnip. Evidence could certainly come from eyewitnesses. Except who in this operation would ever agree to be a witness? A lawyer could subpoena people to give evidence, and they'd have to. They needed their jobs, and it would go hard on them to have to say what they saw. Probably, they'd lie; ones like Hutch and Nat would hardly make good witnesses.

There was Jake, though. She thought she could depend on Jake. He knew Klavan's was a rotten, abusive operation.

Andi was beginning to believe that in order to do something extreme, you had to join the misfits of this world; you had to make friends with the pathological. But making friends with people like Nat and Hutch struck her as being over the top when it came to pathology.

"Sit down right there," Jake said the following morning, pointing to a chair by a desk. "Sit down and let me tell you a few things, Andi."

Andi sat and tried to prepare herself for a world of disappointment. Jake was the only one she knew who showed any signs at all of sharing her feelings.

He sat down opposite her. "Listen: all you're thinking of is these pigs' welfare. But what about our welfare, the ones who work here? We'd lose our jobs if Klavan's got shut down. You'd say, well, we can get other jobs. It's not easy to get one around here. Where do you see jobs unfilled in a place like Kingdom? Oh, we could move to Fargo, but even if jobs were going begging there, that's changing a person's whole damned life."

He went on: "And what happens to the businesses that depend on our employees? We won't have money to spend. You can't seem to take in the domino effect. You change something at the end of a row, and the whole damn row topples. Believe me." Jake sat back.

She just looked at him. "I take it that's a no?"

She got up and left.

★   ★   ★

What she would have liked to ask him was what he was afraid of. If it was nonsense, if it was ridiculous for her to talk about suing Klavan's, then what were they all afraid of?

As she went through her chores that day, she decided she would have to get a bus to Bismarck and would have to find out where she could get one. She imagined Greyhound or something like it traveled U.S. 83.

She did not want to ask Jim or Tom to drive her to where she could get a bus; she didn't want to have to listen to discouraging talk. She called in sick to Klavan's, and as she'd never done that before, no one objected. Maybe they were even relieved not to have her judgmental self around for the day.

Instead of asking Jim for any more information about Bobby Del Ray, she'd called his office and spoken to the secretary. They were called assistants these days, weren't they? Mr. Del Ray's assistant had asked what she wanted to see him about. Andi had been vague. "A job-related matter." She was afraid that the attorney wouldn't see her if he knew in advance what the job-related matter was.

That morning she told Jim where she was going. He was surprised. How would she get there? Andi told him a friend was going that way. And she left.

48

The bus ride took a little over an hour. She had gotten to 83 by means of her most dependable transport: walking, combined with hitching rides. It had taken more than two hours to get there, but she'd done it.

Andi was never bothered by anonymity. It was restful, in a way, no one's knowing you; you felt you could expand a little, let in more air, open a window higher, a door wider.

On her way out of the Bismarck station, she bought a street map and found Main Street. His assistant had told her Bobby Del Ray's office was located across from the old railroad station. "But now it's a Mexican restaurant," the woman had told her. Andi would have walked the distance, but decided that might make her late to her appointment. Door 25 was the transit door; the door next to it, 27, was the taxi office. Here, she got a cab.

"*You're* Miss Oliver?"

The little sign on the woman's desk verified assistant status. She looked Andi up and down as if measuring her for a school uniform. Looking at the woman's dress, which was rather old-fashioned, Andi thought it could easily have come from the Unique Boutique. For some reason, Andi found this poignant and wondered if Bismarck, a dozen times the size of Kingdom, was any more sophisticated.

Andi had tried to pile on a few more years by dressing in a skirt and plain sweater and applying a lot of makeup, going heavy with goldish-brown eye shadow. Makeup to Andi always looked heavy, hence, older. But how young, then, did she look to this woman if people her age didn't hire attorneys?

Hire was the word, too. Lawyers were expensive and she didn't know what to do for money beyond the several hundred she'd managed to save up in the last year. She'd brought money with her, and decided the rest was a problem she could work on if the lawyer said he'd take the case. There was no sense in worrying over money if he was going to refuse.

She sat in one of the chairs against the wall. She was the only other person there. She had been waiting for fifteen minutes when the inner door opened and a man poked his head out and crooked his finger at her, motioning for her to come in.

The assistant wasn't part of this transaction. She didn't even look up from her papers.

Andi followed him into his office and took the client's seat beside his desk. She could not, in sizing him up, take him for a dangerous man at all. He seemed pleasant, like the town itself, pleasant and mild-mannered. He expressed no surprise at her age, or hinted that she was too young to be bothering him.

"I work at Klavan's, that pig-farm facility near Kingdom. I live at Jim Purley's. He recommended you ... well, in a way. He did not recommend you for my case. But that's only because he thinks I'm crazy and no lawyer in his right mind would take this case."

Bobby Del Ray grinned a grin that split his face in two. "I'm hired. Tell me."

What she'd put in by way of an apology was instead just the right tone to take. Bobby Del Ray must love challenges—loved taking on cases that other attorneys might consider unwinnable. He crossed his arms and stuck his hands in his armpits. He was wearing a blue shirt and a dark blue tie scattered about with little images of various dogs, which made her smile. His jacket was hitched over the back of his chair. He rocked a little in the swivel chair, which was badly scarred.

Andi said, "This is all about businesses like Klavan's and a slaughterhouse called BigSun and how they violate all sorts of animal welfare statutes like the Humane Slaughter Act and Humane Transport Act. Probably you've never seen either of these operations."

"No. But I can imagine."

She shook her head. "The thing is, you can't. It's beyond imagining. Let me tell you a few things."

She went on to tell him with the greatest economy she could muster for some of it, since she didn't want to waste his time, his time being $250 an hour. But when necessary she went into detail.

Bobby Del Ray listened to every word (or so it seemed to her) as he ran a lead pencil across his fingers, back and forth, like a drum major's baton.

"I think the Department of Agriculture should take a lot of this blame. Probably, they don't want to step on the toes of the meat-packing industry. A lot of it's down to them, Agriculture, and that's why my first thought was to sue them."

He stopped the pencil-baton. "The U.S. Department of Agriculture?"

"Yes. But then I thought that might be too hard. So I settled on suing Klavan's or BigSun or both. Somebody's got to do something." She sat back, looked past him and out of the window. She shook her head. "Jim thinks I'm crazy."

"Then he's wrong. You've heard of Bell Farms, haven't you?"

She hadn't, but thought she should have and was glad when he didn't stop for her answer.

"An outfit called Sun Prairie—part of Bell—opened up a factory hog farm on a Sioux reservation—Rosebud, it's called. The thing is that South Dakota has environmental and animal welfare regulations, but that obstacle was gotten around by putting the farm on Indian land where they wouldn't have to comply. This Sun Prairie outfit convinced the people at the Rosebud Reservation that the business would be a godsend because of all the jobs it would offer. But what they actually wound up with were poorly paid, menial jobs under conditions so bad that the Humane Farming Association petitioned the attorney

general to enforce the animal cruelty laws that Sun Prairie was breaking all over the place. It was a very long, very detailed description of
the godawful way the pigs were being treated. Rosebud managed to
get out of the contract because of all the violations.

"So, no, there's nothing nuts about what you want. Maybe what
Jim thinks is nutty is that you're one person, not a whole organization
with a couple hundred thousand members. How big is Klavan's
operation?"

"There are five thousand pigs there."

"At Rosebud I think there were a hundred thousand. Workers
were getting sick all the time. Conditions were deplorable. Well, you
know what it's like at this other place, Klavan's. Now, what about possible witnesses? Anyone who would testify to the conditions?"

"Not so far. I asked, but naturally they're scared for their jobs. I
don't blame them really, when they've got families to support. I know
I need what I think's called material evidence. I think I can get a camera in and take pictures. Maybe a camcorder. Would that help?"

"That would help, of course, but not even that would go unchal-
lenged. Try and imagine the weight of the argument that would be
leveled against you. This would be a long time waiting for a ruling."

"How long?"

"Months, maybe, possibly a year or longer."

That truly sank her. She could imagine a case drawn out for
months, but *years*?

"While it would be business as usual at BigSun and Klavan's. This
would galvanize the megabusinesses like Morrel or Smithfield. They'd
stomp all over you; they'd dig up everything on you they could find,
on not only you but your family. Drugs? Sex? Police record? And certainly your emotional stability. If you think your friends who smile and
say 'You're crazy' are annoying, just wait until you get the legal counsel
against you from some high-profile firm of attorneys saying it."

She looked past him and out through the window. It would be
ironic, wouldn't it, if this bank of lawyers should turn over stones and
find her past there.

"Let me get some information about you. Andi Oliver. Age?"

How could she have been so stupid as not to have realized her past, her life, her family, would come up? Then the last two years and every-thing that had happened.

"Andi?"

"Oh, sorry. I'm twenty." She dug into her bag and pulled out money. "I brought enough to pay you for your time."

"You don't have to—"

"Please." She passed five fifties across the little bit of space between them.

"This is only a consultation, Andi. I haven't done anything for you." With his index finger he pushed the money back.

"All right. Thanks. What I'd like to do is go home and think about all of this, what you've said."

He stopped her. "How do you come to be living at Jim Purley's place?"

It wasn't that he sounded suspicious, but more as if he'd just hit on something, something he wanted to figure out.

"I needed a job and since I wasn't staying anywhere in Kingdom, he said I could stay at his house. Then I got this job at Klavan's."

"Why did you choose that place? Did you suspect there was abu-sive treatment going on?"

"Yes."

He looked at her for a long moment. "Where were you before you got to Kingdom?"

She could see it coming. "I was backpacking around the country, West and Midwest."

"Where are you from?"

"New York. Look, Mr. Del Ray—"

"Bobby." He smiled.

Then she did, too. "Could we do this later? I've got to go now."

He rose, shook her hand, said he'd be in touch.

"It's been a pleasure, Andi." He meant it, too.

★   ★   ★

All she could think of on the bus going back was that she'd failed to realize beforehand that her own history, her past, would come into this. It would be examined. She would be found out.

She had never had access to the means of discovery that the legal system would have. She would have thought before that this—the discovery of her past, finding out who she was—would have provided even further impetus to go ahead with the lawsuit.

She watched as the bus passed a Sinclair gas station, no longer used, its bubble-topped pumps empty, and it brought back Reuel and his dog, which he'd found at an old Sinclair station, abandoned and turned out of somebody's car. She wished he was here, to give her advice.

She had pored over newspapers, looking for herself; watched the news, hoping to see her face on TV; all of it a blank. She had little flashes, and they *seemed* like memories, but they could easily have been of dreams that she'd pushed to the back of her mind.

But this. This she might not be prepared for—to have someone else, a lawyer, a policeman, hand over her past in a manila folder, its contents stamped and stapled: this is you.

The thought frightened her.

She leaned into the window and touched the cold glass with her forehead. It felt like winter.

Then there was Harry Wine. The police in Idaho never solved that case, neither the Salmon nor the state police, probably because they didn't really want to. A lot of people were plenty happy to see Harry Wine dead. Police went through the motions, she had heard, but that was all. There would be no reason to tie her to that, really, but . . .

What was she willing to do?

Was she willing to go through all of this, when the outcome would probably be to lose? A fleet of high-powered attorneys given over to discrediting her?

And it was hardly news, was it, this abuse of animals? What had she to add to it?

At this point she was beginning to rationalize and had to stop thinking about the case. She kept her eyes on the shabby scenery of farms and vacant buildings. She turned away, wondering if she was turning away from herself.

They passed a field with bright-faced sheep looking toward the bus, or seeming to. *Do you know you're lucky?* She would have liked to get off the bus and walk across the field and tell them that.

How serious was she about all of this?

In her mind's eye she watched Nat grab up a piglet and throw it against the wall.

She flinched.

She thought then she was serious.

49

She was back by dinnertime. Hitching rides, walking to Kingdom, and then getting Kingdom Kabs to deliver her to her door. Although no ride with Bub at the wheel ever felt like deliverance.

Jim was cooking. He looked around from seasoning the chops, flushed as if he'd been found out in some criminal enterprise, and said, "Howdy."

Tom was sitting with the local newspaper and his usual whiskey. He smiled at her.

Neither of them asked if Bobby Del Ray also thought she was crazy, which was what she'd been expecting.

Trying to sound casual, Jim asked, "You get on okay with Bobby Del Ray?"

She had sat down beside Tom and fooled with the place setting. "Yes. He's very nice." Right then she felt like caving in; she hadn't realized how tired she was.

"Sound a little hangdog about it. He discourage you?"

She shook her head. "No. Well, yes, in the sense he tried to tell me how difficult it would be, prosecuting Klavan's or BigSun. As if I'd be prosecuting Smithfield and Morrel by doing this."

"You would be, in a way. They wouldn't take kindly to your case."

Andi was quiet for a moment, then said, "I just don't understand it, why a farm or a slaughterhouse can't simply operate by more humane standards."

"Of course you do, Andi," said Jim, watching the grease spit up around the chops. "You understand; money, that's the long and short of it. They think running a plant the way these activists want would cut into profits. They'd lose money."

"But that's probably not even true. Look at what they lose when an animal that's still conscious kicks some worker in the head. Then he's off the line and they've got to find a replacement, and that holds up production even more."

Tom looked up. "You ever think that maybe they like it? Though it's kind of awful to think. Maybe it's not just faster and more efficient to push the animals along the line no matter what state they're in—a hog that's supposed to be knocked unconscious but isn't—maybe that's what they like."

Jim poked the chops around the cast-iron skillet and shrugged. "Pretty grim."

Andi remembered Warren, standing up there on the bridge. "Maybe you're right. The trouble is—" She'd been going to say, "my past," but what good would it do to own up to the lack of one? They couldn't help her there, or advise her. And if the case never got to court, her past wouldn't make a difference. She started again: "The trouble is I don't think we'd get anyone to testify."

"No surprise there," said Jim. "Klavan's, that's their livelihood. This is the Dakotas, remember? None of them can just go next door to McDonald's or Wal-Mart and pick up some hours to work."

"I know, I know. I just thought there would be someone—"

"You mean, like Jake Cade? No, ma'am. You give him too much credit," said Jim.

Tom said, "I don't know about that, Jim. My guess is he would do it but he can't."

"I thought you didn't like Jake Cade much."

"I don't. Still, he's got kids; it's hard to do the right thing when you got others depending on you."

"They don't—" she stopped. That was Tom's argument, not hers. "Unlike people not depending on me, you mean. It's easy for me—"

Tom stopped her. "No, it is not, Andi. It's harder on you than on anyone. I'm just saying try not to be too hopeful you'll find some whistle-blower. Probably there are one or two Klavan workers who sympathize with these benighted animals."

Jim said, "What Bobby Del Ray says makes sense. Let's eat."

The next morning Andi watched pigs bound for slaughter, packed snug into an eighteen-wheeler. It wasn't anyone at Klavan's driving; this was one of the independent haulers they hired when the numbers warranted it. She watched as they got the pigs up the ramp and into the truck. Some of them without any trouble, most of them holding back and having to be pushed or prodded or whipped in.

Andi had had a dream the night before that she was with some others who were going to die. The dream was a nightmare and she had woken in terror. There was no violence in the dream, no blood, no threats. It was the inexorability of death that was terrifying. She questioned a man who seemed to be the source of their information, and he had said, "We're going to die." He had said it without emotion. There wasn't a shred of a chance, no possibility of survival. This was how it was for these pigs. For she was certain instinct told them there was no escape.

The truck was nearly full to bursting. The driver, a monolith with a beard, sat in stony place, staring out of the windshield.

She was headed to the sows' hut and saw Jake walking toward the office. She'd borrowed his cell phone to call Jim and needed to return it. Jake, she knew, was good. She still held out hope. Jake had a conscience, though a cruel conscience, by the sound of it.

In the hut, she unwedged a couple of piglets from a new litter who'd climbed on top of the sow. She freed the leg of another that had gotten stuck between the boards.

When she was through with the feed, she leaned against one of the low doors and stood looking at the piglets, who couldn't know what was in store for them; she tried to figure out which would be thumpers. That one, easily, the one whose leg she'd freed. She went into the enclosure, picked that one up, and stuffed him into her jacket. It was quitting time, nothing else to hold her here, so she zipped up the jacket and walked to the road, before she remembered Jake's cell.

Damn. She doubled back to the office, kept her hand over the piglet, and bounded up the steps, cell phone pressed to her ear, speaking loudly to a nonexistent respondent, laughing. Anything to drown out the squeals of the piglet, should they come.

"Yeah. Bye." She flapped the phone shut. "Hey, Jake! Thanks!"

She tossed it to him and got out of there.

When she got back to Jim's, she took the tiny piglet out and put it inside the pigpen and watched the others hurry over to have a look. It squeaked crazily.

She was getting ready for bed when she thought of it: why not *former* employees of Klavan's? Ones who had stopped work, either quit or gotten fired. They'd have nothing to lose.

Norman Black had mentioned one of them. A woman with a peculiar name. Odelia? No. Odile. The last named was something like Tacoma, sounded Indian. Nekoma, that was it. She'd quit because she hated the place, Norm had said. And she had pictures.

Andi lay with her hands behind her head. What was the weight of one witness, she wondered. Then she thought of the nice kid at the motel, Eddie. His testimony—since he'd witnessed only the pigs on the truck—wouldn't be as weighty. She tried to imagine the Klavan defense lawyers interogating him.

"*You saw a truck transport of two hundred pigs and you provided water. How do you know they needed it so badly?*"

"*Because she told me.*"

"*By 'she' you mean the plaintiff?*"

"*Yeah.*"

"*But you didn't see this for yourself?*"

"*Well, no. I mean, you can't exactly see something needs water.*"

Perhaps he couldn't be a witness to abuse outside of the crowded truck itself, but at least he could corroborate there was a truck and the pigs looked in bad shape.

It wouldn't be much; on the other hand, she didn't know the law. Bobby Del Ray might be able to squeeze a lot out of Eddie's story.

Now, if Odile Nekoma had been showing people photos of what she'd seen, then she surely would be willing to come forth as a witness, wouldn't she?

And then Andi recalled Drew Petty saying how lots of Pettys had worked at Klavan's. Had that included Uncle Drew? She couldn't picture him in that environment, but maybe his gentle manner had evolved out of Klavan's merciless abuse of animals. He could testify, she was pretty sure, as he had nothing to lose. And, she thought, he was, for all his quiet manner, fearless. He would come across as decent and honest and not one with an ax to grind or a score to settle. No, Drew Petty would come off as a witness who was anything but a troublemaker.

Unlike herself.

She rolled over, thinking now she could sleep. She'd started out with zero and now she had three witnesses. Maybe. And there was still Jake. She had hopes there.

Tomorrow was a Saturday and she didn't have to go to work. She could begin looking up these people.

50

Odile Nekoma?"

Andi had called Norman and found out where she lived.

"*But don't expect a lot, hear? She's not the easiest person in the world.*"

"*Well, good Lord, Norman, neither am I.*"

The woman had blunt features, as if they'd been squared off with a chisel, and straight-cut black hair. Her manner went with this. She looked suspicious of strangers.

"I am. Who are you?" She was holding on to a can of Red Rock beer, a cigarette in the same hand.

Andi told her and told her why she had come.

"That dump?" She was speaking of Klavan's. "Come on in. Want a beer?"

It wasn't yet ten in the morning. "No, thanks." She followed Odile Nekoma into a crowded room.

"Cigarette?" Odile offered a crumpled pack of Marlboro Lights.

"No, thanks. I don't smoke."

Odile let out an annoyed rasp of air. "Oh, Christ, you ain't a drinker, you ain't a smoker, and I have to spend time with you? Go on, just shove that stuff off the couch and sit down."

Andi piled a bunch of newspapers and magazines onto one end and took the freed-up space. Outside, house and land were bare boards and barrenness, looking swept clean. Inside, it looked like a fire sale. Books and papers stacked up everywhere, couch and chairs either ancient or so worn you could sink almost to the floor, and covered with fancy embroidered silk cushions. Somewhere flute music played and Andi thought she smelled incense. The floors were deep in Native American rugs, bright zigzags of reds and blues. Andi wondered if Odile had a thing for the Southwest and then recalled her last name.

"So you work at Klavan's? How do you stand the place?"

"I can't. That's why I wanted to talk to you. I've got a lawyer and I'm going to sue them. The way they treat the pigs—" Andi shrugged.

Odile was waving her hand like a kid in class who thought she had the right answer. "Hold it, honey. Did you say 'sue'? And you got a *lawyer*?"

"Bobby Del Ray in Bismarck."

Odile whooped and got up. "This calls for another beer! I know Bobby Del Ray. He could get a field full of bulls to line up and listen."

She took her empty can to the kitchen, came back popping the top off a fresh one. "So you want me for what?"

"To serve as a witness."

"Like in court, you mean?"

Andi nodded.

Odile seemed literally to be chewing this over, but what she was chewing was probably the inside of her cheek. She shrugged. "Okay." She took a pull of Red Rock.

Andi was astonished that it was this easy. She hadn't expected anyone to agree to her proposal without a lot of pushing. "I appreciate this. Really. I haven't been able to find anyone who works there willing to do it."

Odile gave a little bark of laughter. "I don't guess. Wait, and I'll go get my pictures."

Andi rose and looked around the room, with its surprisingly warm ambience. There was a tiny cackle and she thought Odile must have come back quickly, until she saw the parrot. It sat on a little perch, swinging softly, eyes closed, air unstirred. Its eye opened and fluttered shut again. No interest at all. That made her smile.

"That fool bird acting up again?" Odile sat down with her snap-shots and her beer.

"No. It's rocking and being quiet."

"Well, then, you got a strange effect on it. That bird never shuts up. Do you cast spells?"

This seemed a serious question. Andi laughed. "Spells? Me? Hardly. I wish I could."

Odile's mouth curved in a sickle smile. "I'm half Indian, you know. Sioux. My mother took spells real seriously."

Andi returned to the couch.

Absentmindedly, Odile was riffling her thumb across the bunched snapshots as if she were a blackjack dealer about to slap down the cards, or tell a fortune. She was silent.

Odile's ancestry. The parrot. The picture-cards. The silence. Her reference to "spells." Anyone might feel spellbound in such an atmosphere.

"Look at these." Instead of passing them over, Odile motioned with her head for Andi to come to them.

Andi looked over Odile's shoulder at what Norman had described earlier. It was a good thing he had, although nothing could prepare a person to look at a hanged animal. Nothing could've prepared her for this witnessing of pigs hanging from posts and metal poles, their necks stretched by chains, their shadows cast across the ground like victims of a lynching.

How could such a thing happen? Her mouth was dry; she couldn't form a word.

"This was it for me," said Odile. "This was it. I couldn't look at the poor pigs in those long, long lines of crates and cages, couldn't look 'em in the face. Yeah, this was a new low." She seemed to forget her cigarette and beer, looking down at the pictures now fanned out on the table, twelve of them taken at different angles and sometimes including Klavan employees.

Andi recognized Hutch grinning all over, making a gun of his hand with the barrel finger pointed at one of the hanged pigs. Andi finally managed to string some words together. "How did you manage to get these?"

"How? Because they're such stupid assholes they probably thought I meant to send them to *National Geographic* and make the sons of bitches famous."

"Do you think I could get a camcorder in there and make a video?"

"Well, that'd be much harder. You could manage some snapshots, I'm sure. The thing is, you they'd take seriously. Me they never did because I was a cutup. Unless they're complete idiots—which is certainly possible—they'd guess you had a purpose in taking pictures. You gotta be careful."

"You're a Sioux, you said. Then you must know about that Rosebud Reservation business and Sun Prairie."

"Oh, *believe* me, I know about it. Several years ago, around they came painting this rosy picture of plenty of work, a lot of jobs. Well, you can imagine the unemployment rate there. It was like sixty percen' of us needed work. To have jobs promised, that was a windfall. So they contracted with the reservation and put up their facility and the jobs were horrible because the conditions were horrible. Not just for the pigs but for the workers, too. People getting sick in the awful stink, some getting permanent lung trouble. The water poisoned by those lagoons leaking into the ground. It was just awful."

"Do you know other people who quit Klavan's?"

"I'm sure there's more than me. There's Drew Petty. He hates the place, too. You should talk to him. He doesn't live far off."

"I'm going to see him next. I've met him. He seems very honest." Andi rose. "I've got to get going."

Odile heaved herself out of her chair and, still holding on to her beer can, got Andi's coat for her. "Those pictures, could I get copies made? I'd want them to show Bobby Del Ray."

"Don't see why not. I'll get them copied for you."

"I really appreciate this, Odile." Andi picked out one shot of the lynched pigs. "Could I take this with me?"

"Sure."

As Andi was going to the door, Odile said, "Thing is, it's almost five years since I worked at that place. Their lawyer would probably make much of that, saying things have changed, things have improved."

"Well, *my* lawyer will make much of the fact things *haven't*." She turned at the door. "Why? *Why* would they kill animals this way? Why hang them? Why not shoot them or even knife them? Euthanasia is obviously not a thing they'd bother with, but there's something horribly perverted about those snapshots."

"Why'd they do it? Power. Because they could."

51

Uncle Drew?"

Andi smiled when he opened the door of the trim little house.

"Well, hello there, Miss Andi. Come on in." He held the door wide.

Inside, she asked him if Dewey was there.

"No, he's not. Did you need to see him?"

"Not him, no. You." She smiled. "I don't think he'd approve of me talking to you about Klavan's."

"Ah. Well, try as we might we just can't please everybody, now, can we?"

It amused Andi that he always acted as if he were in on whatever it was. She followed him back to the kitchen, which must have been the room in which he lived for the large part of the day.

"Now, you just sit down. I'll get you some coffee."

It was a comfort that he seemed not to think her purpose here was suspicious or even odd. She could already feel that mantle of calm settling over the kitchen. It was quite amazing, really, his effect on things. No request seemed to surprise him. She hoped that acting as a witness in a legal suit wouldn't either.

He set down her coffee. It was in a bright blue mug with a happy face on it. Those yellow smiley faces had always annoyed her, but here it seemed right. That smile seemed full of promise.

"What can I do for you?"

"You mentioned a generation of your family working at Klavan's. Did that include you?"

"Yes, indeed. I worked there at one time when I couldn't get a job anywhere else." He added a little cream to his fresh mug of coffee and sipped it.

Andi drank hers black as she waited. From his expression, she thought he meant to say more, and he did.

"I was an accountant and Klavan's just happened to need one. Another one, that is." He spooned a mite of sugar into his mug and slowly stirred. "I guess that was hypocritical of me."

"Why do you say that?"

"Because if I'd worked where Dewey and the others did—I mean, worked with the pigs—I'd not have lasted very long, job or no job." He shook his head sadly and slowly. He said, "But you won't either, will you?" His look was quizzical, as if he couldn't see her in that role.

"No, I won't. We're going to sue Klavan's because they abuse those pigs something awful."

His slow smile suggested he was coming to realize something surprising and wonderful. Then he pounded his fist on the table hard enough to jump the mugs. "God*damn!* It's about time! You're with one of them animal groups, right? They got you in there to spy on the bastards! Excuse my French. God*damn!*"

His animation, like Odile Nekoma's, made her laugh. "You're partly right. But I don't belong to any organization."

"Then who's doing the suing?"

"I am. When I said 'we' I meant my lawyer. His name's Bobby Del Ray. Do you know him?"

He screwed up his face in an effort of remembrance. "Name sounds familiar, but I don't know. So you're saying you're doing this on your own?"

She nodded.

"Well, girl, let me shake your hand!" He reached his out and Andi took it. "Years ago, I called up some animal rights bunch that said it would look into it. They got so many complaints from different people it was all they could do to catch up. It's all these factory farms and agribusinesses. Ones that are ten, twenty times bigger than Klavan's. I read where they kill millions of animals a day. A *day*. Who's eatin' all that meat? Well, we are, but how much do we have to eat? And why anyway do we have to eat it at all? I stopped eatin' pork. Then I stopped eatin' beef and lamb. All I eat now is chicken, but I'll probably have to stop that, too, from what I've heard." Uncle Drew reflected on that for a moment. "Dewey. He won't never stop eatin' meat. He makes a point of tellin' me that, too. I tell him if it's pork chops he's gotta cook 'em himself. He calls me a sissy."

"*Sissy?* That's a new one. That's one I've never heard. Is it manly to whip pigs? Kick and prod them? Hang them?" She took the snapshot from her pocket and slipped it across the table.

"Oh, my Lord." He whispered it almost as if raising his voice would bring the picture alive. He fiddled a cigarette from his pack, stuck it in the corner of his mouth, and lit a kitchen match, all the while with his eyes fixed on that snapshot.

"You worked in the office, then? But you did see things you didn't approve of."

"I saw things, all right. Made me sick, how they did those pigs. Out behind one of the huts they had what they called their 'dead pile.' They'd just toss pigs, some not even dead, just sick—toss 'em on the pile. They probably still do it, don't they?"

"They do." She leaned closer across the table. "Listen, Uncle Drew, what I'm trying to do is get people to be witnesses as to how Klavan's treats those animals. I'm talking about if it comes to a trial. Would you?"

"I sure would."

"Do you know anybody else who worked there and had the same reaction?"

He rubbed his head and closed his eyes. He looked as if he might come forth with some dire prediction about the world. "I do, yes. There was a man named Melvin Duggan quit and went to BigSun. Out of the frying pan into the fire, that was. Then he quit BigSun. What I can do is call him for you. He lives over in Preston. That's where BigSun is. I guess that's the reason he went to work there, even though he figured it'd be pretty bad. But a man has to eat, I guess." He sounded as if he weren't too sure about that. "Want me to call him?"

"I'd really appreciate that."

Uncle Drew smiled. "Of course, if I was to testify, Dewey would probably never speak to me again, but that's just too bad." He shook his head. "Well, it wasn't only that, was it? They fiddled the books, too, didn't they? I think I was there to make it look good."

She called Bobby Del Ray, thinking he probably wouldn't be in his office on a Saturday.

He was. "I work weekends and holidays and pay myself overtime."

"I wanted to tell you I thought about this and I want to go ahead if you're willing. I found two witnesses and might get more." She told him about the day she'd spent talking to Odile and Drew.

"That's good, for a start. Very good."

52

Eddie told her she could get the bus from Bismarck to Minot and that he could meet her there with his car. They could then drive to Preston. He was happy to do it; he wanted to help.

She had only half-lied to Jim about the trip, telling him she wanted to see her friend Eddie and get him to agree to testify. She said nothing about the bar in Preston. Drew Petty had done as he'd said he would, called this Melvin Duggan. He told Andi that Duggan would meet with her, and maybe bring another employee, too. There was a bar called Zero's where they could meet.

"Why would Eddie be a witness?" said Jim. "What's he know about it?"

She had to tell him then about the truck breakdown outside the Stardust Motel.

"My God, Andi—" He'd laughed. "You're more determined than Dakota."

"Maybe that's why we get along."

It might have been the same Greyhound bus, this time going the other way, to Minot. The seats were kind of lumpy, but Andi liked it, probably would have liked it if she'd had to stand all the way. It was transport; it was taking her where she needed to go.

The bus stopped at a crossroads to let some passengers out. The two roads cut across each other as straight as strings; you would think all directions were possibilities. And there was really nothing else in the vicinity except a lone farm, the outline of either house or barn black on the crest of a small hill. No animals could be seen. Maybe a dairy farm, the cows all gone home.

But then she saw a line of buffalo that had been hidden because of the dip of the hill. She hadn't seen any bison since the Theodore Roosevelt National Park, outside Medora. She watched them move laboriously, their big heads dipping with every step, as their hooves sent up dust clouds that fogged the path behind them. They moved in this languorous, almost choreographed line so perfectly that she wondered where they were kept, if they were. Their slow progress made her sad; she watched the line of them as the sun caught fire behind them and the dust they'd stirred up turned to smoke. Moving so slowly with their bearded, bowed heads, they seemed tragic.

In another hour, they reached Minot and the station and filed out of the bus. Eddie was standing beside his car, squinting at the passengers, not seeing her at first. When he did see her, he waved his arms above his head as if signaling a plane or a ship at sea that here he was, in need of rescue.

Andi gave him a peck on the cheek and a hug. "I'm really glad to see you, Eddie." She was, too, for Eddie had gladly shared a part of her life that no one else, except for Uncle Drew and Odile, seemed to want.

They got in the car and Eddie pulled out of the station and headed north. "Where do we go when we get to Preston?"

"A bar called Zero's. It's on the main street. A man named Melvin Duggan; there might be another one, but he wasn't sure."

"Well, do you want me with you when you talk to him? I think it's better if you do it alone, don't you?" He accelerated and pulled out and around an ancient truck.

"I think you're right. But you could still be in the bar."

"Yeah, okay. Damned BMW."

The car flashed by them, silver or star-colored.

"Why do people pay small fortunes for cars?" she said. "Why do they have to do that to feel they're all right?"

"Well, I confess I don't get too excited about driving this piece of junk you are currently in."

"Is it Mrs. Orbison's? She got mad about that when Jake drove it."

"Yeah, but I drive it all the time. She just wanted another reason for being mad at me. Me, I've always hankered after a Ford Mustang."

"That's different; that's being in love with one automobile, not with luxury. And you'd probably take care of it—you know, be your own mechanic. That's different."

He felt better, she could tell. Probably, he'd been lumping himself with the luxury-loving. "Yeah, I guess you're right."

He didn't mind the BMW now so much as it floated down the highway ahead of them.

"What do you think's gonna happen with this lawsuit?"

"I can't even guess. Bobby Del Ray says it'll take a long time to move it forward. A long time."

53

Zero's was one of those bars where the customers—almost all of them men in suede jackets or heavy wool shirts—seemed wedded to the bar like beer-pulls. They looked as if they hadn't been home for a long time and meant to keep it that happy way.

"You know what he looks like?"

"My friend who called him told me to look for a man with red hair who'd be wearing a red wool shirt. That must be him." She nodded in the direction of a man with a broad face in a red shirt. Someone else, another man, was sitting at his table. "That must be one of his friends."

"Okay, I'll sit here," said Eddie. He was standing by an empty stool and being inspected by the men on either side.

Andi went to the back of the room, where two unused pool tables claimed most of the space.

The two men—one was the redhead whom she took for Melvin Duggan; the other, thin-faced and tall-looking, wore what looked like the jacket from an old suit—they seemed to match each other and sat with the assurance that they'd been grandfathered in as far as Zero's went.

They watched her as she came toward their table. Two other men had begun shooting pool. The one who made the break did it clumsily.

"Melvin Duggan?" She held out her hand, smiling tentatively. He didn't look like a man who welcomed smiles. "I'm Andi Oliver."

He nodded and took her hand. "Ma'am. Drew told me you wanted information. You going to try taping this or anything?" He looked at her chest, not with any apparent interest in her breasts, but in what else she might be wearing under her vest.

"No, I'm not." If it had been the Bailey boys there'd be offers to pat her down, ha-ha.

"This here's Tim Dooley."

He was a thin, nervous, polite man a little like Uncle Drew himself. He also seemed friendlier than Melvin Duggan, or at least less paranoid.

"Tim, he worked a ways down the line—"

"Head skinner," said Tim.

"We both worked on the floor. Me, I was a knocker. You know, stun-bolt gun. But I was good at it; cow'd come down the chute to the knock box, it'd only take me one go to knock it out. Well, that's what it's always supposed to be, only others doing that job, they'd hit that old cow two, three times, and even then, some were still conscious." Melvin stopped to draw in on his cigarette. Then he put his hands on his thighs. "Drew said you worked at Klavan's and don't like it. That makes three of us."

"How did you stand it?"

"It was the pay. A person can stand near anything if he can just pick up his pay packet at the end of the day. But then you go out and get drunk just because you *can't* stand it. At least, I was good at it, though it's not much to brag about. What I mean is, I could do it right. If you use the knock gun right, the cow's completely out of it and dies. Do it wrong, animal might go out for seconds, but then he regains consciousness and he's still alive when he's hauled up for the sticker. I've known some knockers drive that bolt seven, eight times into the animal's head and the poor beast is *still* alive and kicking. I mean actual kicking. It's dangerous as hell for the guys near it."

Tim nodded, almost imperceptibly. He struck Andi as not being used to trouble and one who would avoid it if he could. "I recall more than one day when every cow was still alive by the time it got to me."

"Then you had to skin them alive."

Tim closed his eyes and nodded. "Yes, ma'am, I did. And a cow can look at you and the less imagining you do over that look, the better."

Andi saw in her mind's eye the pen outside the plant and the look in that cow's soft eyes. She shut her own. The less imagining . . . Tim was right.

Andi told them what she wanted.

"Yeah, Drew said somethin' about that." Melvin fell back against the booth as if he were broken. "I don't know about that."

"But you don't work there anymore, so you wouldn't be jeopardizing your jobs."

"No, that's true. But we could end up like Johnny Johnson." He turned to Tim. " 'Member him?"

Tim nodded deeply, as if the man were forever implanted in his thoughts. "Trouble was, Johnny had a mouth on him. Whaddaya call it? Whistle-blowing? They fished Johnny out of the Little Missouri up there in Teddy Roosevelt Park. He went up there to fish a lot."

"Fishing accident is what got around. Johnny drowned. First fisherman I ever knew to do that. Pretty funny."

"Was there something to contradict that?"

Melvin cocked his head. "You ever hear of a fisherman drowning in the river he's fishing?" Melvin snorted his disbelief. "What the police said was he hit his head on a rock, slipped maybe and hit his head."

This time Tim snorted. "More likely that old rock was in somebody's hand."

Andi said, "You're afraid something like that could happen to you."

They didn't answer. Melvin finally said, "Aren't you?" His black eyes fastened onto her like leeches.

Andi took to Melvin Duggan in a strange way. Maybe because he wasn't being condescending. She didn't answer the question, though.

Tim said, "Now, that don't mean we won't testify."

Melvin tossed his longish hair back off his neck. "That's true. I was just saying."

"Anyway, it could be a long time before it gets to the point of testifying. I really appreciate your talking to me." She rose. They made an effort to do so, but the table held them prisoner.

"Nice to meet you," said Melvin from a crouch. Tim nodded.

Andi was tired. On the way back, she said, "They're both kind of on the fence. But I can't blame them. They were saying it's dangerous." Andi told Eddie about Johnny Johnson.

"Don't you get scared, Andi? Look at what you're up against."

"I get scared, yes. I think I'll stay at the Stardust tonight. I can't face another bus ride at the moment." She looked in her small wallet. "I've got enough money."

He waved that away. "Be our guest."

She smiled. "Why don't I believe the owner would second that motion?"

"Oh, she's eatin' out of my hand ever since that Jake talked to her."

"Jake's good at that."

54

The next afternoon, she got off the bus from Minot where it stopped along 83 and then hitched a ride to Kingdom. She was lucky and had to flag down only one car; the driver was going all the way to Beulah. From there she could walk if she had to.

She was hungry, hadn't eaten since eight that morning, so she stopped in at the diner.

Norman Black turned to her as she walked in. "Hey, where in hell were you last night?" His smile wasn't convincing.

"Last night?" She couldn't believe her trip to Preston had so quickly become gossip. "Out. Why?"

"Well, I hope 'out' doesn't mean that town where BigSun is."

"Preston. Why?" Something was coming she wouldn't want to hear.

"You never heard about the fire?"

"No." She tried to hold down the panic.

"BigSun. 'Bout midnight. Buildings, most of them, went up like dry kindling. The offices didn't burn so I guess they're glad they've still got their undoubted cooked books. Interesting thing was no animals got hurt. There weren't many in the pens at that hour and the few that were there got released. Pigs, a few cows, sheep. They were over in a field, just wandering around. I never."

She wanted to laugh, or sing, or something. "What caused it?"

"They're saying arson."

She had been half-standing, propped against the counter, and now she sat down, hard. "*What?* Arson?"

"Police are talking about some animal rights group—"

Andi shook her head. "No legitimate one burns down buildings."

"That's what I thought. Of course, they're not ruling out an individual could have done it. They're pursuing 'several lines of inquiry,' as they say."

She hesitated, then said, "You're not thinking I had something to do with this, are you?"

"Your name was brought up. Guess who brought it?"

"The Baileys."

He nodded. "The idea's around."

"My name's 'around'?"

"Why are you surprised? You made no secret of how you hated the place."

"It's a long way from hating to torching." Actually, it wasn't, not as far as she was concerned. "For all I know, it could've been a Bailey just so they could blame it on me." Her heart was racing.

"You know it wasn't a Bailey."

"How?"

"Can you picture them getting the animals out of harm's way?"

He was right. They wouldn't have.

When Mildred came down to her end of the counter, instead of ordering, Andi said that she had to go. "See you later, Norman."

He answered, but she didn't hear it.

In Jim's driveway, the cab came to a stop behind the sheriff's car. That, thought Andi, did not bode well. She sighed and paid for the cab ride and went to the kitchen door.

"Andi!" said Jim. "You heard about BigSun?"

When Harry McKibbon turned to her, she averted her eyes. She felt his look. "Yes, I heard. Don't expect me to be sorry."

"That's the point," Harry said.

Then she looked up at him. "What's that mean?"

"That you might be happier than anyone around."

Jim's slight smile didn't reach his eyes, as if his eyes were taking back what his mouth offered. "Where you going with this, Harry?"

Harry said to Andi, "I understand you took a trip yesterday."

Jim made to protest, but Harry held up his hand like a crossing guard.

"Sheriff, you can't think I—"

"Where were you?"

"Look, it takes hours to get to Preston, if that's what you're thinking."

"It isn't. Where were you?"

She sat down, furious with him for taking this tone because he had good reason to do so.

Jim answered before she could. "She was visiting a friend of hers, I told you, off U.S. 83. He runs a motel there."

"Andi?"

"Well, that's right, that's where I was. You can call the friend if you want."

"I will. What's the name?"

"Eddie Crane. Here." She rooted in her backpack for the Stardust's phone number and handed it to him.

"Thanks." He took out his notebook and copied it. "You spent the night there?"

She nodded. She didn't care what he inferred from that.

"I heard you got yourself a lawyer." He clicked his ballpoint pen a couple of times. "You should be careful, Andi. You're riling a few people with this business."

She said nothing.

He smiled slightly. " 'Fomenting unrest' is the way one person put it."

"I'm surprised, to tell you the truth, anyone would be bothered by anything I did."

"Don't kid yourself."

"Is that all, Sheriff? I need to take Dakota out for a little while."

He nodded and put away his notebook and pen. "Sure. You'll stay around in case I need to ask you anything else."

It wasn't a question.

WHEN TROUBLE CAME

55

The scope of the Remington was zeroed for two hundred yards. Grainger set out the black bull's-eye at that distance. The cover he'd found was two hundred yards from the house, across the road—a hill, treed and layered with red rock. It was the only cover around, but it was ideal. The rock striations reminded him of the Badlands. Layered as the rock was, it formed a shallow, cavelike opening at one point, flat and offering an ideal position from which to shoot.

He was in an area way off the road, some distance from where he'd parked the car, unfortunately not a four-wheel drive; he hadn't been able to find one on the Toyota lot. But it didn't make any difference; it just made him walk a little farther.

He rested the Remington on the sandbags he'd taken from a roadworks section of U.S. 83 at two AM. It was absent of workers. He'd grabbed them from around the orange cones and tossed them in the trunk. It was easier than buying sacks of feed (and someone remembering he'd bought them).

Grainger rested the Remington on the two sandbags, drew the stock into his shoulder, felt it warm against his skin, and fired three shots. They made a neat cluster, but slightly off-center, say, an inch left of the bull's-eye. With the windage knob on the scope he dialed four right clicks, an adjustment an inch to the right. Then he reloaded and fired three shots again. Perfect. Dead center. He removed the casings and dropped them in a pocket.

He got up and carefully placed the rifle in a padded case. He collected the target and the bags and walked back to his car.

It was time for dinner and he was hungry. He headed toward Kingdom.

Grainger knew her the moment she walked through the door of the diner. Young and pretty, but it was the hair that did it. They had said she was a blonde. That word didn't quite do it. It was a blondness so ethereal—the only word he could think of to describe it—it put him in mind of a J. M. W. Turner, the way it picked up light. No, it was more the way it was its own light. It was one of those Turnerlike gauzes, filaments of light.

He was sitting in the booth at the end of the row. The girl sat down at the counter beside a man who must favor the place, as he'd had a half dozen refills on his coffee. Maybe he'd been waiting for her, too. No wonder. They were talking.

Grainger was glad the man was on her right side, for that meant her face was visible to him when she turned to talk to him. Grainger could look directly at her from where he sat drinking coffee, finishing up his apple pie (which was good), and then smoking one of his small cigars.

She'd been smiling, but now she stopped. Her face was serious, grave. He wondered what the guy had said to her. What bad news he'd imparted. He was just as glad he didn't talk to people. He had nothing against them for the most part, only he hated small talk and bad news.

He didn't even need the snapshot, which was bad anyway, showing her from a distance. Anyone else might have said, "Real pretty, ash-blond hair," but he valued precision. It was his business, you could say, to look on things point-blank.

He left the diner by the exit in the back so as not to walk past her, although it made no difference if she saw his face, since she wasn't going to see it from two hundred yards. No difference that he could think of. But there might be one he couldn't.

He walked the six blocks to his black Toyota. Not exactly his, but the one he was currently driving. He'd picked the first one up in Bismarck from a big parking lot out behind a supermarket. He chose it because black wasn't an attention getter, and, Lord knows, not a black Camry. Minutes later he was switching the plates from the first to the second black Toyota Camry on a Toyota used-car lot.

Grainger could make a living boosting cars; it just wasn't very interesting work; it wasn't very demanding, either.

Police would have a hell of a time chasing down that license plate. It wasn't going anywhere.

He had checked into a motel on the outskirts of Beulah on State Road 200. It was ten miles from Kingdom, a comfortable distance. The motel was as anonymous as he was.

Times like this, sitting in some nondescript motel room, he seriously missed the Gulf, though he wouldn't say that to a living soul. Skill had been necessary there. It took more skill to put one shot in the right place than a dozen on jobs like this. The Gulf War, you could expect anytime to have a sniper's gun fix on you from the roof of a building a quarter mile away.

A job like this was just too easy. A hundred thousand was way over what this job was worth, at least to his way of thinking, but that's what he'd asked for, just to test the waters with these people, and the damned fools had shelled it out.

They must really want her dead. She was awfully young; she was just a girl, for God's sake, but they really wanted her out of the picture. He wondered why.

56

It's all over the place, what you've been doing."

They were in the farrowing hut.

"What? What have I been doing?"

"You've gone and got that hotshot lawyer over in Bismarck, and you've been drumming up witnesses for a legal suit," said Jake. "Klavan's suspicious you're coming in here with a camera or something."

"If they aren't abusing these pigs, then why's he worried?"

"Are you kidding? Of *course* he knows we're treating these animals like shit. Only he doesn't call it abuse because as far as he's concerned it's what you do; they're dumb animals that don't know what's going on and wouldn't care if they did. That's if he stops to think about it, which he doesn't. This is just the way farms like this do it. *He doesn't care,* for God's sakes! People don't care."

"You do." Her stare seemed to be what turned him around to head out the door as if she had some witchy power.

"I'm not the bastard who's after your hide," Jake threw back over his shoulder as he walked though the door.

Klavan was right to be suspicious. The digital camera she'd brought with her belonged to Odile Nekoma. It was several years old and too chunky to hide in her clothes, so she carried it in a canvas bag she'd shoved down into one of the sows' crates.

"Take the memory card to some camera store in Bismarck and do it yourself," Odile had told her.

It was easy enough to get shots of the pregnant sows in Hut 5 and the crates so narrow they couldn't turn around. When Vernon appeared, she shoved it quickly into the canvas bag. Vernon had never been very observant.

He said, "You doin' anything useful?"

"Do I ever do anything useful?"

"No, now you mention it." He laughed his raspy laugh as he checked the watering system.

"Are they loading up today?" Andi asked.

"Not likely. I don't think Klavan's got another plant yet."

"Which one can they use besides BigSun?"

"Maybe one of the South Dakota operations. Or one in Mexico. But BigSun'll be back in business soon."

"I'm sure." Andi tossed the canvas bag over her shoulder and left. But at least it was a reprieve, no matter how short a one.

Hutch and Nat were herding pigs somewhere. Slapping the pigs' backsides and bringing the prod into play.

The two of them were standing on one side of the ramp and there was nobody else there except for the truck drivers, who were out of their trucks and laughing.

She had cut a hole in her vest just big enough for the camera's eye; the camera itself was hidden beneath the vest. She had caught a particularly nasty bit where Hutch couldn't get a pig to move and kicked the animal in the face. The blood spattered his sweater and that further enraged him; he brought the steel pipe down on the pig's skull. The pig died with brain matter on the ramp.

What in God's name made them so angry at these animals?

She had started back to Hut 5 when one of the office workers called to her and waved her over.

"What?" she called back.

"Klavan wants to see you." He hitched his thumb over his shoulder. "Office."

Oh, God. She looked around for someplace to drop the camera, but with him standing there watching, she couldn't do that. All she could do was press it against her side with her arm while she called out, "I've got to go to the toilet."

He called back, "So there's one up here. Come on."

Reluctantly, Andi made her way to the office. The fellow didn't wait; he went on ahead. At least she was able to pull the camera from inside her vest and put it in her canvas bag. But what, then, was she to do with the bag?

Jake was there, but trying not to be. She wondered as she passed him on the way to the ladies' if Klavan had questioned Jake and that was why he wasn't looking her way.

She dropped the lid on the toilet and sat down. There was no place in here to stash the bag. She'd been hoping for a large trash can where she could shove the camera down in the paper towels.

There was the coat rack she'd bumped against. She flushed the toilet and ran water in the sink. Then she picked up the canvas bag with the camera and thought, *Hide it in plain sight.*

The coat rack outside the bathroom was crowded with coats and carryalls. It was mobile, like the ones that department stores use, with two metal bars across and wheels. There were hooks and hangers on both sides. She slung the canvas bag over one of the hooks on the side facing the wall and pulled herself together and walked to Klavan's office.

Jake, she felt, was watching her every step of the way.

She tapped on the door, which was open anyway.

"Yeah? Come on in."

Andi walked in but was not asked to sit down.

"You're Andi Oliver?" Klavan sat back and tossed his pen on the desk. "Girl, what the hell do you think you're playing at?"

Andi frowned so deeply her brows nearly met in the middle. "What do you mean, Mr. Klavan?"

"You *know* what I damn well mean. What's real funny is you think you can do it."

Same frown, but now she tilted her head to one side as if a different perspective might illuminate what he was saying. "Do what?"

He leaned forward. "You been stirring things up saying that we mistreat these pigs."

Her look now was puzzled. "We do. Is that even an issue?"

Now he was out of his chair. "They're pigs, lady, *pigs*. They're here for one purpose only: to feed us!"

"Do they know that?"

Klavan picked up the ledger he'd been working on and slapped it down. "Who the fuck do you think you are? You waltz in here a couple months ago and act as if you own the place!" His voice was rising murderously. "You maneuver around my employees like Jake and get him to help you, probably having sex with him—"

"Did Jake say that?"

"Didn't need to. Then you go round Kingdom talking about the awful conditions here. Let me tell you a home truth, girl: I've had DOA inspectors in here and the place passed fine. Only little problem was the lagoon. And we're fixing that. So if you don't stop all this I'm gonna take you to court."

"I don't know what you mean."

Klavan got so red-faced Andi thought he might have a stroke. With his wide shoulders and meaty arms, he rose behind the desk like a mountain.

"Let me tell you something, little lady, you are gonna be sorry. You had best be careful. I mean be careful, for you will be dealt with!"

To Andi it sounded like a voice coming out of a volcano before the lava started sliding down its sides. "I can't think what you're talking about."

"Keep it up and you'll find out!" More lava, boiling. She thought the man would have a coronary, which was all right with her.

"Open that vest!"

"What?"

"Open it up. Unless I'm crazy, you got yourself a camera inside there."

"I do not."

He was coming around his desk. "Either you open it or I rip it off."

"You do and I'll call the police."

"Fuck the police!" He came toward her. As he reached out his hand and grabbed the coat, Andi flung the door back and yelled, "Stop!" The temptation to cry out "Rape!" was strong in her, but she feared that might compromise the case.

To the three stunned people in the outer office, he called out, "She's been taking pictures—"

Andi right away unzipped the vest for all to see and took it off. "I told you I don't have a camera."

That set him back. He took a few steps away from her. "Go on, get the hell out!"

"Does this mean I'm fired?"

He slammed the door in her face. Jake was standing behind her. "Christ, Andi. Didn't I warn you?"

"I think I'm fired."

Jake said nothing.

Feeling an awful sadness wash over her, like rain, she walked over to the coat rack. He followed her.

"You're too good to be working in this place, Jake."

Jaw clenched, he answered, "Some of us got to be practical. You don't."

She hitched the canvas bag over her shoulder. "No, I guess I don't. Good-bye, Jake."

57

He did not know at precisely what point she'd be on the path, only that she'd be on it. She'd walked it, bucket in hand like a milkmaid, every day of the four he'd been here watching. It was always after dinner, a meal consumed at slightly different times each evening. But she was dependable in her visits to the barn and the pigsty. Once she had carried two buckets, all of it feed of some sort for the horses and pigs. She seemed to like the pigs, the way she hung over the fence to watch them.

He'd been watching the house from the rocks across the road at a range of two hundred yards. He had watched her walk that path several times a day, at different times; the evening walk, though, was dependably after their meal. It was still light, with no obstructions. Through his binoculars, he had watched them: the girl and two men. He knew nothing about her.

There was also the barn. In the late afternoon, she brought out a handsome coal-black horse and a mule or donkey. They went rambling off, out across the field, where there was no cover at all except for two very large trees. He had checked that position out.

A hundred feet or so on the other side of the house, there was an exercise ring. She saddled up the black horse and fell off it at least three times before she managed to get herself into the saddle. He loved that. Sometimes she fell off the other side. Finally, she levered herself into

the saddle and rode him around the ring. It was the worst horseman-
ship Grainger had ever seen. This girl couldn't have grown up here
around horses. So the two men he'd seen—the one around most of the
time, whom he'd taken to be her father—neither would be the father,
to his way of thinking. There were no women. There was one short
man with a dark complexion who took care of the horses. Was she also
a hired hand? Also hired to take care of the horses, to breeze them
around the track? Definitely not. He laughed silently.

If this were war, that laugh could have gotten him killed. Silent or
not, his body had moved.

He'd scoped out the bedroom window. This was no prurient act;
he'd just wanted to know what times she did what things. She passed
by the window several times every night. Sometimes she stood perfectly still before it. She had never been naked, and sometimes she
pulled down the shade.

He wondered what she'd done to make it worth this money to get
rid of her. Maybe an inheritance with her standing to collect the whole
thing? Maybe a witness to murder? Maybe a jealous wife?

No, somehow that didn't go with the girl. She wasn't old enough,
didn't seem sophisticated enough, to fill the role of the other woman.

Grainger plucked off his baseball cap, wiped the moisture from his
forehead, and pulled the cap back on. It was cold, but the intensity of
his concentration made him sweat; it always did. That action with the
cap would also have got him killed in Kuwait. He might as well have
stood and waved his arms over there. But here, no one was looking for
him, so the danger was minimal.

He had been here with his equipment for five hours on the fourth
day after he'd seen her in that diner. She just seemed so young to be
in life-threatening trouble. He could wonder, but he didn't want to
know.

He wondered what her name was.

He didn't want to know that either. His contact had said the name
she was going by was Andi Oliver.

The name she was going by. Was she a fugitive? Witness Protection
Program? No comment from his contact. The contact wasn't the one

hiring him. Grainger always insisted on anonymity, not only for himself but for whoever was shelling out the money. He didn't want to know who was hiring him. He didn't want to connect with the bastard who was paying the fee.

He wanted a smoke. The danger of smoking on a job had been hammered into him with such force that he never chanced the thread of smoke. And even though no one was looking for him up here, at least so far, he held to that rule.

What had she done? The less he knew the better. Sometimes the person who hired him was so eager to tell him about the target and what the target had done to him or her, Grainger had to order them right off to keep it to themselves.

"*What? Well, I just thought—*"

"*You thought wrong.*"

She had disappeared for hours the first day he'd been here, which was the day after seeing her in the diner. Grainger assumed those hours when she wasn't here were the ones she worked that job at the pig farm.

He'd scoped that out, too, but why choose a public venue when a private one was available? This horse farm or ranch or whatever it was had her moving in and out, back and forth, by herself a dozen times a day, early morning and evening. But she must not have gone to work today as she was at the house before he was on the hill. Maybe she came home early.

Nobody was watching her back.

He waited. He uncased the rifle and the scope, shot the bolt and dropped the cartridges into it, pulled back the bolt, placed his cheek against the stock, and drew the rifle into his shoulder. He felt as if someone had just settled over his shoulders a suit of impeccable cut and tailoring. There was a strange rush of coming home that he couldn't explain. It was that smooth. He lowered the rifle and sat back and waited.

Waited and thought about the war. He'd had his own team. The one day when four of them had been deployed around the roof of a large house, what was left of an estate, once beautiful, now largely bombed out. The setting had put Grainger in mind of a gorgeous ruin he had seen in a photograph, an old house with an overgrown garden behind, concrete pools, dry then, but anchored by statues in graceful poses, now fallen from their pedestals, some broken. Two of the men had been killed by countersniper fire. The shots had to have come from a thousand yards away, at least.

Here, the sun was setting over the burnished field and the shadowed rocks. He waited for the girl, checked the time. She was not like clockwork.

Late morning wasn't as good because she left at eleven-thirty for work and was always in the company of one man or the other. Perhaps she was visiting for a while. The way she sat that black horse convinced him this wasn't her home.

He told himself to stop wondering, to stop making deductions on the basis of basically nothing.

Ordinarily, he didn't do this. But ordinarily, his targets were men, most looking hard: looking as if they'd be glad to return the favor if he wanted to take it outside.

He didn't get into fights because once he'd killed a man. The fight was fair and square, the killing probably wasn't; he'd told himself to rein it in and he hadn't.

Grainger disliked situations where he was under orders from himself to control himself. So he avoided anything that might give rise to things getting out of hand.

This work was not one of them. He had a target. He hit the target. Always. Never missed. Granted, the targets were easier to hit than in the war. There the enemy would be looking for him. Sharpshooters, marksmen, and especially snipers had to be removed.

What had happened there never should have happened. The camouflage was first-rate. He could barely pick his men out himself. When they had finally got to Willie—and they'd waited until nightfall to do it—Grainger saw what it was that had given Willie's position away. It wouldn't have made any difference if it had been night, but in daylight, it did: the end of Willie's rifle was dead black, and that gave it away. Nature wasn't into black; nothing in it was black. Dark, but not black.

She had come out of the side door. He lifted the rifle and pulled it against his shoulder as smooth as glass. He looked through the scope where the crosshairs quartered her head perfectly. At that second came a sudden jolt and flare of sun and her hair blazed in it.

It was as if the trigger pulled itself. There was the blur, the kick of the gun, and she was still standing.

He'd missed.

The bullet had grazed her head apparently, for she stood stock-still with her hand to it. That second which should have begun her collapse to earth instead had her hand flying to her head.

He'd quickly retrieved the binoculars and watched as she withdrew her hand from her face. She stood absolutely still. She didn't run, didn't even try to make her way back to the house. Frozen with fear, probably; yet he had the sense that she was waiting.

For the final shot? As if she figured she couldn't get away and running would only provoke a gunman into action. But not to move took someone with a hell of a lot of control, or one practiced in the art of confronting danger.

Or (and this was probably the real reason) she didn't know what had happened and stood puzzling over it. She stayed that way for several seconds, not even regarding her hand. There must not have been any blood.

He plucked out the brass case and stuck it in his pocket. He did not put another one in. He waited as she waited.

58

At first, Andi told herself it must have been a wasp or bee sting. Yet something going that fast, torpedoing across her cheek, she doubted could be an insect; an insect didn't move like that. An insect hovered, flew about.

The only other thing she could think of—and she was trying not to—was a bullet. There was a bead of blood, perhaps a tiny scrape.

Someone was shooting at her.

She knew this also from the sudden glint of light. She knew that glint; she'd seen it a dozen times when she'd been practicing at the shooting range. A wink of light on metal. Like the wink of an eye. *Get this.* At first she almost turned and looked across and up—

But stopped herself. It was important that she not turn her head at the ninety-degree angle it would take to look off at the rocks way over on the other side of the road. She didn't want the shooter to know she'd spotted the source, but couldn't think far enough ahead to understand why she thought this.

Why hadn't there been another shot?

Here she was, out in the open, stock-still and halfway between house and barn. She didn't run because it would do little good; it might set off another shot, but while she stood there for the three or four seconds it had taken to think, no other shot came.

She didn't want the shooter realizing she knew he was there.

These thoughts lay like lead in her mind, weighted. Her whole body felt weighted, like a body in a dream that can't run. She had to force herself to move and she did, toward the barn, not the house, although the house was where she wanted to go, to go back to it, to rush through the door and scream and have Jim and Tom take care of it. She wanted to throw herself at someone—Jim, Tom, Jake, Harry, even Eddie—and have him take care of it.

But she didn't because she couldn't. Because she knew there was no way out of anything except to stand your ground.

She reached the safety of the barn's interior, and even though she'd lost no blood, she slid down the wall inside and felt she was leaving a trail of it behind her the way Harry Wine had done.

Her only concession to the danger was that she did not take Dakota and Sam out for their afternoon walk through the field. She knew Dakota was not at all pleased with this change of plan and expressed it in his usual way. When she gave them both an extra carrot, he snorted and ate it with his back to her.

When she finally made the return journey, barn to house, she didn't tell Jim or Tom, who had their feet up, reading the paper. Although for a moment she stared at the telephone and part of her thought surely the sheriff should be brought in on this, given his suspicions about her, Andi wondered if he'd even believe her.

It must be Klavan's, she thought, lying sleepless in bed at two AM. It must be someone from Klavan's wanting to stop her and the threat of the lawsuit. Or maybe an outfit much bigger than Klavan's, Bobby Del Ray had said.

Or was it Waylans? But why this? He could have shot her right there in that barn if he'd wanted her dead, and no one the wiser for some time. But he wanted something from her—the "information"—which he wouldn't get if she was dead.

The Baileys? They were stupid and mean, but she didn't think they were killers. Probably too cowardly to shoot someone. Lucas, maybe, as he was no coward, she bet, but why was it worth landing himself in jail?

An hour later, exhausted with trying to work it out, she finally fell into sleep.

59

Something wrong?" asked Jim, standing at the stove dropping sausages onto the spitting cast-iron griddle.

Andi was getting out the orange juice. She shook her head. "No. Why?"

"Just you look kind of pale. You're not losing sleep over that Klavan job, are you?"

She shook her head. "No, except it *is* pretty upsetting." And it was, thinking of the pigs. How would they get that little respite from being treated like furniture, things without feelings? Anyone who made a habit of saying animals had no feelings should be forced to spend a day in a slaughterhouse.

What would ever happen to the pigs now? "Goddamn it!" Forcefully, she banged her orange juice down on the table.

"What?"

"Nothing."

Jim laughed. "First I ever heard you taking the Lord's name in vain."

"What Lord?" She drank her juice and stared out of the window.

Jim slid two sunnyside-up eggs onto her plate, along with buttered whole-grain bread. "You never do go to church, do you?"

"Why would I go to church?"

He laughed even more. "People do. With some, it's a regular habit. You don't believe, it seems. Why not?"

"Animals and little children. They have no way to defend them-selves, and life comes at them like a train wreck."

Jim went back to the stove. "There's something in that, true."

Why didn't she tell him? She was asking herself the same questions. She should call the sheriff.

Andi finished her eggs and toast and took her plate to the sink. "Are the police any nearer to finding the ones who set that fire?"

Jim shook his head as he slid more pancakes onto a plate warming on the shelf over the burners. "Not as far as I know. Don't you worry, though. You're alibied all over." He handed her a colander of food scraps. "Here's for the pigs if you're going out there."

Andi took it and stood with it circled in her arm, afraid to push at the screen door. She shifted the colander to her other arm.

"Something wrong?" Jim asked for the second time.

"What? No." She looked across the gravel drive and the circle of green and trees to the sty where the pigs were lined up at the fence, waiting. Both piglets had joined them at the fence, waiting with them, probably not knowing why.

The scene made Andi want to weep. Instead, she pushed the door open, looked back at Jim, who was poking at the sausages. "Those eggs were really good, Jim, your best."

"Well, thank you." He smiled and turned back to the griddle.

She walked out into the light.

She tried not to run; running would do no good. He could hit her one way or the other. If he was shooting from that distance, he was a marksman, maybe even a sniper. What she couldn't understand was how he had missed the first time.

The gravel crunched beneath her feet, the sound of it magnified by fear until it was deafening.

Nothing happened. Perhaps the time of day was wrong. Yesterday, it had been early evening. Also, he might be lying low for a while.

But she guessed not for long. She couldn't imagine a shooter hanging around for a week just to get off one shot. No, he'd do it very soon, she bet.

She turned this over while she fed cabbage leaves and corn cobs to the pigs.

She was facing the far-off rocks and could, without shifting her head, lift her eyes to see if there was any movement there, anything like the glint of light on metal. But he wouldn't make the same mistake twice. It was a perfect place for cover. Had she never been up there, she would never have considered that location.

Night, that would probably be his choice now. Her window faced the rocks.

Grainger was eating dinner in a very bad steak house near his motel. He chewed the steak slowly, washed it down with a Heineken.

It hadn't been wind that had set the trajectory off target. Anyway, he always checked the wind. It had been perfectly calm yesterday, the barest motion of leaves, no more movement than if he had breathed on the branches.

So what was it? Why had he missed?

He checked off all of the things that could mess up a shot: weather, imperfect positioning, breathing wrong—all of it, knowing he wouldn't find anything.

So if it was nothing he could bring to mind, then it was something he *couldn't*, something he couldn't examine and consequently couldn't correct. That really worried him.

He remembered the wife who had left him years before, telling him he was impossible to live with; he was such a perfectionist. He couldn't help but smile. If she walked into his life right now she would probably say the same thing.

Was the job simply too easy? He thought again of the hefty fee whoever had hired him was willing to pay.

He wadded up the paper napkin and tossed it on his half-eaten sirloin steak. He took a swallow of beer. He'd go back, this time after dark. He'd try a night shot. But now he stayed, drinking his beer.

His advantage was that she hadn't known what had actually happened. Had she, she'd have hightailed it back to the house to get help. Someone would have called the police. If that had happened, he'd have gone back and checked out of the motel because they'd be popping every motel in sight, looking at the guests, especially the single males.

No, he would go back tonight. This time he wouldn't miss.

Having to tell himself that made him nervous.

Five years ago, she had said, *"You're shooting someone in cold blood and you don't vacillate? You don't equivocate? You don't hesitate?"*

He'd liked Beth's language and smiled.

"And it amuses you?"

No, it didn't amuse him.

"You were a hero, Billy, a hero in the war. And you come back to do this?"

He had come back with a supreme sense of alienation not of hero-ism. How many men had he killed? A countless number. He had also saved a few, the men in his team, but he had done that because he was extremely good at what he did. And he was still good at it. But he hadn't said this, of course. He had said, "There are no heroes anymore, Beth."

A week later she left him and took their son.

60

ssholes," said Tom, echoing Jim's earlier assessment of the Klavan business. "Thing is, it makes them out to be fearful of a lawsuit and that in turn makes them look guilty. Are they that stupid they can't figure that out? Who're they lawyered up with, do you suppose?"

"A whole firm of lawyers, more likely." Andi speared a cherry tomato so fiercely she almost apologized to it.

"There've been a ton of complaints from people who live downwind of that facility. Leah Bond—you know Leah?" When Tom nodded, Jim went on. "She says she gets fierce headaches, worse than migraines, from the smell. I don't see how that place is complying with regulations. I mean, they're supposed to make sure that 'lagoon'—I love that word—is up to standards."

She was waiting for dark. Andi sat on her bed loading a clip with 9mm cartridges. The Smith & Wesson lay on the bed beside her.

The first time she'd shot this gun, back in the Sandia Mountains of New Mexico, it had thrown her to the ground. Now she was a lot more experienced and a pretty good shot.

When she finished, she shoved the clip into the gun and pulled on her quilted vest and then her jean jacket. She started to jam the gun between her belt and the small of her back and hesitated. She pulled it out, removed the clip, and put the clip in her jacket pocket. Then she pushed the .38 into her belt and left the room.

She didn't see them, but she heard their voices in the kitchen, mildly raised, mildly arguing. She had never heard either really get angry with the other.

"I'm going out to the barn," she called.

"Yeah, okay." They resumed their argument.

She saddled up Dakota, who for once didn't shy away from her or protest. Well, almost didn't protest. He tried pretty hard to shoulder her away, but in the end, using a stool to launch herself upward, she managed to mount him fairly quickly, at least for her.

As she rode him down the drive, Dakota would be wondering if this was to be a repeat of the exciting night with the Bailey brothers. Or she liked to imagine that was in his mind: *"Where are they? Where are those two bastards?"* Fume, fume.

"No," she said aloud, "it's not them tonight. It's just a short ride around that curve up there."

The road snaked to the left just past Jim's house. It was a rather sharp turn that would have a car coming around almost at a right angle. There were a few trees along this curve. When she dismounted, she would be at a right angle to the rocks facing the house.

She tied Dakota's reins to a cedar and told him she'd be back soon. At this point the white moon offered enough light to guide her, and too much to conceal her. It was all she had.

She was into the trees and knee-high Indian grass above the level of the rocks that she was pretty certain the shot had come from. There were several old paths that led to that rocky promontory and up here she could see all of them in the cold light of the moon. So the light did serve her purpose.

Whether he would try again tonight she couldn't say. If he didn't, she'd come back tomorrow, in early daylight. Then again at night. The thing was, she didn't think he'd hang around; he'd want to be gone from here.

Andi settled onto the grassy slope where she liked to sit, took out the gun and the clip, and shoved the clip into the gun. Then she settled back to wait.

Of course, she could be dead wrong. The shot might have been fired from any one of several positions up here, but she thought of that glint of metal made by the sun: that had come from the flat rock eight feet below here. At least, that's where she would have chosen.

Well, she'd rather be dead wrong than dead.

She waited in silence, her chin on her drawn-up knees, and studied the dark pattern of the aspen leaves.

There were hunters who could sit for hours, waiting for a deer or pronghorn to pass into range. Although she didn't like hunting, she had to admire such patience. It spoke of the high seriousness of the hunter. There were hunters, she knew, decent men, who would always track a wounded animal, not let it wander around with a hole in its side, bleeding out. She wished she could talk to such a man; she was naïve when it came to hunting, and before you can hate something you should try to understand it. Except things that seemed beyond understanding, like two lynched pigs twisting in the wind.

She checked her watch: ten-thirty. She'd been out here for two hours. Not a sound except for the burr oaks' creaking of branches.

Only it wasn't the trees. There wasn't a breath of wind. She sat forward, listening. A twig snapped; undergrowth rustled.

Trying to avoid leaving any sign of her presence, Andi inched toward the edge of the rock shelf, looked down, and saw a man—very tall, a big man probably in his thirties or forties the way he carried himself. She could see only a bit of his face since his back was to her.

The rifle he carried looked heavily equipped. She couldn't make out its different parts, but the part on top was probably a telescopic lens. He was carrying several small sacks.

She could see now what he'd seen before. Her illuminated window, where she'd purposely left the light on to suggest she was there; the house, the barn, the path lay in darkness, too far away to make out, except for the tiny light beside the kitchen door, which illuminated the beginning of the path. Since there was no one around (he would assume), he didn't have to be especially careful of the silence; nobody was looking for a shooter. Still, he was heedful. His movements were slow, the rifle carefully handled. He took his time getting into position, flat along the smooth rock, his oilskin coat wadded beneath him and the rifle resting on the sacks.

He'd positioned himself only a few feet beneath her. There were several layers of rock between them and almost behind him that she could use as stepping-stones. She could progress silently, but if he heard her and turned around, she could shoot him, at worst, or, at best, disarm him, which she intended to do anyway.

She was glad he had taken a prone position; it would be much more difficult to make a transition to a sitting position or any other that would allow him to shoot her. He'd have to bring that rifle around and he'd be dead before he could aim it. Of course, if he were really good, he might do it in an eyeblink. She had the discomfiting thought that he probably was, that if he heard her, she'd go down before she could catch a breath. He was probably that good. She'd ask him for lessons if she didn't kill him.

She stepped onto the first rock, waited, descended very slowly to the next. She brushed the bottom of her socks in case they'd picked up anything. Then down again. It took her ten minutes to go the eight feet down. In the Sandias, when she'd been searching for coyotes or foxes caught in steel-jaw traps, she had practiced such stealth. She was good at it.

Then she was there. She was standing near his feet with her gun pointing at the sky. She saw him tense up, grip the rifle, and she put the barrel of the Smith & Wesson against the back of his head.

"I'm Andi. Who are you?"

61

Jesus, thought Grainger. He didn't have to guess what it was; he'd had enough guns pointed at him over the years. But he was stunned to discover who was holding this one: the girl.

"Put the rifle down. *Now.*"

He did it.

"Shove it away from you; shove it back toward me."

He did this, too. Andi pushed it farther out of reach, over to the edge of the rock.

"May I turn around? I hate having to talk to someone behind me." If he could see her, he could probably disarm her.

"No."

"Smart girl." He smiled. "Are we going to stay out here all night? My arms are getting tired."

"Put your hands on top of your head and get up. Slowly." After he rose, she said, "The path down to the road—you came up that way?"

"I came up some path, yes."

"That's how we're going down. I want to see if you stashed anything along it. A gun, maybe."

Now Grainger really smiled. "I didn't. But it's not a bad idea." She must have heard the smile in his voice, for she said, "Let's be clear on one thing: if you try anything, if you make a sudden movement, I'll shoot you. I won't hesitate."

"Can I ask you a question? Where—"

"No. Just walk."

He moved toward the side of the rock where the rough patch converged on rock, and where his Remington lay. "What about the rifle?"

"Leave it. I can come back for it later."

"Where are we going?"

"Just move along. Keep your hands on your head."

"This path is pretty rocky; it's hard; if I fall—"

"Pick yourself up, but leave your hands where they are."

"You're full of sympathy, aren't—"

"Shut up. I'm not here to have a dialogue with a hit man."

He kept the laugh to himself. Aside from roots and rocks, there was no real obstruction on the path and they made it to the road without incident.

"You've got a car, I imagine. Where is it?"

"Half mile up the road there." He nodded in that direction.

"Walk."

He did, she following close after. "Look, if someone driving along sees us, won't I look kind of suspicious like this?"

"If a car comes along, you can drop your hands—"

"Thanks—"

"—and put your arms around me."

This stopped Grainger cold. "What?"

"We'll look cute and it's the only way I can tell what you're doing with your hands. But don't worry. I'll still have this gun in your ribs."

He shook his head. "Sugar, you think of everything."

"*Sugar?* Don't you dare call me that!"

He swallowed the laugh. "Sorry. It's one of those Southern ways I've never been able to drill out of me."

"You're not from the South."

No cars came from either direction. Grainger was disappointed. He'd have loved to put the contingency plan into operation. She was such a pretty girl.

Then it occurred to him that he couldn't be positive she was the *same* girl. He turned before she could stop him. Yep. Same girl.

"Keep your eyes forward."

They went on for another fifty feet when he said, "Right there."

His Camry was pulled onto a dirt track that Andi recognized as an old road to the Custises' abandoned farm. Now it was mud and shale, leaves and roots. The house, though, looked perfectly habitable. They were by the car.

"Open it."

"Keys are in my pocket." He nodded toward the left pocket on his canvas jacket.

With the hand not holding the gun, she reached into the pocket, pulled them out.

To him her hand felt like a swift's wing. As if he knew.

She opened the driver's door, managed to work her way across into the passenger's seat, gun on him the whole time. "Go on, get in. You can put your hands down. You'll be driving." As he got in and rubbed his arms, she asked, "Where are you staying?"

"Motel outside Beulah."

"Okay, let's go."

He kept being surprised by her. "My motel?"

"I can't take you into my house, can I? People there might wonder."

He shut the door on his side. "Yeah, right. I guess I was expecting something along conventional lines, say, like the sheriff's office, the police station, that kind of thing."

She shook her head. "Go on, drive. I'd like to see your license."

"See if I'm old enough? Okay. Here, take the whole wallet." He pulled it out of a back pocket, tossed it to her. "You really want to go to this motel?"

"Call it a dirty weekend." While he turned on the engine, she fished into the wallet and pulled out the license. "Your name's not Tom Green, as it says here." She was looking at the license, then at him, back and forth. "It sounds so stagy. Maybe this isn't your license. The photo doesn't look much like you."

Backing the car onto the road he said, "Nobody looks like their photo."

"True, but this doesn't look like your license because it's not your license." He accelerated down the road as she flicked through a plastic sleeve of credit cards. "I'll bet Tom Green never tried to kill anybody."

Grainger kept wanting to laugh at her cocksureness. "And what makes you think I want to kill you?" He squinted into the dark; the moon had disappeared.

"Oh, maybe just the bullet that blew by my face yesterday evening." She stuffed the credit cards back in the wallet and laid it on the seat between them. Across the distant fields the lights of Kingdom showed for a few moments.

He said, "Anything interesting in the credit cards?"

"I don't see it, but we could always ask Tom Green." She sat back, head against the headrest, and was silent.

"You know, you don't have to keep that gun aimed at me." He took his eyes from the road to look at her. "I'm not going to do anything."

"Why would I believe that?" The gun, having momentarily rested beside the wallet, came up again.

There was a several-mile silence, which Grainger rather liked. It was one of those comfortable silences that are rare in the best of circumstance, extremely rare when someone's holding a gun on you. He smiled. The gun wavered every once in a while; she was trying to stay awake.

Not that he planned to do anything except what she told him to do. The situation here was far more interesting than anything he could have dreamed up. Once when the gun lolled downward—and she had her eyes closed—he put his finger under the barrel and edged it up again. He rooted for a cigarette when her eyes snapped open.

"What was that?"

"What? Nothing. I'm just lighting up a smoke. Want one?"

"I don't smoke." She yawned; her gun hand dropped an inch.

"Put that damned gun down."

"Have you got a gun in your motel room?"

"My gun is back there on the rocks."

"You don't have an extra one?"

Extra. Grainger loved that. He flicked the match out of the window. "Why would I?" He had one, but he wasn't going to use it on her.

"You weren't having much luck with the rifle, were you?"

"Very funny."

Miles later, he said, "Motel's right up there."

A big green shamrock dominated the Shamrock Motel's white sign. The A in the neon SHAMROCK flickered, about to disappear for good.

"Is the owner Irish?"

He was pulling into the parking area. "I wouldn't know; I don't chat up motel owners. For obvious reasons."

"I guess. Is this your room?"

He was slotting the car into a space in front of number 19. "That's it."

Andi held the gun close down her leg as she got out and went to the door, which he unlocked and held open for her, as any gentleman would do.

She walked in and sat down on the queen-sized bed and looked around.

As he twisted the cap off a pint of Bushmills, Grainger said, "I call your attention to the Monet on the far wall." He swept his arm in that direction. "And just behind you, the J. M. W. Turner." These were two generic prints, one of dissolving flowers in a pool, the other of trees at sunrise.

She smiled a little. "The Shamrock has good taste."

"Here." He handed her a water glass with a finger of whiskey. Then he sat down at a round imitation-wood table.

The gun lay on the bed beside her. She sipped the whiskey. "How do you know about Monet and Turner?"

"Why, by the brushwork, of course." He pointed to the dissolving flowers.

"You know what I mean. The real painters. I guess I'm surprised you'd know."

"You mean because I kill people for a living? I see no contradiction there."

She rolled her eyes. "Okay, who hired you and why?"

He shrugged. "I don't know."

"What do you *mean* you don't know? You tried to shoot me; someone must've told you to do it. Paid you to do it."

He nodded. "The contact, the go-between. I never want to know who exactly I'm doing it for. Or why." He sat back and looked at her. Her eyes were a shade so light they were almost silver, a silvery blue, he thought, the exact color of the river in Maine he loved to fish. Pure water.

"But that's . . . that's just irresponsible!"

At that, Grainger threw back his head and laughed. "You could say that."

"Then what happens is somebody is sent by the person who wants the job done to give you the details."

"Correct."

"Are you still going to try and shoot me?"

"I wouldn't dream of it." He said this quite seriously.

The answer seemed to surprise her. "Then you'll have to give back the money."

"I didn't take any. I never do until I've finished a job. I take the entire payment then."

She frowned. "But that way, they could cheat you. I mean, you do the job and they don't pay up."

"I don't think so." He smiled and poured himself another finger of whiskey.

"Oh. I see what you mean."

"Now, maybe you can tell me why someone wants you dead."

As he had done before, she shrugged. "I don't know."

"You don't know either?"

"No, but I can guess." She told him about Klavan's, about the lawsuit, about BigSun.

Grainger took all of this in and found it hard to believe that someone would put this girl in a gun's crosshairs because she wanted to help
abused animals. He said this.

"I know. But it's really about money, isn't it?"

"Most things are. So you mean that management loses profits if the
trouble is taken to see the animals are treated better?"

"Yes. That's one reason they might want me out of the picture. But
then there's someone else." She told him about Waylans.

"And you don't know what this man is talking about."

"I don't, no."

"Something in your past—"

"That's the thing. I don't have any past, except for the last couple
of years." She told him some of that, too. Not the end of it, not about
Harry Wine, but most of it she told him. And wondered why she
was so cagey about her past with everyone else, but spoke so freely
to him. Perhaps it was because of the complete incongruity of their
relationship.

Grainger fixed his eyes on her as if her face might begin to dissolve
like the flowers in the painting. Unless she was a total nutcase, here was
a girl who'd been hounded ever since she could remember.

"And then," she went on, "there are the Baileys."

There was more?

She told him about the truck on the highway.

Hounded, harassed, betrayed, threatened. Yet look at her. Beautiful
and held together by razor wire or sheer nerve. Nerve must be where
part of the beauty came from. He fingered a cigarette from the pack
on the table beside him. "Is it safe for me to assume you're not calling
the police?"

She looked at her hands. She seemed to be ashamed at finding
them gun-empty, as if she'd failed to do her job. "No. I'm not." She
looked up. "Because I want you to help me."

He tried not to register the surprise he felt, since the statement had
been made so tentatively. He lit his cigarette and waved out the match.
"Doing what, exactly?"

"One thing is this man Waylans. If you could find him maybe

you—maybe we—could get him to tell why he's following me." As if she had to convince him, she added, "It's bad enough being followed by someone and you know the reason for it, but by someone who's a complete mystery and wants something from you and you don't even know what that is—"

"I know." In a strange way they were much alike, she being moved by forces that were a mystery, he by ones he chose not to know. They both were staring at blankness.

"If you're a sniper you probably know how to find people. You must have to follow them, without them knowing."

"There's a difference, though; I'm given something to go on: the person's whereabouts and, as far as they're known, his movements. Where I'd be able to find him. For you, I got a name, a photo, the house where you were living, the place where you worked. In other words, enough to find you. About Waylans, see, I know none of that."

"But I can tell you what he looks like; I can tell you where I've seen him; he's somewhere around here. He might even be living in that empty house on the Custis property."

Grainger speculated. "That's all?"

"Yes."

He sat smoking and regarding her. "You live one hell of a life, Andi."

Her smile was slight. "I almost didn't."

Grainger looked away.

"If I can just get rid of this Waylans, I could breathe easy."

"That's the least of your worries, sounds like."

"You mean you?"

"No."

He meant the next shooter they'd send for her.

62

hile Grainger waited he thought about Jimmy. He hoped Beth had kept the little chalet and let Jimmy go skiing.

She was so afraid he'd have an accident; she always had been. "God, Billy, look at those slopes! He could break his neck!"

"If you don't let him, Beth, not only will it ruin the one sport he loves, it'll erode his courage."

"Oh, is that what *you* have? Is that what you feel when you shoot a person in cold blood? Courageous?"

He didn't answer. There was no point. She had just found out what he did for a living. "You don't even hate your victims. You don't even *know* them. You kill them for money."

"Yes."

All he could do those five years ago was stand there in their house outside of vail unable to call up a good reason why, in the divorce proceedings, he should be granted joint custody. He wouldn't even get visiting privileges. He might never see his son again and there wasn't a thing in the world he could do about it. To avoid Jimmy's finding out about his line of work, he hadn't contested anything and wound up with nothing.

He hadn't seen Jimmy in five years; it had all been that final with the divorce. It made no difference to Beth that he had been a good father—better than good—at least compared to other fathers he knew.

But all of that congealed like melted wax after a flame was extinguished. What dreadful virus had Beth expected to pass from him to Jimmy?

"Why do you even care, Billy? Unless you're insane. Are you? Your judgment strikes me as a little impaired. Doesn't it to you?"

It was the sarcasm, the ironic tone, that he couldn't stand, as if his desire to see Jimmy hadn't merited a serious response.

Beth went on: "How often must I make the point? I don't want my son growing up with a hit man for a father."

He had almost corrected her. He had almost said he wasn't a hit man. He was a sniper.

He wasn't going to contact the people who wanted this girl dead yet. He'd stall that as long as he could because when they found out he hadn't done the job, they'd send somebody else to do it.

He told himself he was involved in this girl's life because she'd given him no choice. That wasn't true. He could have left at any time after they parted. Just reclaimed his Remington, gotten in his car, and roared off.

But here he was, sitting in his car and watching through binoculars the house he'd seen the man go into.

"*The Custis farm. I think that's where he's staying.*" Andi had told him this.

So, no, he didn't take off. And this bothered him the way missing the shot had bothered him.

The man's Ford truck was parked in the barn, out of sight. When he came out of the back of the house and got into the car, Grainger set the binoculars aside and waited until the truck eased out of the barn and went down the dirt drive.

Grainger followed it.

He followed the truck for ten miles to Hazen. He waited until Waylans parked, got out of his truck, and crossed the street to a restaurant.

Grainger wondered why he was going so far for some food, if that was his reason for coming to Hazen. It looked like a nice town, but he doubted Waylans cared much about nice towns.

After five minutes, he crossed the street and went in. There was the familiar Formica counter, horseshoe-shaped, with booths to the left of it. Waylans was sitting in the first booth with a mug of still-steaming coffee and two sugar doughnuts on a plate before him.

He was sipping the coffee when Grainger slid into the booth. Waylans had had a lot of experience with not letting feelings register on his face. He scarcely blinked. "And you are?"

"About the girl."

"What girl?"

"You know what girl."

Waylans dunked one of the sugar doughnuts into the coffee and ate it slowly before replying. "Nope. Don't know you, neither."

The waitress, whose name tag said Rayette, stopped by the table with a coffeepot. Grainger let her pour a cup for him. "Nothing else, thanks." She went away. "Why?"

"Why what?"

"Why are you following her?"

"I ain't following her."

"Who?"

"Whoever the fuck you're talking about."

"You've been doing it for more than a year."

Waylans picked up and put down the second doughnut. His eyes were as hard and dark as agate. "Now, why would anyone follow a person for that long?"

"You tell me."

"I ain't tellin' you squat, mister." He smiled a thin, sour little smile. Enjoying this.

Grainger was silent for a moment, then he said, "Could we stop dicking around?"

"It's your dick, not mine." Waylans thought this really funny, for he shook with silent laughter.

Grainger had already reached around and pulled the gun from his belt. "I'm prepared to listen." He leaned farther across the table, giving room underneath for his arm to extend until the gun touched Waylans's knee.

There was a flutter of surprise in the eyes, instantly smothered, before he went back to his coffee and doughnut. "You shouldn't be playin' with them things. You could blow off a kneecap. Which I don't think you'll be wantin' to do in here."

Seeing the man wasn't going to scare, Grainger drew the gun back and shoved it into his waistband. No one was watching them; he and Waylans were just a couple of friends meeting for coffee.

"We could keep this up. You know I'll be around again asking the same questions."

Waylans appeared to be considering as he finished off the doughnut and took a big swig of coffee.

Grainger prompted. "You know her."

"In a manner of speaking."

"She doesn't know you."

"So she says."

"What do you say?"

"She knows me all right."

"She doesn't remember anything of her life before a year and a half ago."

"That what she says?" Waylans shrugged.

"Now, what do you want with her?"

"She has information for me."

"She doesn't think so. What is it?"

"Now, that really is none of your goddamned business."

Grainger considered. "Why didn't you go after her when you first saw her? Why the hell follow her all this time?"

Waylans had lit a cigarette and now blew smoke across the table. "So you tell me, brother. Why are you lookin' out for her?"

"She's a friend."

Waylans shook his head and stubbed out his barely smoked cigarette. "Girl don't have no friends." He threw a five-dollar bill on the table and got up. "She used 'em all up. Nice talkin' to you."

Grainger half rose. "Wait a minute—" He knew it was senseless trying to detain him. The man would just talk more and say less. Irritated with himself, he looked at the empty cup, the little plate with traces of sugar. He hadn't handled that well. He hadn't handled it at all, for God's sake. Waylans had done the handling.

He felt somehow weakened by the encounter. By all of the encounters he'd had since coming to North Dakota. Whatever about him that had been intact was now in danger of being breached.

Wrong. It already had been.

63

It's as much as I could get out of him. It's not very helpful," Grainger told her that evening. They were talking in his car. She'd told Jim she was going for a ride with a friend. Grainger picked her up at the end of the drive.

"Yes, it is," said Andi. "At least you got him to admit it. And now he knows he's being watched, too."

"You remember nothing at all before you wound up in Santa Fe?"

"No. That morning in Santa Fe is as far back as it goes."

"You might have left somewhere that's connected with this man, and it happened just before you wound up in Santa Fe."

She sighed and gazed off where the fields burned in the late-afternoon sun. "There must be some way of getting him to say what it is he wants."

Grainger watched her face when he spoke. "There may be."

"What?"

"If he found out you really don't have amnesia. I mean, if you admitted you don't."

Her face was as clear as a cloudless sky. "You mean, say that I was lying? So that he'd really come after me and whatever it is I know." She frowned. "Only, he's not stupid—"

"Everybody's stupid about one thing. Maybe this is his one thing. He's depending on you to remember. I'm sure he'd threaten you if you didn't come up with it; he already has. But he's dependent on you. So he's not going to hurt you until he finds out what he needs to know."

"If I really know nothing, how can I get *him* to talk? I mean, he'd hardly say, 'So you remember the bank robbery after all?' Or, 'the diamond heist.'"

Grainger smiled. "Probably he wouldn't offer up the facts. But if he talks at all, and he'll have to, he'll say something you can build on. And of course you have the advantage: he thinks you have what he wants, or maybe has to have."

"For all I know, he's another hired gun. I'd have the two of you. You'll probably cancel each other out and I'll go out through the same door I walked in."

"Could be. So don't get any idea of walking out on me."

Her laugh was uncertain. "Come on, I'm only kidding."

"I'm not."

She didn't know why she was blushing, and tried to hide it, washing her hands over her face. "Tomorrow I'm going to see my lawyer about the lawsuit."

"Do you think you'll get anywhere with it? Do you think your witnesses are stand-up guys? When it comes down to it?"

"I think so. Unless somebody hired you to shoot them."

"Very funny. I think you should drop this lawsuit, Andi."

"I can't. You've never seen the way these animals have to live. Not to mention BigSun and the way they die. I didn't do it, incidentally; I didn't set that fire."

"I never thought you did. But they probably do. I think you're in danger."

"I'm betting on BigSun, but we don't know who's hired you, since you don't bother finding out why you're killing a person. How do I know that you're not the counterpart of Waylans? He wants something from me, and maybe someone else doesn't want him to get it. I don't know how to meet up with him."

"I'll get the message to him. Incidentally, how do I get messages to you? I'd better not call your home."

She paused, thinking, and jotted down Odile's number. "Call her and she can call me." Then she said, "Maybe whoever hired you is somebody else out of my past who wants me dead."

"Is your life always like this? Trouble coming down the road? Christ, I don't know how you stand it, sugar."

"I stand it because I have to stand it." She slid him a sideways look. "And don't call me sugar."

64

Grainger followed the truck when it left the Custis farm. Waylans didn't appear to be too bothered by someone picking up his trail. Did he think of himself as untouchable? Invulnerable?

For several miles Grainger stayed on the truck's tail before flashing his headlights. He passed the truck, then slowed down, motioning for Waylans to stop.

Grainger got out, walked back to the truck. Waylans rolled down the window and said, "I can ask you the same question: Why the fuck are you on my tail?"

His arm along the roof's edge, Grainger leaned down. "She wants to see you."

This appeared to stump him momentarily. "What about?" He was chewing something, gum or tobacco.

"You'll find out. That field where you took the horse. She's there most every afternoon, late. She'll be there tomorrow evening."

Grainger thumped the roof of the truck twice and went back to his car.

65

The next day was windy, rough, and warm, wind lifting the small branches of the cottonwood and buffeting the sage, lifting Dakota's mane and Sam's tail. In the far fields, in the dark line of trees, something strange was happening. Out of that shimmering blur, too far away to distinguish, it was as if one of the trees had separated itself from the others and the landscape had begun to dissolve.

Dakota stopped grazing for a while and watched this tree move toward them. Sam's head came up and watched, too. At that distance, everything was a blur. They watched the figure approaching.

He walked as if he owned the world. The trees seemed to bow to him and the wind had knives in it.

Andi laced her fingers through Dakota's tether as if this might lend her a strength she didn't feel.

When he came to stand before her, she nodded. He touched the brim of his hat as if they were well met here, introducing themselves again.

"Ma'am," he said.

She felt a chill, a worse one, there being no screen door between them drawing boundaries.

Dakota had raised his head from the grass and stared at Waylans. He appeared to recognize him and wasn't liking it.

"Your friend back there says you wanted to see me."

She wondered what direction, in his mind, he was coming from.

"You want to know . . . Listen, what's this information worth to you?"

He gave her a sharp look, and then laughed. "Well, instead of you blackmailing me, if I was you I'd stop and think about what it's worth to *you*. Start, maybe, with living. You'd like to keep doing that, it's my guess."

"If I'm the only one who knows this, I don't think you'll kill me. As for the others—?" She shrugged.

"The others be damned." But he looked uncertain, she thought.

"Things, people, have a way of coming back to haunt you, you know."

"Girl, keep the haunting to yourself and tell me why you wanted me to come here."

"I'm willing to tell you if you'll just leave me alone."

"Have no call not to, if you talk."

"You remember—what happened back then?"

" 'Course I damned well remember."

Andi felt she was standing not on hot ground but on a skin of ice, ice so sheer the next word out of her mouth would break it and the cracks would run crazily and suddenly beneath her and she'd fall. All she could do was toss out something and hope it stuck. "The ones who were after you—"

"What the hell? Wasn't no one after me."

"Of course there was! My God, were you that unaware you didn't even know it?"

He hesitated. "There wasn't no one else that knew anything."

"Yes, there was."

"Who?"

She simply did not know where to put a foot without tripping. "I don't know the name, but—"

Blood suffused his neck, and she knew she'd said the wrong thing. "Then you don't remember squat, girl." His face darkened; in the distance there was thunder. "Come on. I kept my part of the bargain, now you keep yours."

"Bargain? There was no bargain." She stared at him as it dawned on her. "*You* did it? *You* set that fire at BigSun?"

"Who'd you think?"

She took a step toward him, clapping her hands against her chest. "They think it was *me.* You deliberately did it when I was in town."

"Oh, I think they need a hell of a lot more'n they've got to ever charge you with it." He pulled his gun from the shoulder holster. "It's time you told me what you know."

The gun wasn't more than two feet from her heart. Her mind tumbled. It was like carefully calibrating turns of the combination to a safe. She waited for the click—of the tumblers, of the gun.

She had to say something to save herself. She had been depending too much on his saying something, telling her something on which she could build. All she had to do was make up a story, contrive a plan. Her mind wouldn't throw up a single thing, not a name, not a place.

Then he moved the gun several inches to the right, saying, "Now, we got two nice animals here, so what say I start with them?"

How could she have been so *stupid* as to have Dakota and Sam out here? It was too late now to tell him she'd been pretending and that she didn't know anything at all about Alice. "Look, I can't tell you where Alice is—"

Lowering the gun, he looked at her as if she'd said something utterly surprising. "You can't what?"

"Tell you where she is. Alice. Honestly, I haven't seen her."

Now he looked furious, not in the manner he'd been assuming, which to him was probably jocular. Again he raised the gun. "Donkey goes first—"

She lunged at him. There was a quick crack and the gun flew out of his hand. Blood clouded the air, splattered like rain on a windshield. Half of his head was gone, as if he'd twisted it off and thrown it away. Blood and bone and brain matter sluiced over the ground. Dakota reared up and would have run except Andi had a tight hold of the rope. Sam did run, but not far, and trotted back soon enough.

Andi looked off toward the high rocks on the other side of the road and, despite the river of blood, was thankful.

66

Harry and two state police cars were parked in the field, together with a crime-scene vehicle and an ambulance. The paramedics were bent over the body, its limbs positioned at odd angles like a hieroglyph. Half of the head was gone.

It had been established straight off that this was the same man Andi had told the sheriff about more than a week before.

Harry expelled a breath. "What happened? Guy was packing a forty-four Magnum Colt. Why?"

"To threaten me."

"Why? And don't make me keep asking why?"

"He wanted to know where his daughter Alice was—I mean, I assume she's, she was, his daughter. I don't even know *who* she is, much less *where* she is." She was relieved when one of the crime-scene people came up to the sheriff.

"That shot to the head came from out there"—the technician pointed toward the road—"but I can't say exactly how far off. I will say the shooter was damned good to make that head shot from any distance. The angle probably says the shooter was somewhere up in those rocks."

"Could be a marksman, maybe? Service or ex-service? Maybe a hunter?"

The technician shrugged. "I don't think. Not with the shot he made. I'd say this guy has more than a little experience shooting people."

"Hunters can be damned good shots," Harry said. Then he went back to his crime scene. He said to Andi, "We can narrow this down a lot, this mystery shooter, since he appears to be a friend of yours."

"*What?*" Andi feigned surprise and massive irritation. "Just why does it have to be connected with me?"

"Well it usually is, Andi: In this instance, let's say because he saved your life."

"It could more likely be an enemy of *his*." She pointed to the body now covered by a body bag.

"If this was just a shooter aimed at killing this Waylans fellow, he sure picked a strange split second to do it in. When you were throwing yourself at the guy."

Frantically, she sorted out the reasoning. "Then maybe he was aiming at me because he was someone Klavan or BigSun paid to shoot me."

The sheriff also looked toward the body, doubtful of this explanation. "Well . . . guess it could be—"

"You see?" Her smile was worn thin.

"—except how come this crack shot hit the wrong person?"

Her mind came up with nothing, except, "What do you mean?"

"Just what you think I mean, Andi. He was aiming at Waylans, not you."

She did not know how to reply.

Harry went on: "So your friend's a stone-cold killer."

"He's not my friend!"

"That's kind of a shame. Fellow that watches your back? Man that'd do murder for you? Hell, I don't have a friend like that. Wish I did."

It came through to her even under the current of sarcasm. She wanted to throw herself at somebody in the way she'd done at Waylans, only for the sake of being caught. She wanted to cry for a long time until all of the crying she'd missed out on could be over. The crying, the tiredness, the going from place to place, town to town. She wanted to stop. To stop and go to bed for a hundred years.

Defeat was everywhere. Defeat was in the hearts of the worst of the worst. Even in Waylans. Now she had to include him in her catalog of defeated men. There came to her an overwhelming sense of sadness, as if they were all being crushed under a doomed sky. All of them. They were all together in this. For a moment she wondered if men did live, after all, in the pigs' world.

Waylans had said it right: vagabond. She gazed up at the rocks.

"Who is he, Andi?"

She looked back then, looked hard at Harry McKibbon. "You're the police. You tell me."

She walked off, feeling she was nowhere, she was nothing.

Vagabond.

67

It was less than an hour before Harry McKibbon caught up with her at Jim's. Jim and Tom were sitting with her at the kitchen table. All were bent over cups of coffee.

"Can't this wait now, Harry? Andi's had a pretty bad shock."

Harry's look pretty much said a bed of burning coals followed by a beheading wouldn't shock this girl.

Forgetting to muster a trembling winsomeness, Andi gave the sheriff a dirty look.

He said, "No, it can't wait. I'm sorry if you don't feel up to it, but you were there. Witnesses don't get much better than that." Harry tried out a smile, but it didn't work—not for her, not for him.

"I'm up to it," she said.

Harry looked at Jim. He looked at Tom. Neither of them gave a sign of budging an inch, much less leaving him and Andi alone.

Harry scratched his forehead, looking at the cups and mugs. "You think I could have a cup of that?" When Jim made to rise, he added, "And a glass of that?" He nodded toward Tom's whiskey.

With Jim on coffee and Tom on whiskey, Harry sat down right across from Andi. "Look," he started, then thanked Jim for the coffee and Tom for the drink. "You could make this whole thing a lot easier if you'd just tell me what in hell's going on."

"You make this out to be *my* show."

"Isn't it?"

She sighed mightily. "I've told you, Sheriff. I was meeting that man because he thought I had information he wanted."

"What information?" said Tom.

"I wish I knew." She turned to Tom. "It's a long story."

Harry said, "Just pick up the bits and pieces as we go." To Jim and Tom, he said, "Don't interrupt or I'll never be out of here." To Andi: "I don't get it. You told me over a week ago he'd come to the house, said he was looking for a girl. You told him you knew nothing about her. Why this meeting this afternoon?"

It would make no difference if she told Harry McKibbon some of the truth; it wouldn't compromise Grainger or put him in the sheriff's sights. "Because I wanted to know what he knew. About my past, about my family."

"But he never let on that he knew you at all when he came to your door here."

"Pretense. So I told him that I lied about the amnesia. I told him I didn't know Alice, that I'd never seen her. I assumed that was his daughter. But that infuriated him. I don't know why. First he was going to shoot Sam if I didn't tell him. Then Dakota. Then me."

"Okay," Harry said, letting Tom pour him another drink. "But that still doesn't tell me who shot this Waylans."

Andi's anger started building again. "I don't know. But I *do* know if somebody hadn't shot him, Dakota and Sam and I would all have been lying in pools of blood for sure. I couldn't tell him what he wanted to know because *I didn't know*. But I'd never convince him of that now, not after I led him to believe I'd remembered everything."

"For heaven's sake, let the girl alone," Jim said to Harry, who paid him no attention, didn't even look at him, but kept his eyes fastened on Andi.

Harry said to her, "You know this is a murder case, don't you? Premeditated murder. The shooter was lying in wait. If you do know the shooter, that makes you accessory to murder, and that means you could go to prison for a long time."

Jim was angry. "Now, I know you're the law, Harry, but this is just—"

"Shut up, Jim." His tone was level and deadly. "I let you stay here, you and Tom, but you'll be quiet or get out. Or I'm taking Andi into the station."

Jim's face was mottled pink. Tom murmured some imprecation and rose and went to the coffeepot.

At that moment a car wheeled in beside the sheriff's cruiser. One of the men she'd seen at what was now the crime scene was rapping at the back door.

Jim got up and let him in.

"Sheriff," said the state policeman, his fingers coming to the brim of his hat in some offhand salute. "I need to speak to you." He smiled uncertainly at the people around the table as if protocol for this situation eluded him.

Harry rose, excused himself, and the two of them went outside.

The state cop turned away from the sheriff and looked toward the rocky ledges, now at this late hour dyed a deeper red. "Thing's this. Our ballistics people can't hit on exactly where this shot came from; there's several possibilities up there"—he pointed—"that the shooter could have used."

"Get that ballistics fellow with Bismarck police to look at it. And they're wrong saying it could be anyplace in those rocks. If this guy's a sniper, and I'll bet he is, then there's just one spot that would have suited him. One, maybe two. He sure as hell didn't flop himself down on any old rock up there. No, he chose his place. We've got to search wherever he stationed himself. Have them keep looking. Though I admit he probably didn't leave a hell of a lot behind."

The state policeman went back to his car, tore off as if the devil were behind him.

Harry went back inside.

As if the sheriff hadn't left, Tom said, "I don't quite get your thinking here, Harry. How can this girl be an accomplice or accessory when she herself was in the line of fire?"

"That's my point: she wasn't. Andi?"

She looked up at him, sullen. "What?"

"Take this seriously, will you? It's not a game."

At that she sprang up, upsetting her chair. They all flinched. "*Seriously?* Not a *game?* You're telling *me?* I'm the one just had a gun shoved in my face. It's more serious to me than it is to you, Sheriff. And stop being so goddamned condescending."

A muscle tightened in Harry's jaw. "I guess I'll be talking to you later, then, if you won't talk now."

"I'm sure glad I got a lawyer for those pigs. Maybe they'll let me borrow him." She kicked the chair out of her path as she left the table and the room.

They watched her go, heard the stairs creak as she stomped up them.

Harry could hardly keep from smiling. *Tantrum. Makeshift tantrum.* And it struck him suddenly that she was the most real person he had ever come across, in spite of her cooked-up drama.

Jim and Tom turned to Harry, who picked up his glass and downed the whiskey in it.

Jim quipped with an eye to diluting the tension, "Thought you're not allowed to drink on the job, Harry."

Harry plunked the glass down. "What job?" He raised his hand much as the state policeman had done, said, "Gentlemen," then turned to leave.

68

"Cops will be going to all the motels, rooming houses, hotels," said Grainger. "Getting names of recently arrived strangers. Single men just staying around for a couple of nights."

They were in a room in the downtown Radisson in Bismarck.

"They don't know what you look like," said Andi.

"They will if they ever get around to the restaurant and any of the help who might have seen me with Waylans." He had been cursing himself about that: how could he have been so stupid as to show his face in the company of Waylans? The only excuse he had was that he wasn't used to this kind of development—trying to save the life of someone he was hired to kill.

And Lord knows he'd never had anything to do with the target himself. Herself. He had never been on the run; police had never known whom to look for. He'd been smoke.

He had finally managed to meet with her by going through Odile Nekoma. He had said to Odile, "Tell her to call me on my cell. Tell her it's Billy." That had been another thing he'd never done: given out his number.

He had certainly never done this damsel-in-distress act.

And here she sat, looking so woebegone he wanted to hug her.

"They won't have any trouble getting a picture from his license and they'll be showing that around, asking if someone saw the man in the company of someone else. If they get around to that waitress at that restaurant, she could probably identify me. That won't do the cops a hell of a lot of good, but it at least will narrow the playing field. I'm just saying the chance they'll find me is slim once I'm out of here. And the chance they'll find anything to make this 'accessory' charge stick is near zero. No one saw you at the Shamrock. We parked slam up against the door of the room. What this sheriff is saying to you is garbage, Andi. He's only trying to scare you."

She was sitting on the bed across from him in the room at the Radisson. "I'm not scared. Well, yes, I am, but not of that, not really. Do you have to leave?"

To her embarrassment and to his eternal regret, she was crying. Big tears plopping like cartoon tears on her jeans.

"Andi—"

"Please don't go." She got up and leaned over and laced her arms around him, and it was only the awkward position of her standing and him sitting that kept him from engulfing her in an embrace. Instead, he pulled her down beside him on the bed. "I can't think of anyone worse for you than me."

She had planted her forehead against his upper arm, her own arms around that arm. "I can. Not-you. Not-you is worse than you. You saved my life. You took a terrible chance in doing that."

"That's what you're feeling the effects of, Andi. You're tuned so tight, you could take on Jeff Beck."

"Who's he?"

Grainger smiled. "Guitarist."

"You think I should leave because I'm in danger."

That's what he'd told her. "I do, yes."

"Okay, then why can't I go with you? You could take me with you."

He was swamped with conflicting feelings. "You wouldn't tolerate the way I live for more than a day. You couldn't."

"Of course I could."

"I'm not going to change, you know. I'm a shooter. That's what I am."

"Where do you live?"

"Las Vegas." It was a lie. It was the first place she'd hate he could think of. Fifty acres in Wyoming, which was where he lived, would be right down her alley.

She smiled. "That's hard to believe."

"I like to gamble. Well, that's obvious, isn't it?" He returned the smile as he brushed back strands of her hair. He said, "It's time to go and see your lawyer now."

She glanced at the cheap digital clock on the bedside table and stood up. "It probably won't take more than an hour. You'll still be here, won't you?"

He stood up, too. "Yes." He wouldn't, and he suspected she knew it. It was mean of him, but it beat saying good-bye.

She raised herself on her toes and put her arms around his neck. This time he hugged her back. He felt her loose hair on his cheek. The blue ribbon that held some of it back. Was there actually any other girl in the world who'd use a blue ribbon to tie up her hair? He felt like crying himself.

"The two men in this bar, Zero's. They sound ambivalent, to hear you describe it," said Bobby Del Ray. "And it's a long time before this gets to trial. Months, at the very least. More likely, years. Those two have a long time to change their minds."

Andi nodded. "But I think they'll testify. It took some courage just to talk to me."

"Okay. I still haven't managed to get the county prosecutor to take this up. That's one of the things that takes time. A lot of ranchers and farmers think they've got the God-given right to treat animals any way they please."

"Why does it please them to watch a pig covered in its own blood dumped in a vat of boiling water? Or a cow with its eyes bleeding? Or a sow that can't even walk because of multiple litters trying to drag herself forward because she's being thrashed—" Andi stopped and looked away. "Sorry."

"Because they don't see it, not what you've just described." Bobby held up his hands, palms out. "I hear ya, babe, I really do. But it's like gun control. You can't pass a law to keep assault weapons out of the hands of citizens because the NRA thinks if they give an inch, they'll take a mile. You know. Something as plain, as obvious, as the nose on your face, some people will say, 'What nose?' "

"I don't understand it."

"You don't have to understand it. All you have to do is stop it."

She was silent, looking at the ancient rug on the floor.

"You having second thoughts?" he asked, quietly.

"No. How long did it take for the Rosebud people to settle their case?"

"Years. That discourages you, I know."

"There's something else, too." She told him about the Waylans shooting.

Bobby brought his chair down with a thump. "Jesus!"

Then she told him about Harry McKibbon's threat.

"Balls. I'm surprised he'd say that. I know him and he's good at his job and fair. Accessory? Balls."

"But there is some justification. I mean, if I know who shot Waylans, I should tell him."

"*Do* you know?"

"Yes."

"But you're not telling."

"No."

"Would you tell me?"

"No."

"I'm your lawyer."

"You're the pigs' lawyer."

He laughed abruptly. "The next time you come, bring one along. So you don't trust me, is that it?"

Her eyes widened. "Of course I do."

He didn't look convinced. His chair creaked as he leaned back.

To Andi, it sounded almost sorrowful. "I'm going to have to leave Kingdom. It could be dangerous for me to stay in the area."

He nodded. "But you'll stay in touch?"

"Yes, definitely. This doesn't mean I feel differently about the case. I really want to go on with it."

"You should, Andi." When he rose, he looked at her as if he were seeing something for the first time.

She wondered what it was, and thanked him and left.

He was gone.

She stood in their room at the Radisson and looked all around. He was so gone nothing about him remained; no scent lingered, no impression persisted on the bed he'd sat on.

Andi sat down where she'd sat beside him and put her head in her hands. She couldn't believe anybody could be this gone.

69

But he wasn't gone.

He had no intention of leaving until he'd neutralized the danger.

The first thing Grainger did when he left the motel was to go to a shopping mall, one of the big ones with a huge parking lot. The Kirkwood would do. He cruised around in the Camry until he found something he thought would work—not as down-the-middle-lane as a Camry, but not as flashy as that cherry-red Porsche sunning itself in one of the handicapped slots. Oh, sure.

The Volvo convertible closer to the back of the lot was just the ticket. Solid and sensuous. A bit of flash, like a slit skirt, until the top came up and hid it. He pulled the Camry in beside it. The Volvo's top was down now, providing easy access to thieves—thank you!—and since it was new (dealer price still glued to the window), it would be more likely to have another key. He slid in and opened the glove compartment. There it was, the valet key the dealer leaves in the car and forgets to tell the owner about. An open invitation. He switched plates between the two cars. Then he started up the Volvo and eased out. He wondered if the owner of the Camry would get his car back, poor bastard.

He drove the Volvo around to the other side of the lot to a men's store. Inside, he settled on a black cashmere sport jacket and a Ralph Lauren turtleneck, also black.

Then he left the mall, drove around searching for a map store. He found one, bought the same topographical map he'd used but then tossed in a Dumpster when he was done with it.

With these three items and his newfound convertible, he drove to a Days Inn on the other side of town, booked a room for the night.

The first thing he did was to lie down on the bed, push the pillows up at his back, light a cigarette, and think.

"This isn't good, Grainger," his contact had said.

Grainger's call to him had taken place yesterday. *"No, but it cost you nothing. You can get somebody else."*

The man on the other end sounded as if he were sucking his teeth. *"It's just, you know, the trouble it takes."*

"Sorry."

"Heard you're the best. What happened?"

"I miscalculated. Anyway, I'm not the best."

There had been no way of putting off that call. Actually, he hadn't wanted to: if they were going to hire another shooter, Grainger wanted to be here when he came, and he'd come right away. He knew the psychology. Once they decided on this way of proceeding, they'd want it done immediately. Because dimwits were impatient. They took no care.

Whoever they got—and Grainger knew a few in this line of work—would probably do as he had done: get a room at a motel not in but not too far from Kingdom. What he'd do would be to check out the ones passed up in favor of the Shamrock. He got up and showered, then put on his new clothes. The old jeans were perfectly okay, and to carry that gun at his back, he needed a familiar, comfortable waistband. Jeans these days had such a dropped waistline you could wear them for socks.

From his duffel he removed two little boxes, each holding a different set of contacts. His own eye color was a little too distinctive—silvery, steely, icy, depending on who was describing the eyes, and a lot did. Apparently, too memorable. The contacts in one box were blue-green, in the other an ordinary shade of brown, much like his ordinary hair.

There was nothing he felt safe in doing about his hair. If he dyed it or cut it he would mess up and he didn't want to go to a barber. But the color was so common, it hardly seemed worth changing. What he did do was part it and brush it across his head, over to the left, and let a strand or two fall over his eye. He scraped it back, let it fall again.

He looked at himself in the mirror. Black cashmere, over black merino wool. Dark eyes, steel-rimmed Armani glasses. He smiled. He almost wished there was a woman around to impress. The only one he wanted to impress he had just left.

Grainger scraped the keys to the Volvo off the dresser, yanked his duffel from the bed, and left the Days Inn by another exit.

He made sure to pick up a local paper, this one the *Register*, which carried the account of the shooting on "Purley's ranch" on the inside page. Andi had never referred to it as a ranch; he doubted the owner did either.

He drove north toward Golden Valley, which had nothing by way of a motel, then turned onto State Road 200 and drove west. The following little town was Zap. No motel here, but he drove slowly through it, intrigued by its emptiness. A kid tossing a ball in the air was the only person around. Zap was a very small town, yet apparently proud of itself, for there had been a huge *Z* whitewashed onto a hill and a very large sign pointing out the town's attractions. He still didn't know what they were. He found a cluster of streets, all named for women. Virginia Lane, Sharon Court, Elizabeth Avenue. Some care had been taken, too. The names were not all linked simply with "Street." He loved "Evangeline Lane." All of this reminded him of something, ticked something over in his mind, though he couldn't grasp it, and he was aware that it might be important.

In Hazen he stopped in at the Roughrider, and in Beulah, two motels. In both places he said the same thing: he was looking for a friend who would have checked in in the last, say, thirty-six hours, single guy, probably staying one night. He gave, of course, a phony name, but the answer both times, after a check of the guest cards, was, "No, sir, no man by himself had checked in. Sorry."

Driving that same stretch of road, he saw the pickup truck parked in the lot of a motel in Pick City. It was the sticker art on the back window and over a lot of the truck bed that was so familiar, most of it boosting the NRA, a couple of pro-life stickers.

My God, he thought, Kyle Hanna. Kyle had been one of Grainger's team of snipers and scouts. He was the best shot Grainger had ever seen.

And here he was. The damned fool apparently didn't care that this truck of his could be ID'd in an eyeblink. Kyle always had been so cocksure of himself, it should have gotten him blown away in Kuwait.

Grainger wanted to get to the restaurant. He figured Kyle wouldn't be going anywhere until dark, so he turned around and drove back to Hazen listening to a radio preacher and watching the sun skim like water across the wheat fields.

If he failed to neutralize Kyle Hanna he'd grab Andi and leave. That would be no personal sacrifice for him, but for her, although she didn't know it, it would be a disaster. Her life would be fractured, a detour that she shouldn't take and one that he thought would never get her back to the main road. He had never believed in fate, only accident. But here, his belief tripped up. Nothing that happened to Andi was accidental.

After he parked the Volvo along the main street, he put the map in his pocket, got out, folded the newspaper under his arm, and headed for the restaurant several doors down.

He considered taking a booth as part of this little test, even the same booth he and Waylans had occupied, but decided a counter seat would be more help in encouraging conversation.

Rayette was at the other end of the counter talking to a beefy auto mechanic. The name of the garage was stenciled on his denim jacket in huge letters, as if its employees were prisoners. He sat down a few stools away from the garage guy, but still easily within Rayette's line of vision. Grainger opened the paper in front of him, hit the fold a few times to straighten it.

When she came down the counter he ordered coffee and one of the sweet rolls under a plastic dome on a stand. He unplugged a menu from the aluminum grip beside the sugar shaker. She returned with the coffee and a plate onto which she slid a sweet roll, then returned the plastic dome to the stand.

He said the coffee and roll would be enough, and then said, "Did you read about this?" He shook the paper, half-turned it toward her.

Had she! "Mister, not only did I read about it, I was *part* of it."

"No kidding?" He pushed his glasses a quarter inch back on his nose and looked her full in the face, prepared to listen, fully attentive.

She returned the coffeepot to its burner and dropped her forearm onto the counter so she could lean in. The murdered man had, she said, sat "right over there" and she'd waited on him.

"My God! I bet the cops are making your life miserable."

With a happy "don't-I-know-it?" look, she flapped her hand at him. "I'm quoted in there, you know"—she tapped the paper—"on the second page."

Obediently, he sought out the continued report. She helped, pointing out the bit pertaining to herself. He read it aloud: "'Rayette Jenks, waitress at the restaurant, said she'd been the one to serve Waylans.'" She went on. "I didn't know it at the time. It was him, all right, and the friend who sat with him in the booth." Grainger read, "'The police are looking for this second man, as he might be able to help them with their inquiries.'"

"They wanted to know if the two seemed friendly, or what. I told them, sure, they were friendly, drinking their coffee and talking. But I don't listen in on customers' conversations." She said this with self-righteous fervor. "They want me to describe him for an artist, you know, the way they do—"

Grainger nodded. "You mean like an Identi-Kit?"

"Right. But they have to bring the artist from—excuse me."

She plucked up the coffeepot and quickstepped to the end of the counter and the mechanic, who'd raised his empty mug and was slewing it around.

Grainger wanted to laugh. Of course, he could not have proceeded with his plan if she'd shown the slightest sign of recognizing him. This restaurant had been virtually empty when he'd been here before, so he doubted there was anyone else to worry about.

He drank his coffee and pulled out the map. He was looking to see if going down 83 would take less time than the way he'd come. His eye trailed over the straight-as-a-die Interstate 94 to Fargo, then back a bit, and then he saw it: Alice. *Eunice Street, Elizabeth Avenue:* this is what he hadn't been able to grasp. Alice wasn't a person; Alice was a place. That was why Waylans had been furious with Andi. She had assumed Alice was a girl, his daughter, maybe, and that's how she had talked about it. Something must have happened in Alice—

Rayette broke into his thoughts. "So where're you from?" She leaned on one hand, held the coffeepot aloft. It was flirty time.

He smiled. "Vegas."

"Oh!" she spread her hand over her heart, as if taking a vow as she set the pot down on the counter. "But I've always wanted to go to Las Vegas; I have a friend that loves the slots at Caesars Palace. Have you been there?" Forgetting the other customers completely, she rested her elbows on the counter and her chin on the bridge of her laced fingers in a pose left over from a fifties movie.

He smiled and rose, putting down a ten on the counter. "Maybe I'll see you there, though by then you'll have forgotten my face."

"I never forget a face."

He pushed the ten toward her and said, "Keep the change for the slots." He winked and went out.

On his way out of town he thought about Rayette. If he drew her a map of the Strip and gave her five hundred to play the slots, she still couldn't find Caesars Place.

Now he could focus on Kyle Hanna.

Kyle Hanna was better than Grainger, almost a legend. Only legends don't always get happy endings. Grainger's big advantage was that he knew Kyle was here, but Kyle, if he ever knew, would assume he'd left. Crazy not to.

Kyle had always used a sniper rifle, ever since Kuwait. He could hit a mark from a mile away. His control over his gun and his environment was perfect. The trajectory of a bullet was fragile, and the farther away the target, the more chance the shot could be deflected. In an urban setting, buildings could create a wind tunnel. In the present setting, no.

Unlike Grainger, Kyle didn't research his targets, not the way Grainger did; he had studied her movements for several days. No, Kyle Hanna was in and out. He didn't hang around. He would be told the likely places that the target would turn up at some point: home, work, the bungalow by the sea. He'd pick the most likely and go there and wait. It was a kind of waiting an ordinary mortal simply wouldn't be able to do, not the length of it—hours, days; not the conditions of it— any weather, utter stillness; not the focus, the concentration.

So if Grainger had spotted him today, Kyle would be gone by tomorrow. That meant he'd take the shot between now and then. He'd wait at least until sundown, at most sunup. But Kyle liked night shots. He could see in the dark.

Grainger looked at the map and rubbed his temples. A bastard of a headache was coming on.

A couple of miles from Pick City, he pulled into the parking lot of a pizza joint, went in, and ordered a large pizza with everything on it. While that was baking, he went next door to a liquor store and got a six-pack of Heineken. He went back to the pizza place, waited around, then collected the pizza and took it and the beer to the car.

He got to Pick City and pulled into the motel. The truck was still there, parked in front of the cabins at the rear. Grainger pulled up by the truck.

He took the pizza and beer from the passenger's seat, went to the door of the cabin, and knocked. A voice called out, "Yeah?"

"Pizza delivery."

The lock slid back and the door opened an inch. "I never—"

"Hi, Kyle."

Kyle Hanna was truly flummoxed. He never had been the brightest light on the lot. "I know you?" His eyes narrowed.

"That's not very flattering."

Now Kyle's eyes widened. "Grainger? What the fuck, man! You

modeling for *GQ* now?" He opened the door wider, scraping his straight hair back from his forehead.

Grainger dropped the pizza and beer on the all-purpose table, sat down on the cheap burned-orange plastic and fake-wood chair. "How much they paying you, Kyle?"

Kyle already had a piece of pizza folded over and halfway to his mouth. "Whaddaya mean?"

"Oh, please. You know what. The girl. The one Klavan's paying you to bury."

For a couple of what looked like thoughtful moments, but weren't, since Kyle was no thinker, he chewed the pizza, drank half of the can of beer, and said, "What's your interest in this?" He was still standing. He belched and hit his chest.

"Klavan's a welcher. Hope he gave you your money up front. Him or BigSun—but I don't know the BigSun people."

"Couple of ass-wipes. Eugene Tuttle. I don't know the other one." He belched again and sat down. "Now, you're not sayin' they hired you, too? Why the fuck?"

Grainger shrugged. "Maybe they want backup."

"Backup?" Kyle's laugh seemed to move in his throat like grinding glass. "Not for me; maybe for you."

"You got all your money up front?"

Mouth full of pizza, Kyle Hanna nodded. "I always get it up front. It's safe. I don't miss."

"Can I talk you out of it?"

Kyle stopped chewing, bug-eyed. "Fuck you wanna do that?"

Grainger didn't answer.

"You can't. You think I'm giving back seventy K? You're nuts." He pulled the tab back on another beer.

Grainger was rather pleased they'd got Kyle Hanna cheap. "If I match it, would you?"

"Seventy grand? You got that kind of money?"

"Not on me."

"You're lying, Grainger. Even if you weren't, no, I wouldn't do it. They'd send somebody to collect, you can bet. Maybe send you." Kyle thought this hysterical. His eyes watered from laughter. "So what the hell's the story on this woman?"

"No story." Grainger got up. "Okay, Kyle. Gotta go."

Kyle's look was suspicious. With his eyes narrowed that way, he resembled a wolf. When Grainger was pulling open the door, Kyle said, "Listen."

Grainger turned. "What?"

"Now, you wouldn't be thinking of, you know, taking a shot at yours truly?"

"You kidding? Go up against you? I'd have to be insane." Although that was exactly what he'd thought of doing until he had found a better way to take care of Kyle Hanna.

Before he got in the car, he looked at the truck's plate, memorized the number, wrote it down once he was in the car. The other stuff— the bumper stickers, the trash all over the back of the truck bed, the NRA propaganda—Grainger was familiar with. Kyle kept on driving a vehicle so easy to spot because Kyle thought he was untouchable. Nothing would happen to him.

He didn't want to make the call on his cell, so when he saw the phone booth at a gas station, Grainger pulled up. He brought the Volvo to a stop by the pumps, got out, and went inside to pay cash for gas and get some change.

Outside again, he jammed the handle into the tank, put the tab on the slowest groove, and went to the phone. Inserted coins, dialed. When somebody picked up the phone in the sheriff's office, Grainger said, "Man you're looking for in that Waylans' shooting is at the Sakakawea Motel in Pick City. Blue truck parked outside." He told him the plate number. "Name's Kyle Hanna."

Grainger was hanging up when the eager voice said, "Wait, who—"

Kyle would probably be oiling the damned rifle when the cops burst though the door.

Grainger smiled.

70

Grainger hadn't wanted to see Kyle Hanna, had sooner not have seen him, but it was the only way to find out who was behind this, who had hired both of them.

He fired up the car again and headed toward Kingdom.

It was true, what she'd said, it all looked so benign, the white buildings in the shadow of a sundown that promised to be glorious.

He had gotten out of the car at the slight rise that overlooked Klavan's. Now he got back in. He had spotted the smaller building and the dirt road that led to it and that was where he was headed.

Grainger parked the car, backing it in. He flipped open the glove compartment and took out the .357-Magnum revolver, got out, and walked around to the front of the building, which he took to house the office. He stuck the gun down through the belt at his back.

Inside was a large room with computer equipment, file cabinets, several desks, and a cracked leather couch beneath a wide window. Off to the left was another, smaller office. It must have been after quitting time because there was only one guy in the larger room.

"Can I help you?"

A good-looking fellow, probably in his thirties. He seemed genuinely puzzled that anyone not part of this business would be showing up here.

"I'd like to see Mr. Klavan. He here?"

"Yeah. Only, do you have an appointment?"

For God's sake. As if the man were so much in demand. "No. He in there?"

"Yeah, but—"

Grainger flashed him a winning smile and walked into the smaller room.

Klavan looked up from a pile of papers he was scratching things on, then putting aside. He frowned, said "Yeah?" (Everybody's favorite word today.) He tossed down his pen as if it were the reason for the appearance of this tall bastard, one looking none-too-friendly, interrupting the work, around closing time, too.

"I'd like a few words, Mr. Klavan."

"About what?" Klavan looked suspicious.

Grainger sat down in the wood chair on the other side of the desk. "Girl you fired. Andi Oliver."

Anxiety began building in the man's face as he cleared his throat. "Andi? Nice girl, but a troublemaker. Anyway, who the hell are you to be asking questions? What the fuck's your name?"

"Diver. Dick Diver." Grainger liked F. Scott Fitzgerald and imagined Klavan wasn't reading him. Although it would be fun if he were.

"Well, this Oliver girl was also a thief."

"Oh? How's that, sir?" The "sir" was calculated, a deferential sign for Klavan to relax a little, which he did.

"Well, for one thing she stole one of the sows. Then she went and started stirring people up, and even threatened to sue us."

"On what grounds?"

"The goddamned pigs. This girl didn't seem to know the difference between a pig and the pope. She seemed to think the pigs should be treated like fucking royalty." Klavan leaned as far forward as he could. "Who the hell you working for, Diver? You a lawyer or something? In what capacity are you here?"

"This one." In one smooth move, Grainger brought out the gun.

The expression on Klavan's face, which had gone white, was something to behold. Grainger smiled. Klavan raised his hands, pushed them palms out, and rolled his chair back against a green-blinded window. He cast furtive glances at the door.

"He's busy. Now, don't worry, Klavan. I have no intention of shooting you—right now, that is. But if anything happens to Andi Oliver, believe me, I'll be back. *Then* I'll shoot you. So pray that she doesn't meet with an accident not even of your making. Hope she looks both ways crossing a street and doesn't walk under any falling safes." Grainger rather enjoyed sitting there holding his weapon.

Klavan was looking desperately for a way out of this mess, shot hole-and-corner glances at the telephone and something else in or on his desk, maybe a panic button.

"Don't reach for anything, man, or you will be so dead. Now, do you understand what I'm saying?"

Sweat was forming on Klavan's brow and above his mouth, beads of it. "It wasn't me. It was my brother; I couldn't stop him—"

"I don't give much of a damn which of you's paying a man to kill her. My remarks still stand. So, again, let's be clear: anything happens to Andi Oliver somebody's going to pay for it. Your outfit, BigSun, whatever, whoever." Grainger rose, the gun swinging at his side. "You do get it, don't you?"

Klavan's head was reminiscent of those little bird figures you put on a glass of water, bob, bob, bob. "Yeah."

Grainger stuffed the gun down in his belt again. "Good evening to you," he added pleasantly and walked out, closing the door behind him. The fellow in the outer room was still by himself.

Grainger walked up to him, an edgy smile on his face. "You wouldn't be Jake, would you?"

"Yeah—"

"Asshole." He swung his arm around and delivered a blow that landed with a crack on Jake's jaw. It spun him around before he went facedown onto the floor.

Grainger walked out.

He was back on the highway, stopping once for gas and coffee at a Shell station, driving the next couple of hours as dark collected. In the distance the rather magical cluster of neon stars told him this was Eddie's motel. From this distance they looked like they'd fallen from the sky, stars on the street.

It was after eight in the evening now. He pulled up to the office and went in. "You Eddie?" He looked at the tall, skinny, waiflike young man who'd been watching one of the crappy reality TV shows that turned up all night.

The fellow nearly jumped up. "Me? Yeah."

"I'm a friend of Andi Oliver." Grainger smiled at him.

Eddie didn't know whether to smile or frown, so he took turns. "What do you want?"

"Don't worry, I really am a friend. There's something you can do for me. When you and Andi drove to Preston, you went to a club and talked to some guys."

Eddie was already nodding. "They used to work the line at the slaughterhouse. She wanted them for witnesses."

"Were they happy to do that? Or reluctant?"

Eddie leaned against the counter and fooled with some color brochures, not of the Stardust Motel. "Well, they weren't eager, no. But she thought they'd do it." He stopped stacking the brochures and stood gazing out at the darkness as if someone had simply stolen the light away while his back was turned. "See, she's a girl. It's hard when you're a girl, making men like that listen to you. I guess she thought it was so shitty, the way those animals are treated, then butchered, she needed to do something."

Eddie's weightless shoulders shrugged. His rodlike arms nevertheless did have some muscle to them. "What did you mean," he continued, "something I can do?"

"These two potential witnesses. I'd like a word with them."

Eddie eyed him for a bit, and then a slow smile spread across his face. "What I think is if you have 'a word' with a person, the person listens."

"I strike you that way?" Grainger's smile was perfectly friendly.

"Yeah, you do." Eddie looked pleased that some secret that the night encrypted had revealed itself. "That club's called Zero's. It's just on the edge of Preston. Easy to find, right on Main. It ain't a big town."

He'd been searching his scruffy wallet and now extracted a torn bit of paper which he was about to hand over, but then asked, "How do I know you're who you say you are?"

"I haven't said who I am yet. My name's Billy Grainger. But I've been introducing myself around as Dick Diver. So let's keep this between us."

"How come?"

"How come an alias? In case the state police come knocking." Grainger looked at the piece of paper Eddie held. "Now, what are—"

"The cops are after you?" Eddie found this intensely promising.

"They would be if they knew more."

Even more promising. Eddie opened his mouth to mine this ore and Grainger said, "But that's beside the point, isn't it, Eddie? Do you recall their names? Andi's witnesses?"

Eddie looked down as if the paper in his hand had appeared magically, another sign. "One's Melvin Duggan and the other's Tim Dooley. Here."

Grainger looked at the names, learned them, handed back the bit of paper. "In case you need it sometime." As if Eddie might decide to have a go at them, too. "What do you know about them?"

Eddie's expression grew serious. "They both worked on the line in BigSun's slaughterhouse. One was a sticker—you know what that is?"

"I can well imagine."

"The other, he was a skinner, I think. See, I didn't actually talk to them. Andi told me later."

"But you were there."

"Yessir, I was at the bar."

"Can you describe them?"

"Sure." Eddie had his elbows on the counter, head in his folded hands. "The most distinctive thing about them, I think, is that they were together. I mean, I think that's the way it goes with them."

"Gay? Or just find one, you'll find the other?"

"No, not gay. The second thing. Real friends. The one called Melvin is easy to spot. Really red hair and he wore a bright red shirt that night. And he's been to tattoo heaven. Tats all over, from what I could see. The second guy, Tim, he's a spindly kind of fellow, you know, as if his joints had just come off a lathe and the buzzards pretty much cleaned them out."

Grainger shook his head and laughed. "Eddie, I hope the cops never ask you to ID me. Inside of ten minutes I'd be toast."

Eddie really liked that. "No problem," he said, with a shrug meant to be casual. "Glad to help Andi out anytime."

"She thinks you're great."

His eyes down, again with that shrug. "She does? Well, I can tell you when this case gets to court I'm gonna be there, the first witness. I never thought about animals much, pigs, especially, I guess—as things that had to put up with wholesale shitty treatment—until I saw that rig from Klavan's. I guess she told you. I guess we just don't think about that stuff . . ." His voice drifted somewhere else.

"No, we don't." Grainger looked at the clock on the wall. "I've got to be going, I guess, if I want to get there before the place closes."

"Zero's. It probably never does."

"Thanks for the information, Eddie." He put out his hand.

Eddie shook it. "What do you want to see these guys about?"

"Just to remind them and to see they don't go back on their word. That they'll be witnesses against this place when the time comes."

"If it comes. Andi told me the lawsuit could be put off for a long time. Months, maybe years. They could completely change their minds in that length of time."

"I know. That's why I want to see them. To make sure they don't."

Zero's was a dank bar on a dank street, flanked by a small grocery store on one side and a dry-goods store on the other. Grainger hadn't seen the phrase "dry goods" since he was a kid. The window showed mannequins in dresses and shoes that looked as if they'd dropped by decades ago and decided to stay. He bet they were dusty. The fashion mirrored the town itself.

Why was he standing here looking at unfashionable clothes? There were times when he sincerely doubted himself without a rifle in his hands. He sighed and pushed open the door of Zero's.

You always expect a blare from a drinking crowd, but Zero's was quiet, almost dead and downtrodden. Even so, there were a fair number of customers. He went to the bar, sat down. The bartender came along, heavily bearded, black-patched eye, a ring in his ear, no parrot on his shoulder. Peg leg, maybe, but Grainger couldn't see. He ordered a double Glenlivet, was surprised they had it.

He set to looking around the room. A few women looked back. One winked. He didn't return the wink. One of Grainger's problems was that he saw too much—not just faces and expressions, but what lay behind them—the nuance, the shadow, the lie. It was as if his work—the way he could edit out what was irrelevant—as if all of that rushed in to plague him when he wasn't sighting down a scope.

He saw the corkscrew red hair almost immediately. But the second man wasn't there—yes, he was, just now sliding into the booth beside the redhead, carrying two bottles of beer by the necks.

Grainger picked up his glass and went to the booth in the rear of the room. "Gentlemen," he said.

They looked at him, then at each other, and then around the room, as if trying to place not only Grainger but themselves and the bar.

"We know you?"

It was only half-hostile, as if full-blown hostility wasn't called for, at least not yet.

"No. But I'm a friend of Andi's." When neither appeared to recognize the name, he added, "Andi Oliver, the one who was here talking to you about your former jobs." As if they might have forgotten that, too.

They hadn't. "Oh, yeah, that girl," said the red-haired one, who must have been Melvin Duggan.

"That girl, right. Mind if I sit?"

The spindly one (Eddie had been right) slid over. The one he presumed to be Duggan inhaled a bundle of smoke from his cigarette, exhaled, then laid his cigarette, ember end out, on the edge of the table. The table was ringed by little scorch marks.

"So you want what? You the lawyer?"

Grainger considered saying yes just to speed things up but decided that would only make them more careful in their answers. "No. I'm just a friend."

They nodded. Okay, so far.

"She just wanted me to remind you about the lawsuit. It'll take some time; you can imagine how this sort of thing plays out. Big corporations can stall a legal proceeding for a long, long time. They've got the money to do it. It might even be money coming from one of these agribusinesses. Some of it's certainly coming by way of BigSun. You know a man named Eugene Tuttle?"

"Tuttle? Yeah, sure. Everyone works there knows him. He's a real shit. He's all over the yard, checkin' up. I guess he's manager; he's a real shit—or did I say that? He spends most of his life at the place. He practically lives there."

"Where is he when he's not there?"

"His house? Beats me. But if you're lookin' for him, start with the business. There's administrative offices there."

The black-haired guy was chewing at his lip. They both looked a little nervous. "Yeah, well, we've been talking it over and though we ain't sayin' we *won't* do it, we're sayin' we got to think about it some more."

Grainger smiled. "What's there to think about? You know the issue."

Melvin interrupted: "Thing is, we can't be a hunnert percent sure about this, you know."

"It's important you do this. Without your testimonies, the whole case could go south."

"Okay, okay. Only us, we need jobs. It's hard to get work around here and BigSun's the biggest employer."

"You mean you're trying to get your jobs back?"

"Well, not *those* jobs, but even looking for work in general, like roadwork, say, you don't get hired on if they think you're gonna make trouble—you know, be a whistle-blower, if that's what they call it."

Grainger sat looking from one to the other of them. "Yeah, I hear you. Sounds as if you're between a rock and a hard place." He finished his Scotch, left a couple of crumpled bills on the table, smiled, and said, "I'll be back."

"Who the hell are you, anyway?"

"I'm the hard place."

Grainger walked out.

A more immediate problem was Eugene Tuttle.

To find the place, he could have followed his nose. As he got out of the car, the smell of burned-out buildings was strong, that and animal waste mixed with blood and fear. Fear was palpable; he knew that himself. The air could seem drenched in it. From somewhere, perhaps not from here, but from a distant farm, came lowing sounds. He saw no animals, only the empty space where holding pens had been.

The building on the other side of the pens to this one where he'd parked he took to be the remains of the slaughterhouse. He didn't want to think about it. Let Andi think about it; let her think about it for all of them, for that seemed to be what she was doing. How craven of him. There were lights in a few of the windows. The rest was darkness. The whole operation might have been suspended in time before morning heaved it up again.

The office door was open. To look at Eugene Tuttle, one would think *accountant* or maybe *teacher*, or *researcher*. He was bent over a ledger as if he were examining a specimen under a microscope. God knows, one wouldn't have taken him for a "shit" who ran a stockyard and who was the overseer of a slaughterhouse.

When he looked up, Grainger changed his mind. His face was feral. Sharp, ferretlike features, nose like a knife. His nostrils seemed to quiver when he saw Grainger, as if he were scenting him.

"Yes?"

"Are you Eugene Tuttle?"

"Yes. Eugene Tuttle, yes."

"I was told you were probably here."

"Told? By whom?"

"Friends. If I could have a few minutes of your time."

Eugene looked at his watch. "It's nearly eleven PM."

Tuttle emphasized that as if his visitor might think it was morning. "We've got a problem."

"*We* have?" Tuttle capped his pen. "Who the devil are *you*?"

Grainger didn't know who he wanted to be yet, so he didn't answer. "Basically, you have the problem. I'm just keeping you company with it." Grainger stayed standing; he knew his height was intimidating.

"You're an agent? If you've got a complaint, I'm not the person to see. You want—"

"No. I'm told you're the person to see about everything. I'm not an agent. I believe you know a young lady named Andi Oliver?"

Tuttle's eyes dropped to his desk. Either a security button of some sort, or a gun. But his hands hadn't moved, so Grainger didn't reach behind him for his. "You recognize the name."

Tuttle didn't move. "What do you want?"

"I want you to forget her."

"I don't know what you're talking about."

Grainger sighed as if disappointed in the man's performance. "Eugene, Eugene, I'm also a friend—well, an acquaintance—of Kyle Hanna—"

That arrow hit its mark.

"—and he's decided not to take on the job. Or rather the decision was made for him."

"*What?* What about the—" He caught himself, but not in time.

"The money? Good question. You'll get that back. Or most of it."

The little weasel (awful to badmouth a weasel) sniffed several times as if he were indeed trying to sniff out the truth here. "I don't know these people."

"There you go again, pretending, even as Kyle right now is sitting in a police station. They'll certainly be wanting to know who hired him. Meaning you and Klavan. Now, you might want Kyle taken care of before he tells the cops. See, I know Kyle. He'll stay zipped up tight until his brief turns up. That'd be me." Grainger had removed the card he wanted after a lightning-quick scan of half a dozen. "Here—" He handed the card across the desk.

Tuttle had to look at it. "'D. Diver; Attorney; Delaplain, New Jersey.' So, assuming you're right, what do you want in exchange for shutting him up?"

"Only, let's say, maybe fifty grand. He'll do what I tell him to do. Plus the assurance there'll be no more attempts on the girl's life."

Eugene glowered. "What the hell do you care about her? Why should I agree to that?"

Grainger sighed. "Isn't it fucking *obvious*, Eugene? I have my client to protect, don't I? Anyone else comes along and tries to whack her, it's Kyle who'll be suspected right off."

"He's in jail."

"That's right. Did you have somebody else lined up to send out after this girl in the next ten minutes? He won't be in jail long, dickhead."

Huffily, Eugene said, "No need to be offensive."

Grainger could hardly contain his laughter. *No need to be offensive,* for God's sakes. "What's your job here?"

"I'm one of the owners. I take care of the finances." He was sullen.

"Who takes care of the murders?"

Tuttle heaved himself up. For such a spit of a man, he could make himself appear heavy.

"That's just ridiculous!"

Since Tuttle stood up, Grainger sat down, just to make life seem arbitrary. "What is it about this place here you're so afraid to have discovered?"

"Nothing, nothing at all. The girl's making it up. She's a troublemaker."

"I'd say the trouble"—Grainger rose again—"was already made. Good night, Mr. Tuttle. I'll be talking to you again."

There was nothing else to be gotten out of the man; in any event, Grainger's purpose had been to deliver a message, and he was pretty sure he'd done it. He might not have accomplished much in the long term, but in the short term he had. They'd stay away from her, at least until they worked all of this out. And once they found out she'd left, they'd probably forget the whole thing. It had been hard enough getting a shooter—two shooters—and failing both times.

He thought about all this as he drove back to Kingdom. It was midnight and he was tired. He could have stopped off at Eddie's motel, but he was afraid that something might happen to her if he wasn't around. He had a bedroll; he was used to sleeping on the ground.

71

They'd been over it and over it. Jim was having a hard time with her leaving. Tom wasn't much more accepting of it. Both of them feared for her safety.

Jim was tossing cut-up cooked potatoes into a ceramic bowl. "On the road again."

Andi laughed. "Willie Nelson."

"At *least*, take the car."

"No. I can't take your car. But thanks, Jim; that's very nice of you. I'm just used to walking or taking buses. I like it. You see things when you walk."

Tom said, whiskey in hand, "Like donkeys."

Now Jim was adding large spoonfuls of mayonnaise to the potatoes. He slapped the mayonnaise out of the spoon so hard he might have been mad at the salad.

There came a knock on the door or, rather, a rattle of the screen. It was Harry McKibbon.

"Harry, come on in; you're just in time to take someone into custody and lock her up."

"I take it that would be you." He looked at Andi. "Why should you be locked up? Except on general principles, I mean."

Jim answered. "To keep her from going on with her harebrained scheme to leave here and go to Canada."

Alaska, actually, thought Andi, but saying that would make it worse.

Harry frowned. "I'm sorry." He sounded genuinely so. "But I can't see where it's harebrained." Harry sat down and nodded at Jim's offer of coffee and took a potato chip from a bowl on the table.

Tom leaned back in his chair. "Walking? Walking to Canada? That don't sound harebrained?"

Harry shook his head. "Not for Andi." He bit into the potato chip and said, in a speculative tone, "You getting out because of Waylans getting shot? I can't blame you, only if that's the reason, I mean, if you're thinking the guy might have been aiming at you—?"

"Partly. There's also being fired and not being able to work with the pigs anymore. Klavan will never let me on that property."

Jim, who was still standing with his coffee mug aloft, said, "There's this legal issue, this suit against the damned hog farm. You're not sticking around for that?"

"Bobby Del Ray says it'll be months, more likely a year or two. He can't get the state's attorney to touch it. Klavan must own half the county and BigSun the other half."

Harry said, "But you're not letting up on it?"

"No, of course not. I'll keep in touch."

"Well, the reason I came here tonight wasn't to have a cup of coffee, although I appreciate it, but to set your mind at rest on one thing. We got the shooter."

She froze. The hand she had raised to Jim like a flag sank down. *Billy.* She couldn't speak.

Harry went on. "I'd like to put it down to our expert police work, but it was really because we got a telephone tip that the guy was holed up in a motel, rifle shoved under his bed. Damn fool."

Andi cleared her throat. "Who is he?" She hoped the others didn't notice the break in her voice.

"Fella named Kyle Hanna—"

The name settled over her like balm. But then she remembered he used aliases. She swallowed hard. "Why did he say he was here?" *Surely not; it's surely not Billy Grainger.* "Who tipped you off?"

"Just a voice on the phone. He didn't introduce himself," Harry added drily. "Hanna doesn't say why he's here, I mean, beyond here to hunt, which accounts for the rifle, only, it doesn't. He protests his innocence, surprise, surprise. Claims someone else did it and is letting him take the fall."

That sounded like Billy Grainger. Andi picked up a potato chip and started breaking it into little pieces. "What's he look like?" That didn't sound casual, which is how she wanted it to sound. She ate the pieces, tasting nothing.

"Little creep. Probably five-five or -six at a stretch. Bad mouth on him and a bad case of acne. Why? Some friend of yours? Not that it'd surprise me."

Her face felt hot and she hoped she wasn't blushing. Relief made her so dizzy, she was afraid to get up. "I just wondered if I'd seen him before, if he was following me, too, along with Waylans."

Harry frowned, serious again. "Claims he never heard of you. Trouble is, he had a picture someone took of you outside of one of the Klavan buildings."

Jim slapped down his mug. "Now, Harry, why'd you have to go and tell her that?"

Harry was surprised. "She knows it already." He looked at her.

She nodded. "It's Klavan; at least, I think so. It could be BigSun, too. Now the sheriff has the shooter, maybe I'll find out."

Harry sighed. "And maybe not. He's not talking except to declare he's innocent and wants a lawyer." He took another chip.

Jim said, "You got some kind of ballistics, don't you? You can tell if the bullet that came from the rifle is the same kind that went into Waylans, can't you?"

"That's the problem. We didn't find any casings. He probably took them with him. The guy is a pro."

"But, hell, there must've been one in his body. Or did it go through or what?"

"It went clean through. His head."

Jim just sat back and stared. Andi said nothing.

"We didn't find it. We went over the ground inch by inch. Nothing. There's nothing to match up with Hanna's rifle."

"Well, that doesn't look good for Hanna, does it? If the bullet was from another gun he'd be home free."

"He might be home free anyway. What evidence do we have? None. Circumstantial evidence. Man appears in a motel with a rifle. Hell, he could be hunting deer or bear or anything. But on the other hand, nobody needs an M40A1 sniper rifle with a ten-power scope to shoot a whitetail deer. So I'm keeping him as long as I can by law."

Andi thought: *So he'd been right.* Within forty-eight hours they'd sent someone else to kill her. She looked down at her hands, not wanting anyone to see the relief in her eyes.

"Once he gets a lawyer, though"—Harry slid one palm off the other—"fast."

"But he must be the one, Harry."

"Um. I looked up this Hanna's war record. He was in the Desert Storm operation. He's a sniper. I called a buddy of mine at Fort Meyers who dug up some records. This Hanna was one helluva shot. I mean, how can you zero in on a silver dollar from a thousand yards?"

"So he must be the guy."

"That's a funny conclusion to draw, Jim." Harry smiled. "Waylans was standing maybe a foot, maybe two feet, away from Andi. So how come if he was trying to kill Andi, did he miss?"

Because he wasn't trying to kill me; he was trying to save me. But she kept quiet about that; that she would keep to herself.

The next morning, up early, Andi packed her backpack and went downstairs, to be greeted by a glum Jim, cooking bacon, a lot of it, as if in nontribute to her going. It made her smile.

She went out to the barn, not wanting to stay any longer than a brief good-bye demanded, not wanting to feed them; let Jesus take care of that.

Dakota, immediately upon seeing her, crowded to the back of his stall.

"Oh, don't *worry;* we're not going to the ring. I wouldn't think of putting you *out,* even though you may never see me again."

Dakota moved then to the front of the stall, looking interested, although Andi couldn't tell the nature of the interest. She went over to Sam and patted his side. "I can't take you with me, and anyway, you're much better off here." She wondered what she expected the donkey to do in response to this news. Odds On and Odds Against looked at each other and then at her. Palimpsest shook his head and snorted. Nelson seemed to be chewing something, air, perhaps, just to be chewing.

She sighed and sat down on a fat hay bale and looked at them and they looked back. Andi remembered that pig in the slaughterhouse, covered in blood and still raising its face in supplication to the sticker. She could hardly stand it and bowed her head. *If we deceive them,* she thought, *we're the ones deceived; if we betray them, they look back unbetrayed.*

The horses and Sam kept on looking at her in such a steady way, with looks somber and sad, that she thought they knew what was happening, that she was leaving and they'd miss her.

That, or they wanted their breakfast.

And she was sitting on it.

72

Grainger watched Jim Purley's house from the distant shelf of rock, his vision clouded only by an early morning fog, fast dissolving. He knew she would leave today or tomorrow, if for no other reason than that she'd told him she would. And there were certainly other reasons, although he was fairly sure he'd defused the danger, at least temporarily. No one would try anything for a while. They'd leave her alone, but, then, who could be sure what people would do? He was watching because he wouldn't feel safe about her until she got out of this town.

That's why he hadn't told her about Alice; it would be one more burden that she'd feel she had to take on, and she wouldn't leave. He'd take it on himself.

For two days now, he'd been watching. He tore open a small packet of cheese crackers, ate one, drank water from a jug. He had some fruit and a bag of carrots, and coffee in a thermos. He surely could do with a big plate of bacon and eggs right now, but he wasn't going to get it.

There was movement. He raised the binoculars. In another moment Andi came out of the side door, took the path to the barn, and stopped. She raised her head and looked off toward the rocks, then looked away and walked the path. She wasn't inside for more than ten minutes. Then she came out of the barn, went over to the pigsty, and stood for a few minutes, hanging over the rail. After that, she walked the path back to the house.

He waited.

In a little while, she came out the front door with the two men, neither related to her, but he knew this was going to be very tough on them. She resettled her backpack between her shoulders. It looked heavy. Lord only knew what she had in there—a pig, maybe? He laughed; he couldn't help it. The thing about a girl like this was she made you laugh.

She looked up, looked right toward him.

But she couldn't see him, of course, and wouldn't expect to. No light glinted from his rifle barrel because the rifle wasn't there. There was a good-bye look on her face. Only it wasn't for him; it was for the place, or so he thought. She was looking into yesterday.

She would never know how tempted he had been to do what she wanted and take her with him. He had been merely truthful when he told her she wouldn't be able to stand his life. Now, though, watching her walk away down the road, watching her wave at her friends, Grainger had real doubts. Maybe he should be going with her, parting the waters, holding back the dark—oh, who in hell did he think he was? Andi didn't need the waters parted.

From far away came a keening sound, cry or scream, and Grainger thought: There's an animal out there somewhere being mistreated, dog being kicked, cat being torched, donkey being whipped.

And in that somewhere, somebody's doing it. Brother, say your prayers, for trouble's coming, and you're going to be right in trouble's way.

He watched until the distant road became a line into a blank horizon and she disappeared.

Grainger lowered the binoculars and smiled.

"Go get 'em, sugar."

EPILOGUE

The white horse had either tripped and fallen into the hollow or maybe even been pushed into it. It was certainly not a wild horse come to grief. It looked unhealthy, its ribs protruding. Tripped, probably, although these vast fields appeared to offer little obstruction. Maybe it had sunk down in simple weariness. It was clearly dying.

It had taken Andi four days of walking and one long bus ride to get to North Dakota's northern border. Canada lay beyond.

What she had come upon, what she could see in the distance, must be a horse farm. There must be a couple of dozen barns out there, at least, and big ones; out in the field beyond it a number of horses. As there were no other animals, it was the horses the barns had to be for.

She looked around for some means of pulling the horse out, something to help her gain leverage, a rope tied around a tree, something. But she knew there was nothing, no rope and no tree. And even had there been, it would not have helped the horse.

Nothing in her pack would help the horse, either. There was the painkiller and the armica but she had no idea if these would do any good. The horse was lying on its side, its big eye looking up at her.

Water, for heaven's sake.

Although there was hardly any room, the dying mare taking up most of it, Andi lowered herself into the hole and the little open space between head and torso. The horse looked frightened, and no wonder: what else was coming now to do her more harm?

"—*the white moth thither in the night . . .*"

She thought of walking to the farm in search of help, but she had a feeling help wouldn't be coming, certainly not the sort that would be bringing some kind of equipment to lift the horse.

She took off her quilted vest and bunched it under the mare's head. She rubbed the sweat-damp flank. The hole, she'd found, was nearly five feet.

Water. She reached up to her backpack and pulled the liter of water out. It was half-full, but would be something by way of relief, though she didn't know how the horse could drink if it couldn't raise its head. Images of Dakota and Sam, of Odds On and Odds Against, all slurping up water from buckets, came to her. All she could do was raise the mare's head and try to pour the water into her mouth. She was half-successful at doing this; some of the water dribbled out and down the neck. But it was better than nothing. And the horse at least relaxed enough to close its eyes.

Awkwardly, Andi sat there, legs bunched up to her chin, arm at a difficult angle under the mare's neck. She took it away, refolding the vest to make it a better cushion. She didn't know how long she sat, her mind crowded with images of Grainger, Jim, Tom, Bobby Del Ray.

She kept running her hand over the mare's side, feeling its shallow breathing. The horse was dying and she didn't want to leave it; she didn't want it to die alone. She stayed for a short or a long time, she couldn't say, when her hand felt the breath subside, grow less and less, until the horse gave a quick stretch and it stopped altogether. Andi started to cry, but stopped abruptly and wiped her face on her sleeve.

There was nothing more she could do. She got up and pulled herself out of the hole and picked up her backpack and started walking across the field. It was as if the closer she got to that place, the more it receded from view, as if it were something like a star.

Finally, she came upon fencing, wood and barbed wire and a NO TRESPASSING sign, which made her laugh. Somewhere along here, if she looked, she would find the fence broken down in at least one spot and that would be how the horse had gotten out. But what had caused its death, she couldn't say.

After another ten or fifteen minutes of walking she came to the spread—long barns, something like Klavan's, only not painted white.

She passed an open barn door and halted. She saw line after long line of horses in narrow stalls, each apparently hooked up to a hose and a kind of plastic sack. This, then, was what Jim and Tom had told her about. It was from just such a place that Jim had got Dakota. He'd said there were these horse farms mostly along the state line, most of them in Canada. Pregnant mares' urine. PMU. It was the urine being collected. That meant all of them hooked up were pregnant. This was the way they spent their lives.

Andi stood for a while, thinking of walking into it and yelling at someone, anyone in there about the dying horse, the dead horse. No, she could say and say and it would make no difference.

Beyond the barns was a very large white house. Probably the owners'. To the left of the barn was a whitewashed cinder-block building.

Then a man in big suspenders and a feed cap carrying two buckets came out of the barn, saw her, and stopped. "Help you?" His frown seemed more curious than hostile. "Need something?"

"I just wanted to tell you I found a horse out there"—she pointed off in the way she'd come—"in a hollow; the horse must've tripped into it."

He set down the buckets. "Oh, shit. Excuse me. Got over the fence, I guess. Just where is it now?"

"I can point you the way; then it's easy to find."

He nodded.

"Is that white building back there the office?"

"Yeah, it is."

"Well, if you just go straight, you can't miss the horse. She's in a deep hole. I'm afraid she died."

Again, he nodded and thanked her and walked toward the fence.

Andi tossed her backpack over her shoulder and moved to the cinder-block building and up the three steps. Inside, there was a long counter. Behind it, bent over a newspaper, was a man of uncertain age, tall and spindle-thin. There was another shorter, heavier one at the other end. They were both wearing feed hats.

The thin one looked up, surprised, and then settled into a lascivious look. "Well, hell-*o*, pretty girl." The grin was a leer he meant to be a wicked and sexy smile.

Andi stood there for just a minute trying to decide whether to shoot him or smile back. The only smile she could manage was a twist of her mouth, and she settled for it.

I can point you the way; then it's easy to find.

Then her smile broadened. It was for herself. "*Don't be so goddamned self-righteous*," she could hear Tom saying.

She thought of Grainger. She thought of Alaska, of its cool blue-white seductiveness. How much she wanted to see it.

"My name's Andi. I need a job."

ACKNOWLEDGMENTS

I want to thank the Animal Legal Defense Fund and Sue Ann Chambers for help with the legal issues; the Humane Farming Association and Gail Eisnitz for their tireless investigations into pig farming facilities and slaughterhouses; and John Walker, who can shoot a twig off a tree from an unimaginable distance.